A THIRD KIND

J. C. CAMPBELL

DIVERTIR
PUBLISHING
Salem, NH

A Third Kind

J. C. Campbell

Cover design by Kenneth Tupper

Published by Divertir Publishing LLC
PO Box 232
North Salem, NH 03073
http://www.divertirpublishing.com/

ISBN-13: 978-1-938888-27-4
ISBN-10: 1-938888-27-8

Library of Congress Control Number: 2020947020

Printed in the United States of America

Dedication

*To my family, for all of the encouragement and support
you've given me over the years.*

Table of Contents

Chapter 1 1
Chapter 2 3
Chapter 3 9
Chapter 4 11
Chapter 5 21
Chapter 6 25
Chapter 7 29
Chapter 8 31
Chapter 9 37
Chapter 10 43
Chapter 11 49
Chapter 12 61
Chapter 13 65
Chapter 14 69
Chapter 15 77
Chapter 16 83
Chapter 17 89
Chapter 18 91
Chapter 19 95
Chapter 20 99
Chapter 21 105
Chapter 22 109
Chapter 23 111
Chapter 24 115
Chapter 25 119
Chapter 26 123
Chapter 27 129
Chapter 28 133
Chapter 29 141
Chapter 30 147
Chapter 31 151
Chapter 32 153
Chapter 33 169

Chapter 34...177
Chapter 35...181
Chapter 36...197
Chapter 37...207
Chapter 38...213
Chapter 39...221
Epilogue...231
Also by Divertir Publishing...235

Chapter 1

SCREAMS ERUPTED FROM inside the trunk less than an hour outside of Jacksonville.

Kaleb sighed. He'd been waiting for the girl to come to. Her name was Allie, a twenty-year-old student from Jacksonville, and knowing that only made things harder. It was a stupid mistake to look at her ID—not the first of the night, mind you, but it had happened—and now more than ever he had no idea what to do with her.

He pulled over, grateful for the brooding clouds and heavy rain veiling the night. Stinging droplets and gusts of wind lashed him the moment the door opened. He hesitated, trying to think of what to say. Maybe, *Hi, sorry I abducted you. I haven't decided if I should kill you or not, but I'll keep you in the loop.* Could he even bring himself to do it? Killers, thugs, all-around criminals, sure, but some little wisp of a blonde girl with a bad habit?

He popped the trunk. "Please, stop scream—"

The kick caught him off guard, knocking him back a step. For a second he could only watch the sad little thing attempt to escape. Allie tried to heave herself out of the trunk, but her hand, wet with blood and rain, shot out from beneath her. She fell hard, her head catching an edge with a wet crack.

Kaleb leaned in to take a closer look. If not for the slight rise and fall of her chest he would have thought her dead. There was relief in that, but also anxiety settling into his chest and shoulders. What was better: having a role in another innocent's death, or having to deal with a witness? Tough call.

It could be worse, though—he could be in her shoes. Judging by the cast and tautness of her skin, she was a junkie. Maybe not that far gone yet, but on her way. What a waste, so young to be tainted by that poison. She didn't deserve any of this, but what was he supposed to do? She'd seen him.

As if that was her fault. How many times had he gone hunting? Hundreds? Thousands? And she was the first witness. Sure, others had seen him at times, caught glimpses, but never during a kill. If only he'd gotten there sixty seconds later…or if he would have just found someone else, someone worse…or…if. Or. If. It was useless to dwell on. It was what it was.

"It would be easy to kill you," Kaleb muttered. "Solve the problem. Twist your neck. Or suffocate you."

1

Can you? his conscience whispered. *Can you handle seeing another innocent face when you close your eyes?*

No. He couldn't. Two were more than enough to haunt his dreams.

He could almost hear his conscience hissing with laughter as if to chase off any misgivings that a bit of mercy might make him a little bit more human or a little less hell bound when he finally reached the end of his miserable existence.

A flicker of movement drew Kaleb's attention to the back of the trunk, striking home the truth of the matter. 'Killing' didn't adequately describe what he did. It was too cavalier. This girl was an accident he didn't know how to deal with. Then there was the drug peddler, a thug who made money on the side by pimping girls out whether they wanted to be or not. He was watching this all, eyes wide with abject terror. They were the only part of the man's body that still worked.

The technique had taken decades to perfect. Shattering the vertebrae in just the right way kept the body alive for a few hours—not long, just long enough to harvest. The pain had to be extraordinary, the reality beyond horrendous. Of all of Kaleb's victims, perhaps only a handful deserved such a brutal death. The rest were bad people, predators, but to die like this?

Ignoring the withered, whispering voice of his conscience, Kaleb slammed the trunk shut and turned away. It had to be done.

Chapter 2

ALLIE WOKE UP fighting the urge to retch. Every beat of her heart sent a sickly throb through her head. A whimper slipped through her lips, and she pressed a hand to the back of her scalp. Her hair was clumped and sticky, matted with blood, and beneath was a tender lump split by a ragged gash.

She closed her eyes and focused on breathing, waiting for the pain to subside.

Thunder boomed, rattling windows and jarring Allie awake. She'd passed out—how long ago she couldn't even guess, but the throbbing had eased. She struggled to sit up and peered into darkness that was undoubtedly a blessing given her headache. It was also a curse, concealing all of the hidden terrors of her nightmares. Lightning flashed and the room sprang to life in flickering gray and black snapshots. She was lying on a couch in a cavernous concrete-walled room full of clutter.

This couldn't really be happening. She didn't want to be reduced to a story on the news—just another missing girl whose face would make headlines for a day or two, and then she'd be forgotten like she never existed. This wasn't the way her life was supposed to go!

Allie struggled to stand and collapsed back, cradling her head and trying to stop the spinning. Tears broke free, wetting her hands, and she waited for the dizziness to pass. "God, please help me," she prayed.

Minutes crept by and she looked around again. Her eyes were adjusting, but even so most of the room was impenetrable without the lightning. What she could see was junk—a lifetime's worth of boxes and furniture, layers of dust, and scattered bits of debris. The smell was more than just the moth-eaten couch. It was damp and dust and mold, and a distinct coppery tang that she wasn't quite ready to cope with.

Rain pelted a window above her head, and in a weak flash of lightning she saw the bars. They were thick and square; even if she could somehow reach them, there was no hope in hell she could break out. The desire to fall to her knees and weep was nearly overwhelming, but Allie fought it. Crying would do no good, no matter how badly she wanted to indulge, and she wasn't ready to give in just yet.

With one hand stretched out she wandered the room, searching, passing boxes that broke apart at her touch. A fit of coughing sent shock waves through her body, reigniting the pain in her head and making the floor roll beneath her. Midway through her fall she hit something large and solid, halting her without

3

grace. Her ribs ached where an edge had found them, and a cloud of dust enveloped her, taking away her breath. She clawed at the thing, trying desperately to stabilize herself and stop the spinning. Even as she fought to breathe her fingers found a grip. Wood. Hard edges mercifully worn smooth by time and wear. A dresser or cabinet.

Gradually the dust settled and the dizziness subsided. Amid the faint speckles dancing in her vision she saw a hint of light, so faint that only someone whose eyes had been denied sight for a time would notice it. She crept toward it, weaving through stacks of boxes and dark looming shapes. The path was slow and the room larger than she had thought, feeling more and more like a tomb. Her pulse raced and fluttered, fueling the headache, but she kept moving.

All at once the source became clear: a single, dim, dust-shrouded bulb dangled at the foot of a stairwell. Worn by the tread of countless steps, wooden slabs trailed up and into a murky recess.

Allie waited, straining to hear anything. The room was painfully silent, the only sounds the storm and the thundering of her pulse. She went up the first step and gagged, nausea overwhelming her. Another wave and she couldn't hold it back. A bit of bile splattered into her hand, and she flung it away before wiping her hands on her pants. Specks of light danced before her eyes and she sat hard, waiting for the spell to pass. It would be easy to blame it on a concussion, but the need was also there, the reason she was in this mess in the first place.

She wanted to quit. She tried. But the craving never left, never stopped nagging. All of her bad memories piled upon each other. Every stupid decision she'd ever made and every embarrassing and cruel moment of her life ground her down. Using was the only way she had to block it all out.

The nausea eased and she started up the stairs again, one hand held out in search of the door that had to be close. Cold metal greeted her hand and hope flourished. Praying a little prayer, she twisted the handle. It rattled but wouldn't turn. It shouldn't have been a surprise, really. God had never been there for her before.

Her legs gave out and she crumpled, drawing her knees up to her chest and succumbing to the need to cry. The nausea came back. Dry heaves sent her scrambling down the stairs, and she fell on all fours gagging. The next thing Allie saw was a pale, glowing white light surrounded by a void; a light at the end of a dark tunnel. She reached out, whether to push it away or embrace it she wasn't sure. She hesitated and chose to fight. She wasn't ready to die. Not yet.

Footsteps echoed overhead. A key rattled in a lock.

The dark tunnel widened, dissipating, and the light bulb swayed gently in a damp draft. Allie sat up too fast and nearly passed out, but she was already moving, crawling into the shadows. Terror rose like a living creature within her, biting and gnawing, trying to claw its way up her throat to freedom. Tears welled up, unwanted as they were, clouding her vision. She squeezed between piles of junk and boxes, melting into the clutter.

Footsteps started down the stairs, every soft thump on the wooden steps a haunting knell. He reached the concrete floor and headed for the couch. Her abductor's voice cut through the basement—young, strong, and coldly neutral. "I guess you're still alive then. I'm glad for that. Now come out and we can try to sort this out."

Allie eyed the stairs. Did she dare? Was it even a choice? It was a chance, however slim.

"You can't hide forever," he said, louder. "You're going to have to talk to me eventually." He waited a moment, and sounded almost disappointed when he spoke again. "If I wanted you dead, why would I be keeping you like this?"

She could think of a few reasons. None of them made her want to step out and talk.

Scrapes and the sound of clutter being pushed aside came from the darkness. Allie slid out from behind the dresser and crept up the steps. She grabbed the handle, and again it rattled but wouldn't open. She choked back a frustrated scream and shoved against the door, trying to force it open. It didn't move. Not even a fraction. Allie held a hand over her mouth to silence her crying, turned back to creep back into the shadows, and screamed.

He stood at the foot of the stairs, face lost in shadows.

"Let me go," she sobbed. "Please, please let me go."

"I don't want to hurt you."

"Then why did you take me?" she screamed back.

He was silent for a moment, and then spoke softly. "You saw too much. I didn't know what else to do."

"Let me go!"

"I'm sorry, I can't. I need to figure everything out first."

"I want to go," she sobbed. "I *have* to go."

"Maybe," he said. "In time. Now come back down. The couch isn't much, but it will have to do. I have to go out for a little while, but I won't be long."

When Allie didn't answer or move, he came up the stairs. She shrank away, trying to melt into the wall as he brushed past. He turned back, glinting black eyes boring into hers. "Is there anything I can pick up for you?"

She wanted to claw his eyes out and shove him down the stairs, but she'd seen what he'd done—how he'd been shot point blank and still manhandled the dealer like a rag doll. A knot lodged in her throat. He spoke again, maybe repeating the questions, maybe not. None of it was really registering, except the rasp of the key in the lock and the finality of the deadbolt clacking into place.

It had to be a nightmare. Allie clamped her eyes shut, trying not to listen to his footsteps fade away. Her chest hurt. Even breathing was a chore. Her hands trembled and her skin was crawling. The headache was back with a vengeance, and it was a struggle not to retch again.

She stumbled back to the couch in a daze and more fell than sat. A cloud of dust swirled, setting off a new bout of coughing. Allie drew her legs up, rubbing them, trying to warm them. It might have been that her clothes were still a bit damp, or the chill in the air, but some part of her knew it was shock. She'd heard about it before, on TV, in books, and even in a textbook once. Exhausted, she tried to think and figure a way out. What was she supposed to do? The place was locked up tight.

Allie ran her hands over her feet, trying to work some warmth into her sore muscles. She winced as her fingers touched a patch of raw flesh just above her heel. It took only a few moments for lightning to flash, and she caught only a glimpse, but it was enough. Amid the bruises, a handprint purpled her skin, and a spot the size of a dime glistened wetly.

The events of the night caught up in a rush. The need had sent her out into a shitty, wet night. She remembered the misery of trying to turn back, get her shit together, and maybe even make amends. She owed it to herself and hated what she'd become, but it was so hard.

And then *he* came along. She watched from half a block away, hidden in the shadows, doing nothing as a man was murdered. She'd panicked, given herself away by running. If she'd been smart, clear-headed, she would have crouched low and stayed out of sight until it was all over. Instead she'd bolted.

As if reliving the memories of the night had taken something out of her, she curled up on the dirty couch, lulled by the sounds of the raging storm while crying silent tears, and sank into darkness.

§ § §

The grocery store shone like a beacon. People moved behind glass walls, shopping despite the unpleasant weather. How many times had Kaleb driven by this very store and never once gone in? It was too busy, too bright. Buying online or from magazines was easier.

"Woulda been better if she'd died," Kaleb muttered. He shook his head at the thought. Horrible. Two innocents were more than enough. A third, even by accident, was unacceptable. But if she got away…He couldn't be hunted. Not again.

The sounds and smells of the hundreds of people who had passed through the store recently assaulted Kaleb's senses the moment he stepped inside. Anxiety pressed in, and he leaned against a shopping cart, closed his eyes, and centered himself. No one knew who or what he was. The sensation of the world closing in gradually subsided, and he pushed on, eager to finish up and go back home.

Fruit caught his eye, much of it exotic, the only familiar items being apples and oranges. Saliva flooded his mouth at the oranges, a rare enough treat in his childhood and one of his favorites. He shook off the flash of nostalgia and grabbed random items. People milled about the store, barely giving him cursory glances, oblivious, stuffing carts full of garbage that surely couldn't be fit for human consumption.

Half an hour later he stood in line, not quite sure what he was about to pay for. Cans and boxes, bottles—both plastic and glass—full of ingredients he'd never heard of. Part of him wondered at the frivolity of humanity, and another part just wanted to be a part of it.

The bag of apples he'd stuffed into his cart caught his eye, and he could almost taste the sweetness, feel the crisp crunch of biting through the skin.

Forcefully diverting his attention away from the cart, he stared at the impossibly-slow woman in front of him. Elderly and wrapped in a heavy one-piece raincoat, she shouldn't have been out in such a storm. Time stood still while she rooted around her purse for payment. The teen running the register rolled his eyes.

The debit machine flashed. Code error.

Fed up with the light, noise, and odors, Kaleb resisted the urge to push past the elderly woman and dash into the night. He smiled at the absurdity of it. This was a simple taste of what he'd always craved, a tiny bit of normalcy in an otherwise nightmarish existence. An old woman was nearly proving to be his bane, the straw that broke his back. A joke considering the things he'd seen and done.

Minutes later he was finally on his way home. To Allie. His smile withered to a scowl. She was safe. She wasn't going anywhere. But what the hell was he supposed to do with her?

Chapter 3

WHAT HAPPENED?" a dry voice rasped.

Jason swallowed the lump in his throat. "Someone killed Antony. We don't know who." *Why the hell was it his problem?* It wasn't like he'd actually been there. But everyone else had bailed. Dealers, gangsters, and wannabe made men, all a bunch of fucking punks.

But staring into Amado's dead eyes, Jason felt a bit like a punk himself. There was something behind those eyes, lurking, waiting to break free. Whatever it was, Jason didn't want to be around when it finally did.

"Did you get anything useful? A plate number? A description?" Amado asked.

"They got a plate…"

Amado looked almost placated.

"But it was stolen." Jason sat back on the desk, legs trembling. He resisted the urge to wipe sweat from his forehead.

"That is very…unfortunate."

Jason raised his hands in surrender. "I wasn't there, and it's pure luck that Lee saw anything at all. He was making a pickup, got there just in time to see Antony shoot the guy point blank. Before Lee could even figure out what the hell was going on, the guy damn near tears Antony's head off. At first, I thought, like, maybe he was wearing a bullet proof vest or something, right? But Lee said the guy moved like one of you. And Antony, he's big, a real mean sonofabitch. No human could just walk up and twist his head around like a fucking corkscrew. If not for the girl showing up, Lee might be missing too. He played the only card he had and kept out of sight. Otherwise, you'd have two guys missing and no idea what was going on." Jason swallowed hard. It made sense, and they were usually reasonable.

Amado seemed to stare into him. "Why was he alone?"

Shit. One of the rules broken. It wasn't even his fault, and he had to explain it? His mouth suddenly dry, Jason forced the words out. "Lee was running some errands."

Amado didn't look pleased.

"But, uh…" Jason stammered, "there's always another angle on this."

The vampire settled an icy stare on Jason, waiting.

"Not the first time one of your guys has disappeared." He shrugged. "Who knows. Some morons start dabbling, testing the product, and before they know it the supply is gone and their pockets are empty. Some get caught up in other shit. But maybe this isn't the first time this freak has killed one of ours."

Tension eased out of the vamp, even if it went grudgingly. "Maybe. When was the last disappearance?"

Positive he'd barely dodged being on the menu, Jason clenched his fists to control the trembling in his hands and prayed his voice held. "About six months ago—some thumb breaker."

"How did it happen?"

Jason shrugged. "No idea. He was out doing pickups and drop-offs, collected a few debts, and no one ever heard from him again. We put the word out that he ran with cash and product, but nothing turned up."

The vamp turned his cold look on Jason again. "Maybe," he said softly. "From now on, make sure the rules are followed. I will look into the trespasser myself. Where can I find our young...Lee was it?"

Lee was a good guy, nice to have at your back. Jason didn't want to rat, but there wasn't much of a choice. *Fuck.* "Peeler bar," he sighed. "Twisters."

Jason sagged with relief as the vamp turned and began to walk from the room, and froze, unable to breathe when Amado glanced back. The hunger in the stare, the beast shimmering right beneath the surface, took his breath away. They were businessmen, modern day mob, but they were still monsters.

Jason blinked and jumped up. Amado was gone. The room was empty. Jason buried his face in his hands and sat back hard. "Stupid." He knew better than to stare into those eyes. His hands shot to his neck, checking for bite marks. He was clean, but he shuddered anyways. That stare had left him cold, as though it alone had been enough to drain him.

Chapter 4

LIGHTNING FLASHED, PIERCING the darkness beyond a window covered in grime and dissected by rusted iron bars. For a second or two Allie thought she was home in bed, waking from a bad dream, and then she remembered.

An ominous rumble of thunder rattled windows, and moments later another bolt of lightning sent shadows leaping and dancing, scurrying across a gray and lifeless landscape of old furniture and boxes strewn with dusty cobwebs. The flash faded and a darkness so complete it was profound swallowed Allie whole. It was still night. The storm was still trying to wash the world away.

She sat up and rubbed at puffy eyes. It was all real. She was being kept prisoner by some psychopath. She scratched at her arms, trying to sate an itch that couldn't be sated, and chewed on her bottom lip.

Grateful that at least the headache had eased, Allie still felt like crap. She wasn't cold anymore. Instead, she was burning up, shivering, and slick enough with sweat that her clothes clung to her body. Every last inch of her being ached, and she felt as though insects were slithering beneath her skin.

She slid her legs over the side of the couch with a groan and checked herself over. Her ankle was swollen and hot to the touch. She traced her fingers over the bruise, feeling the raised outlines of his handprint, and pulled away when she found something wet and sticky. If she hadn't already thrown up, she would have now. She flicked her fingers frantically, trying to rid them of the skin that had sloughed off.

The room spun as she stood, and she limped toward the stairs.

Beneath the faint glow of the lone light bulb, she saw a purple and black bruise that covered her ankle as if *his* hand had been covered in ink. At the center of the bruise, the dime-sized scratch had grown to a glistening silver dollar swatch of infection that dribbled yellow and brown pus.

The clutter. Maybe there was something in there she could use…cloth to clean and bandage it. It was stupid and probably a waste of time, but anything that kept her distracted was worthwhile. She had to admit, even sick and wounded, she was more clear-headed than she'd felt in a long time. The panic had lessened. The fatalist glimmers were gone. Both were replaced by grim understanding. She was screwed, there was no arguing that, but she would rather die clawing his fucking eyes out than giving in to whatever he wanted.

She glanced up the darkened stairway and walked on by. She'd tried that. He wasn't stupid. He was calm, collected, and had no fear of her whatsoever. She wasn't his first.

The light faded with every step into the debris. She pulled box after box back to the light and tore them open, digging for anything that might help. She found nothing more than ancient books and newspapers, moth-eaten shirts, and dozens of shoes. Some of the clothes were newer, but most were yellowed by time. Shivers rippled through her and her heart raced, skipping a beat and then catching up with a thud that ached in her left arm. The clothes weren't his. They were all different sizes. Scores of them, but almost entirely men's. A preference, not that it helped her.

She sifted through the clutter, trying and failing to break apart the furniture and finding little worthwhile. One massive tome had some potential. It was leather bound and heavy, written in a flowing silver gild in old English. If she got a clear swing it might stun him.

The going was slow, the searching done by hand and the occasional lightning bolt that turned everything a ghostly shade of gray. Too often her gaze was drawn to the barred windows above, near enough to be infuriating. At best she could wait for the storm to break, pile up enough garbage to stand on, and scream for help.

She shuffled deeper into the basement, following a cluttered path, hands held out, searching. Part of her mind feared the possibility of a moment where her hands would find something, try to understand what it was, and realize it was him. How had it come to this? Why her? Because she made bad decisions, the worst of which was Taylor. She should have dumped him, or better yet, never bothered with him at all. Could he ever go out and not drink? Never. And then it was a hit of this and a snort of that. If she didn't join in she was a pariah.

Then the needles started. That was the limit at first. She drew a line, and Taylor crossed it while she lay passed out. The sting was enough to wake her up, but it was too late. He sank the plunger, and she was melting from the inside out. It was a type of bliss she'd never understood until she experienced it. The first was his fault. The second, third, fourth, fifth, and twentieth were all on her.

The here and now came back in a burst of pain. Her foot collided with something hard, and she instinctively reached for something to lean on. Her hands touched cold metal, and she bit her lip, waiting for the ache to fade while the chill from the metal sank into her flesh and bones.

Dread set in, tempting Allie's imagination, turning her stomach. A freezer, hidden in the back of this dungeon. The possibilities turned her hands clammy and her legs wobbly.

Just do it!

Afraid but needing to know, Allie tugged on the lid. Harsh white light blinded her, and she held one hand in front of her eyes, waiting for them to adjust. It took only a few seconds, and she let out a breath she hadn't realized she was holding. There was no body. The dealer wasn't stuffed into the freezer. There was nothing but boxes of pork chops, steaks, and burgers.

She began to lower the lid, and the dread came back. Hardly six feet away another freezer was nestled against the wall. An old fridge was beside it, and not far from those was a thick wooden table—old, worn, and covered in dark stains.

Unable to turn back and needing to know, she went to the next freezer. The same brilliant white light burned her eyes, and Allie stared, trying to comprehend. Unmarked, brown-paper packages filled the freezer to the brim, crisp and fresh without the rime coating the meat in the other freezer. Her hands trembled while she tore a package open. A bloody, round cut of steak complete with pale white skin and brown hairs pocking the pores glistened in the light.

The meat fell from Allie's hands, clattering on the stone floor. Reality wavered and grew heavy. Her hands shook uncontrollably, but she couldn't turn back. She grasped the refrigerator door and pulled it open. Plastic containers were stacked upon each other, jammed in beside dozens of glass bottles. All were crimson.

Allie threw up without warning, an explosive spray that burned her throat and mouth and splattered what had to be the remains of the dealer. She staggered away and collapsed against the table. The acrid smell of bleach assaulted her and she pulled away, nauseous, realizing what she was touching. She frantically wiped her hands on her shirt.

Allie fell to her knees, whispering a mantra over and over. "I have to get out." She half suspected he was watching her, laughing, and she waited for him to come.

He didn't. In time she stood again, steeling herself. She wasn't going to die here. Not like that. She wasn't going to wind up in that freezer. No way.

Still reeling, she caught a faint glimpse of color. Gloves. Thick, yellow, and as stained as the table they rested on. Behind them was a wooden block with a dozen black handles protruding from it. Allie reached for one and yanked it free. Light caught the edge of the blade, glinting lethally. She threw it away and reached for another, and then another. She refused to think of what the knives had done in their lifetime, but she couldn't stop thinking about what they were going to do yet.

With a cleaver in one hand and a carving knife in the other, Allie used her arm to wipe the dribble of vomit from her chin. She still had a chance. She just had to surprise him.

§ § §

Jordan ran to the basement door and glanced back impatiently at Kaleb, curiosity glinting in her emerald eyes. She'd been making a pain of herself, trying to get into the basement since he'd put Allie down there.

Kaleb brushed Jordan aside with his foot, ignoring her meows and defiant swats. The moment the door opened, she leapt, darted down the stairs past the light, and her coal-black fur merged with the darkness in the blink of an eye. Kaleb sighed and followed.

The basement was silent. "Are you awake yet?" he called. "I brought you a glass of water and some aspirin." It was a small peace offering, but he had news for her as well. It might cheer her up a little to know that her family and friends were looking for her. They'd been on the news two nights in a row. The story was nationwide. Funny how one story would go big while others didn't even make the local paper. But she was a university student from a big middle-class family with lots of friends. Luckily for him there were almost no clues.

If she was awake, she gave no sign. Not surprising really. She'd seen him kill, and then he'd abducted her. Even so, sooner or later she was going to have to deal with him.

He turned a corner and rounded on the couch. Empty. Again, not a surprise. The basement was a junk heap. There were a million and one places to hide and almost no lighting. Most of the sockets had been empty for decades, and there was no way in hell he was bringing a lantern into this firetrap.

"No sense in hiding," he said. "There's nowhere for you to go."

He waited a moment, and hearing nothing, delved deeper into the room. Light caught his eyes, so bright it hurt. *Shit!* He pushed through the clutter with practiced speed. No wonder she was hiding.

"I shouldn't be surprised you found those. I'm sorry you had to see that, but it really doesn't change anything. We're stuck here until I figure this out."

Nothing. Not a peep.

There had been times in his life that were harder to live with than others. This was one of them. He lashed out, kicking a box that exploded like a dust bomb. "I can tear this room apart to find you," he shouted. "But I don't want to do that."

Sickened by himself, he turned back to the freezers, glad to see his supply untouched. He shut the lid and paused. She was close; he could smell the sour tang of sweat and hear her breath coming in fast, shallow gasps. It wasn't as if he didn't expect it. He knew he was a monster. What he did was evil. But it sucked to see it so clearly.

"I know this is rough, but I promise I don't want to hurt you," he said. "Hell, I even went shopping for you. I've got groceries upstairs. Tell me what you want and I'll see what I can do." He fell silent, hoping, and quickly grew disappointed.

The appliances hummed on and wind whistled overhead, finding its way through rotten seals and cracked glass. The noises of the house were familiar, lonesome as they were, but the faint sounds of life were new. His life was solitary. He would often stare out of his bedroom window in the pre-dawn hours, enjoying the scent of the ocean in the air, watching and listening to a silent and still world, and feeling a horrible emptiness. People were out there, alive and sleeping. Yet even when they woke the emptiness would remain. Existence never felt as hollow as it did during those late hours. But Allie's breathing was worse. Here was someone who knew he existed, and still an insurmountable chasm remained between them.

Miserable, he turned to close the other freezer.

She moved nearby, her breath quickening, and Kaleb turned. He flinched, raising one arm in defense. Something glinted cold and metallic. Recognition clicked. *Did I leave those out on purpose? Did I want her to set me free?*

He was quick, but he hadn't given Allie enough credit; he'd taken her sweet and innocent appearance to heart. The cleaver bit into his skull. For a moment he was floating, the floor falling away only to rise up suddenly. His vision blurred and split. Allie towered over him, wide-eyed with adrenaline. She rooted through his pockets, pulled out the keys, and grunted in triumph.

His throat worked, trying to speak, but only pathetic gasps and gurgles came out. Allie bolted, leaving only the cleaver to occupy his thoughts. It bisected his vision, buried in his forehead, cutting down across the bridge of his nose. She'd gotten him good. A chill ran through his body. The pain began to fade.

It was time!

The relief was overwhelming, and tears rolled freely down Kaleb's cheeks. It was finally over. It would be pure bliss, if not for the terror of what was to come.

Keys rattled in the distance.

Good for you, he thought. *Got away clean.*

A piece of darkness detached and crept toward Kaleb. Bright green eyes glittered like gems in the harsh white light of the freezer, and Jordan mewled and sniffed at the blood soaking Kaleb's shirt and jeans.

The brief relief of finality dissipated as devastation set in, not for himself, but for Jordan. It had been damn near thirty years since he'd found her mangled on a road, damaged far beyond any normal creature's capacity to recover. Somehow, she had survived. She was smarter than she had any right to be, almost human in some aspects, and normal animals shunned her. What would happen to her now? Who would take care of her? She stared into Kaleb's eyes, and slid back into the shadows.

Unable to say goodbye, Kaleb closed his eyes and waited for the end to come. What awaited him? An eternity of flames and torture? Forgiveness? Maybe even his parents? Or would it simply end?

Keys rattled again and he grew impatient. Dying wasn't what he'd expected.

People always grew weak and sort of faded away, didn't they? That's what it was always like in movies and books. But he didn't feel like he was slipping away. He was just…numb. Darkness wasn't overtaking his vision. The freezer light burned against his closed eyes.

Allie pounded her fist against the door and screamed in frustration.

Kaleb opened his eyes and stared at the blade screwing up his vision. More than anything it was annoying now. He shifted, wanted to reach for it, yank it free, only his body refused to cooperate . The left side of his body was paralyzed, but his right hand twitched. It rose as he willed it, grasping upward. Sweat broke out on his forehead, and in a surge of effort his fingers clawed their way up his body.

The lock clacked open and Allie cried out in triumph.

Kaleb's fingers inched over his chest, touched the sweat slicking his face, and finally found the cleaver. The urge to retch arose as he yanked at the blade. Every pull, every last little motion, caused a sickly sucking sensation behind his eyes.

Taking a moment to gain a firmer grip, he worked the blade loose. His head jerked up and down, refusing to let the blade free, and dropped as the cleaver finally came loose with a wet squelch. A familiar, salty wetness dripped down his face, and he let the cleaver slide from his grasp.

Disappointment set in. It had felt like it was happening. Death. An end. Things that scared the hell out of him but could never seem to claim him. But if it wasn't…and if he was going to survive…then the girl had to be stopped. To be hunted again, reviled, banished. That couldn't happen.

Allie's footsteps pounded across the wooden floor overhead. She screamed. Jordan screeched. Glass shattered and a heavy thud rattled through the house.

A shiver ran through Kaleb like a winter breeze. Driven by desperation and self-preservation, he reached for the freezer, used it to pull himself up, and lurched toward the stairs on wobbly legs. One staggering footstep after another took him closer to *her*.

Allie screamed and shouted. More glass shattered, and Jordan let out a spine-chilling shriek. A door slammed shut. The front door.

She was out!

Kaleb broke into a run. If he was dead it wouldn't matter, but once again fate had only teased him. He couldn't lose everything he'd worked so hard and done so much evil for. Fear set in, and with it came anger. They worked like a drug, quickening his movement, strengthening his muscles.

He rounded the top of the stairs and shouldered the door out of his way, tossed aside the kitchen table, and tore down the hallway toward the front door. A piece of archway to the living room disintegrated into particles of plaster as he rammed by.

Allie's voice carried over the storm, desperate screams for help.

Kaleb's feet didn't even touch the steps as he leapt across the porch and onto the lawn. Soggy grass flew in clumps. Just a stone's throw away, Allie bolted up the neighbor's steps and pounded on the door. The little junkie was going to ruin it all!

Kaleb was on her in a flash. One hard pull and Allie was airborne, her mouth turned to a comical little O, her eyes wide with surprise. The little color in her face drained away. She landed hard on her back, grunting as the air was knocked out of her.

Kaleb lunged after her, clamped one hand over her mouth, and carried her across the lawn and up the porch steps. Allie kicked and thrashed, grasping for anything to hold on to. She managed to snag the railing and dug her fingers in until they turned white with exertion. One savage yank and the aged wood gave way. Kaleb unceremoniously dumped her across the threshold and swatted her new weapon aside when she turned and swung on him. He knelt and held a hand over her mouth, tempted to twist her head around.

A voice drew his attention, and he dragged Allie to the door, daring a glance outside to see what was going on. The porch light next door was on, and the elderly little lady that lived there peered out at the wretched night. She called out again, and after a few seconds returned to her home. The door thudded shut and the light turned off.

Kaleb eased his own door shut, and leaned against the wall nearly overcome with relief. Helen was a kind woman, always waved or said hello, and best of all she minded her own business. Thank god she hadn't seen anything.

Allie went limp in his arms, trying to use her dead weight to drop free. When it didn't work she flailed again, squirming and scratching, trying to bite him. Kaleb dragged her kicking and screaming through the house. She grabbed everything she could—a light stand, door jambs, and a chair from the kitchen. She fought like a rabid animal when they reached the stairs. All futile attempts. She wasn't strong enough. Only when they reached the couch did he let her go, trembling with anger. Why couldn't he just kill her? It wouldn't be the worst thing he'd done.

The answer was simple; it was because none of this was her fault. She was an innocent, albeit with a bad habit. Of course she was going to try to escape. She was terrified.

Kaleb let the tension slip away. "No more," he said. "I don't want to kill you, but I won't let myself get caught."

She stared back wide-eyed and uncomprehending. "What the *fuck* are you?"

A monster. But what exactly? Decades of research and he still wasn't sure. There was no slipper with a perfect fit.

He ran a hand through his hair, trying to compose himself, and let his fingers linger on the crevasse in his forehead. It was easily the worst head wound he'd ever had. The girl had spirit.

He tried to smooth his shirt out and touched something hard and unyielding. A black handle protruded from between his ribs. He drew the blade out inch by inch, entranced by the thick, seeping blood. Based on the hysterical sobs and whimpers coming from Allie she didn't feel the same.

Nausea twisted his stomach. *What unholy thing could survive this?*

When he spoke again he was calm. "Whatever I am, you should realize by now that you can't kill me. You can barely even hurt me. And most importantly, you can't get away from me. You surprised me tonight. It won't happen again."

He waited, gazing down at her. When she didn't respond he turned away. "Get some rest. Tomorrow we're going to talk."

Allie curled up on the couch, silently sobbing.

§ § §

Bits of plaster cascaded from the walls when Kaleb yanked the basement door shut. It rested crookedly in the frame, set in place but not even close to repaired.

Jordan mewled from atop the kitchen counters wanting something, not that he cared at the moment. She wasn't starving, and he needed attention more than she did. Kaleb made a beeline for the bathroom and stared into the mirror, hardly able to believe the face staring back at him. It was nightmarish: bloody, pale, and waxy. His eyes had sunken into black holes, absorbing light rather than reflecting it. They were the eyes of oblivion, a personification of the void he'd always felt in his heart.

The gash on his forehead was horrific, speckled with tiny splinters of bone and bits of gray. Blood so dark it was almost black had dripped down his face and shirt. But the damage was already healing, the bone knitting. He stripped off his shirt before it could dry to his skin and threw it in the trash basket. A cut oozed between his ribs, a perfect surgical slice already pulling together.

People had chased him before, hunted him. He'd been stabbed, shot, and beaten, but never had he taken such a grievous blow to the head. Never had he appeared so ghoulish afterwards. Stab wounds and bruises were mere irritations. Bullets burned for an instant, a passing sting no more worrisome than the bite of an insect. But he'd always protected his head and heart, unsure if they were a weakness. Now he knew. He'd survived the head shot, or head-stab as it were, but the morsel of knowledge imparted in that one brutal stroke had cost him dearly. Decades of vitality wiped away.

The thought of losing so much hard-earned ground sent him into a panic. He bolted, tearing into the kitchen, yanking open the fridge door, and shoving

Allie's food aside. He snatched up a crimson bottle, chugged it, went back for a raw, bloody steak, and tore in. Chunks slid down his gullet as gracefully as any pelican, and he waited for the euphoria to set in.

It didn't crash over him as it always had but crawled through him crippled and weak. It felt like the drugs they'd made him take as a child, a creeping fog that numbed his mind and body and made everything go away. Hoping, praying that it worked, he walked in a daze back to the only mirror in the house. A nightmare stared back at him with hollow eyes, a jaundiced ghoul dressed in blue jeans and blood.

So much lost in one careless mistake.

He trudged to bed and collapsed. Down pillows had never been so soft and welcoming. It was all catching up. A man could only take so much.

There were things to be done. He would need money, lots of it, and a new place to live. Somewhere secluded that still had access to the highways. Maybe a cabin in the woods. Even with the sun far from rising, Kaleb felt a crushing need to sleep. His mind raced in an incomprehensible way, trying to plan, a thousand thoughts vying for attention and not one able to take root.

Sleep came like an avalanche, burying him beneath a wave of cold white noise that washed the world away. A flash of warmth spread through his chest as he fell asleep, gone as quickly as it arrived and forgotten just as easily.

Chapter 5

THE DYING OF the day wakened Kaleb from his sleep. The sun's dim and waning light brought not the hope of a sunrise and a better day but the despair of yet another sunset and lonely night. His life was hollow.

As always, he regretted the thought. He had Jordan. She alone in this world needed him. She stirred at his side as if sensing his need and snuggled closer. So many years and she still couldn't bear to be alone. She was his shadow…unless she had something better to do.

Contemplating the night before him, Kaleb crawled out of bed, reached for the lights, and thought better of it. He trudged to the bathroom, wondering if he'd overreacted. Unlikely.

A dark figure stared at him from the bathroom mirror, something apart from himself. It was a creature of its own merit, an alter ego that could come and go of its own volition. He flicked up the light switch and watched the monster's eyes open wide in surprise. The spreading veins of corruption had lessened. The horrible gash in his forehead was little more than a pink scar. Even the black, limpid pools of his eyes had returned to a dull and dusty version of their hazel origins. He was gaunter than normal, pale enough to be anemic, and had suffered a setback that may take years to overcome, but those were all small prices to pay.

Jordan wove between his feet, meowing, her tail tickling the back of his knees. He picked her up and scratched her throat while she trilled and purred. If she wasn't kissing ass to get him moving on breakfast, he might have thought she was happy for him.

Two empty bottles and one shared package of meat later, Kaleb sat in quiet contemplation at the kitchen table. Self-loathing aside, he still had a problem in his basement that wasn't going to resolve itself. "Dunno what to do. That girl is a serious pain in my ass."

Jordan cocked her head and then went back to cleaning her paws.

"Lotta help you are," Kaleb muttered half accusingly.

If the girl didn't come to her senses…well, there weren't really a lot of options. She had no idea where she was, but if she got out, went to the police…with a good sketch artist, who knew what could happen? He mused over paying her off, but not with what she'd seen. He couldn't keep her captive forever though. "What the hell am I supposed to do?"

Jordan stared up, silent, though if she had an idea, she wasn't sharing it.

"I can't kill her. I just can't," Kaleb muttered.

The clock struck twelve. Hours had passed. Sitting on his ass was well and fine, but it was only avoiding the problem. Dreading the look that would surely be on Allie's face, Kaleb grabbed a bottle of water and a few apples as a peace offering.

§ § §

The sound of *him* walking around upstairs woke Allie from a restless slumber. At first, she wondered if it was thunder, but as she became aware of her surroundings she realized the storm was dying off. The shrieking of the wind had lessened to a quiet howl mixed with the soft patter of rain.

She curled up on the couch, shivering and bleary eyed, nausea twisting her stomach. The headache was back with a vengeance. Maybe it was withdrawal, or maybe it was still shock, but she didn't think so. She knew what both of those felt like.

The basement was arctic around her even though it was summer and the rain had been warm. The sweats had stopped overnight only to be replaced by chills that set her teeth chattering. She rubbed her arms, shivering, and looked to the clutter. There might be a blanket out there, an old coat, something. If only she had the energy to find out. She was tired, hungry, and exhausted by a night of little sleep punctuated by horrible dreams. Her waking hours were spent thinking of a plan. Nothing good had come to mind. Neither had there been a miracle—a passerby, a delivery man, or a neighbor. No one.

There was no way out. He was a monster. A real one. The bogeyman who used to hide under her bed, waiting to eat her all up. Now he was finally going to do it—and not all that long after she'd stopped believing he was real. She shivered again. This time it wasn't chills, but the thought of being diced up and placed into small brown packages.

She struggled to stand, managing to get halfway up before collapsing. Her legs were cold and numb and refused to do what she wanted. Unable to move, she curled up again, closed her eyes, and put her mind elsewhere. She went home.

A hand grabbed her arm, shook her, and she struggled to wake up again. The numbness had spread up her body, through her chest and arms, and even her eyelids felt weighed down. She managed to open them a crack, just enough to see him looming over her, his face once again obscured. How did he do it? Ever since that first glance his face had been hidden by shadows.

His lips moved, but the sound they made was faint, an inaudible murmuring. He leaned down into a bit of moonlight filtering between the bars above, and she finally got a good look at him. He didn't look like a monster. He was no deranged psychotic. Pale, maybe, a bit gaunt and tired, but…normal. Worry creased the corners of his eyes. He reached out again, gently caressed her arm, and spoke without sound.

In that light touch she felt an odd connection to him, felt sympathy for him, for the sorrow in his heart, for his pain, and through it all she understood him. What he had done was terrible, unforgivable, but he wasn't what she'd thought. She smiled, grateful for this one small mercy, and let the darkness take her.

§ § §

Kaleb shook her again. "Get up. It's time to talk." As usual she didn't listen. Was she just defiant? It didn't look like it. She was sickly, even for a junkie in withdrawals. He pulled at her shoulder, turning her towards him. There was almost nothing to her. *And I tossed her around. Probably gave her a concussion, maybe even a hemorrhage.* He shook her again in desperation, and his heart sank. Allie's eyes were milky, unseeing.

She smiled. And then she died.

For the briefest of moments, he'd felt her mind, an awful sadness at dying mixed with peaceful acceptance. And he wasn't sure, but had he also felt forgiveness? He took her hand and let it fall away; she was so cold. And the smell...

He wanted to believe it was the natural smell of death, bowels letting go, though he knew it wasn't. It was rot. Infection. One of her feet was pale, while the other was black with corruption. The basement floor rushed up to greet him and he sat down hard. It was his fault. Of course it was. But of an infection? Because of an accident?

"No." He shook his head. "No excuses. You killed her. May as well have broken her neck, too."

Grief and guilt gnawed at him. He sat with his back to Allie and the couch. "I'm sorry," he whispered. "I really didn't want to hurt you." It was true, if not the whole truth. He felt as bad for himself as he did for her. He wasn't a good guy. He was a selfish, miserable, murdering prick. The grief was as much for the life he was trying to live as it was for the one he'd just taken. Killing bad guys was an easy out—a mask, twisting him to believe that maybe it even made him one of the not-so-bad guys. But now he'd killed another innocent. He wanted nothing more than to be a part of society, normal, but he was a parasite. And like all parasites, he killed the good and the bad. No matter how hard he tried he would never be normal.

His mind wandered to when he'd become a monster, that critical turning point in his life when he'd believed a lie. He'd been cursed ever since. The creature inside of him craved flesh.

Unable to look at her, he sat in silence and drew her university ID from his pocket. It was a good picture. She looked young, hopeful, and full of potential. Her life had barely begun before he'd ended it. Why couldn't he just kill himself?

Because you're a coward who can't take what you give.

Time passed as it always did, uncaring, and he was finally able to turn and look at her. He stayed that way for a long time, seeing beneath the grime and sickness. She was quite lovely—pretty in a girl-next-door sort of way—and as screwed up as it was, he'd taken some small measure of pleasure in being able to talk to her. It wasn't enjoyment of her fear or having power over her. It was contact, a connection, even a screwed up one.

She was different. Not that he was above killing addicts, but only people so far gone they may as well already be dead. Even then, they were a last resort. Guys like his last victim, the dealer, were preferential prey. It was more than the drugs, even though he'd been selling the hard stuff. No. That guy had been scum, the worst kind of guerrilla pimp with a rep for disappearing girls who tried to quit.

Maybe Allie would have lost herself in addiction eventually, thrown away her life, and become something he might take if he were desperate enough, but no one would ever know. The only certainty was that she'd cast a light not even a burgeoning addiction could dim, and he had smothered it.

A soft groan startled Kaleb out of his reverie. He spun around, hardly able to believe it, and his hopes crashed. Her pallor had worsened to a ghastly, waxy white. She groaned again, and he set his back to the couch once more, frayed. It was only gas escaping. Usually the bodies didn't linger long enough to do that.

The sickly-sweet stench of infection turned his stomach. It would stay until long after she was gone, infused into the dust. Still he waited, rooted by remorse and terrified of something he dared not say aloud lest, like a wish, it not come true.

He waited for a miracle.

Would it even work? The scenarios were so different. They had done it to him on purpose, changed who and what he was. He'd tainted her by accident. Could he even pass the curse on? He'd thought about it—how could he not? But to inflict that misery on another? He couldn't. Not on purpose.

All he knew was that he was different. Alone. A thing so terrible not even the monsters who created him would lay claim to him.

But if it did work…the thought sent flutters through his stomach. A fragile ember of hope ignited, sparked by the possibility of a future not as bleak as the past. Flutters turned to claws. It had taken so many years to return. Everything he'd done…all of the death…The ember faltered, doused by what would have to be done should his worst nightmare and greatest dream come true.

His stomach grumbled despite it all. Beyond the barred windows the sun was already beginning to brighten the morning sky.

Weighed down by a conscience that would crush a normal man, he trudged up the stairs and into the kitchen. He would eat. And then he would sleep. Every step was a misery. But as much as he hated himself, he couldn't fight the hunger.

Chapter 6

THE SOFT SIGH of the wind was a perfect complement to the comforting patter of rain. A cool draft stirred the layers of dust covering the basement and rolled across Allie, leaving goose bumps in its wake.

She shivered and opened her eyes. It was cold—so much colder than it had been. Gloomy gray light filtered through the windows above, a welcome change from the hostile darkness of the previous days and nights. She sat up and tried to wipe the blurriness from her eyes. Had she passed out? She'd been sure she was dying. Then he had come, but the memories slipped away like smoke between her fingers.

Allie tried to stand and fell back. A sickening sensation of tearing skin curdled her stomach. She reached for her leg, sure she had scraped it raw, and found raw flesh strangely cool to the touch and absent of pain. A grimace turned to revulsion when she spied a mass of skin dangling from the side of the couch. Her entire lower leg had peeled like an overripe grape.

Pinpricks of light cut the gloom overhead, and she tried to stand again, wanting to feel the warmth of the sun on her face. She soaked it in, reveling in the heat, until a scent distracted her. Food. Her stomach grumbled, reminded that it had been empty for days. She found it more by smell than sight—apples, fresh and crisp, waiting on a plate near her feet. Skin, flesh, and even the core disappeared in a few greedy bites and she reached for another.

Minutes later the food was gone and the ache in her belly was worse. Spasms wracked her, sending a watery spray of pulp from her mouth and soaking her arms and chest. Not that she cared. Even the insubstantial wisps of memories were gone. She turned her head from side to side, thinning out the smells of dust, old paper, concrete—and mixed through them all was something intoxicating, something she had to have.

§ § §

Jordan sniffed at the door and growled low in her throat.

Kaleb trudged down the hall, calling ahead. "What's up your butt?" He stepped around the corner and saw Jordan, ears flattened, peering into the thin band of darkness beneath the basement door. "Oh." He gave her a guilty shrug. "I know. It's my fault she's dead," he said, his almost imperceptible British accent thickening.

Jordan stared at him, intelligence shining behind her emerald eyes. Glass shattered in the basement, and she turned back to the door hissing.

Kaleb's heart would have thumped if it could. Was it really happening?

He rushed down the steps and paused. It was far too dark. "Not again," he muttered. His entire body felt afire with—what? Not fear, but maybe excitement? It had been so long since he'd felt anything like it.

The predator in him took over and he stalked to the couch, a thrill shaking him to his core when he got there. She was gone, aside from a revolting mass of skin. He hurried past.

It didn't take long to see the light. The freezers. Not like he should be surprised. Even so, he forgot the stealth and plowed through his hoard of trash, uncaring of the mess left behind, taking a quick glance at the table to see that his knives were all in place. As for the rest…a nightmare. Hard work pissed away. Bottles smashed, the blood wasted, plastic containers emptied, and shreds of brown paper and scraps of meat strewn across the floor. Part of him seethed while another tittered.

It was happening. Lost meat was a harsh price to pay, but she was worth it.

Kaleb turned to the maze he had created over the years. She was out there, confused and more dangerous than ever. "C'mon. We've already played this game."

Nothing.

"I get it. I've been there. If you come out, we can talk it over and get you some answers." *Pain in the ass. Why's she gotta be so difficult?* As if he didn't know. "This is stupid," he said. "You're not going to surprise me again, and even if you do, we both know you can't hurt me." What a load. She already had. And now she could bite through frozen meat.

How much time did she have? A couple of days? A week? Every moment was more precious than she could possibly know. He sighed in resignation. Saying so would only scare her more. Patience. That was the only way. Coax her out. Or just talk and let her listen.

Grudgingly, he turned back to the freezer with a scowl threatening to chase away the high of newfound hope. The meat. So much of it ruined. He'd have to go hunting again, and Allie…good lord, she would need ten times as much meat as he did.

It was impossible. Movies were one thing, but the way it was happening… all from a scratch? The implications were terrifying.

He waited, tense. Nothing. No scurrying. No breathing. The only sounds were rain tapping the windows and Jordan's faint growls. Giving the room one last scan before kneeling to sift through the mess, he searched for meat that hadn't been tainted, cursing under his breath the whole time. Garbage. All of it. Months' worth. More.

Arms overburdened with bottles and a few containers from the fridge that she'd missed, he made for the stairs. "I'm sorry," he whispered. He really was. He still remembered what it had been like. The pure terror. The uncertainty. It didn't have to be like that for her.

He grimaced while passing the couch, unable to ignore the gleaming clump of flesh. Time pressed down, reminding him of his own transformation. In a day he'd begun to black out, the patches of missing time growing from one episode to the next. In a week his mind was gone. But this was different. He was no Isabella, and this wasn't part of a plan.

As if summoned by thinking of her, Allie lurched from the shadows, her eyes cold and milky-blue. Kaleb stepped back, trying and failing to stay out of her reach. Meat clattered on the floor. The bottles shattered. Kaleb grabbed her arms and strained to hold on while she twisted and squirmed with a stunning ferocity. "Stop!" he shouted. She bit at his arm, barely missing, and he forced her back, fighting for every step until her arm broke with a wet snap. He let go and waited for the screams, the crying, even a barrage of nasty words.

Instead, she lunged.

For once Kaleb was the prey. A thick strip of muscle tore free, and he screamed, not from pain but surprise. One hand locked on her throat, he shoved so hard her feet left the floor. She hit a wall with a wet crack and crumbled.

Blood gushed down his shoulder and arm, soaking his clothes and oozing between his fingers. She'd done it again. She was still trying. It wasn't possible. Her bones had cracked against the concrete, and there was a dark stain on the wall where her head had connected and split. She crawled toward Kaleb, swiping at his legs, forcing him back. He ran for the stairs, glad to see a black streak racing ahead of him, slammed the door shut, and hammered the deadbolts into place.

Anxiety throttled him mercilessly, making the rooms spin while he rushed to the bathroom. The mirror showed a different monster this time, a frantic creature stained with blood. Bone and cartilage glimmered inside of a gaping red hole where she'd bitten deep and taken a mouthful. Unsure of what else to do, he pressed a clean towel to the wound. Jordan yowled in the hall, a mournful sound.

Kaleb dropped to his knees and set his forehead against the marble sink. At least he hadn't changed this time.

But, Allie. The speed of degeneration…There was nothing left of the old her. He bounced his forehead off of the sink again and again. She would clean out the freezer, and there was nothing he could do about it.

Kill her! The thought popped into his mind as if someone had shouted it.

He couldn't. She deserved a chance, even if it took a hundred years. The opportunity was too important to pass up, the solitude too painful to endure. One bloody piece of clothing after another dropped to the floor. Cold showers. They held no appeal but would serve their purpose.

Blood mixed with water, swirls and whorls diluting and spinning down the drain until the water ran almost clear and only a trickle of blood seeped from the bite. The meat around it was dark, both bruised and tainted. *And well deserved.* If it was toxic, fatal, so be it. It wasn't like he had a cure.

After wrapping up his wounds, he made for the fridge and wasn't the least surprised when Jordan came running. She purred, circling his legs until he sat on the couch, her plate beside his. He ate in silence, staring at the TV, not paying attention to anything until Jordan demanded more. It was too much to handle. Tonight. The past days. Everything since she'd come into his life. If keeping her had been dangerous before, now it was suicide.

Even worse, he was condemning her to as miserable an existence as his own, to being a murderer, a monster, an eater of men. He had no right.

Numbed by the highs, the lows, and having a strip torn off of him, literally, he went back to the fridge. He always healed faster on a full stomach. When he got back to the couch, he offered another piece to Jordan who was more than happy to take it. Without remembering having taken a first bite, he swallowed the last, and realized he wouldn't be sleeping any time soon. He scratched under Jordan's chin, oblivious to the claws kneading his legs, flipping channels with his mind anywhere but on the shows.

Chapter 7

JASON REACHED FOR his phone, already irate. "What?"

"He's back!"

Adam. Again. If it was another false alarm, Jason was going to feed him to the vamps. "You sure?"

"Unless there's more than one guy dragging junkies into back alleys. Over on Woodridge."

"Go find out. And don't hang up, I want to hear this."

"There's a bonus for this guy, yeah?"

"Huge," Jason said, "if it's him."

Jason listened impatiently as Adam and a few others rushed down the stairs and into the street. This was the third call this week alone. The entire state was on watch—the dealers, the junkies, and even the police, ever since the orders had come down a few months back. Everyone was on edge. Two guys had disappeared in Jacksonville alone, the bloodsuckers home turf, and word was at least three or four more were missing in Orlando and Tampa.

Footsteps pounded the pavement as Adam huffed on the other end of the line. A chorus of jeers and threats erupted, muffled and dim.

"What's going on you...*fucking*...MORON!" Jason yelled, face flushing. Gunshots rang out. Jeers turned to screams. The phone clattered and cut out.

"Goddammit," Jason cursed. He punched in Val's number. "C'mon, c'mon."

"Val here."

"It's Jason. He's back, over by the place on Woodridge. I think he killed Adam and his guys."

The phone went dead and Jason stared at it. Did Val really hang up on him? Or was it a disconnect? He tossed the phone away and dropped to the couch, not sure what to do. It had to be a hang up. Part of him wanted to run over and see what was going on. Another part said to stay home where it was safe. The guy was a freak, a soul sucker, a vamp. It was a hell of a risk.

Or a once in a lifetime opportunity.

He glanced at the clock. Only three minutes since the call.

Mind made up, Jason bolted for his bedroom and tore open the closet. A rain of junk flew over his shoulders as he dug for the box buried in the back. He flipped the lid up. Metal gleamed. The shotgun was sawed off, the red shells of silver shot and the blue shells wooden slugs.

He snatched the chain around his neck, drew a silver cross out of his shirt, gave it a good luck kiss, and ran from the room.

Chapter 8

ANOTHER BULLET BIT into Kaleb's chest. Another shirt ruined. The black hoodie was trashed too. He let his struggling would-be victim fall and charged the men that had chased him into the alley. Three seconds to snap the vertebrae, another three to load the body, a few more and he would have been behind the wheel. The trunk was open. The car was ready to go. And now this.

He rushed them, the sting of hot metal no more problematic than the drizzling rain. One hard swing crushed a skull and sent the corpse careening into another meat bag. They collided with a crunch and fell in a tangled heap.

The thunderous booms grew distant, and a blinding wave of electricity ripped through Kaleb's head. It buzzed in his ears, bled the world white, and sent him staggering, searching for someone or something to cling to. With the blindness came panic and a stitch in his chest, a pinpoint of ice. Heart attack? Was that even possible? It spread, down his arms, up his neck, soothing the dozens of holes pocking his flesh and the mangled gray mass in his skull. His vision came back, sharper, brighter, tinged red.

Whatever had happened, he wasn't the only one to notice.

Two of the men backed away, turned and ran. A third went pale, all of his bravado forgotten while he fumbled to swap out clips. A guttural snarl rumbled out of Kaleb's throat, and an animalistic urge took over. *Prey.* He gave chase, running faster than he'd known he could and catching up in mere seconds. One man he grabbed by the shoulder, yanked hard enough to tear the bone from the socket, and sent him rolling through dirty puddles. The other he tackled, forced the man's head back and bit into warm, delicious flesh before they even hit the ground. Hot meat slid down his throat in a wash of steamy blood, the victim's brief shriek a song to accompany the meal.

Warmth flowed through his veins in a euphoric rush. The victim was young, healthy, and delicious. Dizzy with blood lust, he let the body slip from his hands and sprinted towards the others, slowing only to aim a devastating kick. The scum saw it coming, screeched, and almost had time to beg before Kaleb's foot crushed its neck so badly the head almost sheared off. The body twitched, the head lolling at an angle it was never meant to. Blood jetted from torn skin, a severed artery spewing life. The twitches grew worse before stopping suddenly.

Kaleb turned to the last of his attackers. The man who'd managed the head shot was rooted in place by fear, his teeth chattering, hands trembling so badly he'd dropped the fresh clip. Sirens wailed in the distance and Kaleb paused. A sense of dread, some leftover instinct from when man sought the shelter of caves, gripped his unbeating heart and squeezed. He'd felt twinges like it before, but nothing like this.

It was time to go.

But first, the beast inside roared, screaming to be unleashed, fighting the urge to flee. Kaleb rushed the gunman, swinging for all he was worth and reveling in the sound of ribs crackling and the sensation of hot meat encasing his fist. Knowledge from countless malevolent acts guided his fingers as they locked onto a thing so frantic it thrummed like the wings of a hummingbird. One twist and a wrench and the heart tore free with a wet slurp. They both watched, Kaleb enthralled, the gunman horrified, as it beat a few times, and the man dropped. It would be just to eat it like an apple, tasty too, but taking a man's heart was a cruel prospect, and Kaleb dropped it on the body.

He took in the carnage, wondering. How many would fit in the trunk?

Something shuffled in the shadows, and Kaleb spun, ready to kill. A man huddled against a brick wall, the original target, a nearly dead addict. Everything about him screamed death—his smell, his yellow eyes, and his emaciated body. He'd caught a lot of spatter from standing behind Kaleb when the bullets started flying, yet somehow he'd avoided being shot. A guardian angel? He was only the second person to survive a hunt.

What to do with him? Killing would serve no purpose other than covering tracks. "You can go," Kaleb said. "I've had enough for one night."

A voice thick with an almost Spanish accent came out of nowhere. "How generous. Unfortunately, we cannot extend the same courtesy."

Kaleb spun in search, taken off guard.

A similarly accented female laughed. "We should keep this one for a while. It will be fun."

He couldn't see them, but he could *feel* them. They weren't human. They reeked of old blood and death. Kaleb backed up against the car he'd stolen, ready to jump behind the wheel and drive.

The woman's voice dripped with derision when she spoke again. "How cute, I think he intends to run away. We must be scaring him, Renato."

"Move to the street and step into the light, rogue," the man said. "I would see you better."

What was he supposed to do? Listen? Not likely. Make a run for it? Give these things his back? No chance. That didn't leave many options.

"Let us keep him. Please?" the woman begged.

"Adora, be silent," he sighed.

A girlish *hmmph* was her only reply.

The one called Renato spoke again, his voice soft yet commanding, coming from everywhere. "We came here to kill you, rogue, but I have little desire to do so. Give me a reason to let you live. Surrender and perhaps you will receive mercy."

"I'll take my chances," Kaleb said, searching the shadows, desperation growing as the sirens drew closer. Where the hell were they? What the hell were they?

"Don't be a fool," the woman snapped. "If you fight us you will die."

"For your own sake," Renato said. "Kneel before Emigdio and plead your case."

Put his life in the hands of some random monsters? Right. "I have no idea who Emigdio is, and there's no way in hell I'm going anywhere with you. Just let me go. I've killed enough for one night."

Adora's laughter echoed through the night, spreading so it seemed to come from everywhere at once, but he was sure that for a split second it had been behind and above him.

"He has no idea whose ground he's trespassing on," she laughed.

"Take care, Adora. You give yourself away." Renato warned.

The laughter ended abruptly, and Kaleb had a sense of a shadow within the shadows moving away.

"I grow tired of this game. One last chance—will you surrender?" Renato asked.

"No!" Kaleb growled.

"I take no pleasure in this, but you have trespassed on the wrong territory and I do what I must. Michael, Adora…take him."

Kaleb backed up until he hit a brick wall. He'd always known he would meet other *things* at some point. He just hadn't expected it to be quite like this. These had the same feel as the soulless, dead-eyed creatures he had narrowly avoided in the past. Vampires, if he had to guess.

They appeared at the same time, casting off the shadows as though they were shrouds. Adora dropped to the roof of the stolen car, an amused smirk pulling at the corners of her mouth. Had she not been there to kill him, he might have fallen in love with her. Or at least lust. Tall and lithe, she was a stunning raven-haired beauty with a Mediterranean complexion. Her eyes were lost in the shadows, but he imagined they were the color of honey.

The second, a mass of corded muscle with fair skin and cropped golden hair, looked a modern-day Nordic god. All he needed was a giant war hammer. And courage. Despite being a foot taller and a couple hundred pounds heavier than Kaleb there was fear in his eyes.

The last could only be Renato. Even at less than half the size of the giant he demanded attention. The vampire's coat billowed with a gust of wind, and Kaleb realized it was a cape. An actual cape. He almost smiled, and would have if not for the scent. Renato reeked of time and strength. They all smelled of it, but Adora and Michael were softer, lighter.

Adora jumped off the car, landed as quiet as any cat, and revealed the points of her fangs in a playfully malicious smirk. Michael shadowed Renato's movements and took a step closer.

Kaleb used the wall as a launching point before they could box him in, hitting Adora hard and fast, latching on, spinning, using the momentum to toss her. She screamed, the threats and bluster forgotten, and hit Renato like a cannonball.

Kaleb moved faster than any human could have, and still it wasn't enough. He was smashed to the ground, rolling head over feet through water that stank of garbage and oil before sliding to a stop with his face in the gravel and too many stones to count embedded in his skin. Fat drops of warm rain replaced the drizzle, tiny bombs from heaven striking the back of his head to wash away the grime. He grabbed at his hood, forced by decades of skulking to hide his face, and hesitated, enthralled by boots large enough to crush his chest.

Michael.

Kaleb forgot the hood and pushed to his hands and knees. Renato and Adora rushed to Michael's side. Was this how it ended? Soaked in filth, slain at the hands of other monsters? After countless unfulfilled wishes for death, now that he wanted to live was he doomed?

He got up, brushing away mud and dirt, and noticed that his nails were longer, sharp yet cracked, and his skin was bruised and pallid. The vamps were even less impressed. One gasped. Another hissed. Kaleb looked up and saw their fear and confusion, Michael with one massive fist cocked and ready to swing. Shame burned Kaleb's face. He was monstrous even to the monsters.

"What are you?" Renato asked.

"Tired," Kaleb responded. "I've had enough. How about we call it even."

"You are not Vampyr."

"No," Kaleb said "I'm not."

"You must tell me," Renato blurted. "Countless years have passed since I felt surprise. I would know what you are before I kill you."

"Seriously?" Kaleb said dryly.

Michael was a white blur. His fist struck like a sledgehammer, sending Kaleb sprawling once again. Adora leapt into the fray, slipping an arm around Kaleb's neck before he'd even stopped rolling. She squeezed, determined to break his neck. Kaleb struggled to his knees, trying to pry her cold, steely arms loose. Renato closed in, grabbing Kaleb's coat, lifting him and Adora from the ground with one clenched fist.

Kaleb could feel his spine reaching the boundaries of its resistance. The chill behind his eyes dropped a few degrees, and Renato's pity turned to revulsion. Furious, at them, at himself, Kaleb let go of Adora's arms and lashed out at Renato. The vampire's nose burst in a spray of blood, and he fell back in stunned disbelief.

Kaleb threw himself backwards at Michael's unyielding frame, crushing Adora between them and breaking free of her iron grip. He whirled to face the giant.

Michael grimaced.

Too much. Not sure he could even punch high enough, Kaleb swiped at the vamp with his claws. The giant backpedaled, raising an arm in defense, and let out a ghastly wheeze. He felt for his throat and found a waterfall instead. Blood came in a torrent, splashing the puddles of rain, splattering with every choked gasp for breath.

Adora let loose an enraged scream and charged. She sliced and slashed, her fingernails as sharp and strong as any blades. The world tilted. Adora disappeared, and Kaleb found himself looking up at the overcast night sky. Wind hissed in his ears, ending abruptly with a bone-jarring thud against the pavement that reverberated in his bones. They were on him instantly, attacking in relentless unison, pummeling, kicking and clawing.

Kaleb struggled to stave off the blows and stand at the same time, managing to jump up, set his stance, and take a savage blow from Renato. His jaw fractured and at least one tooth popped loose, but he weathered it, surprising the vampire yet again.

The creature inside of Kaleb rose up, fury devouring fear, and his self-control withered. He grabbed at Renato.

The vampire caught his hands, fingers entwining, and a contest of domination began. It might have been an honest battle, as good a way to die as any, if not for Adora circling.

Renato's strength was incredible, his age staggering. What had once been a mere tingle behind Kaleb's eyes turned to an icy blaze. He couldn't say how, but he knew the vampire was at least a thousand years old.

A flicker within the blaze. Adora was at his back, ready to pounce. Kaleb pivoted and called on every ounce of muscle he had, crushing Renato's hands and forcing him to his knees. The vampire stared up, confused. Kaleb rammed a knee into his face, taking guilty pleasure in the sensations of bones and teeth breaking.

They had made him do this—left him no choice. Kaleb gripped Renato's arm and spun, flinging the vampire away. He'd hoped for a brick wall, a grated window. No such luck. A door buckled with a crunch and the spray of dust and splinters, and the vampire was gone.

He should have taken a moment to aim, but…Adora.

The vampiress lunged at Kaleb's back. He'd felt her move in some unknown part of his brain, and without even turning he reached out and caught her by the throat. She spit and snarled like a feral cat, clawing his hands and arms, gnashing her teeth in desperation to get free. When he turned to her she tried to scream, and he squeezed the noise away. With the ancient down the dread had eased and his body screamed for nourishment.

Unable to resist, he bit down, through her leather coat and into the soft, smooth flesh beneath. He lost himself in the gluttony of a fresh, if cold, meal. The blood was intoxicating. Every molecule of his being sang at the unexpected vibrancy of her stolen life force. It was different than human or animal, missing so many of the vital elements he needed but offering something he had never even known existed in return. He ripped chunks of flesh free and swallowed them whole.

The dreamlike high shattered. Adora slipped from his arms, her shrill screams drowning out the sirens. A chunk of lumber slick with blood and scraps of meat pierced the tattered remains of his shirt. He tried to reach for it and couldn't, paralyzed by a wretched ache unlike anything he'd ever known before.

A titanic force slammed into him with a horrendous clang that rattled his brain as efficiently as the bullet had. For the span of a human breath he was flying, and then he landed, skidding across the pavement, leaving a trail of blood and skin. The clang echoed through the night, melting into a ringing, and then a wail. The sirens. So close now.

Battered and broken, he barely managed to turn his head to watch Renato limp to Adora and gently drape her over his shoulder. The ancient tensed, looked at Kaleb as if considering, and rose into the air. His dark figure melted into the cloudy gray sky.

Chapter 9

RENATO RACED TOWARD the mansion, broken fingers aching with the effort of clinging to Adora. "Be still," he soothed. She whimpered and gave one last feeble attempt to writhe free before passing out. Renato dug his fingernails in. He had to hold on, stay conscious. Just a few more minutes.

His vision blurred. By the time it began to clear the ground was rushing to meet him. Willpower alone kept Adora in his grasp. At her age she should have begun to heal already, but the wound was bleeding freely and her flesh decaying with every passing moment. He seethed with rage. Michael was lost, too young to survive such a grievous wound. They were his wards, and he alone had failed them.

Farmhouses and fields below wavered and dimmed. A skewed vision of the mansion came into sight, growing nearer far too slowly. But it was too late. Consciousness came and went.

§ § §

Cristo's heart skipped a few beats. Adora hit the ground with a sickening thump a few seconds ahead of Renato. Neither moved to get up.

Something must have gone horribly wrong for them to come back like this. And it wasn't like he didn't notice Michael's absence. Cristo leapt from the front steps of the vamp's old country mansion, hitting the grass at a sprint, shouting over his shoulder. "Get help!"

For once Adora was silent. A chunk of flesh was gone from her shoulder. The wound oozed yellow and brown, the smell enough to make Cristo gag. It didn't make sense. Vamps could take worse damage and still be standing.

A clamor of shouting and pounding feet from inside the mansion interrupted the peace of the countryside. Claudia and Luther appeared as silently as ghosts.

"See to Renato!" Claudia snapped.

Luther, a bald, wildly bearded brute born in the times when Romans ruled Germania, knelt over Renato and spoke with every bit of accent he must have had when he learned English hundreds of years ago. "He will survive."

Claudia eyed Adora's pustulent shoulder.

"What's wrong with her? Her shoulder smells rotten. I thought you guys couldn't get sick like that." Cristo said.

Claudia drew a one-handed axe from a strap around her waist and scanned the fields surrounding the mansion. Nothing was out there. Only grass, waist-high, gold as wheat, stretching as far as the eye could see. "Take her to Cora."

Cristo moved as fast as he could with a dying vamp cradled in his arms, snapping orders at the other guards. "Stay on the door, and someone call Lucas."

"What the hell are we watching for?" Frank shouted at Cristo's back. Cristo ignored him.

"Faster!" Claudia snapped. She disappeared down the hallway.

Cristo muttered under his breath and broke into a light sweat. Adora was light, hardly noticeable, but Claudia was taking him right into the damned den. From there it was only a stone's throw to the dungeons—Gothic, nightmare-inducing pits of despair. Even up top you could get a whiff of the place sometimes, a stomach-churning nose full of damp, old blood, and whatever the hell it was they kept down there.

He turned a corner just in time to see Claudia vanishing behind a large and ornate gateway to hell. Cristo breathed deep, calming his pounding heart. They wouldn't do anything to him. They couldn't risk a war with Lucas.

The den was bigger than he'd expected and lavishly decorated. Expensive, full of art, murals, tapestries, a couple of paintings, but the lighting was shit—all old-school oil lamps and wall braziers. Fucking vamps.

Claudia stood before a gnarled black throne, talking to Emigdio. Cristo barely withheld a shudder. Emigdio was the worst of them, which was kind of funny. He was so small, scrawny even, but he packed a lot of menace in his slender frame.

Cristo waited for them to finish talking, wanting nothing more than to drop Adora and get the hell out. Most of his shirt was soaked through with her blood and dribbles of pus. They waved him over, and he barely withheld a bodily shudder.

He set Adora on the floor and stepped aside for Cora, the only bloodsucker that didn't make his skin crawl. The oldest of the bunch, she was the most human, or least monstrous depending on how you wanted to look at it. Maybe that was how she'd survived so long with such a lack of power. The elder vamp knelt at Adora's side. Cristo took a hesitant step back, and then another. As little as Cora unsettled him, the others reveled in the discomfort they caused, and it was one of them who turned their attention to Cristo.

The Lord of Florida was calm, uncaring almost. "Call for Vasco and Amado."

Grateful for a reason to leave, Cristo nodded and ran.

§ § §

"What happened?" Emigdio asked.

Renato startled back from the threshold of unconsciousness, briefly entertaining the mad thought to lie. He could come up with an excuse, but he could not and would not lie to Emigdio. "Michael is dead," he said flatly, voice muffled by a broken nose. "The fault is my own. I was reckless."

"Where is his body?"

Renato looked away in shame. "I left him," he whispered.

Samuel stiffened. His gray eyes fell on Renato. He was an enforcer, a true warrior. They were as different as vampyr could be, but his stare held no malice or no judgment. "The trespasser?"

Renato started to speak and stopped, his throat aching. Part of it was remorse, but some of it was broken bones and bruised flesh. "Slain," he finally said. Once upon a time he would have taken pride in that claim, but those years were long gone.

Samuel nodded almost imperceptibly, approvingly, and slipped from the room.

Emigdio went to Adora and dropped to one knee. Blood pooled on the carpet, tainted by the growing infection. Emigdio prodded the wound and wiped his fingers on the carpet, murmuring to no one in particular. "What has happened to our beautiful Adora?"

Cora waved and Rain appeared with a towel and basin of water. The girl hovered at the healer's back, watching and learning as any good apprentice should.

"I don't know. I've never seen anything like this." Cora said.

Emigdio raised his eyebrows. "Never?"

Cora shook her head and swept her gray hair back. She was ancient, even amongst the ageless. If she didn't know…

Cora dipped a towel into the basin and set to wiping the shoulder clean. "This won't heal on its own."

"It's in her blood," Rain said softly. Dark streaks reached across Adora's skin, an etching of lighting rippling through a cloud. Already the flesh had blackened around the bite. No matter how quickly Cora wiped, the pus grew back just as fast.

"She's dying," Cora said. She drew back her sleeve. Thousands of years had taught her the virtue of good aim. She bit into her veins. Two pristine crimson drops welled on the twin punctures, quickly turning into tiny rivulets that ran down her wrist and dripped onto Adora's shoulder. The blood hissed, popping and spitting as it struck the yellow slime. Small puffs of smoke rose in wisps. Adora moaned and squirmed.

Worry creased the crow's feet around Cora's eyes. She watched helplessly as the pinpricks closed up and the blood stopped flowing. Adora fell still on the floor, the gains the blood had made receding before the infection. "I don't know what this is. If I had time, maybe, but—" Cora bit down again, rending her veins wide. Blood came in a spurt, splashing Adora's wound.

Adora awoke with a scream, struggling to gain her feet, railing against Rain and Claudia as they held her down. The wound sizzled and quivered. Acrid smoke permeated the room. But the rot reversed. The dark streaks withdrew.

When the blood slowed to a trickle, Cora rent her arm again as the strain took its toll. The ancient turned gaunt, weak, dark bags growing beneath her sunken eyes. She wavered and collapsed.

Renato ignored his own pain and tried to get up to catch Cora, but Emigdio beat him to it and held her in his arms. Claudia and Rain stepped away from Adora. She'd passed out again. The apprentice healer was nearly overwhelmed by panic. Rain looked from one clan member to another in search of guidance. When none was given, she whispered to herself, nodded assent, and fled from the room intent on some task only she knew of.

Renato waited, every second excruciating. He couldn't lose Adora, too. His failure was already too bitter.

Cora stirred. "Is she healing?"

Emigdio shook his head. "The rot returns."

Cora opened her eyes, beseeching Emigdio. "I'm not strong enough."

Claudia and Luther shared a disconcerted look. If Cora was unable then neither of them would suffice. Cora had no true power, a rare enough affliction, but she was old, ancient, and her blood had the power of time even if she hadn't.

"How far away is Vasco?" Claudia asked.

"Still in New York," Emigdio answered. "And Amado is in Tampa."

Luther gazed at Adora, his harsh barbarian features softened by compassion. "Amado can be back in a few hours."

"Not soon enough," Emigdio said. "Then it falls to me."

Renato cringed. He shared a look with Cora, Claudia, and Luther. Something inside of him almost broke when they nodded in silent assent. Emigdio was the most powerful amongst them, but the gift of blood diminished some vampyr. It was one of the few reasons Emigdio had never made any children. Endangering his power was to risk their lives. But if they would not take care of each other… they would be no better than the clans they had fled from. It was why they had gathered to Emigdio and each other. It was more than simple protection. It was a family. A home.

Emigdio bit into his wrist and lowered it to Adora's shoulder. Luther pinned the vampyress with one large hand and used the other to wipe away the thickening layer of pus.

Adora awoke, whimpering as rich, powerful blood splattered the wound and sent streams of smoke into the air. Blood boiled within the crater, eating the infection. Emigdio ripped open his other wrist and lowered it to Adora's mouth. She resisted at first, but once the blood touched her lips she was lost in the blood lust.

In less than a minute he had done what Cora could not. The wound was still raw and open, but the infection and the dark streaks tainting her flesh were gone.

Rain stepped back into the room, halting as she saw Emigdio on his knees, wrists torn and bloody. She rushed to Cora, giving her a bottle of blood, and not so much handed another to Renato as tossed it to him before bolting from the room again.

Emigdio pried his wrist free and walked doggedly back to his throne. Like any vampyr it had taken something out of him to bleed so much, and still his wrist had healed by the time he sagged into his chair. His hand mindlessly wandered to his neck and plucked at a chain, drawing it up from his shirt until a pendant popped out. It shone like obsidian, a twisted little being warped by insanity and screaming soundlessly for eternity.

The Lord of Florida looked to Renato. "Tell me everything," he said.

Chapter 10

MAXIME GAVE A greasy smile. "So many? And so soon?"

Vasco struggled to hide his disdain. "Business is good." Maxime was unpleasant enough without having to put up with the thrum of music or the stench of hundreds of sweaty, writhing humans just outside of the office. The smell was overwhelming, revolting, and intoxicating at the same time. How could anyone work like this?

Maxime nodded and filled two glasses with wine. "Please, browse the catalogues."

He was a broker. Weapons. Drugs. Women. Whatever was needed. He was scum. Necessary scum.

"Perhaps," Vasco answered dryly. He hated New York. It was full of pretentious underworldlings, young and old. They mixed amongst the humans, hiding in the masses of freaks and geeks. A few like Maxime had been taken into the fold for their unique skills and connections. Vasco tongued his fangs, wanting nothing more than to leap over the desk and rip the flesh from the peddler's face. Instead he began flipping pages.

He shifted, uncomfortable, making mental notes while trying to forget about the buffet on the other side of the wall. The wine had helped. The bottle in his room was of unparalleled artisan skill, blood infused during the fermenting process to make a smoother, richer product, though it still wasn't quite enough to curb the hunger.

Vasco merely glanced at pictures, picking a range of products. He absentmindedly chewed his lower lip, contemplating the twelfth. A blonde or a brunette? Both were young and beautiful. He ticked the brunette and unceremoniously tossed the catalogue to Maxime's assistant, a vampire with tragically orange hair who looked too young to have been turned.

A glimmer of wounded pride flitted across the flesh peddler's face before disappearing behind another unpleasant smile. "Excellent decisions I'll assume. Now let me show you some New York hospitality. Lord Harlow has made it clear that you are to be granted every privilege."

Offering a grim but accepting smile, Vasco nodded. Emigdio had made it very clear that he was to be the consummate businessman. Ties with New York were important. If things worked out well, it would offer a level of protection greater than any of them had ever known. Harlow was one of the most powerful creatures on the continent. But it still pissed him off having to deal with such lackeys as these.

"Kyle!" Maxime snapped. "Get the car. We're going to The Spire." He turned back to Vasco. "The chef was renowned before he was recruited, and his talents have only grown since."

"So I've heard," Vasco admitted. It was the only part of the trip he'd looked forward to.

"I cannot wait to discuss our business with the Master," Maxime chattered, excited. "Good news is uncommon lately. It will be a pleasure to tell him of your expansion."

Offering no more than a complacent nod, Vasco withheld a sigh. Riding in a vehicle left little appeal, though it was a necessary evil in such a busy city. A white Rolls Royce with tinted windows awaited them in front of Maxime's club. Vasco glowered at the machine. It would draw attention. Even so, he had to admit the vehicle had a certain elegance compared to the swarms of nondescript vehicles that filled the modern world.

The bustle of the city was incredible, the noise deafening. Countless humans traversed the streets, unaware of the predators in their midst. Vasco blinked and realized the incessant din wasn't only outside of the car. He nodded at random, barely taking notice of Maxime's words. Instead he marveled at the accomplishments of men and the revolting greed and industrialization which went hand in hand with them. The size of the city and its buildings were astonishing. Humans had far surpassed what he would have considered possible in his mortal life.

The ride took less than fifteen minutes to get to a private parking garage in the subbasement of Harlow's downtown skyscraper. Vasco resisted the urge to press his face to the window as they drew close. Harlow was doing well, and he was surprisingly willing to embrace change. Many of the truly old ones hadn't adapted as well.

They stepped from the car into an elevator. Vasco put his back to the wall, hating to let strangers at his back. He swallowed hard, disliking the small metal tomb. Maxime failed to conceal a smirk and pressed the button for the 99th floor.

Vasco tensed as the doors opened. Two large guards stood at the elevator entrance, their faces pale against black clothing. But they weren't what bothered him. Scents of food and wine filled the air.

As did scents of ancient enemies.

Maxime led the way, Kyle at his heels, and Vasco followed. It was a small restaurant, exclusive, catering to a very select and no doubt wealthy few. The musk of wolves. A hint of feline. Fey and demi-fey, dispelled of their illusions, were entrancing in their natural states. Vasco remained carefully neutral, glancing but not staring at a pair of Golden Ones, glowing with power. Others shifted in dark recesses, solitary monsters, practitioners of unspeakable arts, hidden by shadows that should not have been. Vampyrs tipped their heads in tradition of the old ways, acknowledging his status.

The room tingled with power.

Maxime's smirk returned as he sat down. "I assure you that there's nothing to fear here. You're quite safe in my company."

With a smile that didn't reach his eyes, Vasco turned to Maxime. "There is nothing here that I fear, only that I do not trust." The air thickened with his words. The smile became real as Maxime's smirk faltered. Kyle watched nervously.

"My apologies. I simply meant that no one in this room would dare break Lord Harlow's treaty. Old grievances are to be put aside within the boundaries of New York."

Drawing his power back, Vasco nodded. The worm had gone too far, but he shouldn't have acted so rashly. Emigdio would not be pleased if news of this reached him.

A waiter appeared with a bottle of wine, mercifully breaking an uncomfortable silence. "As requested, the '97 Dom Romane Conti."

Maxime made a 'get on with it' motion and picked up a menu. Against his instincts, Vasco sat with his back exposed and was immediately distracted from any thoughts of danger. A waiter passed carrying a plate of rare, bloody steak. Ravenous, he grabbed a menu and searched for cuisine meant for Vampyrs. Basil Gazpacho, Risotto with shreds of marinated lobster, and spaghetti with a rich red Bolognese sauce, all delicately crafted. Cornish game hen served extra rare, crusted with a crisp coating of dried blood flakes and cracklins on the side, whatever they were.

Maxime swirled a glass of wine beneath his nose. "Merely a suggestion, but the food has a bit of a learning curve. Many of our patrons have to become accustomed. I recommend beginning with the more liquid choices."

"Thank you for your concern," Vasco replied, attempting to sound sincere and failing horribly. There were only four choices for Vampyrs. It was a little underwhelming, even if they sounded magnificent.

As if reading his mind, Kyle cleared his throat. "The menu changes. There are specials on weekends as well as seasonal dishes. If you ever find yourself here on a Saturday, you have to try the sweet and sour soup. It's my favorite."

Vasco stared at the boy. Kyle withered under the scrutiny, and visibly eased when Vasco nodded in appreciation. The boy was young, freshly deceased, but he seemed to have a rare talent. The disappointment hadn't been visible. Too many years of controlling himself wouldn't allow such paltry thoughts to be revealed so easily. This one would outlive many if he honed his abilities. Being able to read people was invaluable.

"The quail," Vasco said to the waiter. The idea brought back a flood of memories; of hunting as a boy with no more than rocks and desire; of his brothers, whom he hadn't thought of for a lifetime. The birds they had eaten were not quail, and did not exist today, but he was eager for a new experience.

The table fell into an awkward lull, all three men sipping quietly at their wine. Vasco began to relax with something in his stomach. He should have fed before the meeting. He was always irritable when he was hungry.

Maxime set his glass beneath his nose and inhaled deep of the aroma, holding it in, savoring it, and let it out in a sigh of near ecstasy. "Do you like it?" he asked.

Vasco took another sip, rolling the liquid over his tongue, tasting the earth it had been grown in. "Magnificent," he said after a moment.

Maxime raised his glass. "To a mutually prosperous future."

Vasco returned the salute, and almost against his will he began looking around the room again. It was baffling. There were mortal enemies here, beasts that once destroyed each other on sight. "How is it that so many kinds come here in peace?"

"We're in a new era. The old feuds and intolerances were a hindrance. Within city limits there are to be no incidents, no mishaps that threaten exposure. It benefits no one to become reality, to become hunted and reviled once again. I rather like this lifestyle, don't you?" Maxime asked. "You know what I'm speaking of. You've survived much of it."

"I have," Vasco answered numbly. "And yes, I do prefer it. It simply amazes me that they have as well. The old hatreds run deep."

"Not everyone plays by the rules," Kyle blurted out before falling silent at a murderous stare from Maxime.

"Don't they?" Vasco asked.

Maxime gave a dismissive wave of his hand. "Incidents are bound to happen from time to time."

Vasco eyed a pair of the Golden Ones, social elites with blonde hair and blue eyes, yet less human than he. He hadn't seen a true Golden One for centuries. Until now he'd thought they were extinct. It didn't surprise him, though. They were notoriously difficult to kill. "An understandable problem."

"Yes…well…I should suppose the bulk of your product is already on the road, and the women will arrive on Monday," Maxime said, trying to change the conversation. "The amount was a little unexpected, though. I thought you produced most of your own supply."

"There have been setbacks. Our contacts with the authorities are not proving as valuable as they once were."

"Ah, yes," Maxime laughed. "Humans. Always prone to greed or those annoying bouts of morality."

Vasco turned his attention to a group of waiters approaching their table. His stomach betrayed him with a grumble. He wanted to tear the bird apart, feel the bones break and the grease of the meat beneath his fingers. If only he could feed alone.

Even diminished by the civility of a fork and knife, the quail was more than he could have hoped for. Kernels burst into clouds of smoky flavor. The meat was perfectly rare. Years long forgotten came back in flashes, faces and smells, the chill of a night beneath the stars and the false safety he had once felt, ruddy-faced, basking in the glow of a fire.

"Excellent, is it not?" Maxime asked, ruining the revelry.

Vasco smothered the longing to dwell on the past. "The chef is truly talented. I would never have believed we could eat food such as this again."

"Marcelle will be pleased. He can never get enough praise."

The red-headed vampyr, Kyle, grinned. He looked a boy, unblooded—weak, soft, and easy prey. Without guidance, training, his second life would be short. As though a message to forgo the thought of poaching the young vampyr, Vasco's phone rang. Course words lingered on the tip of his tongue and flowed freely in his thoughts. This was a business trip. He was not to be interrupted.

The food turned to ash in his mouth. Cristo babbled frantically. Adora and Renato were injured. Michael was dead. Emigdio wanted him home immediately. He shut the cell and stood. "Please give Lord Harlow my apologies, but I must meet him another night." He turned away, not waiting for a reply. There would be no traveling in style tonight. No first class. No more wine. He would fly himself. But that was fine. It was quicker that way.

Chapter 11

THE POLICE HAD swept in with guns drawn, searching for suspects or survivors, shouting demands to men who could no longer hear. All they had found was carnage. Their shouts faded to muttered curses and subdued replies to the harsh crackles and staticky voices over the radio. Their breathing grew fast and shallow as they moved in.

Kaleb held still through it all. What else could he do? Light fell on his back and footsteps splashed through the puddles toward him. He could almost feel the hand reaching for his neck and the sudden recoil. The cop gagged and stumbled back, tripping or slipping and coming down hard. He swore, horrified rather than angered, and a gag turned to a wet gargle and a splash. It was irrational, even crazy, but a nearly overwhelming urge to reach for the cop and shout "Boo" almost made Kaleb give himself away. That would teach the cop some manners. Gag at him, would he?

Spooked by the sheer violence and gore, and having just contaminated the scene, the cops finished checking the bodies and retreated just in time to wave off what sounded like an ambulance.

Minutes later the alley was empty and the police struggled to hold back the gathering gawkers and belligerent social media wannabe-stars, waiting for the Crime Scene Unit and the inevitable appearance of camera crews and reporters.

Kaleb struggled to sit up, even the slightest of movements worsening the nauseating ache in his chest that was so reminiscent of the migraines he'd had in his youth. He hesitated, afraid to look. He didn't want to see it, deal with it, nothing. As if he had the luxury of choice.

A few jagged inches of two-by-four poked through his shirt, slick with black blood and meaty bits, the flesh and skin ringing it pebbled with hot, itchy blisters. He ran his fingers over the slippery chunk of lumber, grimacing as he pushed, pulled, and tried to move it in any way. It wouldn't budge. Maybe if he got up, threw himself at a wall he could force it loose, but not without giving himself away. Or maybe he could wait for them to do an autopsy and take it out for him. A stupid plan. They would have him, pictures, cameras, and witnesses.

Only one choice left.

Kaleb sank his fingernails into the wood, clenched his jaw, and pulled. The stake held firm, refusing to give, and he pulled harder, trying to ignore the growing pressure and fiery ache. He yanked in frustration, his entire body jolting and still not letting go, and gripped it with both hands. Before he could talk himself out of it, he yanked and threw himself backwards.

He blinked, realizing he'd fallen on his side again, and that the stake had grown nearly a foot longer. Fever burned through his mind and body, a sunburn on his soul and a maddening irritation surrounding the wood. He ripped the rest of his shirt off and scratched at the blisters, popping them and unleashing eruptions of weeping, yellow fluid.

Unable to stand the feeling any longer, he gripped the stake with both hands, mustered his resolve, and wrenched. Ribs cracked and the wound tore wide, the shattered two-by-four ripping free in a wash of blood and viscera. Kaleb writhed and shook with the pain, swallowing screams and choking on self-loathing. He was rancid. Toxic. And the stake…most of his heart clung to it, skewered through, a kebab ready for the grill.

He stared at it while the pain subsided, his mind as wounded as his body. When he could move again, he slid the heart free and stuffed it back into his chest, a sense of numbness setting in. It was time to go home. Chances were slipping away with every second and every new arrival at the scene.

Shaky and weak, he rolled onto his belly and pushed himself up, unable to do anything as his heart tumbled loose and landed in an inky puddle. For a moment he simply stared it.

What the fuck am I?

It didn't matter. Not right now. He grabbed the heart, shook the filthy water away, and jammed it back in his chest. "Not again," he whispered, grabbing the tatters of his shirt and stuffing them in too.

A half insane giggle whispered through the alley. It took Kaleb a second to realize it had come from him. It was the wood. Knives and bullets, those were okay, but wood, that was the line. He had something in common with the vamps after all. *Tristan and Katherine…if only you'd known, maybe you wouldn't have abandoned me.*

He might have dwelled on them for a moment, how it had all happened, if not for the buffet of blood and meat surrounding him and the desperate need to heal. Talons sank into his belly, the hunger flaring past the first and second stage and right into the third. Soon his guts would spasm bad enough to tear. Any of the bodies would do, though one held his attention, one with a richer scent than the others. Kaleb crawled toward Michael, unsure if he wanted to eat the vampire yet unable to resist. He bit into meat in a frenzy, shaking his head like a dog with a toy, ripping chunks loose and wallowing in the rapture of flesh and blood.

The high was irresistible, a thread of ecstasy amidst the agony, and he couldn't let it go. He knew he had to, that they were coming, more cops, ambulances, fire trucks, and probably vampires, but it was so hard to stop.

Only by tearing off a fistful of meat to keep gnawing on was he able to turn his attention to the car he'd stolen earlier. A battered old tank of a vehicle, it was as he'd left it, nestled against the back of a building. The police had hardly given it a cursory glance, rattled by the carnage. Not that he could blame them. There was blood everywhere, oozing from seven ravaged bodies, and not a few spilled organs lying about. It was a terrible waste. The only bigger tragedy would be leaving empty handed.

Keeping low and trying to be quiet, Kaleb dragged the vampire to the car and looked back, wondering how many he could fit in the trunk. It could probably take all of them, but he'd already pushed his luck far beyond its limits. Two would do.

The trunk lid closed with a soft click, and Kaleb sighed in relief. He took a step, two, and froze, a nauseating scent permeating the air, a mix of fear, urine, old sweat and sickness. He glanced around seeing nothing, and heard a whispered gasping for breath. There. Beneath shredded garbage bags and a scattering of loose trash. The old man had a hell of a hiding spot, a hollowed-out nook at the base of a crumbling brick wall.

What to do? Kaleb knelt, ready to clap a hand over the junkie's mouth. He peeled back a layer of grimy black garbage bag and stared into bloodshot, yellowed eyes. His intended victim. Homeless. Prematurely aged. Ripe with the sickly-sweet stench of tainted meat and imminent death. He had a week left. Two tops.

He couldn't say why—killing the man would be a mercy—but he suddenly felt sorry for him. The man had seen it all, the murders, the faces, but...Nowadays they said addiction was a disease. Maybe a disease of the weak-willed, maybe a genetic predisposition, but even so...Was it the number of corpses littering the alley? Or was he just growing softer since he'd taken Allie? It didn't matter. There was no anger anymore, nor a need to hunt, only fatigue. Kaleb's face was layered in blood and veiled in shadows, and even if the old man had gotten a glimpse, he was so high that he wouldn't be able to describe his own reflection when he came down, much less someone else's face.

Kaleb set a finger to his lips, "Shhh." The man stared, too afraid to reply, trails of fresh sweat cutting through the grime on his face. Maybe a little bit of mercy would pay off down the road. Karma. Unsure of how, exactly, he was going to escape, Kaleb eased open the driver's side door and swore when the interior lights came on.

Karma was a bitch.

Lights washed over the alley, and a chorus of voices began to shout, not all of them police. The motor turned over with a rumble. The fan belt squealed. The car was old, in need of some bodywork and a new coat of paint, but it would serve. Kaleb tossed it into reverse and stomped on the gas.

A hail of bullets shattered the rear window, and Kaleb jerked as a few found his back. He spun the wheel and the cops leapt out of the way. Steel and fiber-glass crunched in a clash of old versus new. A modern cruiser had no chance of stopping a '69 Galaxy. Two tons of American steel propelled by 390 horsepower plowed into the cruiser and tossed it aside.

Sirens roared behind and in the distance while houses and cars turned to blurs. Kaleb wove through traffic, panic gnawing at his guts. Half a dozen cherries flashed in the rearview. The Galaxy spun around a corner, shuddering as bald tires lost traction and leapt the sidewalk. Mud and grass flew in a spray and Kaleb stomped the gas. For a second the Galaxy hardly moved, tires spinning, digging furrows, and finally lurched forward.

Barely a few seconds and the police were almost on him. Kaleb laid on the horn and drove into oncoming traffic. Cars honked, swerved, and shocked faces passed in glimpses. Most were lucky enough to find a gap to screech to a halt in, a few weren't. One driver was too slow, managing to veer into the next lane only to take out a cruiser and send a handful of others spinning to stay out of the crash.

Feeling worse, something minutes ago he would have thought impossible, Kaleb hoped no one had died, that no innocents were in the cars. Against all instincts he had the urge to pull over and surrender, let fate play itself out—but he couldn't, just like he couldn't stop killing and eating. He had to get away; fear wouldn't let him do anything else.

The crash had bought him a minute, maybe two, but they were closing in again, undoubtedly closing off streets with barricades and spike strips. Sooner or later his luck would run out and he'd make a wrong turn. Kaleb spun the wheel again, frantically searching for a way out. Time slowed for an instant, a sign flashing in the headlights, there and gone in less than a blink. The stadium. It gave him an idea. It wasn't much, a Hail Mary if anything, if he could only go the distance.

The Galaxy roared and surged forward.

§ § §

Samuel watched from above, curiosity piqued.

Mere moments—that's all it would have taken to recover Michael's body before the police arrived. Now there were too many witnesses, too many chances for things to get even worse. Lackeys such as the ones on the ground better served their purpose when they didn't know what it was.

But what was the creature? A starving vampyr? Was the entire chain of events as simple as someone encroaching on their territory? Or was there something more to it? Perhaps another clan testing the waters.

The car barreled through Jacksonville as though the fool wanted to draw the attention of the entire city. It made no sense. The carelessness. The excessive kills.

The emaciation. Such strength meant age, and such age meant power enough to feed without killing or the prey ever realizing they had been bled. And the vehicle, why? Was he unable to levitate? Such things were uncommon but not unheard of. Still… it felt wrong. No vampyr would make such a scene, regardless of their motive.

Samuel grimaced at the debacle playing out below. The police were inept, unwilling to take greater risks lest they wound or kill the wrong person. They were unable to comprehend the greater justice. Not like they could stop a vampyr, but it was the principle of the matter. Better they should lose a hundred humans than allow such a predator to get away and kill thousands. "Run little mouse so I may kill you myself." With luck it would play out so. His role was to 'apprehend' if possible, to allow Renato vengeance for his lost child. If the creature could not be subdued, well…then the pleasure of execution would fall on Samuel.

Either way there would be blood. Vampyr were clannish creatures; there would be others, a hidden den.

The trespasser's car took a hard turn and barreled toward an oncoming police vehicle. The two played chicken for a few long seconds, and Samuel spat in disgust as the cruiser turned first. *Fleshy cowards.* He watched, intent, certain that something had changed. The turns were no longer random. The trespasser was headed south. Samuel looked ahead and realized why.

§ § §

Kaleb pushed the Galaxy to its limits, weaving through the downtown core, forcing his way through the city in the hunt for Bay Street East. He'd been there before, years ago, and prayed nothing had changed.

The deafening chop of a helicopter drowned out the sirens, and a voice thundered above even that. A beam of light blinded Kaleb, so bright and white it was hot against his face, and he veered away, trying to see beyond the sizzling white spots in his vision. The corner came fast, in leaps of time and place, and the car slid on wet road, cutting across four lanes and bouncing off a curb.

A small delay was all they needed. Holes appeared in the windshield in tandem with the cracking of a rifle. The bullets all struck home, punching through Kaleb's body. He fought through it, the car swaying from side to side as he tried to straighten out.

And there it was. That apartment building. Bay Street.

One of the cruisers made its move in a burst of speed, pulling close enough to go for a pit maneuver, smashing into the tail end of the Galaxy and rocking both vehicles. For a second it seemed the chase might be over, Kaleb losing control of the steering wheel and his chance at freedom. If not for luck, karma, perhaps someone below looking out for him, the bumper might not have sheared off and disappeared beneath the cruiser in a spray of sparks. The cop car veered from side to side, brakes squealing, and the tires blew out with a bang. Kaleb watched it all unfold in the rearview, cackling with laughter.

The undercarriage scraped pavement, the oil pan striking so hard it had to have cracked, but it didn't matter anymore. The Galaxy was over the curb, tearing a muddy strip through the park. A few late-night romantics taking a stroll in the drizzle scurried out of the way and shouted choice words after him. Red and blue lights streamed down either end of east Bay St. They'd nearly had him.

A chain link fence was no more an obstacle than the no trespassing sign dangling from it, and the planks on the dock rattled their discontent as the makeshift tank rolled over them.

What they must be thinking.

A moment of weightlessness, and the car slammed into the river, not the soft, yielding landing he'd expected but an abrupt halting that made his guts roll. The motor flooded, dying in a sputter, hot metal cooling with pings and pangs. Water gurgled and bubbled in, turning to a flood when he cracked the door. An instant, maybe two, was all the car needed to slide beneath the surface and let the murky water shield him from the world.

By feel alone he pulled himself to the trunk and peeled the metal open with his bare fingers, reaching inside and grasping a corpse with each hand before pushing off, away from the wreckage.

The constant drag of the current tried to tear away Kaleb's hard-won prizes. He held tight, wandering in the darkness, giddy at his unexpected escape. It wasn't over though; sunrise was only a few short hours away, and he had a long way to go, longer with every minute he spent going the wrong way in the Saint Johns River. Every step taxed his strength. Icy water invaded his wounds, washing away his blood, sapping his strength. Beds of weeds gently slapped Kaleb, snaring his arms and legs, doing everything they could to steal his dinner.

Despite the struggle the world beneath the waves felt timeless, an eerily comfortable, never-ending age of silence and darkness. What was it, maybe five minutes under? Ten? Half an hour? He had to know. Kaleb kicked up, tearing free of the weeds, and breached the surface. The sounds of the city rolled over him, deafening after the silence, a different universe parted by a razor thin boundary of water. Not even a mile away, the shore was alive with scurrying figures, lights, and sirens. The helicopter ran its spotlight up and down the river.

Such little distance to have traveled for what felt so long. Fighting was futile, something he should have known already. Sometimes it was better to simply go along. He silently slipped back beneath the surface and let the current take him.

In the watery universe below he was weightless, drifting aimlessly, peacefully. There was nothing to fear down there, no one hunting him through the gentle swish and swirl. If this was what death was like, it would be easy to let go and allow the river to wash him out into the North Atlantic. Freedom. An end.

It wouldn't work. Death had its appeal, but it was terrifying…what might happen after. Never mind that with his luck he'd probably just wash up on some distant shore and start his horrific journey anew. And besides, he owed Allie, and Jordan.

Keeping track of the minutes proved impossible, and after a time he knew he had to rise again. Kaleb shook off the half-hearted desire to float away and rose to the surface. There were no sirens, no helicopter, and no people at all. The far shore was still bright, clustered with buildings, and the nearer empty with a wall of trees behind. Exhausted and burdened with the leaden pull of the nearing dawn, Kaleb thrashed to shore, feeling ten times heavier out of the water, and stumbled into the inky shadows of the woods while he tried to ignore the sloshing and constant trickle of water seeping from his chest.

The solitude was brief, no more than ten or fifteen minutes until light showed through the leaves and branches. A building loomed to his right, three or four stories high, dozens of darkened windows and more than a few still bright. An apartment built in the woods? What part of Jacksonville was he in?

He glanced left to the other patch of light. There were no buildings he could see, no signs of life at all, yet something was there. The buzz of a motor filtered through the trees, headlights appearing in glimpses. It drew near, and began to fade.

Hope mixed with dread and he looked back at the apartment for a moment before trailing after the car. He knew where he was.

§ § §

A bounty of cars and trucks were just waiting to be stolen. The apartment was student housing. Good old Jacksonville U. So many cars to choose from was a gift from above, and yet there was no place more likely to have late-night, or rather early-morning joggers about. Students were young enough, resilient enough to not care about the weather, worried more about how their yoga pants made their asses look or how ripped their abs were.

He dropped the bodies and ran from the cover of trees in search of something to steal. A Toyota grabbed his attention, not quite as old as he would have liked but battered and unkempt. He made the sign of the cross and pressed his hand against the glass, pushing until it cracked apart. No alarm. *Thank you.* He popped the lock and flopped into the driver's seat.

The inside was worse than the outside—dirty, garbage all over the seats, floor mats hidden beneath a layer of filth, but it wasn't like he was adding to the décor. Whoever owned this deserved to have it stolen. The steering column crackled and broke. Wires sparked and the car reluctantly sputtered to life.

"Thank you whoever is listening," he muttered. He closed his eyes for a moment, resting. Getting caught had always been an expectation, an inevitability really, and somehow he'd avoided it until now. Until... *Allie.* It always came back to her. She was ravenous, insatiable. She was why he'd been found by one of the *others.* But what choice did he have? He couldn't hate her. It was either wishful thinking or sheer stupidity, but when he looked at her, he saw who she could be. He could even sense a bit of that person in her, a consciousness. They had a connection.

He reached to adjust the rearview mirror and froze. Metal scraped against metal, the Toyota dragging against a parked car. Kaleb was beyond noticing, unable to look away from the creature staring back at him. It was nothing like the last time. His stomach churned. This was worse. He flipped on the interior light, and the sickness grew to revulsion. His skin was green, stretched thin like a rubber glove pulled too tight. It looked as if his muscles had liquefied. And the face—it belonged to a body months' in the ground—not long enough to dry out, only enough to rot, for meat and sinew to dissolve and putrefy. The monster turned its head from side to side. Kaleb couldn't look away from it, from the mossy lips and the dark veins beneath its parchment skin.

"What the hell are you?"

It didn't answer.

Kaleb wrenched the rearview mirror off and threw it out, not caring how loud the shattering glass was. He smashed the overhead light and pulled up his hoodie. No matter how much he tried to build the illusion that he wasn't the bad guy, it always fell apart. Who was he kidding? He was an abomination. As if agreeing, his stomach grumbled, reminding him to pick up the bodies.

Even an abomination needed to eat.

§ § §

Jason had laughed when the cops ran from the alley all pale and shaken. Even funnier had been when the sucker smashed a cruiser and took off. Just the thought of the cops leaping out of the way made him laugh.

The chase had gone halfway through town. Dozens of cars had been hit. He'd heard it even if he hadn't seen it. Stupid to follow too close. That many pigs...it made his skin crawl. Instead he had watched for *them.* It hadn't taken long. It was tough to spot, but someone was above, a gray figure masked by a brooding sky.

Jason followed.

He hoped it was Vasco. Vasco was terrifying, but it would be awesome to see him in action. With a bit of luck the cops would be dumb enough to get in the way.

The rush of the chase already wearing off, Jason snagged the chain around his neck and drew it out. A crucifix dangled from the chain, a special possession, made of silver, blessed by a priest, and with a secret no cop had ever figured out. He twisted it a little, pulled, twisted again, and a piece detached. Inside was white powder, not a lot, no more than an emergency supply really. Jason dumped most of it in his nose and the rest onto his gums and howled, unable to hold it in. It was his turn! His time! All he had to do was find a way to help and he had an in with the suckers. Immortality. Power. Money. Anything he wanted. In time he could even start his own crew. He could already see it, working out of a club, his own personal army—and women, whoever he wanted, whenever he wanted. No one said no to a vamp.

The dream blew apart, punctured by reality. He had to do something worthy first. Far above, the shadow in the sky turned as well, but not following the chase. Jason watched, confused. What the hell was it up to? Giving up? Letting the guy get away with it all? Torn by indecision, he trusted his gut and chased the shadow. Suckers didn't let shit go.

§ § §

After what felt like an eternity of creeping through town, Kaleb slid into the comfort of his own car. The Mercedes started with a whisper and slipped away.

The radio babbled some inane, pointless pop music, and he poked the CD button. Massive Attack came on, merciful after the pop, but even that couldn't distract him. Killing himself. That was an answer he'd spent too many hours thinking about, but he could never make the leap. The instinct to survive was so powerful, it was almost a living entity of its own residing in his heart and mind, unable to be overcome even in the lowest of moments.

Jacksonville's outer limits offered no relief. Nothing could. Not with the sight of rotten green hands gripping the steering wheel or the cracked, jagged nails jutting from his fingertips. Claws more like. Unable to resist, he looked into the rearview mirror again, despising what he saw but finally broken enough to truly see it. If it wasn't already in pieces his heart would have shattered. Nothing good could come of his existence.

Deep in the back of his mind an icy blue ember waxed bright. It wasn't the first time he'd felt its chill. In the past it had shown up when other creatures were around, things with dead eyes, blank faces, overwhelming vitality or a sense of wrong so deep Kaleb barely kept from bolting. Until now it had always gone away. Why? The body in the trunk?

The ember flickered and exploded into a flame that ran down his spine.

A gray shadow dropped out of the sky ahead. A ghostly face glared as Kaleb swerved and sped by. The front tire exploded, and the car veered hard. Kaleb fought the steering wheel, barely keeping from spinning right off the road.

They'd followed him!

The Mercedes skidded to a halt. Kaleb trembled with anger behind the wheel. Enough was enough. They'd attacked him for no reason, and now they threatened his sanctuary. If they found his home he would never be at peace.

He opened the door and got out to face the lone figure in the middle of the road. Kaleb tried to sense if there were others. It didn't feel like it. "I've had enough for one night," he shouted.

"Then you should not have hunted on our grounds."

"*Your* grounds? What makes them yours?"

"Florida has been ours for four hundred years," the figure said matter-of-factly. "You have interfered with our business and risked exposing our existence."

"*I* have! If not for your friends I would have been long gone. No police. No helicopters. No cameras or media."

The figure contemplated for a moment and then spoke. "Perhaps, but our claim is irrefutable. You are not welcome here."

Their claim? Like they owned the entire state? "What are you going to do about it," Kaleb snapped. "Your friends tried. There were three of them, one older than you. How did that work out?"

The vampire stiffened, anger roiling from him. "You defeated two newly turned and an old historian. I am a warrior, a Knight of the Rose. I have killed legions." The vampire reached over his shoulder and drew a sword with a glittering razor edge. Cold eyes watched from behind an unruly tangle of silver hair, searching for fear, weakness.

Kaleb would show him none.

"I would have more time to bleed you, to make you suffer, but the light comes. Kneel and submit, beg Emigdio for leniency, or I will destroy you."

Beg? Not in this life. "I've never begged for anything. I won't start now."

Not so much running as flying, the vampire rushed Kaleb, skewering him through and rending the blade from side to side. Ribs cracked apart. A lung deflated. Skin and flesh sizzled and spit at the touch of silver. It had come so fast, so flawlessly, that Kaleb couldn't stop it.

One hand gripped the blade of the sword as the other locked onto the vamp's shoulder. The Knight of the Rose strained to free his blade, twisting, tearing, and mutilating, scraping the flesh from Kaleb's finger bones.

Stunned at the speed and ferocity of the attack, Kaleb could only barely keep his grip on the blade. He couldn't let go. If the vampire got another swing the fight would be over. He would be eviscerated and dismembered. He'd gotten cocky, let his anger take charge, but he wasn't the only one. Was that uncertainty flickering across the vamp's face? Fear? Too late the Knight realized his error.

Kaleb dug his fingers into the knight's shoulder and began drawing him in inch after relentless inch, bloody foam frothing on his lips. "One…problem…" Kaleb gurgled.

The thinning clouds broke, and moonlight shone down revealing all. The Knight of the Rose was an aged warrior, not quite into his sunset years though as strong and healthy as a man half his age. Dozens of scars crisscrossed his face, some shallow, some to the bone, a few that probably should have been fatal. He'd seen battle, true battle, the kind told of in stories.

Cowled in a tattered black hoodie, Kaleb felt the touch of the moon on his hands and wanted more. That was fair, wasn't it? The vamp wasn't hiding who he was, what he was. Trembling with frustration and anger, he threw back his head and let the hood fall away.

The knight recoiled, trying to comprehend what he saw.

Kaleb grinned ghoulishly. "That won't kill me."

Dawning realization flitted in the knight's eyes, and Kaleb lunged, burying his teeth in cold flesh. Stubble scraped against his tongue, and the vampire's cheek tore free. The Knight of the Rose screamed and thrashed, twisting the blade again.

And something inside of Kaleb broke. The stress of the night, of his life, welled up, washing away his sanity. There had been too many lifetimes spent alone, of being a walking nightmare and trying to deny it for every single moment of his cursed existence. Tonight, the illusion had been dispelled, and the realizations had left him hollow. Tonight he had met monsters, real ones, and even they recoiled at the sight of him.

Unrelenting rage took over. The vampire fell before a flurry of fists and teeth. Kaleb rode him to the ground, raining brutal blows, shattering bones, rending flesh, and enjoying every splatter of blood.

Even after the moans and screams stopped Kaleb kept attacking.

He came back to himself slowly, shuddering at his own ferocity, his rage spent. Bile rose in the back of his throat as he saw at what he had done. The face was a mash of unrecognizable features. Arms and ribs had been broken dozens of times. What remained was little more than pulp.

He stood on rubbery legs and pulled the smoldering sword from his chest. His hands burned and stung where they touched the blade, and he let it fall to the ground.

The highway was dark and empty, but someone would come sooner or later. He walked wearily back to his car and stared at the damage. The tire was destroyed. The window was broken. He sighed and walked around to the trunk. He pulled the bodies out and fumbled beneath the tarp. The spare was smaller than a normal tire. He stared at it balefully. He hated the donut. The ride home would be lopsided.

Chapter 12

YOU SHOULD NOT have sent us both away," Amado grumbled. They should be out hunting, backing up Samuel.

Emigdio settled a cold stare on him. "Now is not the time."

"Amado is right," Vasco said, "One of us should always be here." He glanced at Renato. "It left us weak."

How Vasco had returned so quickly was astounding. It had something to do with his power, and perhaps a gift from Emigdio as well, yet neither had ever been explained to Amado. Even among clan, vampyr were apt to keep their secrets.

Amado shoved his curiosity aside. A mistake had been made. Renato had been reckless, and his progeny paid the price. The entire clan had paid the price. Losing Michael. Adora's injuries. Renato's defeat. Their power had been undermined.

"He behaved like a vampyr," Renato said, unable to meet anyone's gaze. "He hunts at night, feeds off the living, and moves as we do. But whatever he was, he is dead now. I ran a stake through his heart."

"He flees from the police as we speak," Vasco spat.

Renato finally looked up, stunned at the news. "How? My aim was true! The stake pierced his heart."

The contempt in Vasco's eyes spread to his voice. "Then your aim must be as bad as your judgment."

"Irrelevant," Emigdio snapped. "Go find Samuel. He will not answer our calls."

Amado glanced at Adora and Renato, wondering what could have injured them so gravely and killed Michael. Poor judgment or not, it was difficult to believe there was something so powerful hiding under their noses. Michael and Adora were young but strong, and while Renato was no warrior, he was cunning and could move with stealth enough to put the greatest predators to shame. More than a few creatures had met their demise at the historian's hands. "What might it have been?" Amado asked.

Renato shrugged, trying to make a mask of disregard, but he couldn't hide the shame and misery in his eyes. "An Immortal?"

"Never," Cora answered. "An Immortal that looked so would destroy itself."

Amado had to agree. "A lich perhaps?" He shook his head, abandoning the idea. "No, there would have been minions, and none would have been so strong."

Emigdio sat back, contemplating. "Could it have been Fey? Was it a creature of the old world?"

Renato seemed to consider it for a moment, and then shook his head. "I know of no such Fey. If it was Fey, it is of this land, something I do not know. It looked… ghoulish, but there was no fel energy, and it was intelligent, cunning." An intelligent ghoul would indeed be something. They were mindless savages, carrion eaters and snatchers of babes.

Exasperated with talk, Vasco spun away with a wordless sound of disgust and made for the entrance.

Amado hurried behind, catching up at the main entrance to the mansion, pointedly ignoring the guards' wariness. Normally he would have enjoyed their fear, savored it, and sipped it like an exquisite rare blood, but not tonight. Vasco rose into the air, and Amado began his own rise when someone shouted at his back.

Valentine charged down the staircase. For all of his lack of grace, he may as well still have been human. "Wait!"

Amado hesitated, staring at the open space where Vasco had been only a moment earlier. He turned to Valentine, irritated at the delay. "What?"

"It's Jason…"

"Who is Jason and why should I care?"

"He's one of our dealers, runs a small crew that cuts and distributes in town. He's on route ninety-one just outside of town, said the guy just took out Samuel."

The little blood Amado had ingested drained from his face. "Go tell Emigdio, and call Vasco, tell him to wait for me." Before Valentine could answer, Amado raced from the house and leapt into the air. The night was cool but warmth tingled against his skin. Dawn was nearing.

Renato maybe, but Samuel? Incomprehensible. Samuel was a skilled warrior, fierce and unyielding, birthed for the purpose of death and destruction.

Dread grew along with the weariness the sun brought. The clouds were dissipating, and the night sky was growing pale. Amado found Vasco kneeling over a bloody mass on the road. Headlights illuminated Samuel, and an insistent dinging echoed from an empty vehicle. Two of the doors were ajar, but the humans were nowhere to be seen. Amado sniffed the air and looked to the quiet fields. Vasco had killed them; a man and woman with the age-old problem of being in the wrong place at the wrong time. It had been stupid. Reckless. But Amado understood. He swallowed hard, trying to quell the emotions struggling to rise.

Vasco ripped open his wrist and held it over a ragged hole that had been Samuel's mouth. A familiar old pain struck Amado. It had been many years since he had lost a loved one. He'd thought he had no one left to love, or rather he'd managed to convince himself that he didn't. He'd thought admitting it would make him vulnerable, but he was wrong—the ache of losing someone close was no easier because he'd not dared admit to caring.

Luther arrived in a sigh of wind, Cora in his arms. Ancient as she was, the power of flight eluded her. She knelt beside Samuel and tended his wounds as best she could while the barbarian stared down the highway, knowing the creature that had done this was getting away. "We have to go."

Amado simply nodded, not trusting his voice.

Cora cradled Samuel's head in her hand, tears running down her cheeks. She said nothing, and that was more than enough.

Vasco laid a hand on the healer's shoulder. "Go. I will carry him. Prepare for our arrival."

Nodding reluctant acceptance, Luther picked up Cora and raced away.

Vasco picked Samuel up as carefully as he could and began to rise into the air, a stark figure against a pale moon, and gave chase. Amado lingered a moment. There were few cities down this road, but enough territory that it might be difficult to find this thing should it hide away in some dark cave or swamp. But he would search. They all would.

Flight was always invigorating, the chill of air rushing past both comforting and exciting, a gift that never fell from favor. Yet now it did little to ease the growing discomfort of daylight glowing on the horizon. Amado tapped into his power, a secret that not even his clan knew of, and raced to catch up to Vasco, uncaring of the cost.

It took only minutes to catch up, and Vasco's quizzical expression was reward enough for revealing a centuries old secret. Amado smiled, grateful to distract his oldest friend from their mutual pain if even for only a few moments. They shared a look, an understanding of the flaws of vampyr, the secretive natures, and of their unspoken friendship.

"Go," Vasco said.

A simple order, though not one Amado could obey. They both knew there was no time. The mansion was close, but dawn was closer. Perhaps Amado could make it, perhaps not, but to do so meant to abandon two of his clan. They could go to ground, find a place to hide, but to do so meant letting Samuel die, something neither was willing to do. They would try to beat the sun.

The horizon turned to a molten, razor thin band of beauty and pain. Vasco averted his face. "Leave us!"

Amado ignored him.

"This is not a game," Vasco snapped. "There is no need for you to stay."

Amado bristled. Vasco was Emigdio's lead enforcer, his word law, but it was a matter of pride. "If I face the dawn today, so be it. I have too few friends left in this world. I will not abandon either of you."

The look on Vasco's face, the malevolent fury, was almost worth it. Amado smiled, knowing how irksome he was being, how maddened Vasco was at being indebted, even to a friend and clansman.

Vasco's irritation was cut short. Samuel thrashed in his arms.

They would face the sun together, but for three to die was an unnecessary tragedy. Amado dashed ahead and cast his cape wide. He tore it from his neck, let it billow in the wind, and let go. It engulfed Vasco and Samuel, blinding them even as it shielded them.

Amado spread his arms wide, using his body to protect those he loved, and faced the dawn. The colors were amazing, breathtaking. The first kiss of light was a burning caress, and then a flare, and then the sun crested the horizon and struck like the hand of god.

Amado fought for his dignity, tried to refuse the screams—to deny the pain—but as his skin sizzled and smoked, melting away and revealing muscle and bones beneath, he lost his battle. Smoldering in sunlight that had not touched his skin since the fall of the Visigoth Kingdom, he screamed, thoughts of anything but the agony banished. His strength fled as the sun seared into and through him, setting him aflame as he fell in a meteoric descent.

Chapter 13

BY THE TIME Kaleb returned to St. Augustine the sun had long since risen and the clouds had fled. Sunlight spilled through the windows, glaring, baking, and revealing. His bloated hands glistened on the steering wheel, long yellow nails twisted like claws. He'd turned up the rearview mirror, unwilling to see more than he had to.

A swaddling blanket of darkness enveloped him when he pulled into the garage. Finally home, he pulled away his hood, anxious to be free of the cloying feel. He eased out of the car, wincing at every little movement. He wasn't healing.

He stumbled toward the door, stopped, and turned back. The bodies. But it was already too late. They were hours dead, the blood useless. The meat would keep for a while though.

An exhilarating wash of icy air engulfed Kaleb the moment he stepped into his home, soothing his aches and pains. Jordan mewled a greeting, caught a glimpse of him, and bolted. He had to admit, it stung. Not that he could blame her. He'd run from himself if he could.

He staggered through the house, one hand trailing the walls to stay upright. The bedroom called with a siren song, irresistible except against the hunger. The floor wobbled and rolled beneath Kaleb and the walls rippled. He tore open the fridge and rummaged for food, ravaging meat and chugging blood uncaring of the mess left in his wake. There was no joy to it, no euphoria, only necessity. The meat disappeared in a few quick bites, and he reached for another steak.

The second disappeared as quickly as the first, and despite the poor welcome home, he dropped a few pieces for Jordan. She peeked from around the corner, emerald eyes glowing in the dim light.

With gravity and a belly full of meat doing their best to take him down, Kaleb had to lean against the wall to make it to his room. His legs trembled and faltered, and by the time he reached his bed his entire body was leaden. He didn't lay down so much as fall, dead to the world before he touched the mattress.

§ § §

Once again sunset came too early. Kaleb blinked and stared at the crumbling stippling on the ceiling. His stomach grumbled. He tried to sit up and collapsed back, his entire body throbbing. Was it that bad? He couldn't remember hurting like this before. By willpower alone he crawled out of bed and hobbled to the light switch. Flashes of the other night hit him, almost real, shots of his hands, the horrifying face in the mirror, the vampires, and he hesitated. He didn't want to see. Never again. But he had to know. He flipped the switch and fell to his knees in relief. His hands were stained black and red, crusted with the lifeblood of half a dozen men, but they were normal.

And then he noticed the trail of gore. The bed was ruined. No amount of cleaning would help. Bits of flesh and spatters of blood spotted the carpet, trailing into the hall, no doubt all the way back to the Mercedes. Not that it mattered. New sheets and carpet were a small price to pay, and right now all he wanted was a shower and a change of clothes.

He noticed Jordan sitting in the darkened hallway, glaring up in indignation. "What's up your butt?" She didn't answer. She just turned away, tail switching back and forth, showing her furry ass.

Curious and slightly annoyed at the unexpected treatment, he looked down as he stepped on something rubbery—a tail, a mouse, maybe even rat. That was a first. Jordan wasn't a hunter. Not anymore at least. The little princess enjoyed the finer things in life. He scratched at his jaw, wondering, and dismissed it. Shower first.

A few steps later, the twist of a shower knob, and tepid water splashed across the tub. He considered it for a moment and cranked it to hot. When was the last time he'd done that? Years? Heat would make him smell like roadkill, but the air conditioning would cool him off quick enough. Waiting for the old plumbing to warm up, he went to the mirror to get a fresh look at himself. How had he made it all the way home without anyone calling the police? Head to toe he was splattered with blood. He sighed. His clothes were ruined again. The hoodie was in tatters. *Thank you, Adora.*

Worse than the clothes was the face in the mirror. It was gaunt and sickly, laced with dark veins. It was the face of a creature badly wounded, weakened. It should have taken months of hunger to hit this level of degeneration.

Steam clouded the mirror, spreading and thickening until it shrouded the creature within, and Kaleb blinked and shook his head. The fog. It was creeping in like it always did when he waited too long to feed.

He fought the daze and slowly began to strip. Muscles spasmed in protest. The hoodie and jeans fell to the floor. The shirt came off in little more than ribbons. He picked at a lump of cloth stuck to his chest and gasped in pain. Dried blood cracked and crumbled, and fresh blood dripped down his stomach. He pulled at the tatters, grimacing, and remembered. He'd stuffed it in there on purpose. The wound had closed around it.

Kaleb eased into the shower, gritting his teeth at the hot sting even while he exulted in it. A river of crimson swirled beneath his feet as what seemed like gallons of blood washed away. The rags in his chest leaked a steady stream of red as the water soaked in and ran out, diluting and fading beneath the scouring showerhead.

Time melted away. Kaleb rolled his shoulders and neck, enjoying every pop and crunch. The trickle from the shirt turned a pale pink. He wound one finger into the material and began to draw it out. It came slowly, every inch eliciting a groan, finally sliding out in a purge of congealed blood, splinters, and bits of meat.

It was done. A knot of sickness had been drawn out, yet something was wrong. Deep, vicious slashes marred his chest and stomach, gaping wounds where the sword had nearly ended him. Normally they would have sealed up already, scabbed over as soft pink scar tissue formed beneath, but these still carried the sting of the blade, something he'd never felt before, and raw flesh oozed with dark blood.

Kaleb stepped out of the shower, gave the towel a quick glance and decided it was too much work. He staggered down the hall like a drunk, wincing as a rattle of chains erupted in the basement. She was hungry. She could wait. He strained to open the fridge door and looked wistfully at the last bottle of blood before grabbing it and plopping down at the table. He took his time with it, sipping and savoring, not sure when there would be another. It would be a while before he could hunt again.

Jordan rubbed against his legs, purring madly.

"Sure, now you're my friend," Kaleb muttered. He scratched behind her ears, and then went to get a steak to split with her.

Chapter 14

PLEASE LET HIM *survive*, Renato thought.

As though mocking his prayer, Rain gently wiped Samuel's brow and cast a worried glance at Cora. "He's getting worse."

The elder didn't respond. She'd already done everything in her power. They all had, and at best the spread of the disease had slowed. The wounds were too many, the damage too severe. "I don't know what this is," Cora admitted.

"How long?" Renato asked.

"A few days. A week at most," Cora said, turning her attentions to someone she could help. Vasco rested on a bed not far from Samuel, wounds different though just as grievous. Under her careful touch bandages peeled away to expose charred flesh and cracks shining with red meat. His return was a miracle, even more so because he had Samuel with him. To face the sun…Renato shuddered, remembering his own brief encounters, and wrinkled his nose at a dank reek of mold and fouler things. Cora lathered a salve across Vasco's blackened flesh, noxious and slimy, but she swore she could keep him alive long enough to heal.

Renato watched silently, alternating between his fallen clan mates. Was it even possible for Samuel to recover? Adora had. But Samuel had been more than just hurt—he'd been ravaged. In a matter of days he'd become little more than a rotting corpse. The decay was unstoppable. Emigdio, Cora, Claudia, and Luther had bled themselves nearly dry. And Amado…he was gone. Vanished. Vasco had managed a few words, conveyed what had happened, but they would not give up so easily, not without proof.

It's my fault. Everyone knew it. The first words he'd spoken should have been about what the intruder was, or rather, what he wasn't. He slipped from the room as silently as he'd arrived. It was his responsibility to find a cure, or at least the nature of the beast. The archives, his archives, held thousands of years of lore and history, a compendium of his own work detailing the creatures that inhabited the world.

The basement melted into the subbasement. Electric lights grew into pitch braziers, and carpeted floor turned to cold stone. Gruul lunged from a dark recess, talons outstretched to rend flesh. The dungeon's custodian saw Renato and turned away with a squeak, slipping out of sight in an instant.

Renato curled a lip in contempt. Why did Emigdio insist on keeping the wretched beast? Gruul was more hazard than help, more liable to torture and kill the pets than tend them.

He was reminded when he reached the cells; no one else wanted the job.

Gradually the light of the braziers began to fail, so many broken or empty, and Renato lit his lamp knowing it would be dark where he was going. Few ventured to the tunnels beneath the dungeon. Oddities and prisoners grew restless at his passage, only a portion of them placed there by Emigdio, the rest too unknown and potentially dangerous to release. A massive double door rocked as he strode past it. The steel frame shook and sent motes of dust cascading through the stale air. Whatever was kept in that cage was large and very angry. The echoes of its body thudding off of the door chased after Renato long after he passed.

A wordless gibbering in the darkness hastened Renato's pace. The lantern in his hands made him a target, and even old and powerful, the dungeon made him nervous. Doors creaked, unknown horrors skittering and chattering behind them. He jogged determinedly towards his archives, stored away for centuries but not forgotten; books that had been acquired through blood and pain. Once he had prized knowledge above all else. Now his collection was his shame.

Renato blinked. A solid, cast iron door pocked with rust had appeared before him. He glanced around, unsure of where he was, and turned down the dark hall. He faltered, and his gaze was drawn to the heavy bars crossing the door. He knew this door. It was forbidden. No one was to enter this hall.

A voice whispered in his ears, a pitiable pleading, asking him to come in, to talk, to be rewarded.

His hands moved on their own, reaching for one of the many rusted locks. His skin touched metal, and a snap of energy numbed his arm to the elbow. Not electricity. No magic that he knew. A strange power, vile and dirty. He stepped back, and the voice pleaded frantically. Renato pulled away, shaking his head, trying to quiet the noise.

The door shook. Rust fell off in a fine dust, and the voice shrieked in rage.

Renato staggered away. In that scream he felt its pain, its longing for freedom and the hopelessness of centuries of isolation. Its hunger brought his own, and the thirst turned to agony. The bond dissolved with every passing step, and the voice soon fell silent. Renato leaned against a rough stone wall, trying to still his shaking. The encounter had left him cold, even for a vampyr. Emigdio would have to be told. Whatever he kept prisoner in there was not bound securely enough.

After a time, he began to hunt for the archives again. The areas beneath the subbasement were no place to linger.

He smelled it before he saw it, the inimitable scent of a library, of old parchment and leather-bound books. How he loved that smell even while he hated what it represented.

§ § §

Cora stood before Emigdio's throne, struggling to find the right words. She had failed. Samuel was beyond her capabilities. "It won't be long now."

Luther grunted his displeasure. "Vasco?"

"Sleeping. He will heal, but it will take time."

Emigdio looked tired and almost skeletal. "Is there no way to save Samuel?"

"Not that I know of," Cora said quietly. "The infection is spreading slower than it did with Adora, but it's relentless."

Valentine stared back at Emigdio with an insolence that would have bought him a horrendous end had their lord been a weaker or more malicious vampyr. "We need help."

Emigdio dismissed the idea outright. "No."

Guilt worried at Cora. First, she had failed, and now they all held their tongues while Valentine said what they all wanted to, the youngest among them the only one brave enough to speak up. "He's right," she said. "Someone may be able to help."

Emigdio sighed and slumped in his throne. "And how long will it take for the consequence? Is any one of us worth that price? Especially while we are weak?"

Luther and Claudia both looked at the floor when Emigdio turned their way, while Rain froze under the scrutiny. Cora did not. Valentine moved to her side, too young to know what might come. She stared back, defiant. "Yes," she said. "We can't afford to lose him. Michael is dead. Vasco's recovery is slow. Amado is still missing, and we can only assume the worst. If Samuel dies, we are nearly defenseless."

"I know these things," Emigdio snapped. He closed his eyes and tilted his head back. He was stubborn. He knew she was right. He just didn't want to admit it.

"You're no fool, Emigdio," she whispered. "Rumors are already spreading."

Claudia found her voice and joined the rebellion. "The money is already slowing down. We have a fortune amassed, but blood and bribes are not cheap. It will not last forever."

Their ruler turned to Luther. "And you. Are you willing to risk it?"

A serious question. They had all escaped a past, and Luther was no exception. He was born of a nightmare, a true ancient who existed only for the lust of blood and death, whose clan had once ruled as dark gods and been responsible for the deaths of countless unknown throughout history. Luther was the last born to the creature, the last allowed to be born, and only Emigdio's dark abilities and the odd assortment of the clan's powers had kept his father from coming to claim him. Haunted by a past he refused to speak of, Luther nodded.

A defeated sigh escaped Emigdio. He nodded almost imperceptibly. "Then we do as we must."

Not giving him a chance to change his mind, Cora motioned to Rain and dashed from the room. For once in her long life, time was not her friend. "Go to Jacksonville, speak to Suzanne, and tell her what has happened," Cora ordered. "She may know something. And ask if she has anything that might help Vasco. I'll make some calls from here."

Rain ran to do as she was bid.

"Landon!" Cora yelled.

The guard wolf came running, a pair of others on his heels.

Cora waved the others away. They backed off but didn't leave. Not that it mattered. Even if she took Landon into her office, their damned wolven ears would probably overhear. "I need you to speak to Lucas. Ask him if he knows anything about Samuel's sickness or what may have caused it."

"Alright, I'll call back if I find anything out," Landon said. "Anything else?"

"Go!" she snapped.

A thrill ran through Cora. The despair wasn't gone, but it was at arm's length. Asking for help was a minor injury to her pride, but unnecessarily losing a friend would destroy her. In a vampyr's life, mistakes are eternal.

Her hand hesitated over the phone. Their three most powerful enforcers were out of commission. Luther and Claudia were strong enough to ward off many of the clans and creatures of the dark, but not all. There were things out there to make a vampyr shudder with fear.

§ § §

Val turned away when Cora began making calls. You knew things were bad when she melted down. Five years since they'd made him, and this was the first time she'd ever so much as raised her voice. He shrugged at the disgruntled guards and ran after Landon.

Landon startled and tore his arm away when Val grabbed for him. "Dammit, you scared the shit outta me."

Val grinned. "Where we goin?"

Landon ran a hand through his hair and jumped in his battered old pickup. "The Pack Master. He's gonna be at The Penalty Box tonight, shit-ton of games going on." Landon turned on the stereo and cranked up the country music. Val didn't know which was more painful, the volume or the music itself. At least the Penalty Box wasn't far.

The roar of a raucous crowd rolled out into the night to meet the truck from miles away. From the parking lot the bursts of cheers and screams of outrage were at levels that assaulted Val's senses. People here took their sports seriously.

He trailed behind Landon, letting the wolf clear a path through the crowded bar. He slowed, almost losing him when a pretty waitress smiled and fluttered her eyelashes. Val's eyes wandered down her body and back up. A tight flannel shirt, tied above the belly, and very short shorts. A tiny diamond twinkled in her navel. Probably a tramp stamp, too. She didn't seem to mind the look. She did look a little pissed when he shrugged and turned away, though. He wanted to hear what Lucas had to say for himself. The wolves around the mansion seemed like decent enough guys, but that didn't mean they were trustworthy.

Landon pushed his way to the counter and thumped a fist on the bar. A barrel-chested man leaned in and nodded. The local pack leader, slab-armed with hands that looked as if they could crush a human's head, which they assuredly could. Lucas disappeared into the kitchen. Landon followed.

Val slipped through the crowd like mist compared to Landon. Half a dozen kitchen staff scrambled to cook wings and dry ribs, the essence of any good bar. Landon slavered over the food but pressed toward the back of the building. Hungry himself, Val gazed at a prep cook a little too long and got a dirty look for it. He turned away, embarrassed, but he still ran a tongue over his fangs. They all smelled good, tasty, but the prep cook, he smelled spicy. He sighed, reminiscing on hot wings and Pho.

Things should have been different. Being a vamp was supposed to be ro-mantic, magical, wasn't it? But no, it was nothing like that. Food at the mansion consisted of bottled blood, edible, but with a bitter anti-coagulant aftertaste. The others were old enough to break the rules, sneak out and roll a human for a sip or two. Only Cora and Rain suffered with him, and they did it willingly.

He pushed his thirst away and stepped into Lucas' office. It was small and cramped, with none of the swagger of a vampire's lair. Centerfolds and sports ar-ticles filled the walls. It was a cave. Man-cave? Wolf-cave? Whatever.

Lucas eased his bulk into a chair behind a cluttered desk. "What do you want?"

Brusque. No grace. An envoy from Emigdio deserved better.

"Cora sent us to talk to you," Landon said, stepping in before Val could say something he might regret.

The pack leader's eye twitched, and he didn't try to mask his irritation. "Why?"

"There was an attack a few days ago," Landon replied. "Michael's dead, and they think Samuel is dying."

"And you're just telling me now?"

Landon squirmed under his pack master's predatory stare. "I'm on guard duty this month," he said nervously. "When we're there the vamps are our first prior-ity…right?"

Lucas smiled dangerously. "I suppose they are."

You're in deep shit now, buddy. Val almost felt bad. Landon had been a stand-up guy so far.

73

"What does this have to do with me then?" Lucas said. "I'm not kicking up any more guards. The deal is for eight at a time, Valentine."

The last word, his name, had been delivered with a lot of mustard on it. The name was bad enough in itself. And why the hell everyone insisted on using the full version was annoying. The vamps were terrible for it, but this guy? "Just Val," he said, ditching diplomacy. "And we don't need any more guards. I still can't figure out why we need them at all to be honest. But I could use some information. Emigdio sent me to find out what you know, if you have an idea of what's been hunting in our territory or how we might be able to save Samuel."

The bear of a wolf grunted, understanding the purpose of the unexpected visit. "How the hell am I supposed to know?"

"Ask around, maybe one of your people has seen something. You still have that witch doctor, magician, or whatever he is, don't you? Maybe he knows something."

"Him?" Lucas said. "What would I get out of it?"

"I think it's more important that you ask yourself what Emigdio might do if you could have helped and didn't," Val said.

For a moment Lucas was unreadable. And then he smiled. It was a sinister thing, hungry enough to contend with a vamp any day. "Careful now, I hear you're short more than Michael and Samuel nowadays. Not sure who's gonna come running if you start screaming for help."

He knew. Had from the start. Not surprising really. The guard's true loyalty was to their pack. Val smiled. "We have more than enough to handle whatever comes our way. I pity the creature that picks a fight with Emigdio, Claudia, or Luther." Val had no doubts about what he'd said, but right now it was him and Lucas, and he had no chance against the pack master.

Lucas's smile stretched until too many teeth were showing. He stayed that way, frozen, silent, probably imagining all of the ways he could kill the impudent little vampire before him. Sweat trickled down Val's back, and the wolf blinked. "So what am I supposed to ask about? What are you looking for?"

Oh, Thank God. "Someone's been disappearing people all over the state. About 5'8" to 5'10", dark hair, white guy, young and strong. First, he took on Renato, Adora, and Michael all at the same time, and then later he got Samuel. Mike's dead. Samuel's got some kind of rot spreading through his whole body. Renato said that the guy who did it looks like a starving vampire, decomposing, wasting away, but he's something else."

Lucas leaned back and crossed his arms over his broad chest. "How do you know it's not a v?"

Loathing to give up more information, Val sucked it up as a necessity. "Renato staked him, straight through the heart. He thought it was dead, but it shook off, made a run for it, and took out Samuel in the process."

The pack master grunted, his interest piqued. "Rotting, huh. Sure it wasn't a zombie? A hit to the heart wouldn't do shit to a z."

Was the wolf trying to be insulting, or was it just so second nature that he couldn't even see it? "They're too slow, too stupid, and not nearly strong enough."

"You got a lot to learn, boy," Lucas said. "There's shit out there that you can't even begin to understand. I've heard stories, seen things, and I promise you there are z's out there that can rip your ass in two."

Inklings of doubt stayed Val's tongue. Was it true? He'd heard different, but after spending time in Emigdio's mansion could he really rule anything out with any conviction? He'd only been down to the first level of the basement, carrying stuff for Cora, but even her little pets had been a surprise. Still…"Maybe," he acknowledged, "but this wasn't one of them. It talked. Drove. Maybe there are strong zombies out there somewhere, but I can't imagine a smart one."

Lucas scratched his jaw. "Interesting. Then I have no idea."

"Ask your pet Voodoo freak," Val said.

"You ask him." Lucas laughed. "You're lucky, he just happens to be around."

"Fine. Where is he?"

Lucas unleashed a happy, malevolent grin. "Landon knows. He can take you. I'll set it up. Tomorrow night, no earlier. You really don't want to turn up unexpected."

"Fuck," Landon whispered under his breath. He looked almost ill. He shot a dirty look at Lucas that only broadened the pack leader's grin.

Val grimaced. Landon was a guard, one of *his* guards, and he was scared of some mumbo-jumbo priest. "Don't worry, Princess. I'll protect you."

Lucas was silent. He just smiled his malevolent grin.

Val turned away. He had to let Emigdio know. But once he was outside of the bar, he still felt that grin on his back—that smug, shit-eating, knowing grin.

Chapter 15

JORDAN TRILLED AND meowed, tickling Kaleb's face with her whiskers. She pawed at him, fussing until he opened one eye to glare at her. "Okay, okay." Aches blossomed into dull agony when he tried to sit up. Thick, rough scabs made a stitch work of his chest, and the ragged hole left by the stake had finally closed up. He ran a finger over the knitting flesh and swore when dozens of tiny splinters tugged against the skin.

Jordan let out an anxious meow, a shout to hurry the hell up.

"Ease up, fur ball," Kaleb muttered, plucking the splinters before getting up to toss on a bathrobe.

The jaunt to the kitchen may as well have been climbing Everest for the effort it took. Something crunched underfoot and Kaleb glanced down. Tiny bones gnawed clean. And further down the hall, a scatter of feathers and the same rubbery tail he'd stepped on last time. When he finally turned into the kitchen, he headed for the fridge and nearly tripped over Jordan. She pranced around his legs, making a ruckus like she was starving.

He pulled the fridge door open, and his hopes of a quick meal were dashed. The roast was going bad, the color off, and the smell a bit worse than his own on a bad day. There was a time when he wouldn't have given it a second thought, but those days were over. He had the luxury of choice now. It didn't make sense though. The roast wasn't that old…Unless. It clicked. The spoiled meat. The feathers. The tail. He looked to Jordan. "How long was I out?"

Her only answer was a mewl and rubbing her face against his leg.

The flap he'd set in the back door drew his attention. It was useful. Jordan used it to come and go as she pleased, and obviously it had kept her fed for the past days. But with all that had happened, did it have to go?

A barrage of meows and squeaks turned him back to the fridge. The meat went in the garbage, and he took a look in the freezer. Not much remained: One lonely roast and two generous gang banger steaks. A solid inch of frost surrounded the entire interior and would have to be dealt with eventually. Slim pickings, but steak would—

The bodies!

How the hell could he have forgotten? Everything he'd gone through, wasted!

Jordan didn't care. She attacked, a flurry of strikes against his leg. He leaned against the fridge and banged his forehead on the freezer door. So much risk for nothing. Anger and regret lodged like a bone in his throat, and he choked them both down.

Meat thawing in the microwave, he held his hands out for Jordan. She jumped up, and he clutched her close, scratching her throat. How could someone as old as he was fuck up so badly and so consistently? Luckily, Jordan didn't hold it against him. She purred and snuggled, as much as she could without taking her eyes off of the microwave.

Almost dwelling on the events leading to this moment, he noticed the phone. The blinking green light meant someone had left a message. He played through them, more curious than concerned that he had three messages waiting when he hadn't been expecting any calls. The last time that happened was a phone scam.

The first call was from the neighbor, Helen, whom Allie had almost brought into this mess. The elderly woman asked about Jordan, who had shown up for a few meals lately. Kaleb allowed himself a weak smile. Helen was a nice lady, enjoyed her privacy as much as he did his, but she always had a wave and a smile for him, and as much petting and scratching as Jordan could revel in.

The next two messages were from Mark, the manager Kaleb had hired to run the St. Augustine Meat Market, inquiring about an order that had come in days ago. When had that been due in? Wednesday? He thumbed through the phone, marking the dates, and realized that things were worse than he'd imagined. Six days were gone.

As disconcerting as that was, there was a grain of good news in there; no one had found him. Some of the weight on his shoulders slid off.

The microwave beeped, cycling down. Jordan yowled and wriggled free. Chains rattled in the basement as though Allie could smell the meat, and a familiar ache settled behind Kaleb's eyes. *Allie.* Her hunger was insatiable. Worse, she still attacked him at every opportunity. She was mindless, a need-driven beast. No matter what he said, how he tried to communicate, nothing got through. She could wait.

Headlines blared while Kaleb and Jordan caught up on missed meals. The Jacksonville police department was still searching for information related to the downtown bloodbath. A nationwide warrant had been issued for the arrest of the brazen driver who had fled the scene, though they still suspected a body would turn up in the river.

A vague sketch flashed across the screen, and Kaleb sagged in relief. A figure in a hoodie and an approximate height. They had nothing. He'd been trying not to think about it, what could happen, but it was always there, waiting to pop up whenever it could.

The story changed to a mystery. Animal conservation officers were looking into the sudden disappearance of wildlife surrounding Jacksonville. The alligator population was dying off, along with snakes and birds, and all without an apparent reason. Suspicions were running towards some type of outbreak, but a suitable corpse had yet to be recovered for testing.

Mildly curious, Kaleb forgot the story as Allie thrashed against her chains. He was tired, sore, sick of the stress, but what choice did he have? He'd made a terrible mistake, and now he had a terrible price to pay for it. But all he had to do was look at her and he could sense a spark inside of her, a kindred spirit, and it gave him enough hope to keep striving.

He reached to the coffee table and grabbed her driver's license. She was such a pretty girl, had a great smile and beautiful blue eyes. She was a national head-line; the second-year psych major who came from a good family, had a promising future, and apparently was clever enough to keep her dirty little habit a secret.

Chains rattled again and he pushed to his feet. The bodies would be spoiled, but she wouldn't care. They wouldn't be a total waste after all.

The sight of his Mercedes battered and abused brought fragmented flashes of that night. He pushed them aside and stood near the trunk, not sure what awaited him. The human had died of a crushed skull, though he would have spoiled already anyways, but the vampire…Kaleb had ripped out his throat, tore off a chunk of meat. The flesh around the wounds should have been excised right away. Surely infection had spread through the entire body.

Kaleb opened the trunk and was greeted by a stink of rotting meat and bowels let loose. The vampire was a pale contrast to the discoloration of the human, a creature of the night versus a monster of the day. The human was bloated and discolored as expected, however the vampire was a surprise. Infection had taken root, blackening the pale skin, yet the spread was slow, only rising halfway up the face and sinking a few inches below the clavicle. A natural immunity? At the least it was a blessing.

Chains rattled and brackets groaned when Kaleb made his way down the basement stairs. Allie struggled to break free, clawing at the air, eager to feast. The human's corpse suddenly smelled pleasant next to the unholy stench in the basement. Layers of kitty litter did almost nothing to help. If only he could open the windows without the risk of someone seeing his dirty little secret.

"Allie?"

She gnashed her teeth and clawed the air between them. Cloudy eyes followed his every movement, always able to sense where he was. Kaleb watched her with a weary detachment, wondering when she would acknowledge him as something other than prey. She had to feel it too. They were opposite sides of the same coin, the only two of their kind in the world. There was something in her mind he could almost speak to, some buried bit of her old self that he could actually *feel*.

He dumped the corpse at her feet, the sixth in just a few months. Six murders, not counting the Jacksonville nightmare. How long would it take? Would it work at all? He was flying blind, making guesses based on movies and myths. This wasn't what he'd been through. He had no idea what they had done to him beyond that first bleeding and taste of undeath.

She tore into the body and Kaleb turned away, loathing the wet ripping and squishes. He couldn't tell if his disgust was for her or for himself, because for all of her bestial savagery, he'd been there too. The only difference was that he'd grown into a picky eater.

Allie ignored him when he came back with Michael slung over his shoulder. Grateful for at least one trip in which she didn't try to kill him, he set to work dismembering the body, trying not to spend too much time worrying about if he could, or should, eat it.

A familiar scraping filled the basement. The butcher knives clinked and rasped over the whetstone. The meat could be salvaged even if the blood was a loss. Hardly any of it remained anyways having been spilled in a dirty alley.

Eager to get the task done, Kaleb chopped relentlessly, his hands moving as nimble as any surgeon's, skimming fat and nicking cartilage in just the right places. His shadow was a ghoulish mockery on the wall, a sick imitation of puppetry. The light at his back felt too bright for the ugly task at hand, but he'd learned his lesson: no more shadows to hide in. Packs of brown paper stacked up around him. The garbage bins under the table slowly filled with discards, either useless or unpalatable. The one saving grace was the size of the vampire. It would keep them fed for a while. If he wanted to eat him that was... Adora had been a rush, but that had been in a moment of weakness. This was more deliberate. There was time to think. Time to worry.

Routine took over and his mind wandered back to Jacksonville. It felt surreal, like it hadn't quite sunk in. The entire sequence was a half-remembered dream. Adora had been absolutely malicious. And Michael—the man was a behemoth. The worst of it, though, was that he couldn't get over the vampire's fear and disgust.

Renato had been an odd character. His question rang over and over in Kaleb's mind. *"What are you?"* He wished he knew.

The present came back in a rush. Blood seeped from his hand, a thin strip of skin and muscle sliced clean off. He stared at his meat, comparing it. He was darker than they were, somehow tainted. A beautiful roast had come from the vampire's thigh, perfectly marbled, absolutely delectable, but he still couldn't shake the uncertainty.

Bones ground to mulch in the grinder. The worthless bits were drawn in one end and spit out as a noxious slurry at the other end. Swamps surrounded St. Augustine. Mix a little dirt and dye into the splinters, and no one would ever give them a second glance.

Tired from the chore, Kaleb sidestepped Allie. She ignored him, oblivious as long as she had food in front of her. The stench of torn bowels was almost enough to put Kaleb over the edge. He pushed past and ran up the stairs, slamming the door shut behind him, cutting off the sounds of the feast. He sagged back against the door. He was tired. So tired. At the rate she was going the body would be gone in a few days.

Chapter 16

VAL PUSHED THROUGH bushes and branches, swatting mosquitoes. Landon crashed along the path ahead, hidden from the moonlight by a canopy of old, gnarled trees and rampant undergrowth. Every step the wolf took was loud, cracking branches, thudding in the soft earth, announcing their presence to whatever creatures still lingered in a Florida swamp. A panther or gator would be bad enough, never mind legend and lore.

The crashing stopped abruptly. "What the hell was that?" Landon called out, voice high and verging on panic.

Val stopped midstride and listened to the music of the swamp—the bats, the birds, the rodents, and things that slithered. Bayard had them all, and more. An inhuman shriek raised goosebumps on his arm and Val pushed on, unnerved by how close the scream had been and how quickly it had been silenced. "Keep moving."

Landon held his ground, staring into the distance. "I hate this place. I mean, I *really* hate it out here. The smells...they're so *wrong*. Why can't this idiot live in the city like everyone else?"

"Go," Val whispered. He nudged Landon's shoulder. The wolf turned with a sweat-streaked face and nodded before disappearing back into the undergrowth. Val kept close. Something *was* following them, and it was no alligator. He'd caught a glimpse. It kept its distance, shadowing their movements, always back and to the side.

It grunted. Others returned the noise. Too many to count. And for the first time since he'd been made, Val began to sweat. Shapes moved in the shadows, too large to be animals, too disfigured to be human. Val glanced at Landon's back. *Screw him.* Val began to rise into the air, desperate to be anywhere else, and dropped backed down. *Fuck.* He was still too young and unpracticed.

"Fuck it," Landon said right before breaking into a run and disappearing into the brush. Val stared after him, too stunned to say anything. *That coward!* Not eager to be left behind, Val raced to catch up, smashing the path clear and punching through a tangle of vines, nearly eviscerating himself on the rusted spikes topping a decrepit wrought iron fence. He leapt, wondering when he'd had a tetanus shot last, and shook his head. That wasn't a problem anymore.

His bladder loosened, and for a moment he wasn't sure if he wet himself. A ghostly face snarled down at him from atop a mausoleum, only a gargoyle he realized after a moment, but not soon enough to spare himself the scare.

Landon was crouched halfway across the estate, panting hard and eyeing a centuries-old mansion. Grateful the wolf's attention was elsewhere, Val took a moment to compose himself. No matter how much he slapped and dusted his clothes they were ruined. He looked a mess. Very unprofessional. It was Landon's fault, though. The so-called guard's fear was catchy.

Under control again, Val took in his surroundings. The place was crumbling, long abandoned by the looks of it. Whoever had built it had a sinister streak. The gargoyle on the mausoleum had nearly scared the piss out of him. He paused at a fountain. Weed-stricken and mossy , it still worked. Dirty water spilled from the eyes of a disfigured imp holding a bow to its chest in a disturbing parody of a cherub.

The estate was expansive, old and secluded, a private Babylon some aristocrat had attempted to carve out of the swamp centuries ago. A few had tried. None succeeded. Swamps always took back what was theirs.

A knot formed in Val's throat at the sight of the mausoleum. It was bigger than he'd thought. And it wasn't empty. More gargoyles adorned the roof, obscured by veils of vines and moss. Constantly shifting shadows watched from the blackness within, pale eyes flickering and fading.

THUMP! THUMP! THUMP!

Val leapt, trying to fly again and failing. His fangs lengthened before he could control them. He searched for the source of the noise and saw Landon pounding on the mansion's front door. To kill wasn't explanation enough for what he wanted to do to the guard. The only thing that stayed his fangs was the thought of having to walk back alone. He could always kill the mutt later.

Faded and cracked, the front door opened at Val's approach, forcing him to bite his tongue. He glared at his cowardly guide dog and shoved him across the threshold. Double cross? He waited, almost hopeful, and scowled when nothing devoured Landon.

In fact, there was nothing at all inside. The foyer was as empty as it was cavernous. Stairs led to a second floor, and darkened doors rested to the right. An archway to the left shone with the soft flickering of candlelight.

Val pushed by Landon without a word. After all, this was what he'd been made for, to be an intermediary, an ambassador of sorts—or 'the expendable one' as Vasco had not-so-joking called him for almost a year. Even so, times like this were a small price to pay for the gift he'd been given and the death sentence he'd been spared. He'd sort of come to terms with dying, as much as anyone could when they didn't have a choice. The way he was going, the constant degradation of his body and life. Every minute he lived was a gift from Cora.

The candle-lit room was a mix of parlor and library. Chairs and a sofa wrapped around a blazing fireplace. Candelabras burned precariously close to innumerable books set about bookshelves and tables. The room emanated a warm glow brought on by a mix of natural wood and walls painted the palest shade of blue. The paintings were intricate and old, possibly pre-Renaissance if Art History 100 had taught him anything. Cherubs danced in fields of flowers and drank in gardens of Eden. Angels watched over mankind and battled the darkness for their souls.

Val forced his eyes from the paintings. A young man watched amusedly from an oversized armchair. Long blonde hair tied behind his head left a handsome face unfettered. This was what Landon was so terrified of?

"I've been expecting you," Belial said pleasantly. "Lucas asked that I try to help you, though he wouldn't specify with what."

Val nodded. "We are trying to deal with this problem as discretely as possible."

"Information would have helped," Belial admonished half mockingly. "A little extra time to consider matters never hurts. But no matter. Please, sit."

Val sat on the edge of the couch. Landon moved quietly to sit beside him.

"So, the Vampire Lord asks for help," Belial said. "The problem must be serious."

"One of our clan is dead. Another is dying of an illness we can't seem to cure."

Belial nodded in sympathy. "To lose immortality…such a shame." He began to speak, hesitated, and went on. "I hate to bring up such an unseemly issue but, as is the nature of my business, payment will be required."

For a second Val was taken aback. He'd expected this, but not so boldly.

"You really didn't expect me to provide such a specialized service for *free*, did you?" Belial said.

"What do you want?"

Like the snap of fingers or the flick of a light switch there were calculations working behind the sorcerer's eyes. "I would like to view Emigdio's collection before I choose."

This wasn't what he'd been expecting. Landon said the wolves dealt with Belial in cash. Only Emigdio fully knew what was in those basements. Not even clan were allowed to explore. Cora ran an arboretum and Renato kept books down there, but no one else had set foot past the first floor of the dungeon. Val shook his head. "I can't make that deal."

The pleasant demeanor faltered and melted away. What was left was cold disdain. "Then we have nothing to discuss."

Val settled back on the couch. He was beginning to understand why Landon was unnerved.

"What I can do is take your offer back to Lord Emigdio. The collection is his. It's only fitting that he decides what he's willing to pay."

"Something he should have thought of before sending a lackey to barter with me," Belial snapped.

Shadows outside the windows drew Val's attention. Landon shifted nervously. The wolf reeked of fear. Thank god the witch doctor couldn't smell it.

It took a few seconds to notice what Landon already had. Val struggled to keep his face a mask. He'd thought it was the shadows, but it was more than that. The room had shifted, just a bit. Some books were gone, replaced by jars and bottles. The pale blue of the walls had grown dull and dirty, laced with cracks. "My apologies," Val said, "But I'd understood you dealt in money."

The half-amused smile returned to Belial as though it had never left. "I suppose that's an understandable mistake. My agreement with Lucas has always been based on monetary terms. Unfortunate Lupines, they have nothing else to offer."

"Can you help then?" Val asked, eyes darting back to the windows.

"Perhaps. Tell me everything."

Val recounted what he'd been told. The kills. The fight with Renato. Samuel's demise. Belial closed his eyes as he listened, arms tented, fingers locked, interrupting occasionally to ask for details.

When the story ended, he sat back with a sigh. "I believe I can help, though I doubt the knight can be saved. Perhaps had you come to me sooner..."

Val slumped back. Samuel was doomed? Then it was a waste of time. "I came here to save Samuel," he said. "If you can't help him, we have little to discuss."

A flicker of something twisted crossed Belial's face. Hatred? Anger? Both?

"Take my offer to Emigdio, and when you do, ask him if it is worth a fraction of his wealth to know what you are fighting so that you lose no one else when you hunt this creature down."

"You know what it is?"

The witch doctor settled back into his chair, contemplating the question. "Possibly. If it is as I suspect, you are in more danger than you know. I will have to look into the matter to be certain."

In other words, this third-rate conjurer wanted to get paid before he said a word. No matter. They would need a night or two to prepare a hunt anyway. "Fine," he said grudgingly.

Belial struggled with some internal battle. Val knew he should be more courteous, more charming, but he'd been off his game since he set foot in the swamp.

"Go then," the witch doctor snapped. "And come back tomorrow night or not at all."

Val returned the cold stare, wondering. Did Belial look different? Had his hair been light blonde when they'd first arrived? And he'd been younger, more vibrant.

The house changed with every step away from Belial. Cracks spread and paint faded and peeled. All that remained were the candelabras, now illuminating shelves full of dusty tomes and jars filled with unknown liquids and unspeakable things.

Val dared once glance back and wished he hadn't. Belial's stare was dark and grim. Their host had aged and lost the welcoming aura he'd exuded earlier. The healthy light beige of his skin had faded to jaundice. Bruises grew beneath his eyes as deep crow's feet spread beside them. Belial flicked one hand dismissively at the windows and turned back to Val. The shadows fled. Something let out a blood curdling wail. All that remained of the young man from earlier was the smile, but now it was forced and without a hint of sincerity.

The swamps were silent when they stepped from the house. Unable to resist, Val wandered toward the window.

"C'mon, don't." Landon protested. "Let's just get the hell outta here."

"In a second," Val said. He peeked through the window and cursed himself for making the same mistake twice. Belial sat in his chair, an aged tome in his gnarled hands. The room around him had turned to rot and disrepair. Paintings of cherubs and angels were now disturbing nightmares. Movement caught his eye. For the first time since he'd been dead, Val's heart leapt. Belial looked up from behind the tome. The witch doctor was shrunken and shriveled, sitting in a half-rotten chair like a tumor growing from the disintegrating fabric. The look in his eyes was one of madness and spite, as if he was ready to leap up and chase them howling into the night. Val spun away, racing back to the car. Landon called after him, begging him to slow down. The pathetic shouts were irritating, but after a while Landon was so far behind that Val couldn't hear him anyways.

Chapter 17

UNABLE TO FALL asleep or get up and get something done, Kaleb lay on the couch in his bathrobe, flipping through a hundred channels and finding nothing to watch. Cable was abysmal. What the hell was he paying a hundred and fifty bucks a month for? And what was he going to eat? Animal flesh wasn't cutting it anymore, and short of going hunting his only choice was snacking on Dracula tartar.

He reached out to scratch Jordan's belly. She slept on the fringe of his robe, paws to heaven, enjoying a lazy snooze despite having only woken an hour or so earlier. She flinched and squeaked, turning an accusatory stare on him. Unusual for her—she normally enjoyed being woken up for attention or treats. As unforgivable as the trespass was, she stretched out for a belly rub. Kaleb grinned and indulged her while still flipping through the channels.

The sci-fi channel caught his attention. A *Planet of the Apes* marathon in half an hour. It was old and cheesy, but classic old and cheesy, as good a way to waste a day as any. All he needed now was a snack.

He got up with a groan and hobbled to the kitchen. A little over a week since the massacre and he still hadn't healed. Was it the extent of the damage? The use of wood, silver, and claws? For sure he wasn't eating the right stuff. Even so, today was better than yesterday, and much better than the day before that.

Opening the fridge was a futile effort. There was nothing in there, but he looked anyways. A few assorted cans, two boxes of baking soda, and some wrinkled fruit he'd never been able to give to Allie. What he wouldn't give for a few bottles. The freezer was just as dismal. What had he expected, for meat to suddenly appear? He'd finished off the last steak yesterday.

He closed the freezer and glanced reluctantly toward the basement. Go out or raid the deep freezers? Stupid questions. Going out wasn't an option unless he could wait until night and hope he found a really slow-moving victim. What was he scared of anyways? He'd eaten of them twice already and nothing bad had happened. In fact, they had been intoxicating, energizing. Or was that what he feared?

He crept to the basement door and slipped quietly down the stairs. Allie knelt over a dark and twisted treat, gnawing the scraps off a forearm. As much as Kaleb wanted to try to reach her, his hunger was flaring. He slipped past, allowing Allie to enjoy her feast.

A dusting of frost covered the brown paper packages, glittering in the white light off the freezers. The packages were plain, simple, and a little bit ominous. *No choice. It's either this or go hunting.*

Arms full, Kaleb stopped by Allie. She wavered on her knees, the flesh before her forgotten. Hardly more than a glimmer of her eyes could be seen through the tangle of her hair, but Kaleb felt the weight of her attention nonetheless. "Allie?"

Did she twitch at her name, or was he imagining it? Wishful thinking?

"Allie?" Kaleb said again. "Do you understand me?" She stayed as she was, swaying back and forth, and Kaleb sighed with disappointment. It was far too soon.

She lunged. The chains reached their limits with a clank; a bracket tore loose, jolting her a bit closer.

Kaleb lurched back, resisting the insane urge to take her hand. Despite her gnashing teeth and straining to break loose, he had the feeling she only wanted to be close. Foolish to say the least. He glanced at a few packages that had slipped from his arms and fallen within Allie's reach and made for the stairs. A bit of meat wasn't worth the trouble.

"When are you gonna wake up?" he muttered, knowing the answer all too well.

A minute later the microwave was humming, a few steaks spinning round and round. Kaleb's stomach growled and went through the first stage of true hunger. Spasms ripped through his abdomen, muscles clenching and threatening to tear apart. He barely resisted the urge to double over and fall to the floor. The first stage was unpleasant, but it was only a gentle reminder of what would happen if he didn't eat.

The microwave beeped, cycling down, the last five seconds until he could eat, and Jordan purred, winding herself around his legs, appearing like magic. It was more than her being jet black in a dimly lit house, it was as though she could move unseen when she wanted to. Black magic.

"I should have named you Minnie, you mooch," he said.

Chapter 18

ELP!" Rain shrieked.

Footsteps pounded down the hall, and the door exploded in a spray of splinters as Emigdio burst into the infirmary, Cora and Luther hot on his heels. A handful of guards clustered behind them.

Emigdio had one hand poised to strike, and even though she was fighting for her life, Rain was entranced by the smoking tendrils rising from the dark aura that encased his body. Fangs gnashed inches away from her face, and she twined her hands in Samuel's hair and yanked his head back. At best it bought her a few more seconds, and even that was impressive. He was simply too strong.

An arm wound around Samuel's neck. More locked onto his arms and tore him away. Rain let go of his hair and scrambled out of reach.

"Chains," Cora snapped at the guards. "Now!"

Samuel flailed, trying to break free. His teeth clacked together, narrowly missing Luther's hand. Two guards bolted from the room while the others pinned Samuel down. Even then he struggled, almost breaking free until Emigdio jumped in.

The guards rushed back in, juggling silver chains that sizzled and smoked against their skin. They threw the chains over Samuel, wrenching them tight. Like the wolves, the silver burned Samuel, melting his flesh and sending up smoke where they touched. Unlike the wolves, Samuel didn't care.

Rain startled when a hand touched her shoulder. Cora knelt beside her, carefully looking her over and questioning her at the same time. "What happened?"

"I don't know," Rain said. "I was just trying to feed him."

"You must take the deal," Luther said.

"It is already done. Valentine left at dusk."

Luther set a hand to the back of Samuel's head. "Whatever he used to be is gone. We can only give him peace and honor him with vengeance."

The room fell to silence. Eyes drifted to Emigdio. "Shackle him in the dungeons." The vampyr watched, their spirits wounded and their hopes all but gone.

"Save him," a dry voice rasped.

Cora was the first to react, rushing to Vasco's side. "You're awake!"

Vasco groaned and tried to sit up.

"Lay down!" Cora ordered. "Old fool, you've been in a coma for days."

Vasco gasped and collapsed, charred skin flaking to show the meat beneath.

Cora went to him, a small bottle in hand, and tipped it at his lips. "Put your mind away and be still. All things will pass, this pain included."

"Do you remember any more of Amado?" Emigdio asked, gentle but insistent.

Vasco struggled to open his eyes; the liquid Cora had given him already taking effect. "He hasn't returned?" he rasped. Crestfallen, he closed his eyes again, red trails cutting tracks across the cracked and burnt landscape of his cheeks.

§ § §

"Jesus Christ," Henry cursed. He dropped Samuel and hopped out of reach of the fangs chomping at his legs. "Someone cover this asshole's face up."

The others let Samuel fall to the ground. Jeff pulled his belt loose and looped it around the vamp's face, reining him in.

"What the hell is wrong with him?" Devon asked. "The chains are melting his skin and he doesn't care."

"He sure wants a piece of you," Jeff said with a laugh to Henry. "Whaddya do? Make eyes at that girlie again?"

Henry felt the blush working its way up from his throat. Rain was cute. But wolves and leeches didn't mingle. They'd made that clear quick enough.

"Cut the shit," Roger snapped. "I don't wanna spend any longer down here than I have to."

"How deep we goin?" Devon asked.

Grateful for the distraction, Henry grabbed Samuel's ankle and started dragging him. "Just one floor. The cells."

Roger darted in and grabbed Samuel's other ankle. At least one of them wasn't a complete idiot.

"Just watch our backs," Henry said. He breathed through his mouth to avoid the stale, clammy air of the subbasement and kept a close watch on the dark stretches between wallowing puddles of light. For every lit brazier there were four or five that had gone out.

"What the hell is that?" Devon whispered.

Henry gave Roger a sideways glance and strained to hear. There was nothing.

"Keep goin," Roger hissed.

Henry nodded and pushed on. The room they needed wasn't far. Rooms fell by one after another, every empty doorway looming. After a few minutes the hallway opened into a cavernous room adorned with dangling crow's cages and rusted stretching racks. How many sorry bastards had perished here?

"There it is again," Devon said.

Henry's hackles rose. This time he heard it; a sibilant snickering in the darkness. It faded, and a new noise began, the soft scraping of a knife against a whetstone.

Devon swung a brazier in search of the source of the noise and sent shadows careening across the walls.

"Ignore it," Roger snapped. "We're almost there."

Henry wiped the sweat from his brow and eyed a long stretch of darkness ahead.

Roger sensed the hesitation and stopped, turning on them all. "It's the dungeon master, groundskeeper, whatever you want to call it. Cristo mentioned it once."

"I don't care who it is, I want to know *what* it is!" Devon snarled.

Roger shook his head. "Not sure. Cristo didn't know. Only that they keep nasty shit down here and it keeps tabs on the place. Now can we finish this up and get the fuck out of here?"

Everyone fell silent and stared ahead grimly.

"Wait," Jeff said.

Devon looked around with wild eyes. "What?"

Roger answered. "Nothing," he said. "There's no sound anymore."

Henry took a deep breath to relax. He was drenched in sweat. His heart was thumping. What the hell were they doing? They were wolves for Christ sake. "You pussies. We really gonna sit around scared of a noise in the dark?"

The others bristled at that. He should have thought of it sooner. Devon and Jeff weren't exactly tough, but they had pride, lots of it.

Roger shadowed Henry, dragging the vamp out of the light. Samuel thrashed and chomped, straining against his chains and gnawing through the belt. They were halfway through the long stretch when Jeff screamed and bolted for the next lit brazier.

Henry cursed and hauled Samuel as fast as he could, imagination running wild with thoughts of the chains falling loose or those fangs cutting through the belt and sinking into his hand or leg. Blood pounded in his ears, his beast struggling to rise. Fear was bad. Any strong emotion could bring the change, but fear was weakness, and weakness could get you eaten alive.

Jeff stepped from the shadows and into the light of a brazier. Blood stained his jeans. Three slashes split the denim and the flesh beneath. "Little fucker clawed me good." Jeff complained.

Laughter hissed through the shadows.

The sound of dry twigs being trod upon crackled behind Henry. He spun around. "Dev, stop! It's too soon!" Devon either couldn't stop or wouldn't. His body twisted and jerked as the bones broke and shifted and instantly knit back together.

"Pull it together, Devon," Roger shouted. "It can't hurt us."

Whatever they kept down here took offense at that. A rock flew from nowhere and struck Roger's forehead. Blood trickled from a jagged split. Henry pulled away from Devon, struggling to control himself. The idiot was going to make them all shift.

A low growl trickled from Devon. He dropped to his hands and knees. The hall filled with the sounds of his clothes and skin ripping. It was too late. He'd gone Werewolf on them. Yellow eyes gave off a faint glow, and he turned his head from side to side, scenting the air before settling on the dark recess of a doorless room.

The laughter stopped. A heavy silence clung to the dungeon. Devon bolted with a savage snarl. Their tormentor shrieked in fear and raced away. Devon thundered after it. Henry grunted and crouched on the balls of his feet. He'd nearly shifted. His body ached with tension and the desire to let go.

Roger leaned heavily against a wall, one hand pressed to his split brow. "I can't believe that idiot, scared of the fucking janitor. Cristo said it's a nasty little thing, but it's more bark than bite."

"My ass!" Jeff said. "Little bastard shredded my leg!"

Henry stood up and glared at Roger. "When Cristo's gone, I'm next in line. You ever hold back information like that again and we're gonna have a real problem. Got it?"

Roger glowered but didn't talk back.

"You ladies can take up this little dance later if you want, but I'm about ready to go if you don't mind." Jeff said. "If Dev wants to play hide and seek down here that's his choice, but I want out."

Still pissed, Henry grabbed a handful of Samuel's hair and with the others began to carry him down the hall. The vampire writhed in the chains, no doubt agitated by the smell of fresh blood.

The cells were redolent with the time-faded stench of bodily fluids. More than one poor bastard had wet or shit themselves down here. They worked in silence, removing the silver chains and replacing them with ones of hardened steel. Henry grimaced and held his breath. Samuel's skin clung to the silver in gooey melted clumps that stretched like hot cheese, smelling sickly sweet.

As one they threw Samuel back and let the last chain fall to the floor. Free, the vampire lunged at them, unaware of his injuries. A forlorn howl echoed up the halls, calling them to join in the hunt, calling for help. It sounded far away and far below, lost in the bowels of Emigdio's cold, damp hell.

All three turned away.

By the time they reached the stairs the howls had grown so distant they could barely be heard. Henry watched Roger and Jeff trot up the steps and turned back. He didn't want to leave one of his own alone in this pit of despair, but he couldn't go deeper. Face burning with shame, he went up the steps and closed the door behind him.

Chapter 19

A LAZY SENSE of satisfaction set in as the credits began to roll. An entire day blissfully pissed away. Almost. No matter how hard he tried, Kaleb couldn't completely relax. One moment he was into the movie, and in the next an hour had passed. He couldn't turn off his brain. What the hell was he? And what had happened to him in Jacksonville? He'd changed before, grown gaunt, pale, sicklier, but nothing compared to the cadaver he'd seen in the rearview mirror.

It happened when he fought the vampires. That was when the chill overtook him and the hurt faded. Strength flowed through his rotting limbs like he'd never felt before.

Until they'd staked him anyways. The blow had been as excruciating as it was crippling. The knight's sword had a sting to it as well. A wooden stake. A silver blade. Humanities' defenses against things that went bump in the night.

And then there was Allie. She'd nearly split his head in two. It had hurt, until the chill came, and then he'd been able to work the cleaver loose.

But there was more to it than all that. When he changed, he could sense things. The vamps had felt like something tangible inside of his head, their age and strength. He could smell them, taste them, each a distinct flavor marinated by time and power.

Kaleb examined his hand. It looked normal enough, but the strength within was anything but. His entire life he'd tried to hide what was inside of him. He'd made himself weak by denying it, by not understanding his own capabilities. As much as he hated himself, he wasn't ready to lie down and die at the feet of some arrogant fucking mosquitoes.

There had been a time when he might have let them kill him, but now he had a future. There was Jordan to worry about. Allie to take care of. He had responsibilities beyond himself. He had a duty to protect them, and if that meant facing what he'd become, well then, so be it.

A few minutes later he stood shirtless in front of the bathroom mirror taking in the raw, pink gashes covering his body and the lingering kaleidoscope of bruises. He steeled himself, trying to muster his courage, and brandished the butcher knife he'd grabbed from the kitchen. Cold sweat dotted his chest. The knife looked too big and sharp. It was funny, really, to hesitate. He'd felt so much pain he was almost immune to it, and a cut like he was thinking of wouldn't do any real damage…but it was taboo. Self-Harm. Suicide. Forbidden fantasies. Once upon a time he'd been a Christian. Obviously not practicing any more, but he still had a healthy fear of the afterlife. No amount of penance would make up for his sins.

But he had to know.

"Just do it you chicken shit."

The reflection listened. The knife slashed across the open palm of his hand. The blade cut deep, and droplets of blood fell, bursting and splattering on the porcelain basin. Kaleb caressed the wound and watched his reflection for any changes. Seconds ticked by, the pain dulled, and nothing happened.

He sighed. It wasn't going to be so easy. He hadn't really expected it to be, only hoped. Before he could rethink it, he plunged the knife through the palm of his hand, embracing the familiar sting of a cut or bullet wound.

The reflection stared back at him, pallid and sunken, the monster still in hiding.

"You're crazy you know," Kaleb said. The man in the mirror gave a weak, lopsided smile. And then before Kaleb could think about it, he yanked the knife free and plunged it into his belly. Muscles clenched, rending deeper around the serrated edge of the blade. A sickly throbbing ache radiated throughout his body. He pulled the knife out and pressed a hand over the cut. Dark blood trickled between his fingers.

A chill ran down his spine like an autumn breeze. Goosebumps rose on his arms. And the breeze turned to a cold wind that seeped into his flesh and burned behind his eyes. The pain eased. The creature in the mirror degraded before his eyes. Skin and muscle sagged, blooms of green, blue and yellow blossoming even as the veins beneath darkened into intricate webs.

In seconds the reflection had become a monster. The eyes that stared back belonged to a nightmare, withered and inhuman as they were. It wasn't a man that stood before him; it was a visage of death.

Kaleb stared, fascinated. It was different this time. Before it had been nastier, juicier, and revolting. It had been the body of someone dumped in the water. He prodded at the cut. It had withered like the flesh around it. Dark sludge oozed from the nearly imperceptible slit.

Shifting was a strange sensation, a release of heat and an embrace of cold. The life slipped away, leaving a horrible emptiness in its place. It was a worse version of what he felt standing alone at his window at four in the morning, gazing at a sleeping world that was forever out of reach. It was an empty ache without hope. But it was also comforting and familiar. The devil he knew.

He closed his eyes. It always happened before when he slept. He willed the world away and thought of nothing. Thought became white static and everything else melted away. He felt when it began; a flicker of warmth in his chest. It crept through his body, chasing away the cold, banishing the numbness and extinguishing the icy spark caged in his skull.

A man was in the mirror when Kaleb opened his eyes. The stab wound in his belly had already stopped bleeding. Satisfied, he taped himself up and headed back to the couch.

He'd learned more about himself in the past week than he had in the hundred years before it.

Jordan stirred as Kaleb flopped onto the couch. She yawned and stared sleepily, trying to decide what to do, and crawled onto his lap, purring while he scratched beneath her chin.

Chapter 20

GET OUT. Now!" Val ordered."

Landon crossed his arms and shook his head. "Nope."

What the hell was this shit? Val leaned into Landon's open window. "C'mon boy. Wanna go for a walk? Huh? C'mon! Let's go!"

The Were tensed, setting his jaw.

"Enough fucking around," Val said. "Get out. You're a guard, now fucking guard me."

Landon shook his head again. "Nuh uh. Our job is to guard the mansion. That's the deal you guys made with Lucas."

It was bullshit and Landon knew it. "The deal is for muscle to watch our backs."

Landon refused to look at him. The wolf was soaked in sweat, and his attention constantly jumped from bush to tree to shadow, searching for hidden threats. "Daytime guardians are what I was told. This ain't daytime and it ain't the mansion."

A loose interpretation at best. "C'mon," Val said. "This thing is your contact."

Landon ignored him. Val curled a lip in distaste and turned away. "If you think I'm covering for you twice you're delusional."

The swampland along the path was eerily silent during the jaunt through the undergrowth. There were no noises this time—no chirps, splashes, or odd grunts. Branches clawed at him, snagging his clothes and scraping his skin. Val broke out in a slightly bloody sweat and noticed after a moment that there weren't even any mosquitoes to harass him.

A splash startled him and shadows deepened. Gnarled trees threw sinister figures on the ground that grasped with cold and crooked fingers. Val pressed through a cluster of thorny bushes and onto the sprawling estate. Free of the path, he squatted, hands on his knees, vowing vengeance on Landon. The back of his neck burned under countless hostile eyes, and the estate itself seemed malevolent. The fountain imp smiled garishly, still crying black tears.

Val did his best to smooth his clothes, glad he'd learned his lesson well enough to wear all black this time. Whispers followed him to the front door even though there was nothing to be seen. He turned, scanned the decrepit yard, and honed in on the mausoleum, sure at least some of the sounds were coming from inside. The gargoyles loomed atop the structure, massive creatures of alabaster with large, unseeing eyes.

Branches crackled on the path behind.

Val stopped gawking at the grounds and walked briskly to the front steps. *Landon you coward, you should be here. If nothing else, you'd be a distraction.*

Before he could knock, the door creaked open and set Val's stomach fluttering. Once again, the foyer was empty. He waited a moment, forcing himself to calm. *C'mon chicken shit. You're a vamp now. You've killed wolves, cats, ghouls. What's one demented old man with a few illusions?* A fragile sense of confidence welled at the reminder.

Belial waited in the same chair as before, nose buried in a book. The tattered state of the mansion was restored to its prior shining glory. The witch doctor set his book down, beamed a sickening, self-satisfied smile, and motioned to a chair. "Please, I expect we have matters to discuss."

Val sat but couldn't manage more than a grim smile. His chair was lower than Belial's. A petty trick from a petty man—a futile attempt to unbalance the negotiations, or maybe a way to feel superior. Likely both.

The mage glanced at a towering grandfather clock. "You've returned later than I expected. I'd almost given up on you."

"My apologies," Val said. "But I'm here now, and I have Lord Emigdio's approval to make a deal with you."

Belial leaned forward, eyes sparkling with greed. "He's accepted my terms?"

"Not exactly."

The smile wilted into spurned anger. His handsome face reddened and shifted. A hint of the twisted creature hiding behind the façade emerged, and a ripple rolled through the room, dulling the paint and dimming the shine.

"But we do have a few items for trade that may pique your interest."

The witch doctor motioned impatiently. "Speak!"

Unnerving as Belial was, it would be a joy to rip his throat out. "Of course," Val said. *Maybe I'll come back and eat your fucking heart tomorrow night, you prick.* If he brought Claudia and Luther with him anyways. "Lord Emigdio has heard of your penchant for collecting. He believes your collection may even rival his own."

Belial smirked.

"I have a few options for your consideration. You may choose any one of them in return for information." The mage contemplated the offer for a long moment, and gave a curt nod. At least the freak was willing to negotiate.

"The first offering we have is a very rare specimen. The Begonia Tessaricarpa, thought to be extinct for over a century. As I'm sure you know, it was used medicinally as well as for more nefarious matters."

Belial waved his hand in annoyed dismissal.

Val slipped into his second pitch. "Perhaps you might be more interested in a prize more endearing to someone of an alchemical profession. Cora has a pleasant little terrarium in which she has been able to recreate the proper living conditions for the Epipedobates Tricolour, better known as the Phantasmal Frog. Wild, they exist only in the Andean slopes of Central Ecuador, and even there they are incredibly rare. For such a tiny creature they pack quite a punch, containing enough venom to kill twenty men. Their secretions have two hundred times the potency of morphine and act as a muscle relaxant, able to still a beating heart."

Belial met Val's eyes and waited.

Val jumped into the third pitch. "Considering your extensive library, Renato has kindly offered up the collective works of a man known only as Khaldun."

There. That one caught his attention—a dilation of the pupils and a momentary tension. Val pretended to read the binding of the tome in Belial's lap. "Not much is known about the man," he went on, "other than he was a practitioner of the dark arts. Renato has confirmed the book's authenticity."

Val met Belial's cool, unimpressed gaze. That moment of surprise, he'd been interested. Was he playing coy?

"And last but certainly not least, your habit of collecting guardians has garnered you quite the reputation. I admit we did a little research on you, for the right reasons. We wished to find out what you might want or need. With that in mind, we have found someone willing to sell us a pair of Asan Bosam. Legend has it that Asan Bosam were once a powerful race of vampires that fell to ruin when their worshipers were wiped out. They were symbiotically linked to their humans and fell as one. Now they are little more than animals, but trainable animals. They make for quite the intimidating guard dogs, or so I hear."

"Is that all?" Belial asked.

Val smiled. It was his business smile, pleasant, apologetic, and disarming. He'd driven Michael nuts practicing it. Not like he'd had a choice. Getting it right was a bitch when you had no reflection.

Belial leaned back in his chair, staring at the ceiling and letting the offer sink in. He spoke more to himself than to Val. "And if this is what he offers, what is he holding back?"

Val answered him anyways. "I'm afraid I'm not privy to such information."

"Fair enough. I suppose some of what has been offered is interesting enough."

Val glanced at the windows. How long did he have before sunrise? "Have you made up your mind?"

The mage dismissed the question with an irritated wave of his hand. He chewed his lower lip, mulling the decision over. He brushed curls of light blond hair away from his eyes and agreed suddenly. "Deal."

A triumphant surge of elation welled up. He'd done it. He'd bartered the deal. "Excellent. What would you like as payment?"

Belial beamed with excitement, for once seemingly happy and sincere. "You've done your research too well. I cannot pass up the Asan Bosam."

"Done." Val held out his hand. He gritted his teeth, keeping his smile by sheer force of will as Belial shook on the deal. The man's skin was soft and doughy, vile to the touch.

Val pulled his hand away. "Now what do you know?" he asked eagerly.

"Without examining the specimen for myself I can only guess. Clearly, he's undead. It is possible that he's a breed of vampire, a necrotic, but I think it more likely he's a zombie of sorts."

This was it? It was Val's turn to be irate. "We've already considered the possibility and dismissed it. He speaks and thinks. Zombies are mindless, need driven." Val didn't even try to hide his displeasure.

Hardly the reaction Val expected, Belial grinned crookedly. "*Some* are mindless. *Some* are *not*."

Val waited impatiently.

"Most necromancers can do little more than aim their summoned dead like a weapon and watch the havoc it wreaks. A strong enough necromancer, however, can not only raise but control a corpse, even possess it in very rare instances. Add to this such mysterious strength, enough to prevail against a vampyr, any vampyr much less a warrior such as Samuel.…. Your enemy is either exceptionally powerful or not working alone."

Nothing they hadn't considered, though the possession bit was a surprise. "Is that all?"

Belial contemplated for a moment. "Any hope for Samuel remains in questioning the creature, or its master."

Val bit his tongue, afraid of what he might say. If that was the case there was little hope. Samuel was a goner; they were going to have to destroy him. Taking that *thing* alive was too dangerous.

Samuel. Michael. Amado. Dead. Vasco wounded. The clan was crippled.

"If it is only a zombie," Belial carried on, "traditional means of destroying it are really quite simple; severe brain trauma or fire. If it is something more, you may need to decapitate the creature or reduce it to ashes. Either way I suggest burning it, as to be sure."

Val slouched at the news. "Emigdio and the others will be upset."

"You were warned that Samuel might be beyond redemption," Belial said coldly. "You do not want to renege on our agreement, vampyr. And you miss the obvious. You have greater problems than you've realized. This creature may be the least of your concerns, the first in an army of undead. You have to find the source. Anyone foolish enough to unleash a zombie needs to be dealt with immediately. They are notoriously difficult to control. Sooner or later they break loose, and then questions will be asked. I would begin with crypts and cemeteries. Necromancers are cowardly beings. They shun life and surround themselves with the dead."

An army of undead rotting beasts, each strong enough to kill an enforcer? A chilling thought.

The conjurer raised an empty hand, turned it from side to side, and revealed a slip of paper out of thin air. He handed it over with a hollow smile. "An address. Or more of a loose location. It took considerable effort, but I have discovered a Satanist who is known to dabble with death magic. With the combination of those two arts, he might be the only living person capable of creating the creature you seek."

Belial was an unpleasant character—abrasive and unquestionably untrustworthy, but he'd given them something to work with. No one had mentioned necromancers being able to inhabit a corpse. And certainly no one had known of a living necromancer.

Val tipped his head in acceptance. "Thank you for your assistance. The Asan Bosam will be delivered within forty-eight hours."

Belial offered his hand. "Excellent! I cannot wait. It is not every day that one has a bygone god serve at his feet."

Val used his business smile. *You love the idea of a vampyr serving you, don't you?* "I'll inform Lord Emigdio immediately and see to the details myself." He cringed at the touch of Belial's hand. Already soft and vile, it now burned sickly hot as well.

Val pulled away and made for the door. He had a call to make.

Chapter 21

A BLOOD CURDLING scream shattered the late-night silence. Kaleb jolted awake. He was on his feet, one hand clenched into a fist and poised to strike. Disoriented, he spun about in search of danger. Jordan was already halfway across the room, ears flat against her skull and paws splayed out, ready to flee or maul at a moment's notice.

Kaleb struggled to cross the threshold from sleep to consciousness. The room began to focus. Ominous music drifted through his barely conscious fugue, and everything snapped into place. He groaned and dropped back to the couch.

Jordan glared at him irritably and began to groom herself.

A young woman cringed in bed as Dracula descended upon her. The music grew shriller and more ominous with every inch the vampiric figure closed. Kaleb rubbed his eyes. When had he passed out? The last thing he remembered was some shitty slasher flick. Lots of blood and guts and too many mistakes to count. It had been kind of funny really. You'd think that someone could have at least looked at an anatomy book.

Still tired, he stretched out on the couch with a few pillows stacked beneath his head. The scene shifted to a man being chased by a snarling wolf. It was old and cheesy, and memories came flooding back. In its day it had been terrifying. Girls had shrieked and turned away. Young men had gone scampering off into the night after the movie let out, wary of every shadow. It was kind of funny really how times had changed. People back then were tougher, harder, had dealt with the sorts of challenges that didn't exist anymore, at least not on the same scale. And yet they were more susceptible to fear of the unknown, or lore and legend. A healthy respect for death? Or a much deeper need to escape into a fantasy in which you could tell who was a monster just by looking at them?

He poked at the remote control until the time showed. 3 A.M. His sleeping habits were screwed. It was his own fault for staying up all day. He adjusted himself, mindful of the countless cuts and bruises peppering his body. The healing was off, too slow, especially the stuff done by the vamps, but slow was better than not at all.

The movie drew his attention again. It was nostalgic. Too nostalgic. Too much of his past was grim and easily stirred up. Somber memories came flooding back. Dracula was malevolent, but he was nothing compared to the real monsters. The real monsters were better liars. Isabelle had been charming. Her promises fueled by his own desperation. All lies. Dracula would have been more humane.

The worst of it, though, was wondering about Tristan and Katherine, the only friends he'd ever had. Their time together had been brief but well spent. Were they still alive? What had become of them? Kaleb curled up and wrapped his arms around his knees. And why had they broken their promise? What had he done to make them abandon him?

"We were fools," he whispered. Who else could believe the promise of immortality? He'd wanted the romance of eternity, of watching humanity grow and change. For the first time in his life he was going to live.

It wasn't entirely Isabelle's fault though. She'd given a warning, however vague.

As though she could sense his mood, Jordan climbed onto the couch and mewled in Kaleb's face. Presumably forgiven for such a rude awakening, Kaleb scratched her ears and made room for her. Whoever said black cats were bad luck didn't have a clue.

By four the movie had run its course. The original Frankenstein was just starting to roll when Kaleb shut off the TV. His tolerance for nostalgia was used up.

He worked himself into a sitting position and sighed. He'd been too reclusive the past few months, and now there were too many things to take care of: clean the car and hit up the deli for the double whammy of making an appearance and picking up an order. It would take hours to put on enough makeup to pass for human.

A groan forced its way out when he stood. Muscles popped and his back sounded like bubble wrap being jumped on when he stretched. He patted his belly. When had he eaten last? An early supper last night?

The sound of paper ripping brought Jordan prancing into the kitchen. Kaleb tore off a few small pieces of steak and dropped them to the floor. He eased into a chair, gnawing raw meat, occasionally tearing off another piece for Jordan, and thinking. If he could get to the store by six-thirty he could be done before the staff arrived.

He swallowed the last of breakfast and made his way to the shower. The bathroom light assaulted his eyes, painful after the comforting, dim glow of the television, and he turned it back off. A shower he could take in the dark. He reached for the faucet and hesitated. *Hot or cold?* Too much heat and no amount of deodorant would cover his rotting meat smell. *Screw it.*

He untied his bathrobe and ran a finger over scabby lumps that were all that remained of the hole left in his chest by Renato's stake. The slashes left by Adora had healed into scar tissue, and the bullet wounds and bruises that had turned his hide into a hideous rainbow of brutality were nearly gone.

He couldn't help but grin. A mere day ago the damage had still been shocking to look at. Maybe today wasn't going to be so awful after all. Kaleb gritted his teeth against the sting of hot water and took the pain until he adjusted to it. Tension slid from his shoulders and neck, down his back and legs, and swirled down the drain.

Eight full days since Jacksonville and no one had come looking for him. The manhunt was at a dead end. The icy tingling hadn't returned after driving away from the Knight. All of a sudden he felt better than he had in years. He twisted and turned, testing his limits. The scabs and scars were a little unyielding but manageable.

Before he knew it, the water was running cold. The boiler was old and bulky, but it could go for what, nearly an hour before running out of heat? More lost time. At least it had been worth it. A lot of stress had melted away and his neck no longer crunched at every little movement.

He dried off and opened the bathroom door, moving it back and forth to clear the fog so he could start the necessary evil of putting on a layer of makeup. He wiped the mirror down, turned on the light, and reached for his kit. Primer in hand, he leaned in, ready to start, and tried to comprehend what he saw. The stranger was gone. That unpleasant creature that stole lives and terrorized the living was nowhere to be seen. The heavy, dark bags under his eyes had faded. Black veins had disappeared beneath skin that was no longer so deathly pale. And there seemed to be a long-missing spark of life in his eyes.

And then he saw it.

What he should have noticed first. Kaleb raised one trembling hand to his neck, feeling what his eyes couldn't accept. What did it mean? And why now?

Realization clicked into place, and he wasn't sure whether to smile or cry. The smile won. Kaleb leaned heavily on the sink, fingers pressed to his carotid, feeling the steady, rhythmic beat of his heart. A fool grinned at him in the mirror, and for once Kaleb didn't try to deny that the creature was him. For the first time in centuries he was almost himself again. He was almost human.

And all it had taken was eating a vampire.

Chapter 22

RENATO HURLED ANOTHER book across the table. Hundreds upon hundreds of books, and not one of them useful. Yet. One would have something, some crucial bit of information. It had to.

He slumped forward and rested his head on crossed arms. When had he slept last? Days tended to meld when lurking so far below the surface of the earth. The lull of the sun was faint, but he still felt it come and go in the waxing and waning of his strength, and in the weight that would settle into his bones when he denied the call of the grave.

All of the time he had spent poring over his books—blurry, useless days of failure. He couldn't quit though. Everything that had happened was his fault. Hunger and sleep could wait.

He pored over his collection, tome after tome, so many crumbling with neglect. This too was his fault. How many creatures had died for these books? And this was how he repaid their sacrifice? It was his hidden shame. Perhaps only one tome was worth it; the compendium he himself had written, a thick volume of every fel, fey, and unnatural creature he had ever been certain existed—and an entire section of things only rumored. And yet all of the other books and their owners had contributed to that work, each gaining a footnote for their contribution. A sad end to a life, being reduced to a footnote.

You have had nothing but time, he chided. *You murdered and stole, and you couldn't even have been bothered to care for the spoils of your crimes?*

Sensing his fatigue, the creature behind the steel door reached out again. It had tried the day before as well, a feeble attempt, and this was even weaker. The creature was waning. Renato clenched one hand into a fist, digging nails into his palms to wake himself. He could not fall asleep, not with that creature trying to sway him.

By the light of a candle he reached for another book, a dusty old tome bound in human skin. Enough years had been spent hiding in places darker and danker than Emigdio's dungeons. Renato had no desire to stay any longer than he had to.

He'd just turned the first page when a howl echoed through the dungeon. A chortle escaped Renato. A wolf shifting so early in the cycle of a moon was not uncommon, but one so weak it could not shift back was indeed a pitiful creature. What would happen should the creature behind the door reach out to a wolf so weak of will…

Chapter 23

REMEMBER TO BUY bleach," Kaleb muttered to himself. As with every hunt the trunk had been lined with heavy duty poly, though a bleach spritz never hurt. He brushed shards of glass off the driver's seat, one eye twitching at the sight. A new interior was going to cost.

As foul as his mood was, a stunning October morning waited for him on the street. Sunlight fell across his hands, warm and natural, and every glance in the rearview mirror lessened the impact of the previous couple of months. A smile came unbidden and unstoppable even if it did feel awkward. There was no longer a *thing* staring back at him when he looked into a mirror.

Maybe it also meant he wouldn't have to hunt as often, for himself at least.

He felt good today. Actually *good*! St. Augustine was brighter than normal, more vibrant, as though a fog had lifted. By the time he pulled up behind the Meat Market not even the sight of a car parked in an employee space could dampen his spirit.

Kaleb opened the back door and peered inside. Mark popped out of the manager's office, a vaguely worried look on his face, and cheered up as soon as he saw it was only Kaleb.

"Thought I forgot to lock that," Mark said. "Was worried for a second."

"Just wanted to swing by, grab my orders, and get out of everyone's way before it gets busy."

"Paperwork's in here," Mark said, nodding at the office. "Boxes are still in the walk in."

Beef. Pork. Bison. Garbage compared to Michael. "Great," Kaleb said. "So, how's business? Been a while since I've been in."

"Steady as always."

Before Kaleb could try to find an excuse to cut the small talk, the phone saved him. Mark sighed, exasperated by whoever would call so early, and went to answer.

True to Mark's word the paperwork rested in neat stacks on his desk. Kaleb slipped in and snagged the new order list. It was the same old crap, all except for the turkeys. Kaleb thought it over and grimaced at the thought of chewing on that thick, rubbery skin.

Before he'd picked out half of what he wanted for his next order, the back door swung open. Employee's he'd rarely met nodded politely, moving past and setting up shop. Robbie and Stacey chatted out front, laughing, seemingly happy at work.

Had he ever really spoken to either of them? A polite hello maybe, but anything more than that? Not that Kaleb could remember. Listening to their voices, he suddenly wanted to know more about them, who they were, what they aspired to, and why they enjoyed life. Their laughter drew Kaleb, and both fell into guilty silences at his approach.

Stacy gave him a shy smile. "Good morning, Mr. Adams."

Kaleb had always liked her. She was a lifer, ten years plus with the deli and just one of those easygoing, charming people, as opposite himself as a person could be. "Morning," he said, "And call me Kaleb."

Her smile spread. "Okay then. I'm glad you're feeling better. Mark said you've been out sick with a bug or something for a while."

Yeah, Kaleb thought dryly. "Something like that."

"Thanks for the time off, brother," Robbie chimed in. "I spent it all on the beach."

Right. He'd given everyone a bit of extra paid vacation as a little bonus for putting up with summer hours.

"Me too," Stacey said. "I took my girls out four days in a row. We had a great time."

Kids. I should have known that. "I'm the one who should be thanking you," Kaleb said. "You're the ones who keep this place rolling."

Robbie beamed a smile. He still looked a bit gaunt and rough. His one-year anniversary with the deli was coming up soon. Most people wouldn't think so, but having a steady job was huge for Robbie. Not many places were open to prisoners on the work release program.

Kaleb struggled to keep his face a mask, suddenly feeling ill. Robbie was a quiet guy, soft spoken and generally harmless, at least to others. If he'd continued down that bad track he could have easily wound up in a freezer. *Is that what I'm really doing? Stealing people's chances at redemption?* The thought of killing Robbie like so many others made Kaleb nauseous.

Overwhelmed by a sense that he shouldn't be around people, Kaleb got back to task. "Just need to grab a few things, sign my name, and all that."

The pickings turned out to be slim. Most of the product still needed to be cut. He glanced back at Robbie and Stacey, both busy slicing meat, prepping for the lunch rush. He couldn't ask them to do that too.

His stomach grumbled, enticed by the smell of fresh, store made pastrami, and he did a double take. Since when did pastrami smell so good? Another side effect? Could he actually eat cooked meat now? He briefly considered trying some and dismissed it. That was something to try at home.

A knocking on the front window drew everyone's attention. A middle-aged man in a suit waved. "He's a bit early," Robbie said.

Stacey shrugged. "No matter. We can cut to order. Won't be the first time." She jogged to the door and twisted open the locks.

The man stepped in and smiled apologetically. "Sorry to bother you. I know I'm early."

Stacey stepped back behind the counter and gave him an infectious smile. "Don't worry about it. We're just filling out the displays."

"I'm just on my way to work and thought I might surprise my staff today. It's been a rough stretch, but things are starting to look up."

"Amen," Robbie cheered.

"I know a lot of my staff buy lunches here during the week," the man said. "I was hoping I could set up an order for lunch today."

"Of course," Stacey said. "What do you need?"

The man smiled apologetically again. "About a hundred sandwiches, assorted."

A hundred extra sandwiches? Kaleb pushed away the darkness trying to encroach on his day and reached for a pair of thick rubber gloves. One last dark thought flickered through his mind—at least he hadn't forgotten how to cut meat.

Chapter 24

SARAH GLANCED AROUND the expanse of Harlow's penthouse suite, afraid to make eye contact with anyone. They were all so old and powerful. She clasped her hands together to still the trembling. "That's what I was told," she said in a wavering voice.

Aedan settled an indifferent gaze on her. It was impossible to tell what he was thinking behind those dark blue eyes. Midnight eyes as she'd come to think of them. "When?" he asked.

"A few minutes ago."

"And they have no idea what's happening?" Aedan asked.

The others had all fallen silent and were watching her, searching for lies or incomplete truths. She withered under the scrutiny. She shook her head rapidly. "No. Cora asked for help, to see if anyone here might know something. One of their clan is on the verge of true death. His mind is already gone."

Aedan fell back into his natural indifference. "Amazing. Emigdio asking for help."

"Even more amazing that they don't know what's going on," Onwyn interjected. "Samuel should understand."

Sarah clenched up. She'd forgotten! "I'm sorry," she stammered. "He's the one who's fallen ill." She wished she could die again as their stares fell heavy on her. Cora had told her it was Samuel.

Onwyn spared her. He gave her a sly wink. "Even so," he said. "There are others who should know."

Aedan shook his head. "Not necessarily. Some are less...sociable than others. And it didn't happen everywhere."

"Backwater hermits," Maedoc sneered. "They deserve their fate."

Sarah dared not move. She didn't belong here. These things were well beyond her pay grade, and the old ones scared her. Maedoc was a brute. Onwyn an unpredictable jester. Aedan cold. And Harlow—beneath his calm demeanor he was ruthless.

The Lord of the city stirred at last. "Perhaps. But I will not allow it. It took humans a long time to forget. We don't need them reconsidering."

"Forget what?" a lilting voice inquired from near the tinted glass wall overlooking the city. Constance, Harlow's latest plaything. She'd been so quiet that Sarah hadn't even noticed her.

"It was before your time," Aedan answered. "It was a disease. The Black Plague. It decimated Europe and many other parts of the world. Countless humans died."

Constance's brow furrowed as she tried to process the information. A beautiful creature, Harlow did not enjoy her for her mind. Aedan watched Constance trying to puzzle it out and cracked a hint of a smile.

"And it cannot happen again," Harlow stated. "It took centuries to quell people's fears and make ourselves the things of stories once more."

"Yes," Aedan agreed. "The world needs no more inquisitions."

Sarah swallowed hard. Should she ask? No. But her curiosity got the best of her. "What happened back then?"

Aedan turned back to her, and she instantly regretted drawing attention. She was no one. Newly turned. A maid. To her surprise Aedan answered with sorrow in his voice.

"It was a sickness, but not as most people know it. The worst happened after the plague. Humans hunted our kind nearly to extinction, and they slaughtered hundreds of thousands of their own in the most horrible ways. The corruption was absolute. It still lingers to this day."

"Then go and make sure it does not happen again," Harlow ordered. "Take Maedoc, Onwyn, and whatever else you need."

"We haven't been invited. Our presence will not be wanted," Onwyn said. He glanced at Maedoc and back to Harlow.

Maedoc cut in. "They're too weak to fight a war with us. And besides, I've never heard of Emigdio."

Aedan turned a cool stare at Maedoc. "Sometimes silence is the better part of valor."

Maedoc grinned viciously. "I'm surprised you know what valor is."

Harlow raised one hand in irritation. "Enough."

"I knew Samuel," Aedan said, staring through Maedoc at something only he could see. "And I know enough of Emigdio to be wary of him."

"Was Samuel a friend?" Harlow asked.

Sarah kept as still as she could, wanting to hear more of their history. For a moment it seemed Aedan was not going to answer, but then he nodded, a hint of his true self showing beyond the façade.

Harlow turned his attention to Maedoc. "Aedan is right. Do not underestimate Emigdio or his people. Make it clear that you are there to help and not hinder. This creature must be destroyed."

Constance was almost in a tizzy. "What is it?"

An adept question from an inept girl, not that Sarah would ever say that aloud. Even so, she listened intently. It made no sense why she or Constance were allowed to hear any of this. It had been what, two years? And this was only the third time she'd seen Harlow.

"It's possible the creature lied," Onwyn mused.

"To what purpose?" Aedan asked.

Onwyn raised one eyebrow and smirked. "Desperation? Fear? For the fun of it?"

Aedan rolled his eyes, annoyed. "If they staked it through the heart it was no vampire."

"*If* they staked it through the heart," Onwyn agreed. "If I missed, I'd probably lie about it as well." Aedan refused the bait, and Onwyn almost deflated with disappointment.

Constance crossed her arms. "I asked a question."

"And I chose not to answer," Harlow said.

"It's alright," Onwyn said, giving her a pitying look. "Just go watch TV. Cartoons should be starting any time now."

Sarah kept her face a mask. Constance glanced from one person to the next, mortified and furious. Onwyn turned away guiltily when Harlow shot him a dirty look. Aedan's barely seen smile made another brief appearance. And Maedoc grinned unabashedly, uncaring of Harlow's displeasure.

Burning with indignation, Constance stormed from the room. Sarah stared at her feet, hiding the mirth in her eyes. The last thing she needed was to make an enemy of Constance. Harlow's toy was gone in a moment, leaving nothing but smiles and the echo of a slamming door in her wake.

In the end, even Harlow succumbed to mirth. He slouched in his chair, a modern-day throne of custom leather reclined in front of one of the biggest televisions Sarah had ever seen. "Just take care of it," he said. "Leave as soon as you can. I will handle business here."

Aedan, Maedoc and Onwyn gave quick, assenting nods, and left the room.

Sarah kept still and silent, unsure what to do. She hadn't been dismissed, but she had no orders at all. If being surrounded by the most powerful vampires in New York was scary, being alone with the single most powerful one was terrifying. Her skin tingled from being so near Harlow.

He turned on the TV and flipped through the channels, settling on a travel show. People laughed in the sun and baked on powdery, white sand beaches.

Harlow set down the remote and spoke without looking at her. "Go with them. You've met Cora before. Stay close to her."

Go with them? Why? Not that it mattered. She had no choice. She belonged to Harlow, mind, body, and soul. He ordered. She obeyed.

Chapter 25

TV SUCKED. Kaleb skimmed channels, finding nothing to distract him from the events of the day. It had been good getting to know the staff, getting a glimpse of the people of St. Augustine. Contact with the outside world. Robbie and Stacy had treated him like a normal human being, and for once he'd felt like one.

He didn't deserve any of it. It only added to the nagging sense of impending doom that had haunted him since walking away from the Knight. The Rose Knight. Ironic. Supposedly they were a sect of the Knights Templar. It would have been nice to talk to him, ask how he was able to stand this immortal dark life after once being so close to God.

Finally settling on the news, Kaleb picked at the scraps of the porterhouse he'd eaten for supper and contemplated getting more simply out of boredom. He tossed the bones on a plate and patted his belly. No more food. Immortality was no reason to let himself go.

Now there was a concept. Letting himself go. The shift had felt like that, like he was slipping his skin, and in a way he was. Whatever imitation of life he possessed fled before the chill.

Kaleb raised a hand in front of his face and concentrated on it, trying to find that power again. Almost too easily a cold spark flickered through his body and butterflies fluttered in his stomach. It was happening. The spark flickered again, longer this time, and grew into an icy speck behind his eyes. It spread as he willed it, flaring, a chill flowing down his arms and into his hands, turning flesh ashen and shriveled. The cold crept into his chest, both alien and familiar. It chased the life from his body, faltering when it reached his heart, attacking the source of life and warmth, forcing it to skip, to falter, and to stop. Kaleb clutched his chest, unnerved and sickened by the sensation. At the last second he tried to cling to life, but it was too late.

In moments the change was over and the winter fire in his mind reached out to sense his surroundings. It was the same feeling he'd had in the alley only stronger, the light of a match versus that of a bonfire. There were no vampires now, nothing that might harm him…but there was something. He turned to Jordan and saw her staring back at him. She was alive, but not alive as were the humans in the houses around him. She was something he'd never sensed before, not even in his past glimmers of other things.

Images from the past assaulted Kaleb in a rush, hazy flashes of swamps, a thousand different moments of lurking on the borders of towns and cities, hunting, an endless parade of lonely days and nights. Suffocating on the memories, Kaleb wanted—needed—the warmth and life he'd felt over the last day. He shut his eyes and tried to still his mind. Too many problems pressed in and he shoved them away. The past. Allie. Vampires. White noise enveloped them all.

Warmth ignited in his heart and flowed through his veins in the tingling rush of a pulse. When he opened his eyes, he had come back from the cold. He clenched a trembling hand into a fist. He could do it at will!

Shaken by the experience, he had to wonder what good the power was. It's not like there was a practical use to looking like a corpse. It might be nice to call on if he stubbed a toe or cracked his elbow on something. Of course, it would help if he got into a life or death fight again, but god willing that wouldn't happen anytime soon. He reached for Jordan, grateful when she didn't flinch or run away at his touch. "Didn't expect it to suck so bad," he said.

He eased off the couch. Allie still needed to be fed. She hadn't eaten since last night. Or made any noise, which was beyond odd. Normally he couldn't even go in the kitchen without her making a racket. She was worse than Jordan.

There was also the matter of what to feed her. Maybe the vamp meat would be good for her, or maybe it would be lethal since she wasn't old enough or resilient enough to handle it. Taking a slow approach seemed best.

Roast in hand, he made for the basement, stopping just long enough to swap the dim bulb with a brighter one. Light flooded the stairs and corner of the room. His heart skipped a beat when he rounded a pile of clutter and saw broken chains.

"Allie! I brought you food." Vaguely hoping she would answer, he crept along, not sure what to expect. The trail was easy enough—slightly wet foot marks, rank with all the joy a rotting body could provide. "Never gonna get that smell out of this place," he muttered.

Every step towards the back of the basement brought a growing dread with it. She was loose, and she was headed for the freezers.

What waited was worse than he'd imagined. The fridge was emptied. Bloody containers had been scattered about. Only one freezer was open, and for a second he had hope. Which one was *he* in? The hope bubble burst. *Of course.*

Kaleb threw the roast away. "Goddammit!" he screamed. "Fuck!" Everything he'd gone through, everything he'd done! If he'd been smart, portioned it out, the vamp would have lasted years.

He finally noticed Allie standing in the shadows, watching him and for once not attacking. One small mercy. He wanted to hate her for what she had done, but he couldn't. She was only as he'd made her.

He kicked a freezer hard enough to cave in the side and bounce it off of the wall. It wasn't enough. He wanted to rage, to scream, hell, even to cry. The meat was irreplaceable. Or was he supposed to turn vampire hunter? Kaleb Van Helsing? It did have a ring to it.

On the verge of either a tantrum or tears, Kaleb stared helplessly at Allie.

Chapter 26

RENATO HUDDLED ON the couch, brooding over ill-spent time in the basement. He'd found nothing. Nothing! His once-precious books had failed him. At best he had a few educated guesses. It could be an inexplicably intelligent ghoul, or perhaps a lesser daemon, or more likely a possession by something other. Valentine had returned with a plausible idea, and yet Renato was skeptical. An unheard-of breed of vampyr called a necrotic? Zombies and necromancers? A necromancer this powerful didn't simply appear out of nowhere. But the Satanist...perhaps there was a truly evil force involved.

Even more shocking had been Cora's queries outside of Jacksonville. To Renato it was a sign of strength and devotion, but others would see it as a sign of weakness. There would be consequences.

The venom in Claudia's tone drew his attention. "So, whose enemy is this? Which of us has brought this down on our house?"

No one replied. They all had a past. Even Claudia. She was simply angry, struggling with the lack of control they all felt.

"It does not matter," Emigdio said. "An enemy of one is an enemy of all."

"Ha," Luther snorted. "I have no enemies. I killed them all, and their friends and families. No loose ends."

Renato kept his face impassive, but inside he cringed at the bold claim. To tempt fate like that...Perhaps Luther didn't have enemies, exactly, but he had family that wanted to reclaim him into their fold, and with Samuel, Amado, and Vasco out of the way, they might be able to.

Then there was his own list, a compendium all its own, the loved ones of those he had slain in his many years. This was not a conversation he wanted to have.

Weary from days preparing remedies and treatments in her own section of the basement, Cora spoke with a harsh edge in her voice. "Old enemies or new, we need to prepare. It may be the only way to save Samuel."

"Have you heard news?" Luther asked, already knowing there had been none.

"Soon," Cora said, making a promise she might not be able to keep. She had a specialist looking into things, Parisa, a Magus of the Light—an odd ally for a vampyr, but one very interested in an active Satanist and Necromancer.

"I have no faith in the information that Valentine brought back," Claudia said. "At most there is a kernel of truth in what he said. The rest was empty talk to justify payment."

Luther rested a hand on her shoulder. "We must consider all possibilities."

Claudia leapt up, wrenching out of Luther's grasp. "Enough considering! We need to act!"

Emigdio shifted on his throne. "We wait until we are sure. We deal with this threat first, and if the conjurer lied, he will be next."

"And we should wait for Vasco," Luther said. He shrugged at the reproachful look from Claudia. The lovers, forever at odds but together forever.

"That could take months!" Claudia snapped.

"No," Cora interrupted. "Vasco is able to feed himself now. The healing is faster. I'm hopeful that he will recover within weeks."

"You speak as though we can sit back and do nothing," Claudia said, exasperated. "We would be fools to give it time to attack again."

Emigdio turned the conversation, knowing that Claudia would not be swayed, but neither would she act without consent. "What news of Amado?"

Renato looked away guiltily.

"None," Luther said. "We have everyone working on it. The authorities. Our street pawns. Lucas sent his best trackers trying to find a trail. I've even brought in bounty hunters." He shook his head, saddened. "I don't know what more to do."

"Cowards!" Claudia snapped. "You're all afraid to admit it. He's dead! Why else would he be gone so long? He faced the sun. His ashes are in the wind!"

Luther slipped behind her and laid a hand on her shoulder. She glared and softened, resting her own hand over his. "We don't know that," he said.

It was a horrible thought but one everyone was thinking. Amado was a fighter and fiercely loyal. Nothing short of death would keep him away. Unless…

"Unless he was captured," Renato thought aloud. "If this creature isn't acting alone, it is possible."

"All the more reason to act," Claudia said, subdued.

Is she right? Renato thought. *Lord help me, I don't know what to do.*

Quiet contemplation was broken by shouting outside the den. Wolves snarled. The sound of wood cracking and snapping echoed from the front entrance.

Another attack? The creature come back to finish the fight?

Heavy footsteps thudded toward the den, and the burly frame of one of their guards blocked the doorway. Veins throbbed on Martin's neck and arms, rapid and strong. Entrancing. Renato stared at the pulse hungrily.

Martin was nearly feral, eyes wide and nostrils flaring. "Vampires. They forced their way in."

A shadow of fury flitted across Emigdio's usually placid demeanor. "They entered uninvited?"

Consequences were expected, but so soon? Renato shared a glance with Claudia and Luther. They were the enforcers now.

A wolf snarled in pain, and Martin disappeared from the doorway. A group of intruders stood just inside the main entrance. A guard lay sprawled on the floor, unconscious, his breathing ragged. Cristo cradled a broken arm, glaring up at a brutish, dark-haired vampyr.

Out of respect for other vampyr, Renato had not included them in his lengthy compendium. He had, however, created a secret book not even his clan knew of. In it lived his compulsion to catalogue names and stories, and through it he knew the intruders.

The brute was Maedoc. One of Harlow's men.

One of the guards snapped the leg off a table and threw the makeshift stake to a pack mate.

Emigdio slid to the fore, casting a warning glance at Luther and Claudia when they tried to move with him. "You enter uninvited, unannounced, and injure my guards. Give me one reason why I should not destroy you."

A tall thin vampire with long blonde hair began to speak. *Aedan*. He clenched his jaw shut when Maedoc answered first.

"You're welcome to try," Maedoc said, voice thick with arrogance and condescension.

"Maedoc, enough!" Aedan snapped. He tipped his head to Emigdio. "My apologies, Lord Emigdio. We are not here to fight you."

Luther fingered the hilt of his sword, an inscribed two-handed executioner, a sword of justice. "A fine way to show it."

Emigdio's face darkened with anger. "I've yet to hear a reason."

"We're here to clean up your mess," Maedoc spat.

Emigdio lowered his head, as if contemplating, and closed the distance between himself and Maedoc in an instant. He raised one hand to the large vampire's chest. The air rippled between them, shimmering translucent waves, and a hollow boom shook the room. Maedoc was flung into his companions, knocking over all but Aedan.

Claudia and Luther moved as one, drawing their weapons and poising themselves to attack. The wolves followed suit, raising their stakes, ready to plunge them through ancient, dead hearts. Valentine and Adora appeared at the second-floor banister, ready to leap into the fray. Renato drifted closer to Emigdio, preparing to intervene at the first sign of reprisal.

Aedan held his ground, unshaken, ignoring the hostility. "Excellent. Perhaps now we can discuss why we are here." There was sincerity in his voice, and of the others only Maedoc had shown aggression. From what Renato knew, Aedan was honorable.

The intruders held their breath, watching for Aedan's lead. But Maedoc shook off stunned disbelief and leapt to his feet, bones shifting beneath his skin. His face

125

stretched wide. Fangs erupted past his lips, narrowing and splintering. The change was fast, and what remained was something Renato had never seen. Maedoc was an old breed, and rare. He was primal. High cheekbones pulled his face taut, and bleeding red eyes glowed balefully. Fingers melted together to form talons. But it was his mouth that drew the eye, a nightmarish maw filled with rows of jagged needle teeth.

Emigdio raised his hand again. The air between them rippled. A translucent bubble grew, folding in on itself, expanding and condensing. Aedan saved the brute's life, lunging for him, kicking out his knee, and locking an arm around his neck. The others scrambled to action, swarming the big vampire.

"Enough!" Aedan roared.

Another held the door wide, smiling amusedly. *The jester. Onwyn.* Maedoc was dragged out snarling and growling, clawing at his own. They threw the primal down the steps, and Onwyn closed the door.

"My apologies," Aedan said. "We mean no harm. There will be no more antagonizing on our behalf."

Everyone waited for Emigdio's lead. The tension eased when he lowered his hand. The bubble dissipated.

Aedan relaxed. "My name is Aedan. I am here on the command of my lord, Harlow." He smoothed the wrinkles out of his jacket, a well-made bit of Armani. "It wasn't supposed to be this way. Maedoc is…" He sighed, trying to find the words.

Onwyn finished his sentence for him. "An asshole."

Aedan pressed on with no more than an irate glance at his companion. "He lost his temper when one of your wolves barred us entry. I will not condone his behavior, but his hatred for lycanthropes runs deep. Had I known you used wolves as guards I would not have brought him."

"Why," Emigdio said calmly, "did Harlow not negotiate your arrival?"

Aedan hesitated, and Onwyn cut in, a smirk pulling at the corners of his mouth. "There was no time for formalities. We know what's happened here, and Lord Harlow sent us to end it before it gets out of control."

If Claudia's looks could kill. "We can handle our own problems," she said, ice in her voice.

"With all due respect, we don't believe that you can," Aedan said. "Onwyn has the right of it. Time is of the essence."

Onwyn nodded politely at Cora. "You've told us Samuel is ill, probably dying, and you're unable to help him. Of all of your people to get injured, it was a great misfortune for it to be him."

"What he means to say," Aedan added, "is that Samuel may have been able to tell you what you're up against."

Aedan waited while Emigdio considered his words. The anticipation was excruciating for Renato. It had been so long since the world held any mystery.

Emigdio nodded his acceptance.

The New York vampires visibly eased. "Thank you," Aedan said. "But I think it would be better to discuss this in private."

Renato's mouth was suddenly parched. Emigdio was actually considering it?

Emigdio turned without a word and strode briskly towards the den. Aedan followed. Onwyn motioned the rest of his clan to stay where they were and trailed after. Renato began following and stopped short. Luther was already a step ahead of him. A moment too slow. The pain of it was worse than broken bones.

Even with the temporary truce the tension was palpable. Claudia glowered at everyone, a battle axe gripped in either hand. The wolves radiated hostility. The remaining vampyr intruders waited in a stony silence, their egos bruised by Emigdio. Only Cora and Rain seemed immune, falling back on their chosen profession to tend to the injured guards.

Minutes stretched painfully long, the only sound an uneven rasp of the unconscious guard. At best it was a concussion. Renato wondered what would happen if the guard died. Such an assault couldn't go unanswered. An eternity seemed to pass before the heavy oak door to the den swung open. Luther beckoned.

Renato resisted the urge to run and walked at Claudia's side. He gave a passing glance to Valentine and Adora, regretting leaving them behind. With just wolves, Rain and Cora, they would be hard pressed if this were a ploy.

§ § §

Onwyn's attention kept wandering, to the massive blackwood throne, to paintings older than the vampires that owned them, and to tapestries that should have turned to dust a thousand years ago. They were exquisite artifacts of a different era, evidence of cities and creatures and people long since disappeared from the face of the earth. Emigdio had nothing modern in his den. He really was a backwater recluse. Good Lord, the one called Renato even wore a cape. Somehow they were surviving despite their antiquated ways. Few lived so long without embracing the times, at least those who chose to live in modernity. There were more than enough who lived in obscurity, hidden in the old world.

Even so, the collection was astonishing. There were stories of war and courage and love and loss. Some were simple fables, others heartwarming scenes of humans celebrating the birth of a child, the passing of an elder, or a festival whose origin and purpose had been lost in annals of time. He stared in wonder at one long tapestry more faded than the others. In it were half a dozen ancients that were little more than whispered rumors.

A knot grew in his throat at the next tapestry. The creatures were so realistic he half expected them to come to life. He walked toward it in a daze. Memories

127

came in a rush, overwhelming his sense of time and place. He was suddenly a child again, hunting with his father and tribesmen. Spears flew through the air, and they swarmed the animal, snarling and roaring like beasts themselves. He again felt the remorse as the dragon cried out in pain and faltered. It wailed pitifully and thrashed to free itself, but the wounds were brutal and blood gushed. His gorge rose when they tore its heart out and gave him a piece, but he did what was expected of him and ate. He was a man that day. It was the first and only time he had ever seen a dragon. It was a buried regret, even if it was one of his greatest. Time did not heal all wounds. There was nothing but shame in bringing such a noble species to extinction.

Aedan cleared his throat and the reverie was broken.

Onwyn swayed, on the verge of illness, and composed himself. The poet was watching him. Emigdio sat on his throne, the lovers on either side. Luther. Where he came from, what he came from, was known, but little else. Claudia had a more marked history, or at least her clan did. No one knew the role she played, only that those who made her had begun a war that killed nearly eight million people, and quite a few other creatures as well. Those vermin had turned thousands into undead fodder, and she had been one of those pitiable foot soldiers. From her waking moment she had been thrust into battle. She probably had more blood on her hands than anyone else in the room.

Onwyn stood beside Aedan. For once in his long life subdued, his mirth was buried beneath regrets and his safety questionable now that he had met Emigdio and his handful of collected misanthropes. The gravity of the situation set in. While Maedoc's actions had been entertaining, their hosts were less than pleased. Emigdio was slight, but he was much more than he seemed. Harlow's orders had been to get it done at all costs, regardless of Emigdio's assistance. There was only one small flaw in that simple plan. No one had really considered the possibility that the Lord of Florida and his clan might be more than they could handle.

Chapter 27

JASON PINCHED HIS leg in a desperate attempt to stay awake. By now half of his body had to be black and blue. It worked, for a couple of seconds at least. He rubbed at raw and gritty eyes as if he could wipe the sleepiness away, and startled so bad he almost peed a little. A face was smushed against the window, teeth and fangs bared and tongue squirming.

Jason scrambled for his shotgun and was nearly pissed off enough to use it when Val pulled away with a laugh.

Asshole! He rolled down the window. "About fucking time you showed up!"

Val looked around. "Which house?"

What would happen if he shot Val in the head? Was that enough? Jason resisted the urge to find out and put the gun back down. Even if the shot didn't finish it, a double tap with wood slugs to the heart would. Not that he could ever try it out; the others would hunt him down like an animal. "End of the block. Last on the left."

Val leaned in, and quickly took a step back. No doubt it was ripe. Several days without a shower and a floor littered with junk food would do that.

"You're gonna have to send one of your guards to take over," Jason complained.

"What happened to your brothers?"

"Idiots bailed. Said they weren't wasting their time if I wouldn't say what for."

Val nodded. "Probably better that way. You're in a unique position, Jason. Only a handful of people know what you know, and it needs to stay that way." Val leaned against the car and looked up and down the street. At its busiest it had been quiet, and at 3 A.M. it was desolate. "I can't believe he lives here. It's so… mainstream. No one else coming or going?"

"Nah," Jason said through a yawn. "Nothing. Doesn't mean no one else is in there though. He's only left the house a couple of times and both were during the day. Seemed like basic errands, aside from the butcher store. You think that's what he's killing people for? Like that hot dog guy from Germany."

Val still didn't say anything, just kept staring at the house. It was the only one with signs of life. Light danced off of the walls through a window. He was watching TV again.

"So? What's the plan?" Jason asked.

Val leaned back down. "Nothing for now. Keep on him."

Shit. "I can't." Jason groaned. "I'm fried. I'm gonna pass out, and someone will call the police when they catch me sleeping here."

Val grinned and tossed Jason a bottle of pills. "I'll see about sending someone out. Until then call me the next time he moves. It doesn't matter what time. He doesn't leave your sight."

Jason popped the cap and took a few pills. He didn't know what they were. He didn't care. He watched Val slip down the street and disappear as smooth as any phantom. It would all pay off soon enough. They were down at least four vamps, and he was handing them the monster responsible for it all. Val had all but told him he was going to get made.

He stared dreamily and bleary eyed at the house, imagination running wild, waiting for the pills to kick in. Flying would be a blast. Drinking blood, though, that might take some getting used to.

§ § §

An uneasy silence permeated the suite Val had set up for the mission in St. Augustine. One of the guards from the mansion was nearly asleep on the couch, and the big vamp glared at him from a chair not far away. All in all, there were far too many bodies in the room for comfort, an unforeseen problem since he'd reserved five rooms. It came down to trust: no one had any, or at least not enough to let the others out of sight.

Val's cell went off, and he answered it before it had a chance to ring twice.

"He's moving," Jason said. He sounded tweaked.

"Where?"

"Dunno. Same roads as last time. To the butcher store maybe."

"Call back when he stops." Val hung up before Jason could answer and looked at Renato. "Five hours and change until sunset. That's a long wait."

Frank got up from the couch. "Boys are in the bar. I'll grab them and head over. We can handle it."

Maedoc made a disgruntled noise and glared at the wolf like he was something to be scraped from the bottom of a boot. "No. We take him tonight. We can't risk him getting away."

Val waited for Renato and Luther to weigh in. They were running the show. Supposedly.

"We do both," Aedan broke in. "Send the wolves to set an ambush. We can't just lay siege to his house. This needs to be quiet."

"You would leave it to the dogs?" Maedoc spat.

Aedan was immune to the outrage. "Yes."

Luther grunted in amusement and nodded at Frank. "Take the van. It has everything you need. If he comes back early take him down, hard, but keep him alive. If he's not back by dusk we'll meet you there."

Aedan looked to a darkened corner of the room. Dax sat there, as quiet and petite as ever, shrouded in black robes. He hadn't spoken once during their stay. "Go with them."

Dax left without a word, Frank trailing behind. Val couldn't blame him; he didn't care much for the little creeper himself.

They were getting close now and they were all feeling it, the energy amping up and tension winding tight. All they needed was time and maybe a little luck.

Val grabbed his phone and started dialing. "Yeah. It's happening. Slow him down, make sure he doesn't get back until after dark."

Chapter 28

KALEB STORMED INTO the garage and slammed the door behind him as if Allie might actually understand that petty act. He couldn't stop dwelling on it—the meat, the fucking vampire miracle meat. A human was bad enough, but how the hell was he supposed get another vampire? The only reason he was still alive, sort of, was pure luck and bad judgment on the vamps' part. They weren't going to make those mistakes again.

And how in the hell had that little belly taken it all in? She'd eaten her body weight in meat, and what she hadn't eaten she'd done a thorough job of tainting. Anything gnawed on was spoiling, something he knew about all too well. For the most part practice had taught him care. He didn't wear gloves to cut meat because he was afraid of some goddamn germs.

He inhaled, held it, and breathed out. It wasn't her fault, it was his. He was getting used to saying that, almost making a mantra of it.

The donut drew his attention, too small and goofy looking. He lashed out with a kick before hopping in the Mercedes. "Get it done. A quick in and out." Yeah right. A new window, a tire, and checking out the upholstery. A few hours minimum.

Two houses. That was all it took to remind him about that little nagging thought that had been bugging him for days now. Something to do. Something coming up, forgotten with all of the other shit going on. Great big leaf-stuffed orange garbage bags littered front yards, and bats and ghosts filled windows.

And then there was his house. It had nothing. *At least on the outside.* Inexcusable. Halloween was one of the few days when he got to talk to people. His neighbors thought him odd enough without adding miser to the list.

§ § §

Half an hour later, Kaleb slipped out of the dealership waiting room while the desk girl was busy. She was cute enough, and he was pretty sure she was flirting with him, but what the hell would he do with her? Take her out hunting one night? Or maybe an evening in with Jordan and Allie? Might be tough to explain. She'd probably have an issue with necrophilia too. *Snob.*

He snuck a glance back and instantly regretted it. She was watching him, phone in hand, looking disappointed and a little spurned. Today was turning out even worse than he'd thought.

He wandered the lot, checking out new vehicles. Maybe it was time to treat himself to a new car. The silver SLS AMG caught his eye the instant he saw it, but it was flashy, and two hundred grand was a touch steep.

§ § §

Ninety minutes and two disappointed salesmen later the desk girl stepped from her office with a forced smile and waved him over. Kaleb fell in behind and caught himself staring at her ass. A masterpiece, it stirred something inside of him never dead but long dormant. There had only been one woman in his life, and that had been centuries ago. Katherine had been more than merely cute, though. She had been one of a kind, spectacularly beautiful, at least in his eyes.

Kaleb snapped back, realizing he'd let his mind wander. The desk girl's smile had once more become genuine, and he realized she'd caught him staring at her backside. Blushing madly for the first time since he was a teen, he had to stand there and take her knowing smile while she printed up the papers. Thankfully she didn't make him talk; he wasn't sure if he could manage anything more than incomprehensible noise.

"Someone's pulling the car around front," she said with a sly smile.

Not until he was sitting behind the wheel of the Mercedes could he let out a shout of frustration. "Shit!!!" Why did he have to choke so bad? It wasn't like he was going to do anything stupid like ask her out, but did that mean he couldn't even talk to a pretty girl without making a complete fool out of himself?

Trying to forget his pathetic display, he unfolded his receipt to see what he'd actually paid. It was bad, but not as bad as the quote had been, and more importantly there was a name and number scrawled at the top. Brandy. It fit.

He wouldn't call. He couldn't. But it was amazing how good it felt. Karma couldn't decide what to do with him today. One woman had brought him low, and another had raised him up. He stared at the number, wondering. Could he? Where would he even begin? He sighed, letting go of the idea. It wasn't realistic. To be honest, it scared the hell out of him. Nothing was stopping him from dreaming about it though.

With his mind stuck in a fantasy of normalcy, he drove from memory and pulled into a parking spot behind the deli not remembering if he'd stopped at lights or cut anyone off. A bit of a terrifying prospect. The last thing he needed was grabbing even more unwanted attention. Even so, he was here, and he had only one errand left after this.

Robbie waved a friendly hello while a new girl rushed to fill orders with a harried look on her face. Mark was on the phone but nodded and motioned to the freezer. Lingering here and there, poking around where he didn't need to, Kaleb found himself without attention, relatively useless, and almost dejectedly went for his order.

Arms loaded up, he stepped from the cooler and glanced around, almost hoping someone needed help. It wasn't to be. No one even looked his way, and he couldn't decide if it was sad or funny that he wanted to stay.

Sad he decided after a minute. He needed more out of life.

It wasn't until he was a few paces from his car, boxes balanced in one hand and keys in the other that he stopped short. One side of the Mercedes hung low, both tires flat. He spun, searching for a culprit. One tire maybe. But two?

Finding the lot barren, Kaleb ran his fingers over the tires, searching for nails or debris and instead finding narrow punctures. The choking grasp of paranoia set in, and he closed his eyes and thrust out his power. There was no tingle, no flicker of ice behind his eyes.

"Goddammit." He flipped open his cell and punched in a number. "Hello. This is Kaleb Adams. I was just in the shop."

"Oh. Hi." Brandy said, a girlish lilt in her voice. "I thought you'd call my cell."

Damn. Kaleb held his breath, realizing what he'd done, and worse, what he was about to do. He bit his lip, unsure of what to say.

"…Hello?"

"Uh, yeah…I'm actually calling to get a tow."

"Oh…"

"Someone slashed my tires."

The lilt disappeared. Frost crept through the phone. "I'll transfer you to automotive."

Kaleb slumped against the car and sighed. He really was a dumbass.

One brief conversation later he was assured that a tow truck would be there to grab him soon. He sat behind the steering wheel, idly jumping from one radio station to another, despising himself for a whole new set of reasons. How could someone who'd lived so long be so stupid? For a few brief moments he'd felt giddy that someone was interested in him. And literally a matter of minutes—not hours—minutes later, he'd screwed it up. It would be impressive if it weren't quite so fucking pathetic. It was his curse. *Karma.* Every time something good happened, the universe was there to slap him down. Not that he didn't deserve it.

He waited patiently, unable to do anything else. If she wanted to be frosty about it that was her choice. It wasn't like he could have had a more legitimate reason to call the dealership again.

Minutes ticked past, turning into half an hour, an hour, and then a little over two hours before the tow truck showed up. *Karma.* Anger wasn't an option, not real anger at least; he'd pretty much burnt himself out on that with Allie, but even so he didn't return the driver's wave.

Kaleb forced a smile and got out. He leaned back, arms crossed, hardly daring to imagine what might go wrong next.

It didn't take long. The driver swapped out his tires. Kaleb got in, anxious to stock up for Halloween and get home to make supper, and turned the ignition. The Mercedes turned over smooth, always a pleasant sound, and sputtered. The motor rattled, coughed, and died.

§ § §

Home rarely looked so inviting. Usually it was a forlorn place, safe and secure if not lonely. Tonight, it felt like…well…like coming home was supposed to.

The cool air of the garage set Kaleb at ease with its dusty familiarity. The day's tension began to drain away. No one to slash his tires here or dump sugar in the gas tank. But there was still the matter of who had done it. Vandals? Or someone with a motive? He'd taken the long way home, continuously checking the mirrors. No one had followed.

Arms burdened with bags and boxes, he made for the door. *A quick outing, a few chores, a few hellos. Yeah right.* The entire day had been pissed away. Even the mundane seemed to have it out for him.

He crossed the threshold and stopped short, wrinkling his nose. The house's smell was funkier than usual. Not the rancid odor of Allie downstairs, or even of Jordan's litter box, but choked with sweat and musk. The lights were off, the blinds closed. Cold fire flared behind his eyes a second too late. Someone lurched at him—tall and broad-shouldered. Kaleb threw his bags and boxes at the intruder and backpedaled. Strong hands latched on and yanked him back inside. The intruder wasn't alone. They crowded in, pinning Kaleb's arms and slamming him to the wall.

Kaleb wrenched one arm free and grasped at the people holding him. Bones broke beneath his fingers with wet snaps. A man screamed in pain. Half a moment of freedom and they were on him again in a rain of kicks, punches, and grasping hands. The lights came back on, and Kaleb saw five strangers in his home, three holding him immobile, one cradling a broken arm, and a small figure lost in a robe.

None were human.

Kaleb stopped struggling.

One of the men rammed his elbow into Kaleb's neck. "Sucker's not that tough after all, is he?"

"Tough enough," the one with the broken arm said through gritted teeth.

"Got him?" someone asked.

"Yeah."

One of the men stepped away and trotted down the hall, returning a few seconds later with a duffel bag in hand. He reached in and drew out glimmering chains that clinked almost musically. *Silver.* Kaleb breathed in their scents. They smelled wild. Like animals. All but the little guy who smelled of nothing. Like a ghost.

They spun at a spine-chilling growl. Jordan crouched at the end of the hall, a furry ball of jet-black malevolence, snarling, hissing, and spitting with her back arched and an eerie glow in her emerald eyes.

The men stared dumbfounded. One of them laughed. Another growled savagely and stomped in an attempt to scare her off. Jordan hissed in reply.

She'd given him a chance and Kaleb wasn't about to squander it. He called on the cold lurking inside of him. Life fled, rushing away in a wintery breath that left him chilled and numb.

They felt it too. They turned back, but it was too late. Kaleb shoved with everything he had. They hit the wall in a tangle, smashing drywall and two-by-fours, punching a hole into the bathroom behind. One of the intruders hit the porcelain tiled floor and quivered in the throes of death, thick blood leaking from his ears and jagged bits of bone shining white where his crushed skull had torn through his scalp. The other was embedded in the wall, stunned into a stupor.

The silver chain cracked like a whip, splitting Kaleb's cheek open. Black blood splattered. The man holding the chain bared his teeth. A ripple ran through his body, warping his face, making him less than human. *Werewolf.*

The silver left a fleeting sting that was easily ignored. Kaleb charged, reaching out with a cold and withered hand to grasp the wolf by the face. For all the beast's strength its neck snapped on the first twist. It twitched and shuddered, its body failing, its strength faltering, doomed yet not quite dead.

A blade sprouted from Kaleb's neck, burning as the Knight's sword had. The little guy drew another blade. An inhuman roar shook the house. The wolf with the broken arm snarled and hunched over, his body writhing beneath his clothes, skin stretching and tearing. In the bathroom, the stupefied wolf shook off his daze and struggled to get free.

Kaleb bolted, past the laundry room, the closet, and into the living room. He eyed the front door and dismissed it. A freak fight on his front lawn? Abandon Jordan and Allie to these beasts? Give up the life he'd worked so hard to create? He'd die first. He set his back to the wall and waited. If they wanted him, they were going to have to earn it.

The stupefied wolf was the first to come. No longer dazed, the wolf smiled maniacally, undeterred by his dead friends, exulting in the thrill of the chase. Jordan was a streak of black lightning, bolting from beneath an end table. Her eyes flashed in the dark, and she squawked as the wolf's foot struck her body.

The wolf stumbled. He clawed the air for purchase, found none, and smashed into the glass coffee table.

Time slowed to a crawl. A million shards of glass exploded into sparkling shrapnel. One large piece survived, twirling, dancing through the air, biting into the wolf's neck, slicing deep, deeper, and passing through completely. The body twitched and slumped. The head hit the carpet with a bounce and rolled, eyes wide with shock. The sentience within dimmed and then disappeared altogether.

The small man strode around the corner, a blade in each hand and a snarling werewolf at his back. Kaleb pressed against the wall, unable to look away from the towering werewolf. It's damn head almost scraped the ceiling. The hand that had been broken was almost knit. Kaleb glanced at the plate glass window. *Screw the neighbors. I want to live.* The beast's yellow eyes narrowed and it moved to cut off the escape.

The little man took the moment to throw back his hood. He was middle-aged, Asian, delicately featured, and he looked like he didn't give a shit about what was going on, as if it was only boring, regular business. A streak of white raced through his hair, branching out and turning his skin ashen. Splits emerged on either side of his face, trailing down, widening with wet tears until red flesh bubbled and oozed. Something moved within, writhing and growing, reaching outward to burst free in a spray of blood. Limbs erupted, straining until two bloody clones pulled apart from the host body.

The hair on Kaleb's arms and neck rose.

One hand held out, the ashen creature made a flicking motion, and a vase whipped at Kaleb, tossed with an invisible force. The room came alive with swirling bits of broken glass and anything not nailed down in a whirlwind of traitorous knickknacks.

The trio lunged with uncanny unison. Kaleb grabbed the only thing available and swung the couch hard enough to shatter on impact and reduce the clones to gobbets of meat. The ashen creature bowled ass-over-head, collapsing beneath the ruins of the couch. The whirlwind faltered.

The werewolf growled and Kaleb met its yellow eyes. He had to break past it, nothing more. Before he could act, cold fire overwhelmed his senses. The front door burst open and the picture window imploded. *They* flooded in, cold and dead, reeking of age and power, their pale faces angry, their cruel eyes knowing no mercy.

He was caught. He could fight, but he couldn't win. There was too much age in the room, too much power. A flicker of emerald caught his attention, and he strained not to look. Jordan huddled beside the love seat, watching and seeming to understand. She was something he'd never thought he would have again—a friend. The least he could do to return her love was to distract them. He owed her that much.

The moment wasn't what he'd expected it to be. It wasn't like last time, ambushed by the vamps. Then he'd been so surprised, shocked at the discovery even if he'd been afraid, but he'd also had hope. This time there was no hope, only death, and it was strangely liberating. There was still fear, of what would happen *after*, but being caught, it must be what an escaped prisoner felt like. The sense of impending doom was gone. It gave him a certain courage. All that remained was how he would go out.

Kaleb could feel Jordan's gaze on him, and from the corner of his eyes he saw that same eerie glow he'd caught a glimpse of earlier.

The wreckage stirred with the little man crawling loose. The distraction was momentary, a flicker of the eyes, but it was enough. Kaleb made his move; a wild sweep of his arm that sent the TV flying. The entertainment unit followed close behind, hurled with everything he could muster. His hope to throw them off was dashed when a large, severe looking vampire stepped into the attack and smashed the entertainment unit to splinters.

For a moment it was as if nothing happened, and then one of the vampires gurgled and coughed. Blood spilled from his lips. He dropped to his knees, one hand clutching his chest. A spot of red bloomed on his shirt, soaking through and spreading, splattering all over the carpet. He turned to his comrades, frantic, and one rushed to press a hand over the wound while the others offered nothing but pity. A thin piece of wood from the entertainment unit, hardly more than a shard, had pierced his heart. The vampire was dead in seconds.

The others watched in stony silence.

Kaleb leapt for the window. Fresh air tickled his face, and for a heartbeat he was free. Hopes to make a break for it and lead them away from Allie and Jordan burst into being and imploded even faster as his momentum stopped with a brutal jolt and he was slammed to the floor. The vampires pressed in, a terrifying, twisted mob with wicked fangs and ungiving grips. Even then, as horrid as they were, they still had an aura about them, a shining, infuriating dark beauty.

The black-haired thug smiled sadistically and dropped an iron fist. Kaleb glared in defiance, managing to take four of the savage blows before the fight was knocked out of him. Dazed and drifting on the brink of passing out, he hardly noticed as he was bound and gagged.

Chapter 29

WHERE IS YOUR master?" The bald one they called Luther asked for the hundredth time.

Kaleb stared straight ahead, ignoring their questions, tuning out their musings and whispers. He would give them nothing. Well, almost nothing. The bastards had stripped him to his boxers, so they had that bit of personal info.

Freaks.

It made him wonder, though, if this is what they were doing to him...what was happening to Allie?

He turned his mind back to escaping, though it didn't seem likely given the situation. They had him in a dungeonesque room, dangling against a cold stone wall with his arms drawn up over his head and his feet inches off the ground, chained and shackled with silver. The bright metal burned where it touched, no longer a mere irritation. The room had only one way in or out, an ancient wooden door that would take a tank to destroy. Sure, the door had a window, but he'd have to bust out the bars and chop himself into at least three pieces to fit through.

Of all the manners of dying he'd considered over the years, this wasn't one of them. In a warped way it felt like justice. A myriad of faces flashed before his eyes, all of the sickly souls he'd murdered and fed on. He had sinned. Atrociously. Maliciously. Of necessity, perhaps, but did that make any difference? He was an unholy thing, an abomination before god, and the devil would soon have his due.

Of all his sins, passing on this curse to Allie was the worst, and these bloodsuckers would do him a favor by ending her dark life before it truly began.

A lilting laughter drew Kaleb's ire. *Adora.* She deserved to die more than he did.

Luther struck with an open palm hard enough to rattle Kaleb's teeth. "Creature! What is your name?"

The black-haired brute cracked his knuckles. "Leave me alone with him."

Luther ignored the request. "You *will* speak. Things will go better for you if you spare us this inquisition."

Never. Kaleb yawned in reply. He pointedly didn't watch Luther head for the table. The vamps had yet to dip into the array of tools and weapons gleaming in the shifting light cast by a few antiquated braziers. Most were silver with oiled leather handles. A few were cold iron.

Luther turned back with a silver gauntlet on his fist. The blow that came next was enough to make Kaleb's vision swim. Luther was almost as strong as the brute, and the silver added a shock to the blow, a crackle of heat and energy that seeped through flesh and into bone.

Luther leaned in. "Answer me."

Kaleb held on to his mask of disregard.

Luther leaned back, readying himself for another swing.

"Luther!" Adora snapped. "I'd never imagined you could be so uninspired." She snatched a barbed hook off the table and threw it at him. "Speed it up."

The bald vampire caught the hook and tossed it away as if it were something unclean. He curled one lip in disgust at Adora, threw the gauntlet at her feet, and stormed from the room leaving her flushing at the reproach.

Renato stepped from a shadowed corner of the room where he had been watching and listening, undoubtedly hoping for answers that had previously eluded him. The flickering light revealed a solemn face. "Tell them what they wish to know," he said in a hushed voice. He waited a moment, his hope for an answer palpable, and seemed to shrivel in defeat before trailing after Luther.

Adora fumed at their departure and gave nervous glances at those who remained. The brute noticed and gave her the sickliest smile Kaleb had ever seen. It was predatory and obscene, like he was imagining not only taking off all of her clothes but her skin as well. Adora met his gaze without flinching but slipped away nonetheless. The brute laughed and grinned at a slender vampire with his hair tied in a ponytail.

"You're supposed to be playing nice, Maedoc," the slender vampire said.

The brute, Maedoc, shrugged. "I thought I was." He toyed with blades on the table and picked one with a serrated edge. His gaze fell on Kaleb, and the humor was gone. He blinked, shook off whatever sick idea was running through his mind, and threw the blade to one of his companions. "Adrian, you can go first." He smiled at Kaleb. "It's only fair. You did kill his brother."

Great. As if things weren't bad enough, now a personal vendetta had been piled on. They'd attacked him, drawn first blood, and now this? The look in Adrian's eyes made Kaleb long for Maedoc's madness. A knot formed in his chest. He just didn't want to disgrace himself any more than he already had. A sliver of pride was all he had left. Unfortunately, that was the only thing Adrian seemed to want from him.

§ § §

Maedoc sat on the couch and set his boots on a table. "He still hasn't spoken."

"His capacity for pain is amazing," Onwyn said, gazing at the paintings.

Amazing wasn't the word Aedan would have chosen. The creature had taken Luther's treatment and a full day of Adrian's retribution. Its nature was a certainty. "If it hasn't broken by now, I doubt it will anytime soon. We should destroy it."

Emigdio dismissed the suggestion with an irritated wave of his hand. "We have nothing but time. Give him no mercy or respite and he will break."

Aedan cringed inside. They were playing with fire.

"Pain does not make him cry out," Maedoc said. "Fear of death does not make him beg for his life. We need to be more persuasive."

Renato stirred. The old poet had spoken seldom since their arrival, preferring solitude more often than not. "We cannot sink so low."

Maedoc cracked his knuckles and rose to his feet. "I'll relieve Adrian."

The historian had a point. But they could do this for days, weeks, maybe years. All of the evidence pointed in one direction, even if Emigdio wasn't willing to accept it. Aedan worked over the information carefully, considering what to do. Harlow would be angry, furious even, but he'd also said to get it done at any costs. Waiting only created an opportunity for the situation to worsen. He sighed, fearing what must be done. There was no choice. They had to know in order to understand. "This will only get worse," he said.

"Our clan is crippled," Claudia snapped. "How much worse can it get?"

Aedan considered what he was about to do and looked to Emigdio for permission. The Jacksonville leader gave a curt nod, and the other vampires went silent, their curiosity piqued.

"We've not told you the entire truth of the matter," Aedan admitted. "Lord Harlow, Onwyn, Maedoc, and I have seen this once before, many years ago. A new sickness was ravaging humans, burning a trail from Asia to Europe. The people of London lived in fear, hiding behind their doors, shunning the ill. We ignored it all, waiting for it to pass, more concerned with our own problem. A man named Filius had emerged with an army of Fey, Human, Mystical, and Supernatural creatures, all eager to drag the world back into darkness.

"His three highest ranked soldiers, Mattias, Mercia, and Khaldun, were all practitioners of the dark arts. One of them was a rarity—a Necromancer—unnaturally powerful, able to raise and control the dead. He also had an unheard-of power, the ability to inhabit the bodies at will. While most Necromancers struggle to control a single undead, this one raised thousands.

"And while the minions were strong, their leader, Filius, was greater than his disciples combined. The necromancer raised an army of the dead, and Filius...he corrupted humans.

"In 1346 Filius began his war. First it was the young and weak who disappeared, human or vampyr, not uncommon occurrences in the time of monsters and hunters but for the scale of the matter. It wasn't long before the city was under siege, overrun by a type of undead we had never seen before. They carried a pestilence that spread through humans like wildfire. Many simply died, but many others turned. Even some vampyr fell prey to the sickness.

"He almost won. Had he taken his time and limited the outbreak the tide may never have turned, but as it was, he lost control of his undead army. His preternatural creatures fled. The walking dead became an epidemic that raged out of control. It took decades and countless lives before the sickness was brought under control. The atrocities of those days were beyond comprehension. The sick were burned, often before they died."

A hush fell over the room in the absence of Aedan's voice, broken by an unusually subdued Onwyn. "We had to kill as many again to cover up the truth behind the Black Death."

Valentine visibly struggled to comprehend what he had heard. "What the hell is he then? A zombie? A Necromancer? Or a Necromancer inhabiting the body?"

"And what was Filius," Cora asked.

Adora scowled and interrupted before Aedan could answer. "You said 'corrupted.' As in…infection?"

Valentine cut in again. "So a necromancer raised zombies, they started biting everyone, and an epidemic broke out?"

"It would explain Samuel and the girl," Claudia said.

Aedan waited patiently for the barrage to end. "He is not a zombie, and I do not believe he is possessed by a necromancer. There are rare cases of undead who rise on their own due to reasons we do not always understand—viruses, curses, perhaps even demonic influences, and there are those raised by necromancers. Those who rise on their own are pestilent, easily infecting humans, but they are not dangerous to vampyr. Those raised by dark magics are at best shadows of their old selves, more likely to be used as obscene tools for petty purpose, and they do not carry the pestilence at all."

"Neither explains what is happening to Samuel." Cora said.

Aedan glanced at Adora. "No, they do not. It is only through incredible luck and the strength of someone with enough power that Adora is still here. Few have survived such a bite."

Cora settled a fierce gaze on Aedan and repeated her question. "Filius. What was he? And how do I save Samuel?" She was angry. She had every right to be. She believed information had been held back that could save one of her own.

Aedan let his eyes carry his compassion and bowed his head slightly. "I'm sorry, Matron, but you don't. If not treated almost immediately there is nothing to be done. All we can do is give Samuel the release of death."

"So," Luther cut in, "you believe this creature is Filius?"

"No," Onwyn said. "Filius died in the fires. But this creature is like him, and it needs to be destroyed immediately."

"Answer Cora!" Claudia snapped. "What is he? You've kept us in the dark, lied to us, and still refuse to answer." She jumped up. "Emigdio, why did you allow this?"

Luther grabbed her arm and coaxed her to sit back down. "Because," he said, "Aedan explained it to us earlier. We thought it best not to tell everyone such a dangerous secret."

Claudia spun on him. "You knew?" She pulled away and struck out.

Luther's head whipped back with the impact. He barked laughter and wiped blood from his nose, smiling approvingly. Even so, he backed out of her reach.

It was a mildly amusing display, even if the timing wasn't quite appropriate. There were serious matters to settle. Claudia wasn't the only one upset. Cora, normally the calmest, most reasonable vampyr Aedan knew of, was furious. Her lips were thin white lines, and her bony old hands were clenched tight. Rain backed away, shaken by her mentor's anger.

Aedan looked to Emigdio for aid. The vampire nodded. "Are you sure?" Aedan asked. They were traveling a dangerous road.

Emigdio didn't flinch. "Yes."

"As you wish." Aedan turned back to the others. "I'd hoped to spare you. What I am about to tell you may never be repeated. It is forbidden knowledge, and for your sake I give you this one chance to leave." He paused, waiting, and sighed when no one moved.

"Shall I?" Onwyn asked. Already tired, Aedan nodded.

"The creature in your basement is exceedingly rare and dangerous," Onwyn said. "As Aedan has said, there are different types of the walking dead. The first kind are those who come alive due to a virus or fel influence. They, like so many undead, hunger for the life they have lost. The second kind are those who are raised. They are mindless servants. And then there is a third kind. They are contagion personified, able to infect even vampyr and other supernatural creatures. Their sickness is borne through bite and sometimes scratch, spreading with dangerous ease, killing in mere days and creating new hosts. There were claims that Filius' bite could infect, kill, and raise in mere hours."

Onwyn paused, trying to find the words. "This creature in your dungeon, one of the third kind...he was meant to be our brother."

Shock rippled through the room. Emigdio's clan exchanged tense glances, finally beginning to understand.

"Vampyr?" Cora asked, stunned.

Valentine shook his head. "What the hell. I thought you said he wasn't a vampire? And Renato staked him."

"He was meant to be," Onwyn said. "Something went wrong. They awaken as we do, and then they begin to fall apart, deteriorate. In days they are little more than mindless, ravenous cannibals. Conventional weapons and methods of killing them are nearly useless. Even silver or wood through the heart cannot stop them, only slow them down, and they are unnaturally strong. They are aberrations."

"He is more than that. He thinks, speaks," Renato said.

Aedan startled and barely hid it. He'd forgotten Renato was there. The poet had been so still and silent, and more than that, it was like he'd faded from mind as well as sight. "I've never heard of one coming back so far. Even Filius could never have hidden amongst humans."

The poet struggled to come to terms. "He is our brother, and still you would have him destroyed? He knew nothing of our laws. He killed Michael, my ward, but he was fighting for his life. I cannot fault him for that." Adora glared at Renato, no doubt wondering if he would be so forgiving had she died.

"Yes," Aedan said. "He should never have been allowed to live in the first place."

"Why," Cora asked, aghast. "If they can come back, why must they die? Will Samuel return?"

Aedan swallowed hard. He hadn't even told Emigdio or Luther that possibility. "Maybe. But it would take centuries, and one scratch, one bite, and the infection spreads. They cannot be controlled. They are too dangerous."

Fully aware of Emigdio's displeased stare on him, Aedan was grateful when Onwyn cut in again.

"Others have tried. They want to save their loved ones, or worse, to use the creatures as weapons. It is disastrous. Even the newly turned can be formidable."

"You need only look to Filius," Aedan said, determined. "Hundreds of millions died because he was allowed to live. *Hundreds of millions!* It *cannot* happen again. I already fear to think what would happen if this one has Filius' intentions."

"Aye," Onwyn said. "And there's no way to predict how they grow. We know they develop as we do, over time, with sustenance, but the extents of their powers are unknown. None survive long enough to find out."

Luther turned a wary eye away from Claudia. "We have all heard rumors of masters destroying their own. I'd always thought it was in some sick torment."

The burden of the secret finally off his chest, Aedan sat back. "It is a well-guarded secret. A law of the eldest amongst us, passed down only to powerful Lords." He glanced at Emigdio. "At least those who create their own clans. Since you have only adopted strays and have never turned anyone yourself, they have not felt the need to tell you. Samuel knew, and that was deemed enough."

"All we truly know of these creatures," Onwyn said, "Is that they crave flesh and they don't care if it comes from vampire or human."

Cora sagged in defeat and half-heartedly allowed Rain to grasp her hand. "Then we must destroy Samuel."

Emigdio stirred on his throne. "It would appear so. First, we need to know if there are more of these creatures."

Chapter 30

FAR ABOVE HIS head, beyond layers of stone, earth, and wood, Kaleb felt the sun begin its ascent. Fatigue settled into his bones, wearing on his battered and abused soul, a deep instinct tied to the abhorrent thing he had become.

Adora prattled on enough to make him yearn for quality time with Maedoc. The brute had barely said a word, letting his fists speak volumes. Adora would not shut up. It was the more painful of the methods so far, though that was about to change. She drew a fire poker from a blazing forge. The iron rod glowed red hot.

Kaleb closed his eyes, trying to put his mind far away as Adora pressed the poker against his flesh. Skin sizzled and melted like plastic. She trailed it up and down, enraptured, and when the glow began to dim, she stabbed the poker into the depths of his belly. He could resist the need to scream. He could keep from telling them what they wanted to know. The convulsions wracking his body though, those he couldn't stop. The beatings had been bad. The instruments worse. The pain of being staked excruciating. But fire, that was a new level of hurt.

Despite the torment, Kaleb's hunger flared, and he recoiled. It was the smell. His flesh burning.

Adora drew the brand out. The orange glow was gone, smothered by black blood, the metal drained of its searing heat. Kaleb let the convulsions run their course, and went limp in his chains, letting his head sag to hide the tears dripping down his cheeks.

"Answer me!" Adora snarled.

Kaleb ignored her as he had the others.

Adora screamed wordlessly and lashed out with the brand. The blow rattled Kaleb's brain and sight, fracturing his skull and driving splinters deep into gray matter. Even that couldn't seem to kill him. They'd done things to him that he'd only read about in books: thumbscrews, clamps, and racks. And the suit of armor—Adrian had made a show of it, displaying the dozens of silvers spikes within. Even that was nothing compared to Adora's tender touch.

Adora broke out into another rant about Samuel and Michael. "You murdered them! You almost killed me! You dare to steal from our lands and risk exposing us all! And now you think you can defy us? Your torment has only begun—"

Enough!" Kaleb shouted before he could stop himself. "Please, go back to torturing me. Cut me, burn me, anything, just shut the fuck up already!"

For a second his wish was granted. Adora gawked, blissfully silent, and then she screamed in fury and spun to the table of instruments, searching for something she hadn't yet tried.

It was almost worth it.

Any pleasure the outburst had given Kaleb disappeared when she returned to the flame. She smiled sweetly and turned her back to hide what she was doing. It didn't take long. A few moments at best. The evil bitch had found a set of tongs, and within their metal grip a piece of coal burned bright.

"Come," she said. "You must be hungry by now."

Kaleb clenched his teeth together and twisted his head in a useless attempt to resist. Adora laughed, that same lilting, girlish laugh, so out of place it was jarring, and plunged the coal into the wound in his abdomen. It was more than he could take. He screamed and thrashed against his chains. She back stepped, still laughing. The coal was agony, roasting him from the inside out.

An ache like nothing Kaleb had ever felt radiated throughout his body, a sickly pulse, as if he had to vomit. His strength fled and his body went limp. Why did it have to end like this? Such a miserable final chapter to cap off a nightmarish existence. Darkness threatened, the room fading in and out, and voices whispered in Kaleb's ears. Prey begged for their lives. Tristan and Katherine made promises. Isabelle offered eternity. And woven throughout, murmurs wriggled like worms into his brain.

Kaleb jolted awake. If the change came while he was unconscious there would be nothing to dull the pain. Every broken bone, bruise, cut, and burn…it would break him. He tried to call to Adora and managed a dry rasp. He swallowed hard, dampening his throat, "Hey."

She turned back, a malicious smile turning up the corners of her pouty lips. "I don't care," she admitted. "I don't want to know who you are, what you are, or if there are more like you." She hefted a piece of pipe. "I only want to hear you scream."

Laughter bubbled out of Kaleb's throat, striking Adora like a slap to the face. "Do you think that will even things out? Is my scream going to make you forget yours? Will it silence the sound of Michael's dying wheezes or the splatter of his blood on the ground?" Kaleb smacked his lips. "He was a pussy for being so big, but damn he did taste good. Made myself some nice kebobs, burgers, steaks, tossed in a few spices. Mmm-mmm. Delicious."

A tremor ran through Adora. Her hands shook. Her fingers clenched tight enough to bend the pipe. Kaleb grinned again and chuckled low in his chest.

The humor died on his lips, speared by a pipe shattering his ribs and piercing a lung. Adora spun back to her fire, and a chill shook Kaleb's body. It wasn't the chill of the change, or of chancing upon some unknown supernatural being, but a shiver of fear. She was hateful, spiteful, dedicated, and creative. She turned back with the tongs clutched in her hands again, and within them a small blackened pot filled with bubbling liquid silver.

Kaleb strained against his chains, pulling and tearing with everything he had. Every attempt sent jolts of electricity through his arms and legs. Skin ripped and blood spattered, but the chains held strong. Adora watched the feeble attempt, smiling with glee and savoring the moment.

"Kill me," he threatened. "Or before god, if I ever have the chance, I will peel the flesh from your bones while you beg for death."

She gave him that same sweet and malicious smile again, grabbed the pipe, and started pouring.

Chapter 31

THE WORLD HAD bled to darkness. Allie could barely see, but her other senses were overloading. She was in a different dungeon now, tied with different chains. All around her, above, below, and in chambers beside were strange beings—creatures so alien she couldn't even begin to understand them. And close by was another prisoner. His mind was corrupt, a thing of writhing snakes and a terrible, ravenous hunger like her own.

She turned rheumy eyes to the locked door, waiting for *him* to come. The one who brought her food. The shadow man who had abducted her. *Kaleb*. She could sense him nearby, no longer something to be feared.

When she was dying, he had reached down to brush a few errant strands of hair out of her eyes and then gently held her arm. Allie had seen inside of him, tasted his sorrow, and knew what she meant to him. In that brief touch his soul was laid bare. She understood him better than she had ever understood anyone else, and in knowing him, she forgave him. She caught glimpses of how *they* had lied to him, of his creation, and of so many lonely years after. The memories were as real as if they were her own, the undeniable heartache, the overwhelming hope, and the excitement when she came back to life.

And then emptiness had swallowed her whole.

Allie wasn't sure how much time she'd lost. All she could remember was waking in darkness, her knees resting on cold pavement and bits of frozen meat in her mouth. Now everything was a confused jumble punctuated by brief moments of clarity, easily lost when her hunger quickened. In her few lucid moments she felt mostly fear, of slipping back into that place where no memories took root. Those hours and days were lost to her, except for a few fragments of light and sound and taste that were difficult to understand—a glimpse of Kaleb retreating from her approach, the taste of blood in her mouth, and a stench of rotten flesh that only made her hungrier. She hadn't wanted to attack Kaleb or eat the corpse he'd laid at her feet; she just hadn't been able to stop herself. And after, always after, it felt as though she was waking up, banishing some evil, invading force that had possessed her.

Kaleb always forgave her though. He loved her, and he would come for her.

After so many years alone, surrounded by people who claimed to be friends and family, he was the first person who wanted—no, who truly *needed* her. Her family was large, eight kids, and she wasn't the smartest, or the prettiest, and neither the youngest nor the oldest. She was the one who slipped through the cracks. She had friends but no best friends, no one she really connected with. And to her boyfriend she was arm candy. She had a type—strong arms, ripped abs, extreme extroverts to her extreme introvert, but again, nothing ever really clicked. None of them had ever really understood her. Sure, everyone would be upset with her disappearance, they would cry, go to her funeral, and then they would move on. Kaleb wouldn't.

Allie could still feel him out there, suffering. She wanted to go to him, tell him she forgave him, that he wasn't a monster, but her body still wasn't her own. She couldn't speak, could hardly control her movements, and patches of time were still disappearing, growing longer and darker.

Her dungeon mate struggled against his chains, lost in the grips of starvation, and Allie turned to him, trying to touch a consciousness that was nowhere to be found. She felt something inside of him, something like herself, and also something that was one of them, one of the people who had taken her captive and tied her in chains that burned.

Allie closed her eyes and focused on Kaleb. He was hurt, waning, but he would come for her.

Chapter 32

A S KALEB HAD feared, the change had come while he slept. He awoke, his entire body throbbing like one massive open wound. He writhed in his chains, screaming almost without sound. All that came out was a rattling wheeze of ruined lungs. Lancets of fire tore through his chest with every movement, searing liquid heat that seemed to be melting him from the inside.

Desperation set in, and he called his power, begging it to come. A spark flickered to life behind his eyes, began to spread, and snuffed out. Kaleb sobbed in silence, his strength and willpower spent.

A rock flew out of the darkness, splitting the skin on his forehead and sending blood trickling into one eye. Something moved within the shadows, a misshapen, stunted shape, hiding beyond the reach of the torches. It chuckled wetly, and another stone narrowly missed Kaleb's face. *It* slid from the shadows with a hiss, claws outstretched, luminous orange eyes glaring up with cruel intent. Pustulent yellow skin glimmered in the dim lighting, and the creature's stench assaulted Kaleb, a rancid odor of offal and garbage set to ferment under a summer sun.

Kaleb lashed out, trying to kick the beast. Whatever the creature was, it understood the constraints of the chains and shackles. It bared broken, rotten teeth and raked its claws over Kaleb's legs, digging furrows and stripping away skin before retreating to the shadows.

Ugly little fucker, Kaleb thought. He gave a weak attempt to stand up tall and failed miserably. His fight was gone, broken by the searing agony of the metal within, now cooled and solid. His vision was fading, blurring around the edges, narrowing to tunnels, and his thoughts were getting jumbled.

And beneath it all his hunger grew.

Stone grated against stone and Kaleb managed to lift his head in search of the rancid little beast. If his heart was still beating it would have skipped. Adora sat in a chair near the dying torches, almost hidden from sight. For a moment Kaleb wondered if the creature was acting at her behest, and then he realized she was unconscious. The sun was up, and she was too young to resist its lull. In her dead slumber she had a deceptive, peaceful innocence. He should have finished her when he had the chance.

Stones scraped, and a brick came out the darkness, shattering Kaleb's ribs and jarring the now-cooled metal within his chest. He sucked in air, gasping, driven almost to the point of insanity. His power came slowly, drawn by the pain, kissing along the nape of his neck and raising the hair on his arms. It built into a cool breeze that slid over his flesh leaving death in its wake. Cuts and gashes stopped oozing as his blood thickened and turned black. The chill settled over the injuries like a salve, easing all but the oppressive mass of silver sitting like a cancerous growth in his chest.

The little monster snuffled, sensing the change. It stepped into the light, curiosity dawning on its dim face. It moved closer. Kaleb grimaced again. The creature was foul. Even in his undead form the stench was overwhelming.

It crept closer, sniffing, and darted in.

Kaleb held still. It wasn't attacking him. It was just curious. It looked up at him, grinned, and licked his leg. A long, forked tongue probed an open gash, and Kaleb lashed out with a kick. It scrambled out of reach, spewing a string of grunts and snarls. It began to pace, agitated, growling, and sharpening its claws on the floor.

"Piss off you nasty little fucker," Kaleb hissed, eyes flickering towards Adora. The last thing he needed was to wake her again.

It glowered at Kaleb with an undeserved malevolence. Dim or not, it was smart enough to latch onto his fear of Adora. An idea growing in its feeble mind, it crept warily towards the vampiress and rooted around a scattering of tools on the floor. It came up with a long, serrated blade, hooked at the end, and jabbed the air in practice.

It was too much. The vampires were bad enough, but now this fucking thing? Kaleb strained against his shackles, cringing at the sensation of skin stretching and melting like microwaved cheese. If Allie could break her chains, he could break these. He braced himself, pulling the chains taut, mustering every last ounce of strength he had left. Sooner or later something would give. The creature watched his display and broke out in a sibilant laughter. It stepped closer, brandishing the knife, trying to scare him, and stopped suddenly, alert, its humor gone.

The weak flames of the braziers fluttered in a chill draft.

The creature gave Kaleb one last malevolent, contemptuous look and threw the blade at him before scampering to a corner of the room and pushing into a crack in the wall, its body squishing and contorting to fit into a space far too small for the revolting beast. In a moment it was gone, only a greasy sheen showing where it had passed.

Kaleb stopped struggling and listened to a faint tap of footfalls echoing down the halls. Adora's relief. Time for round four. Five if you included the nasty fucker. Who was it going to be this time?

Keys jingled and the lock clicked, and the Renato stepped into the room, stopping short while he took in all of the once-shiny blades and devices now dulled by blood, and then at the wounds they had caused. He looked to Adora slumbering in her chair, and gently lifted her up. "Do not worry about the—*mamoncete*—the little bastard," he said. "I will be back before he finds the courage to return."

Renato's footsteps faded into silence. Kaleb struggled against his chains again. Skin sloughed away with every ineffective thrust. Smoke rose in wisps, the smell of his own meat searing. Minutes later and with no progress to speak of, Kaleb flinched. Renato watched him from the hall. There had been no tread of his steps this time; the vampire had moved as quietly as a specter.

"Why do you not speak?" Renato asked.

Kaleb lowered his arms and clenched his jaw. They didn't need to see him struggle, and he had nothing to say.

Renato grabbed the chair Adora had been sleeping in, set it before Kaleb, and sat down. "I doubt you have a master, or even a clan. So, what are holding you back? Are you so willful? Or is it hatred? I understand both, but you can spare yourself this pain." He shook his head, genuinely saddened. "I am sorry for what has been done to you. Please know that I was against this outrage."

Renato waited expectantly, and sighed, seeming to realize the conversation was destined to be one-sided. "I wish it were not so," the vampire said after a while. "My hands have too much blood on them already. I would see you go free, but the others would not." He met Kaleb's eyes. "Answer my questions and I swear you will be treated humanely and given a swift death."

Kaleb searched for a lie within the words and could find none.

Renato eyed the array of bloody tools. "Who did it? Adrian? Maedoc?"

Do you really want to know? There was a hint of worry in the question, like the vamp was afraid of the answer. "Adora," Kaleb croaked.

Renato flinched, closed his eyes, and muttered quietly to himself. "It is one thing," he said, "to realize that your parents are bastards. It is so much worse to realize that you have sired one. She has taken Michael's death hard. Still, I cannot believe she would be so fiendish."

Good. At least she felt some pain.

"We are not innocent," Renato admitted. "We attacked you, all over a matter as irrelevant as territory. But it is the way of things. Emigdio and the others believe you are a threat. Aedan and his clan journeyed a long way to destroy you for fear of what you might do."

Aedan? For what I might do? Kaleb let the confusion carry to his eyes.

"You have questions as well. I should not be surprised. You were shaken when we first appeared, though it was not fear, was it? It was surprise. On my life, on my honor, I will keep my word. Tell me your story and I will answer any questions you may have."

Why was it so important to him? He didn't just want to know about a master or a clan, but a life story? What the hell for? Why read the book when he already knew the ending?

The idea of sharing his life with the dicks that were about to kill him wasn't exactly appealing. Then again, if they could answer some questions, maybe he could have some peace of mind before dying.

He struggled to draw a breath, whispering. "What about…" No one had said a word about her, and he hadn't asked.

"Unharmed," Renato said, understanding. He couldn't meet Kaleb's eyes when he spoke again. "She will receive the same fate as you."

A swift death for him and Allie. That really was the best he could hope for, wasn't it? And it wasn't like he had much left to lose. His home was trashed, Allie caught, and he'd spent the last how many hours being tortured? His only regret was Jordan. What would she do without him?

Spasms wracked Kaleb, shaking him in his chains. His vision dimmed, and the abyss pressed in. He clung to consciousness, determined to die as a man and not a mindless animal. Had any of the others offered the deal Kaleb wouldn't have listened. He shook his head, sickened at what he'd dragged Allie into.

"Okay," Kaleb whispered. He tried to draw a breath to say more, and almost doubled over coughing. The agony began anew as the metal inside his chest shifted and found new flesh to burn. Blood splattered from his mouth, and he managed one more word. "Food."

Renato raced away. Kaleb sagged against his chains, too tired to try breaking free again. Darkness closed in, trying to crush him beneath it. He held on. No more than a few minutes could have passed before the vampire's return. He tore the cap off of a bottle and tilted it into Kaleb's mouth.

Kaleb drank greedily, slurping and sucking, trying not to let a single drop go to waste. His stomach quivered with delight. The blood was human. The person it had belonged to had been healthy and strong. There was no bitter taste of drugs or disease. It set to work immediately, regenerating his body and will. His lungs sealed, drew in air, but not even the blood could help with the silver.

He struggled to draw a breath, ignoring a tickle that threatened to set off another bout of coughing. "Metal," he gasped.

Renato nodded and began checking him over. A sharp pain stabbed Kaleb's abdomen. He craned his head to see what Renato was doing and gawked. A silver pin slid out of him, at least a foot long. A dozen more silver tips gleamed, all skewering him through. *Bitch*! She'd made a damned pin cushion out of him.

The vampire pinched the silver tips between long fingernails and drew them out one by one. Every pin was a thorn of liquid fire, diminishing the moment they pulled free. Renato scanned Kaleb again, and stepped back, nodding.

Kaleb enjoyed the respite. Everything hurt so badly he hadn't even noticed the pins until they were gone. His eyes slipped shut, the little strength the blood had given him used up. He licked his lips, wetting them, and whispered, "More." The snap of a bottle cap brought a flood of saliva. Kaleb guzzled as greedily as he had the first bottle. Renato stared expectantly, eager for the story. *Not yet*, Kaleb thought, trying to muster his courage. *One more thing to do first.* "Chest…inside."

The ancient muttered in a strange language, distraught. He reached for the gaping hole in Kaleb's chest and hesitated. "It is true only your bite and scratch can infect?"

Was it? Bites and scratches for sure. But just blood? Lord knew the vamps had enough of his blood on their hands, and they seemed fine enough.

The same thing must have occurred to Renato. The vampire explored the wound, fingers probing for the metal. After a minute he pulled back. "I cannot feel it. If I am to remove it, I must find proper instruments."

Like proper tools would help. Unless they were taking him to the hospital for a surgery there was no easy way to do it. Kaleb shook his head. That would take too long. "Now."

The vampire pushed his fingers back into the wound, past the ribs and then further, bursting meat and skin as his entire hand slipped in. Renato found the silver and yanked his hand free, sucking air between his teeth while he cradled smoldering fingers. Kaleb fought not to scream, his body rigid and straining the chains in an attempt to burn off the surge of energy that came with the pain.

"Adora?" Renato hissed, outraged.

Kaleb bristled at the name and nodded.

Whatever it was that made a person or creature what it was left the vampire's eyes. His body remained, but his mind, his consciousness, departed for a few long seconds, and when it came back Renato was silent, unable or unwilling to hide the shame he felt at what his child had done.

"Finish it!" Kaleb snarled.

"Will you survive? The silver has attached to your innards. It will not be a clean removal."

Who fucking cares! At the moment dying would be better than living. Kaleb nodded again, unable to speak.

Renato tore a strip from his shirt and wrapped his hand. He hesitated again, and plunged back into Kaleb's chest, fingers squirming, searching and probing, sliding over things never meant to be touched. Kaleb's gorge rose in revulsion. A jolt ripped through his chest as the vampire found the silver again.

The ancient grunted, gripped the metal, and wrenched it free. He threw it to the ground, shaking the viscera from his hand. The cloth hadn't been enough. His flesh smoked where the metal had touched it. They were more allergic to silver than Kaleb was.

Kaleb was frozen, locked in one massive, body-wide spasm. He vibrated, sinew and bones creaking, muscles bulging and threatening to tear. The moment broke. Blood shot from his mouth and nose. He flailed in his chains, somehow managing to draw enough air to let out a ragged scream. Everything he felt, every bit of misery that was his life, every inch of pain and hatred welled out of him and into the dungeons. It was liberating, a release of pent up rage that left him hollow.

Renato was a phantom, trying to comfort him, to stall the bleeding, trying to help him drink, but Kaleb could barely see him. The chains loosened and clattered to the floor. Kaleb collapsed, still bound, but able to sit.

§ § §

The vampire's voice drifted through a haze. "Eat."

Kaleb turned his head away. Eating meant getting strong, and all he wanted was to survive long enough for a merciful murder. Was that really too much to ask? He pressed his lips shut, trying to ignore the smell and taste of the raw meat pressing against his lips. The hunger flared. His mouth opened against his will. *No!* His jaws chewed. *Stop!* His body ignored him.

"Good," Renato said. He pressed more meat to Kaleb's mouth in a shocking display of trust. One bite. Just one, and he would die a miserable death. Why was the vampire doing this? All to satisfy his perverse curiosity? His help was more pain than the other's torture had been.

Kaleb fought to open his eyes. Renato looked ill with worry, hovering like a mother over a sniffling newborn. He really wanted that damn story.

The meat began to work. But it wasn't enough. Not nearly. Kaleb savored it. *Beef.* He swallowed a few more pieces and waved away the next bite. "Blood."

Renato handed him the bottle.

Kaleb sipped at it, letting it slide down his throat. *Human.* It worked better than animal blood, soothing raw flesh as it trickled deeper and deeper. He could almost hear the hiss as it extinguished the fire in his chest inch by inch.

Renato spun the chair so he could rest his arms against the back of it and still watch Kaleb. His long fingers tapped relentlessly.

Aches and pains dulled. The sear eased to a throb. The blood felt ice cold as it trickled across and into the multitude of wounds within Kaleb's body. A seal formed over the cuts and tears in his lungs, and he drew a rattling breath that set off a fit of coughing.

Renato waited for the fit to pass before giving in to the need to know. "Please," he said softly, "let us end this atrocity."

It would be good to screw him over. What would the vampire do if Kaleb refused to say anything? *Would serve you right,* Kaleb thought, knowing he wouldn't. He was a monster of his word. If he didn't have that then he truly had nothing.

"You'll answer my questions, too?" For all the good it would do in his last few hours of life. Still, he'd spent so many years not knowing what he was.

"Yes."

Crushing weight lifted from Kaleb's shoulders at the promise of answers to questions that had plagued him his entire second life. Renato's voice startled him, and he realized his eyes had slipped shut. "What do you want to know?"

"Everything. I would know it all."

They broke me after all, Kaleb thought. Not in the way they'd expected but broken nonetheless. Kaleb pushed away the resentment of being forced to share what was his alone.

"When were you born?" Renato asked.

A long, long time ago. "1758. Bristol. I can't remember much of my life there, only bits and pieces. A big house with servants. A room full of toys. A hound. My father. My mother…sometimes I imagine I can almost hear her voice as she sang, but it never quite comes.

"Most of what I remember happened after I was six or seven, when my parents sold everything they had and bribed our way onto a ship owned by one of my father's friends from his years as a Dragoon."

Renato closed his eyes, absorbing the story.

"It was my fault. All of it," Kaleb said. The story, never spoken aloud, spilled out more easily than he would ever have thought possible. It *was* his fault. "I was a sickly child. I always had something—a fever, a flu, a cold. One of them nearly killed me, though I don't remember which. I couldn't have been older than five or six when the doctor said I didn't have much time left. 'The damp air,' he said. Not the best thing to hear when you're a Brit.

"My parents—they were good people—they loved me, perhaps too much. They were desperate when they decided to cross the ocean to the 'savage lands' hoping to give me a chance at life. Their friends spoke of driving the Spanish out of settlements and claiming them for the Crown, and it wasn't long before we were loading onto a ship filled with supplies and settlers bound for the new world.

"St. Augustine was little more than an outpost when we arrived. My father bribed soldiers and hired peasants to begin construction of our new home, a ways inland, away from the damp of the ocean." Kaleb smiled sadly at the fond memory.

"It took years to finish, and I can't even imagine the cost. All for me. The voyage had been rough, but in time I began to recover. Compared to Bristol I was thriving. My bouts of sickness were shorter and less frequent. I even began leaving the house, exploring our new lands, watching ships come and go in the port. I'd always loved watching the boats. They made me think of faraway places, strange people, sea monsters, and pirates."

A memory struck Kaleb, forgotten until now. "I remember once telling my father and his friends that I wanted to be a privateer like Frobisher and loot ships from France. They laughed, even my father, but I'll never forget the look on his face."

Kaleb fell silent, stung by memories that even centuries later were still open wounds. Renato's voice drew Kaleb out of his thoughts. "Did you ever travel?"

"No. The only wonders I saw were in books. I lived, but my life was empty. At least until we had been there for a few years. That was when I made my first true friend. All of the other children were peasants at first. I must have looked like a fool in their eyes, frail and proper, always clean and accompanied by a servant. But then some of the soldiers started bringing their families to the settlement. That was when I met Katherine."

Just saying her name made Kaleb smile. He could still see her as he had back then, a raven-haired, blue-eyed and fair porcelain doll. "I must have looked a fool to her as well, though she was always kind. I'd worried it was because of who my father was, or because she wasn't allowed to play with the peasant children, but even after higher born families began to arrive we stayed good friends.

"Within another half year I'd found my second friend, Tristan. I'd expected my parents to be glad I'd made a new friend, and at first, they were, until I said his name. They forbade me to see him again and wouldn't tell me why. Naturally I rebelled, and when I told Tristan what had happened, he wasn't the least surprised. It was his father, the family trade; they made their fortune on human misery, trafficking in slaves."

Kaleb looked to Renato and shrugged. "But Tristan wasn't guilty for the sins of his father. He hated the man. He rarely spoke of it, but Tristan had a wound inside of him, and bruises on the outside. His father was a hard man.

"I held nothing against Tristan, and in return he held nothing against me—not my parents' dislike of him, or that I was younger by a few years, and not once did he complain about having to slow down so I could keep up. He didn't mind my silence and awkwardness, and I was happy enough to hear him talk for the both of us.

"What amazed me most about Tristan was his envy of how my parents treated me, letting me follow my own pursuits, and the education they were giving me. He was full of questions, curious about the world, and was awestruck when I showed him my library. His father didn't approve of anything more than basic writing and enough math to keep records. I helped where I could, read books with him, told him whatever interesting snippet came to mind. He was fascinated with stories of Rome and Greece, of gods, heroes and battles."

The memories were both sweet and bitter. Tristan, the only true friend he had ever known, and Katherine, the only woman Kaleb had ever loved, had betrayed him.

"Inseparable as children, we began to drift apart during our teen years, not from a lack of friendship, but rather from family pressures. Tristan was to join the family business. Katherine was to behave like a lady and stop consorting with boys.

"I saw them less and less, and alone, cooped up with my books and dreams, my health was in decline. The journey to St. Augustine had proven only a brief respite. Katherine and Tristan explored the world around them, while I could only study it from an armchair.

"It was only natural when Katherine told me she was in love with Tristan. He was tall, handsome, a grown man by the time he was seventeen, and I was pale and weak and likely wouldn't see twenty. Even then I couldn't hate him. I would have given anything to be like him."

The words were dry and too big for his throat. "That didn't stop it from hurting. I'd known for over a year. They tried to hide it, but I could tell, from the glances, the lingering touches." History overwhelmed Kaleb and he couldn't speak for a minute.

"I cut them out of my life. Even when I wasn't ill, I had the servants say I was. It was around then that my father passed away. His heart, the doctor said. His death hit me hard, unexpected as it was. Or maybe it was denial. He was fifty-seven, a ripe old age back then. And my mother…it hit her even harder. She died less than a year later. I wish I could say I was surprised, but life had taught me well how unfair it could be. At sixteen, I was suddenly alone.

"I inherited the estate, more wealth than I'd imagined possible. They had spent so much starting over, but no one could have expected my father would do so well in the colonies. I could have anything money could buy, and nothing it couldn't.

"Amazingly, I saw my twentieth birthday, and that evening Tristan showed up at the door, refusing to leave until he'd seen me. They had both tried to visit from time to time, but this was different. He spoke of his intentions with Katherine, begged my blessing, and I realized he had no idea. Katherine hadn't spoken of what happened between us. Burning with envy of his health, his strength and even beauty, I think I hated him in that moment. He had everything, including the woman I was still in love with, and I gave him my blessing simply to be rid of him.

"That might have been the most miserable night of my life. I stopped caring. I felt I had nothing. Petty as it was, my only consolation was the feud breaking out between their families. Slavers and officers did not mingle. Katherine was on the brink of being shipped back to England to an arranged marriage. Twenty-one and single; it was shameful."

Isabelle's face pushed through the memories. She had been a beautiful and persuasive liar. Kaleb stared at Renato until the vampire looked up. "We didn't even have to search for a solution. She came to us."

"Wherever there is such tragedy," Renato said, "there is bound to be a vampyr. We are opportunistic creatures with a penchant for the finer things in life. You would have been irresistible."

Opportunistic. That wasn't quite the word Kaleb would have used. Maybe parasitic. "Her name was Isabelle. She approached Tristan first, promising immortality, to be able to watch humanity achieve its aspirations, and to travel and discover the wonders of the world. Brash as always, Tristan accepted immediately. He spoke to Katherine, who thought he was insane, but she agreed when she met Isabelle for herself.

"I laughed at first, thinking him a lunatic, driven to madness by the pressures of his family. But when the laughter faded, I was furious at the cruelty of offering a dying man immortality. I told him to leave and never come back.

"The next night *she* was at my door, and I realized Tristan had spoken the truth. She would not come in without my invitation. She even looked otherworldly. I sent the servants to their rooms and took her to my study. She told me what she had told Tristan and Katherine. And more. She promised me life. She promised that I would be healthy and strong. I would be able to see things I had only dreamed about and others not yet discovered by mortals. And all I had to do was take her hand and give her my every mortal possession. A beautiful ruse, but I saw her for what she was. I knew she was a monster, and I didn't care so long as she remade me in her image. I was willing to sell my soul for one reason: Katherine. I agreed to her terms.

"They came the next evening. I'd given all of my servants a healthy severance and sent them away. Tristan and Katherine were giddy, barely able to contain themselves when Isabelle arrived with two others, Saban and Dorian. I'll never forget the journey that followed. They *flew* us. I couldn't make out the ground below, only occasional flickers of light that Saban said were farmhouses. The wind was so cold it stung.

"They took us far from St. Augustine, over lakes and miles of trees, finally arriving at a crevasse hidden in the middle of a forest. They half-dragged, half-carried me into the pit, at least as far as they could. Soon enough there was room only to squeeze through cracks, blindly following the sounds of those in front of us. And from one step to the next we had entered a cavern that felt enormous in the darkness, like we'd been swallowed by a massive beast from another world. A lamp was lit, and the light couldn't even begin to reach the ceiling or walls. We went by dozens of passageways, and took one that almost looked hewn, mile after mile, deep underground until we reached a cold stone chamber in the heart of the world. Three rough stone slabs waited for us, dusted with earth and root and water.

"The magic was already fading by then. Reality was setting in. But I was determined. We all were." Kaleb met Renato's eyes. "I was sure I was trading my soul to Satan, but all I had to do was glance at Katherine and sense fled.

"True to his nature, Tristan asked to go first. I wanted to go running into the darkness when she bled him. It was so unnatural, so *evil*. Katherine was in tears. Cruelly, she hugged me for comfort, but when it was her turn there was no hesitation.

She lay on a slab next to Tristan and gave Isabelle her neck. A piece of me died when the light went out of her eyes. I wanted to destroy Isabelle for killing something so precious. I was nearly mad with grief. Their bodies were pale and lifeless and immaculately beautiful.

"Isabelle sensed that I wasn't alright. She waited, talking to me, their blood drying on her lips. She was kind when there was no reason for her to be. Any one of them could have crushed me like an insect. Do you know what she said to me?"

Renato shook his head.

"She told me that a better life was waiting for me. One free of sickness and frailty, where I never had to lose someone I loved if I gave my love wisely. A life where I could be more than I was. Where I could be more in the eyes of those around me. And then she warned me that the life of the risen was neither easy nor even assured, but the rewards were worth the risk. I misunderstood what that meant at the time.

"I nodded my assent, and her fangs slipped into my throat and drained my life away. At the last moment I struggled, but she was an irresistible tide and I a drowning man. I awoke in darkness so deep it was like light had never existed. I heard voices speaking excitedly. I heard their softest movements. Katherine and Tristan must have heard me wake because they called to me almost instantly. I sat up, astonished. I'd never felt so good. In death I felt for the first time truly alive.

"Sparks fractured the darkness, and then fire chased it away. Katherine and Tristan glowed in the lamplight. I could see an aura around them, a faint phosphorescence. It didn't take long to realize that the room was sealed. Isabelle, Saban, and Dorian had set a massive boulder into the single pathway. I still don't know why…"

"To make sure you did not kill yourself," Renato said offhandedly. "Some change their minds, driven mad by their beliefs, and some wake ravenous and would go running into the sun so desperate are they to sate their appetite."

An answer after centuries of thought, as unsatisfactory as it was.

Kaleb nodded, "Jailed for the time being, we talked about the possibilities of our new existences. Old grudges were forgotten. We were friends again. They begged me to stay with them no matter where they went. Hours raced by. We talked of the new hunger growing within and wondered what it would be like to feed on blood; something I'd tried to ignore earlier. Trusting in Isabelle, we waited.

"A full day must have passed, and neither she, Saban, nor Dorian returned. We started to worry. The boulder was too heavy for us to move."

Just speaking about it was making it real again. The moment when he'd realized they were different twitched like a phantom limb, something long gone yet somehow still present. Kaleb hung his head to hide his misery.

"That was when I noticed that I was different. They still had a faint aura while I was fading. I blamed it on the hunger, but as I waned and they did not I knew it was something else. The hunger pains grew stronger, more intense, until my entire body would twist with great, wrenching spasms. My skin grew jaundiced and began to bruise. My blood and veins blackened.

"By the third night we were all desperate. I could smell the fear radiating off of them. I was terrified myself. Gaps of time were missing, inexplicably gone. I was losing my mind. That night I awoke flat on my back with my head aching and bleeding. I had no idea what had happened. My last memory was of sitting with Katherine while Tristan struggled with the boulder again. They refused my questions and huddled as far away as the cramped room would allow. We all watched the wick burning low in the lantern, knowing that soon we would be trapped in the dark with a mountain between us and freedom.

"I couldn't handle it. I raged. I hated Isabelle, Saban, and Dorian. They'd taken everything—my wealth, my freedom, even the last few years I might have lived as a human. It would have been kinder to murder us.

"As angry as I was, I couldn't live in fear of what I might do if I blacked out again. Katherine being afraid of me…I couldn't bear it. I snapped, picked up the slab I had been reborn upon, and slammed it against the boulder. The slab shattered, and with it, part of the boulder. It was enough to fuel the fit. I hammered stone against stone until my hands were bloody. I don't remember stopping, only waking in darkness. Alone."

The dungeon held its breath in response, even the flame in the brazier unflinching. Kaleb stared at that small flame seeing it in another time and place, ignoring the tears cutting trails down his cheeks. After a time, he looked to Renato, and was amazed to see red trails leaking from the vampire's eyes. Renato let his tears fall unabashedly, not caring to wipe them away or hide them, absorbing the story as it was given.

The vise that had been growing in Kaleb's chest finally clamped shut, amazing in how it could hurt worse than anything else that had been done to him in the past days. Now more than ever he was ready for death.

Renato stirred, wiping his face with the palms of his hands and doing little more than smearing bloody tears. "I'm so sorry," he said in a choked whisper.

Kaleb didn't answer.

"It is unforgivable," the vampire said.

Kaleb resisted the urge to tell Renato to fuck off. He didn't want pity. He'd only kept his word. Now it was Renato's turn to keep his.

The ancient wouldn't look him in the eye. "Isabelle did not abandon you."

What the hell did that mean?

"I remember her," Renato went on. "Or at least I remember a woman as you described her, with two male companions. It was in those very same days, and outside of St. Augustine. Emigdio had already claimed this land long before the British ever set foot here. Our clan was smaller then, merely Vasco, Claudia, myself, and a few guests."

Kaleb stared, stunned. They'd killed her.

"She was trespassing. We killed one of the males. She escaped with the other."

It took a moment to sink in. She hadn't abandoned him. "What about—" Kaleb started.

"No," Renato cut in. "We knew nothing of them, or of you."

The newfound thread of hope was severed. Isabelle was one thing. She'd been little more than a compelling stranger. But Katherine and Tristan had still abandoned him. He couldn't tell what hurt worse, the betrayal, or the love he still felt for them.

They both waited a while, recovering. The lump in his chest eased, and Kaleb started again.

"After that I don't remember much. I was scared and falling apart, rotting at the seams, thinking I had been betrayed by Isabelle and the only friends I had ever known. Somehow, I found my way out of the caves, but I was hopelessly lost. The last memory I have was of splashing through bogs and swamps, and then waking with a snake wriggling in my hands as I sank my teeth into its flesh. It struck too many times to count, fangs pumping venom into my face and neck, but I couldn't bring myself to stop feeding.

"The next years are lost. I've never been able to remember them, not even a fragment. Over a century passed before I woke again." Pain turned to shame. "It was like slipping from a bad dream into a nightmare. I was kneeling over two ravaged bodies, a young couple, my mouth full of their flesh. I realized what I'd done, and I think I went a bit crazy. I was cursed, a ghoul, a murderer, and a cannibal. I wanted to kill myself, would have, except I still wanted a burial, last rites. The church, they always said it was the one unforgivable sin, if you did that it was a straight shot to hell. They wouldn't even let you be buried on hallowed ground.

"That was sometime in the 1920's. The next few decades I existed by hiding, living on the flesh of beasts and rodents and an occasional human. I tried to ignore the hunger, but in time no amount of animal meat would suffice. I would begin to fade, and that was more frightening than anything else.

"I spent years in Miami, lurking in dark alleys, trying to work up the courage to kill myself—and always breaking down and killing someone else instead. I tried to justify what I was doing by choosing my prey carefully, taking murderers and thieves. Miami was a busy port, full of sailors and newcomers. It was easier to make a human disappear than livestock.

"Years ticked by, and I grew to pass for human once again. In the 20's I was an animated corpse. In the 40's I could pass for a vagrant if I were filthy enough. In 1951 I moved back to St. Augustine. The hunger seemed to lessen as I aged, and thirty years of ill-gained wealth was enough to start my own business, a butcher shop. Employees to run the business, a cover for all of the animal flesh I would ever want for, and a place to live…a home. It was more than I'd ever expected to have again."

"And the girl?"

Allie. "An accident. I was careless. I didn't even know I could turn someone until her."

Renato sighed, letting it all sink in.

"Can't you let her go? She's done nothing."

Renato shook his head, pained. "They cannot let either of you live."

Bullshit. "Because I trespassed? I've been here for hundreds of years, and it was never a problem before you made it one."

"How could you have known?"

"What?"

"What you are. What you are capable of."

They knew? Kaleb swallowed hard. He'd been skirting around that. He did want to know, had spent countless hours in research, digging through the internet, books, fairy tales, and fables, but nothing ever seemed to fit. "What am I?" he croaked.

"You are dangerous. A harbinger of the apocalypse. You are the Horseman bearing down on humanity with pestilence."

Who would have thought the vamp would go biblical on him. "What have I done to make you hate me so much?"

"I do not hate you," Renato whispered. "I fear you, what you may do, even inadvertently."

"I haven't done anything!" Kaleb snapped.

"I had hoped you were something else. I may have been able to save you, but I cannot. The risk is too great."

As quickly as it had come the frustration was gone. "Please…" Kaleb said. "What am I?"

"An aberration. The dead returned to life without that which makes us vampyr. You have an affliction that is only myth amongst our kind, akin to a revenant in some ways, only so much more."

An abomination even amongst monsters. Afflicted. An aberration. Something like a revenant. So that was why he hadn't found an answer? Because he was a freak, a mutation? He'd read about revenants, seen some similarities, and too many differences.

Knowing wasn't as satisfying as he'd thought it would be. It was more like finding out the cause of a fatal illness, giving it a name but being impotent to do anything about it. He slumped against the wall. Aberrant. Figures. "How will you kill me?"

"Dismemberment and immolation."

Fun. So much for humane treatment.

The vampire read his mind again. "It will be done as quickly as possible."

Kaleb wrapped his arms around his knees. Dying he deserved, but at the hands of the vampires? They deserved it as much as he did. And Allie? Corrupted as she was, she was still innocent.

It's okay, his conscience soothed, for once on his side. *It's better this way. She'll never know the shame of murder, of feasting on that which she once was. She sleeps, and she will never awaken.*

Satisfied with the story, Renato gave him one last somber look, and left Kaleb to his last hours.

A Third Kind

Chapter 33

ONWYN ROLLED A throwing knife through his fingers, over and under his knuckles, faster and faster until it was a stream of sparkling liquid mercury. Aedan couldn't turn away. It was hypnotizing the way Onwyn did it, so casually, without so much as a glance.

"This is pointless. We should kill him and go home," Maedoc grumbled.

Dax pulled back his hood. "Agreed. I have other business to attend."

Aedan turned his attention from the flowing blade to Dax, unimpressed that even he was now a voice of dissent. Maedoc, of course, would complain no matter what. Onwyn was a tossup, still unpredictable after a millennium of comradery. But Dax? He should know better. "It is not our decision. We are guests here."

"It would be best to remember that," Claudia said, scowling.

"Claudia, easy," Luther admonished.

Maedoc eyed Claudia, grinning when she noticed. Claudia fingered the hilt of the axe hanging from her hip. "Every moment it lives is a chance for it to infect someone else," Maedoc said.

Was this what it had come to? Maedoc being the sensible one? The brute sipped at a bottle of blood, grimaced, and spat it back into the bottle. Aedan felt his pain. The food left something to be desired. It was old fashioned, and after a hundred lifetimes of it, old fashioned wasn't quaint—it was revolting.

"We may know more now," Luther said.

They had all heard the scream echoing up from the dungeon. Cora and Rain had slipped away, shaken, Sarah chasing their heels like a puppy.

Valentine was the first to speak. "What the hell is Adora doing to him? I mean, after Adrian and Maedoc...what did she come up with?" The novice shivered at the thought.

"Not Adora," Luther said. "Renato took over for her hours ago."

The historian? Surprising. But everything about this place was surprising.

Maedoc snorted. "Him? What did he do, throw a book at it?"

"You heard the scream," Onwyn said. "Don't remember you getting anything out of it."

Maedoc glowered. Onwyn shrugged. "Just saying."

"Speak his name and he appears," Emigdio said. "How very devilish of you, Renato." The historian sat in a chair, having simply appeared from thin air.

Maedoc grinned. "I hadn't thought you had it in you."

A trace of irritation flittered across Renato's face. "I'm sure there are a great many thoughts you haven't had."

"Anything?" Luther asked.

Renato seemed to think it over. He knew something. When he spoke, he had eyes only for Emigdio. "He has no master. It is only him and the girl."

Emigdio stirred on his throne after hours of unmoving silence. "Are you sure?"

"I am. He told me everything."

"You?" Maedoc snorted derisively. "Why would he tell you?"

Renato bristled, something dark and dangerous growing in his eyes. He was said to be one of the weaker members of the clan, yet he had an ability to fade from sight or show up without warning. That was an ability not to be underestimated, and neither were the rumors of his exploits.

Before the danger could take root, Aedan turned Renato's attention. "Is he what we feared?"

The historian gave a sharp nod of his head, still staring daggers at Maedoc.

Onwyn was on his feet. "Great. Let's kill him and go home."

Adrian leapt up at the promise of blood, eager to avenge his brother. "I should be the first to take a limb," he said, "and the one to set the fire."

"No!" Renato snapped. He turned to Emigdio. "We must give him a clean death. I gave my word."

Adrian spun on the poet, outraged. "My brother is dead! So is half of your clan. Why would you show mercy?"

"Adrian, be silent," Aedan warned, tired of the insolence.

"We're here on Lord Harlow's behalf, and we're going to take orders from these rejects?"

The words floated in the air, buoyed by the animosity they wrought. Claudia looked absolutely venomous. Onwyn met her wrath and shrugged. "Not agreeing with him, but you don't even have a TV. It's barbaric."

Emigdio shifted on his throne. He rolled his pendant through his fingers, staring into its dark and twisted depths. There was no outright malice, no anger or threats, but the tension thickened when he spoke. "He lives or dies as *I* choose, not you, nor your companions, nor Harlow."

"*Lord* Harlow," Maedoc sneered.

"Get in our way and Lord Harlow will skin you alive and set you to blister in the sun!" Adrian threatened.

Aedan winced. He should have sent them home already. Maedoc was incorrigible but a powerful ally. Adrian, though…he was still too young, and the loss of his brother had hit him hard. *He has been tried, he has been measured, and he has been found wanting,* Aedan judged.

Emigdio was a small man, slender and no more than a hundred forty pounds.

The gnarled black throne he sat on was grandiose enough to border on ridiculous. Earlier Aedan had nearly laughed, thinking he looked like a boy prince pretending to be king, but Emigdio didn't look so childish anymore. The throne was too large for him, yes, but it hadn't been made for him. He'd taken it.

The lamps and braziers flickered. The tension boiled over. There was no stopping it. Aedan could fight, or he could stand aside. He set his hand on the hilt of his sword and stepped out of Emigdio's way. Emigdio darkened and grew gaunt. His shadow writhed across the floor and reached out with wriggling tendrils that stretched and grasped.

Maedoc and Onwyn backed away, while Adrian was as oblivious as he was brash. The flames fell low. The shadows surged. Oily fingers slid over Adrian's feet and up his legs, melting through his pants and skin and biting into flesh with a hiss. Adrian screamed and tried to lurch free only to have the shadows tighten and cut deeper, spilling blood and drinking it. The more he struggled, the more entrapped he became. The tendrils moved like living things, cocooning his body, trapping his arms, and hovering over his face, no longer shadows but solid and real.

The shadows plunged into his mouth, cutting off his cries. The hiss of melting flesh was drowned out by a choked, warbling shriek. The shadows quivered and burst into mist, and Adrian plunged to the floor retching blood, his mouth a red maw, his tongue skinned. Flames shot back to life and the haze lifted.

Aedan hid his relief behind a mask of impartiality. Adrian was only bruised, a fair punishment. The worry came back in a flicker as the flames bent low, rippling in an unseen breeze. Had Emigdio just been warming up? Was it Maedoc's turn now? Or was he going to finish Adrian off?

Aedan's mind slipped to another place, one where the world flowed at a different pace and everything but the moment ceased to matter. Adrian had been punished; death was inappropriate. He couldn't allow one of his own to be executed, no matter the transgression. He gripped the hilt of his sword, readying himself, and looked to the Lord of Jacksonville only to find him him just as wary.

Footsteps pounded down the hallway. A guard burst through the door while others shouted from the foyer. "Something's outside," the wolf panted. "Dunno what. Never smelled anything like it."

"You were saying?" Maedoc snarled at Renato.

"That's what we get for pissing around," Onwyn sighed.

Luther was already up, striding towards the door. "Jeffrey, what happened?"

"I heard a weird noise outside and went to see what it was. Kevin and Paul were supposed to be out there, but the porch is covered in blood. There was so much. They've gotta be dead."

Claudia let out a peal of laughter, pleasant despite the callousness. "How long did they make it? Two hours? Lucas will not be pleased."

"What now?" Cora asked irritably, stepping past the wolf. She saw Adrian and rushed to his side. Tossing Emigdio a dirty look, she helped the young vampyr up only to have him tear away.

Luther took command. "Go, lock the house down. Barricade the doors." He closed his eyes and tilted his face to the ceiling.

Aedan had already checked. Dusk wasn't close enough.

The Were pounded down the hall, the Jacksonville clan behind him. Not to be left out, Aedan motioned for his men to follow. What waited was beyond ridiculous. The wolves were a ragged band of broken bones, cuts, and concussions. One had shifted. Another couldn't even manage to heal the bloody scratches lacing his face. Others were either missing and likely dead. At best two or three of them would be able to fight, and only the one named Martin had grit. Useless. The so-called guards were more likely to get in the way than help.

Cristo peered through a window, half hidden behind a curtain. It was cowardly, unbecoming. "Movement in the grass."

None of the vampires went to see for themselves.

Emigdio scowled. "What is it?"

"Not it, they, and I can't catch more than a glimpse. They're in the fields. They're small and there are a lot of them."

"Ugh," Maedoc grunted. "Real dogs would be better; at least they bark."

"Oh, I don't know about that," Onwyn remarked. "I think Henry here has proven that he can do anything a dog can. He's even got the yelp down. I'm surprised he didn't have to stop to piss on a fire hydrant on the way back."

Aedan shook his head and took a deep breath. They would never learn. At least their hosts didn't seem to care. Claudia and Valentine were even smiling. Henry, however, blushed, his dignity wounded.

"What do we do?" Cristo asked.

"Go ask what they want," Maedoc suggested. Even Aedan had to smirk.

"We wait," Emigdio said. "Night is coming."

§ § §

"What are they playing at?" Onwyn asked.

Aedan had been wondering the same thing. The sun was lowering behind the horizon. It made no sense to squander the advantage of sunlight.

Maedoc leaned against a wall, slightly less irritating with the prospect of impending bloodshed. "We should destroy the aberration while we can."

"No," Emigdio said. He shot Renato a severe look. "He will die last. It will not be quick, and it will not be painless."

The shifted Were dropped to all fours, snuffled at the door, and whined.

Onwyn leaned over, hands on his knees. "What is it, boy? Did Timmy fall in the well?" The Were bared its teeth and snarled.

Martin swatted at the air. "Oh man, what is that stink?"

At first Aedan didn't know what he was talking about. The mansion was dusty, and there were things other than the aberrant in the dungeon—but those were faint, covered by the pureness of the country, the grass, wildflowers, and fields of clover. Then it struck him, driving him back. A stench invaded the foyer, a tear-inducing mix of methane, ammonia, and things Aedan had never smelled before. The wolves struggled to breathe, their sensitive noses taking the brunt of the assault.

"Valentine!" Luther shouted. "Anything?"

The young vampire ran in from a hall. "Nothing. Phones are dead. Cells and landlines. We're on our own." He recoiled as the smell hit him. "What the f—"

"Maedoc," Onwyn said. "He's lactose intolerant. Must have eaten someone who drank milk." He shrugged. "It's an unspoken epidemic. Tragic really."

"Onwyn, a thousand years you've played the fool," Aedan said before Maedoc could do something stupid. "Shut up already."

Onwyn grinned sheepishly.

"Uh…" Cristo said. "Someone's out there."

The wolves clamored for spots at the windows. Aedan risked joining the guards, wary of the last rays of the dying sun. Someone stood at the edge of the grounds, half hidden by the waist-high grass, hooded and unmoving, waiting. The grass rippled around him. Only around him.

That was when the power went out.

The mansion went dark. Everyone spoke at once. Luther boomed above the others, screaming for lights. Like most unnatural creatures, vampyr could see well at night, but not nearly as well as some of the nightmares that still walked the earth. The sun slipped beneath the horizon, leaving only brilliant hues of orange, yellow, and red in its wake. The figure stood as it had, a malevolent scarecrow, unflinching, menacing, and merging with the growing darkness.

Rain shouted from upstairs and rushed down, arms overburdened, Sarah on her heels. Matches flared. Torches and lamps burned bright. A chill ran up Aedan's spine. The stench was worsening. He reached for his sword.

Maedoc stretched his arms. Bones popped, skin grew taut, and claws sprouted where his fingernails used to be. He stalked toward the door. "Let's see who was stupid enough to bring the fight to us."

Aedan waved him back. The shape was moving. "No need. He's coming."

The front door rocked. The windows on either side burst in. Aedan threw himself back, narrowly dodging gray talons that slashed at his eyes. The werewolf at the other window wasn't so lucky. It howled and thrashed in vain as it was dragged through the shattered window. Over in an instant, bits of glass covered with dripping bloody fur were all that remained of the wolf.

Aedan scrambled away. A creature watched him, a twin of the one which had taken the wolf. Its jaws chattered like a cat eyeing an unsuspecting bird, fire-light dancing off of glossy, cast-iron skin. It tensed and leapt. Fire exploded with a tinkling of breaking glass to envelope the creature mid-leap. It shrieked, an all too human wail, and fled back through the window.

Sarah fumbled to light another lamp.

The house exploded into chaos. Emigdio was furious. Claudia spat a name. Valentine looked stunned. Any sounds they made were lost when the door fractured and split wide open. Dozens of small creatures with mossy green hides clamored to get inside the mansion, their bright red eyes shining with glee. Misty gray shadows flooded through the windows. Goblins and wraiths.

Landon fell beneath a tide of green flesh. The goblins attacked like a swarm of piranhas, stabbing and slashing, ripping off bits and pieces, feasting. The wraiths reached out, trailing cold fingers over flesh, draining vitality with nothing more than the barest of touches and the softest of whispers. Dozens poured in only to be driven away by fire. They circled above, hiding in dark recesses, waiting for the moment when the flames would falter.

Cristo swiped at the wraiths with his bare hands like a fool and paid the price. They dragged him screaming up into the darkness. He fell back a moment later, foaming at the mouth, eyes wide with terror, clawing at his swollen, bulging throat.

Green and red blood competed to see which could paint the house quicker. The goblins went mad, as did Maedoc. The brute waded through the little beasts, sending flesh and blood spraying with every vicious strike. Dax used his odd brand of magic to replicate while Luther, Claudia, and Onwyn cut down everything in their path.

An explosion rocked the room, blasting goblins, vampyr, and furniture alike. Dozens of the rancid little beasts disintegrated into green mist and bits of bone, painting everything in a slick coat of faintly luminescent grass-green blood. Emigdio was a specter of death, infuriated and focusing his strength into another wavering, translucent ball of rippling energy.

A foul wind blew. The goblins flinched and glanced back at the door. The stench rolled in worse than ever, thick and overwhelming. The room fell to near silence. The goblins chittered and recoiled. Something outside groaned.

Aedan couldn't comprehend what he was looking at. *It* oozed across the porch and filled the doorway. Boards broke beneath its fleshy wet bulk. Dread fought for a place beside the revulsion churning in his stomach. Light, the cure for so many fears, only made *it* worse. Mottled brown skin jiggled gelatinously as it squeezed through the broken entrance.

Emigdio set off another blast. The creature rippled and bent, but the skin refused to break. It opened a massive toothless maw in a groan and then sniffed the air. Its eyeless head wandered from side to side until it caught a scent, and eager to eat, it slid toward Aedan.

Rain shrieked. Aedan glanced her way, irritated. *Why was she screaming?* He was the one about to be supper for a giant grotesquery. But it wasn't the hideous blob she was afraid of. Rain stumbled backwards, her terrified gaze locked on a pale, amorphous creature floating in through one of the broken windows.

"What is it?" Rain squeaked.

Aedan had no idea.

Cora did. The old healer stared grimly. "A Bhuta, though how it got here is another matter. I've never heard of one on this continent before."

One of the wolves, Henry, threw his torch at it. The flames passed through as if it were only a mirage. "What the fuck!" Henry shouted. "How do we kill it?" The Bhuta floated lazily into the mansion.

"An exorcism," Cora said, backing away.

The vampyr were forced back against the tide. One of the wolves roared and started to shift. Skin rippling, fur sprouted and grew thick, healing dozens of bites and cuts. It was a neat trick. Aedan could see how it would be handy, but just the thought of being a Were—it was too horrible to dwell on.

"There are too many!" Jeff screamed, throttling a ghoul in either hand.

A cold breeze blew against the tide. The stench of the blob was pushed back. The flame on Aedan's torch bent low, and he spun, already guessing.

The master of Jacksonville grew even more skeletal. Dark shadows writhed around him, reaching out with ropy tentacles. They snapped out with the crack of whips, wrapping around the Bhuta. The ghost let out a marrow-chilling ethereal wail, a sound that had no place in the world of the living. Noxious yellow smoke rose where the tentacles melted through its semi-tangible body. The tentacles pulled tight, severing the ghost to pieces that fell away, turning to dust and powder before touching the floor.

The house shook. The crack of lumber snapping like twigs cut through the tumult. The broken doorway was hammered again. A white behemoth burst through, splintering drywall and wood effortlessly. It rampaged through the room, trampling anyone and anything in its path. Valentine tried to sidestep and took a clumsy slash at it with a sword that was clearly out of place in his hands. The lumbering beast swatted him like a gnat and raced on, past everyone, into the hallway towards the den. Another behemoth charged in, snarling, seeking prey. Maedoc stepped back, a brief flash of fear and uncertainty in his eyes. That alone was almost worth dying for.

Aedan turned back to his own fight. The blob was almost on him. It had resisted

Emigdio's bursts, sliding over glass and jagged pieces of wood with no ill effect. It was time to see how it dealt with fire.

Aedan summoned his gift; a thing all creatures feared. It warmed his heart and flooded through his fingertips, a haunting memory of life. White soul fire engulfed his hands. The light it cast sent Wraiths shrieking away. The blob came on.

Aedan set his hand out. Mottled brown skin wrinkled and blackened on the barest contact, sizzling, reeking of burnt rubber. Onwyn attacked in tandem, his swords flashing almost too quick to follow with the naked eye. The blades lashed out over and over, leaving only shallow cuts in their wake.

The blob cringed at the fire but didn't even seem to feel the swords.

Aedan reached out again, struggling to control the bile fighting its way up his throat. Soul fire sent streams of rancid fluid cascading down the blob's jiggling body like melting wax. The creature cringed and tried to shrink away. Aedan pressed the attack, realizing a moment too late that he should have let it go. It was too slow, unable to retreat, and it seemed to realize that as well. It surged forward, crushing Aedan into a cluster of goblins at war with Adrian, riding them all to the ground.

Chapter 34

THE GROWING CHILL behind Kaleb's eyes marked the arrival of countless creatures above; each was an icy snowflake coalescing into a howling blizzard. The braziers had fallen low while he lay in a stupor-like state of disconnection where dreams and reality intertwined and time flowed differently.

Some found their way into the dungeon, things with no life to their presence, no aura at all, only a gaping emptiness that sapped his strength and will. Shadows more felt than seen raced by the barred window of the cell door with no more than rustling and indecipherable whispers. Kaleb shivered in the midst of a hunger that dwarfed his own, and realized it was more than a chill behind his eyes; it was a physical change in the room. Ice crept in around the seams of the door and frosted the window's bars. A few shadowy figures lingered, evaluating Kaleb with eyes that waxed and waned like lightning bugs.

Slumped against the wall, he played dead. Or at least more dead than usual.

One by one he felt the shadows move on. "What the fuck was that about?" he muttered. He sagged, playing dead once again as a chattering mob whisked toward him, rattling every door in their path and invading the rooms. Kaleb peeked through slitted eyelids, waiting for them to pass.

The door rattled. A horde thrummed against it in an ungodly racket, pounding, kicking, clawing, and shouting. They gave up after a minute or two, and clambered over each other to fight for a place to press their small green faces against the bars. Kaleb nearly gave himself away. Beady red eyes focused on him, and the creatures shrieked in excitement. The assault on the door renewed. Had Renato lied and let these creatures in to do the dirty work? Then why not give them the keys?

A heavy tread cut through the din, each step a thud marked by the click of nails on the stone floor, and Kaleb's anxiety blossomed into full-blown panic. He'd heard a similar tapping of claws on linoleum or hardwood, Jordan, only this sounded a thousand times larger. The red-eyed beasts abandoned their assault and melted away when the steps drew near. Something chuffed, a throaty noise that put a grizzly to shame, and a monstrosity reared up and pressed an orbish white eye to the bars. Kaleb kept still, resting with his back against the wall, still shackled. The face was ghastly, the eye glistening like white marble, without iris or pupil. The monstrosity pulled away, and two pale gargantuan paws eerily similar to human hands gripped the bars and wrenched. The metal shrieked and squealed, but it was the door that broke first, cracking with a sound like a gunshot and tearing apart.

Kaleb's bowels turned to jelly, and he wasn't sure if they'd let loose. A sliver of hope said the beast was far too large to squeeze through the doorway. That desperate belief was snuffed out almost instantly as the behemoth used immensely broad and powerful shoulders to batter the thick stone walls to bits. It burst into the room in a spray of stone shards. The beast chuffed and sniffed Kaleb up and down. A gentle prod with his snout, another chuff, and it reared up with a roar and brought its massive paws smashing down, ripping furrows in the wall and fracturing the floor.

Kaleb fought to keep from flinching as the stony muzzle snapped an inch away from his face. Intelligence shone in its eyes. Maybe it knew he was faking, could smell it or something, or maybe it wanted to make sure he was dead. Either way, it grabbed Kaleb in its giant paw and pulled the chains to their limits. Silver shackles ripped into Kaleb's wrists and ankles, sending jolts of electricity through his bones, and the creature tightened its grip and hurled him with everything it had.

§ § §

Even the darkness was spinning when Kaleb opened his eyes. He lay stunned and broken, his body reverted and reduced to pure agony. He choked back screams and called out to his power, letting it flow through him, chasing away life and the pain that came with it. Only then did he open his eyes and allow himself to dwell on what had just happened. He could only guess, but he didn't think Renato or the other bloodsuckers were involved.

Shouts and grunts echoed from deep within the dungeon, punctuated by the clatter of breaking and shattering. *They're ransacking the place! What happened to the enemy of my enemy is my friend?* he thought, bitter.

He gingerly sat up and looked himself over. As battered as he was, only his leg was broken badly. It would slow him down, but it wouldn't stop him. The shackles would have to go though. Two were already gone, broken when he was torn from the wall. He picked through the tools scattered about the floor until he found a blade thin enough to fit into the keyholes. Decades of thievery had its uses. The locks popped. The shackles fell free with strings of melted skin stretching after them.

Kaleb limped to the door and peered into the hall. Which way was he supposed to go? The direction the things had come from? More would be waiting upstairs, hundreds of them judging from the ice storm raging above. And the white thing? Going another round with that behemoth wasn't an appealing thought. And there was Allie to think of. He could feel her out there, somewhere, lost in the muddle. Kaleb looked to either side, torn, wanting to run but not wanting to abandon Allie.

The choice was made for him. Something was coming.

Kaleb hobbled by room after ransacked room, chills not so different from those he'd been ill with as a child coming and going, letting him know when other things were near. Twists and turns took him deeper into the dungeon, leaving him disoriented. It didn't take long to get lost in the maze of branching hallways and tunnels.

He paused to get his bearings. Everything looked similar, except the braziers—there were fewer and fewer of them. Voices hissed nearby. Kaleb pressed against the wall, trying to hide in a dark patch between braziers. A trio of the red-eyed beasts jogged down the hall and paused, bickering. Shadows crawled on the walls behind them, barely seen, but clear enough to make out horns and skeletal torsos that tapered into long, roped tails. One after another they disappeared into the shadows.

Kaleb huddled as he was, waiting until they were long gone before moving. Goblins? The red-eyed things fit the description. Those he could handle. Probably. But the floating things? They kindled a different kind of fear in him, an echo of angst and depression, of being all alone in the world.

He closed his eyes and called on the cold fire, trying to fan its flames, to find Allie. He could almost see it, a pale blue flame like that of a candle, flickering and swaying, struggling to exist. As hard as he tried, it wouldn't grow. The auras, energies, whatever they were, remained indistinguishable. Kaleb fell to his knees, exhausted, hardly able to stay upright. He was too weak, too scared, and as much as he hated it, and himself, there was nothing he could do for her.

The cold fire flickered again, and Kaleb forced himself to stand, wincing at the ache in his lower leg as he hobbled down a steeply sloped tunnel that reeked of unknown creatures. Soon enough the sounds of the swarm faded, and *things* stirred in his wake. The doors were thicker here, barred and overladen with locks. Inhuman voices called out in strange languages, and bodies smacked against the doors, railing against captivity.

Kaleb kept glancing over his shoulder, sure that sooner or later something would come for him. A voice called out behind a steel slab and he paused. What was it saying? Was it begging? He could feel the pain in its voice, the desperation, but without knowing what it was and what it might do...

A lack of braziers forced Kaleb to stumble along, one hand resting on the wall to keep him standing. The stone had grown colder and wetter with a film of slimy moss. Everything was a shade of black. The walls were pitch, the doors soot, and the empty passages yawning chasms.

A door trembled when he touched it. The wood bent out, forced by some terrible power on the other side. Kaleb rushed by, not wanting to hear any more wordless pleas. He leaned heavily on the wall, using it to push himself along, wall, long stride, wall, long stride, wall…nothing. For a second or two it felt like being swallowed by a black hole, and then the physical world intruded. A sharp edge. Blunt stone. Snapping bones, scrapes, and gouges.

He landed hard and lay still, stunned yet unsurprised at the turn of events and unsure if he had the will to get back up and keep going. If not for the feel of soil and gravel beneath him and the dank air he couldn't have been sure he was still earthbound. The dark was absolute and suffocating with the fear of the unknown.

Chapter 35

EMIGDIO STRAINED TO control his fury. Belial strode into the mansion as though it were his own. The alabaster gargoyle padded after the mage like a pet. An Asan Bosam followed, crouching to feast on the buffet of chunky green meat littering the floor.

Belial would suffer for this.

Coils of liquid shadow twitched, eager to be unleashed. They were sentient in a manner, living only to destroy and drink pain. Emigdio ached to let go and allow them to wreak havoc, but without control, without his will to guide them, the results would be devastating. They would kill everything.

The mage stood at the ruins of the front door, a smug smile spread across his face. Belial's army had bayed them all. Aedan and his had put up an impressive display, but they were overwhelmed and cornered. The one called Dax became a dozen that had in turn killed scores, and still it had hardly stemmed the tide. How was it possible? First the undead in the basement, and now this, a legion of monsters defiling his home?

His clan was wounded—some were dead—and now they suffered beneath his own roof. Luther had been badly frostbitten by another Bhuta. Valentine could barely stand, and only two of the wolves still lived.

It was humiliating.

Still, Emigdio was proud of his clan. Against this army, everyone had done well, even young Adora, Rain, and Valentine. They were strong, even if he wasn't. Rain fumbled to light more torches to replace the faltering ones. Wraiths swirled above, skirting the light, their whispers frenzied.

Belial was waiting for the acknowledgment, the surrender. Emigdio looked over his clan. Cora and Sarah were doing what they could to tend wounds. Renato, Claudia, and Adora stood resolute at his back.

Emigdio choked down his pride and swallowed his rage. "They are in the dungeon. Take them and go. Run while you can." He nodded toward Aedan. "These vampyr have come from far away to destroy them. Even should you kill us, more will come."

That piqued Belial's curiosity. "They? Do you mean the creature that killed your men? There is more than one?"

Emigdio couldn't look away from the smile. The arrogance. One way or another, the mage would die.

"Such creatures are beneath me. I'm power-hungry, not mad."

Emigdio could almost feel Renato's relief. His old friend had been right; this was not a betrayal by the aberration. What was this about then? Supplies? The collection? Or was he striking first, knowing that reprisal was coming for his lies? "Why are you here?"

Belial smirked. "Your collection is infamous. Had you simply let me see it for myself rather than waste time with that ridiculous offering all of this could have been avoided."

He was lying. He couldn't be that foolish. Emigdio spread his hands, motioning to his clan and guests. "No one has died yet. Tell me what you want, and perhaps we can come to an arrangement."

The mage laughed. His bright blue eyes twinkled with mirth, and his golden curls bounced. "Still trying to barter? Why should I? You're beaten. I can take anything I want."

"No," Emigdio said softly. "Taken by surprise, perhaps, but not beaten." He flexed his will. The tendrils around him snapped out, lashing the walls and floor, leaving smoldering cuts wherever they touched.

Belial chuckled again. "An interesting ability. I've never heard of a vampyr with such a power. Did you come by it naturally?"

"One last time. What are you searching for?"

The humor slipped away, and Emigdio caught a glimpse of the unpleasantness Valentine had spoken of. "Such an inhospitable host," the mage said. "But as you wish. I'm here for the book."

Book? Renato's collection? "What book?"

"The book!" Belial snarled. "The book of Khaldun. Do you take me for a fool? I want it! Now!"

"And if I give it to you, will you leave in peace?"

"Peace?" The mage contemplated it. Goblins ran by in a steady stream, coming and going, running out into the night with arms full of plundered treasure. They were cleaning the basement out, but they still hadn't found Renato's library. "My pets. They're loyal, they do as they are bid, but they are not terribly clever," Belial said. "I have no wish to be here any longer than necessary. Fetch me the books, all of them mind you, and I will leave."

Too many lifetimes to count had given Emigdio many gifts—not the least of them was an understanding, an ability to see through people, to gauge their worth. Belial had none. The mage would take what he wanted, and then he would kill them all. As if sensing his anger, the writhing darkness tested his will again. Emigdio fought it back, whispering a single word. "Renato." His old friend, the poet, the historian, the vampyr so many thought weak, was more than he appeared. Renato had survived through cunning and intelligence; he was their best hope.

Renato took off at once, a pack of goblins clamoring behind.

"How did you obtain it?" Belial asked with a smug grin. "Such a book in the hands of vampires is perplexing."

Wanting nothing more than to rip out the mage's throat, Emigdio smirked. "Off of Khaldun, of course."

Belial's grin faltered. "How?" he scoffed. "He was a powerful mage. He should have been beyond mortal death."

"Nothing is beyond mortal death," Luther said. "Even mages and witch doctors."

"Such a shame. His knowledge would have gone far beyond mere books."

Valentine leaned heavily against the banister. "If the book is so valuable, why didn't you just choose it?" he snapped.

Belial smiled sweetly. "The Asan Bosam, of course. I'd thought them extinct."

"Almost," Emigdio said. "They are few, remnants of a lost race, kept as curiosities and guard dogs."

"Guard dogs undoubtedly, but mere curiosities? I think not. With proper training they are formidable pets. Did you know they can withstand the sun for short durations? The metallic nature of their skin gives them an incredible advantage. They are stronger, faster, and more resilient than any other breed of vampire I've ever seen. If they weren't so stupid, I have no doubt they would be masters."

Every passing minute drained Emigdio's strength. If he sent the tendrils away it would show weakness and doom them all. If he didn't, they would break free and act on their own, killing anything they could reach. The power flexed again, searching for a way out. It succeeded for a moment before he could rein it in again. A shock wave rolled through the room, sending shivers through every last man, beast, monstrosity, and vampyr.

"Remarkable," Belial said. "I can't remember the last time I felt fear. I shouldn't be afraid, and yet I'm apprehensive. It has been ages since a vampire's tricks could sway me."

Emigdio said nothing. The mage was too close to guessing. Even so, he was surprised when Belial stared him straight in the eye. Part of him wanted to try to roll him. Another part reminded him of the risk. He had no strength to spare. He resisted the urge to wipe his face as beads of sweat broke out on his brow.

§ § §

A knot of sick dread lodged where Kaleb's heart should have been. The subterranean depths were unnerving, too reminiscent of a horrible time in another place deep beneath the earth. He'd lain on the ground, listening for a little while. There had been a few faint noises, but they were far away, and it was impossible to tell which direction they were coming from.

He was born in darkness, made for it, but here he feared it. The chill behind his eyes had changed, grown almost painful. There were things around him that he couldn't explain, things that made his dead skin crawl. It was what he'd imagined purgatory to be like, an all-encompassing abyss where there was nothing to do but reflect and worry about devils creeping in the darkness. The only exception was the slight breeze occasionally tousling his hair and the tatters of his clothes.

Air was getting in.

The simple act of getting up may as well have been the thirteenth labor of Hercules. Hopelessly lost, he waited for the next breeze. It came like a fetid chilled breath, stinking of damp and earth and beasts unknown, but also laced with a hint of water and fresh air. It caressed his face, lasting only a few shorts seconds, and with its passing he had an idea of where to go. Hands held out and grasping, he hobbled deeper into the caverns, trailing walls when he found them, shuffling blind when he could not.

Without light or a sense of how far he had traveled, time dragged on. The ground became rougher, more jagged, and the scent of dirt, moss, and water became suffocating. He paused, the hairs on his neck and arms rising. It was muffled, nearly imperceptible, but something was sobbing. It gave off no chill or aura, and neither did it react to his presence as many of the other things had. Quite a few of the creatures in the dungeon scared Kaleb, but this was the first to truly disturb him. He reached out, feeling for a door, a lock, anything to mark another cage. He found nothing. So, either there was another tunnel nearby, or…it had been sealed.

Sickened by the sheer depravity of the vampires, Kaleb pushed on, trying to forget the pitiful crying.

Too soon he crossed another door, and a skittering noise made him grateful for the barrier between him and whatever was on the other side. Then again, he *was* hungry. Seconds later he blinked and realized he was fumbling with the door, trying to pull it open. He backed away, horrified. His mind was fading.

Kaleb rushed away, ignoring the clack of the broken bone in his leg. Between that sound and his worries, he almost didn't hear *them* until it was too late; goblins, their torches painfully bright points of light after so long in the darkness. Not knowing when he would be able to turn or hide, he broke into a crippled jog that was less than his best idea. If they hadn't heard his footsteps, surely they noticed the crack of his face striking stone and his body thudding to the ground.

The chill breath came again, tickling across his face, all the colder against the wetness seeping from splits and scrapes. Rattled and barely understanding what he was doing, Kaleb found himself crawling on all fours. He found what he'd run into, a band of stone maybe a foot wide, and empty space to either side. A fork in the road.

If he'd even been a few inches to either side he wouldn't have clobbered himself. His fucking luck. He paused, waiting for the breeze to tell him which way to turn and listening to the chattering gibberish drawing dangerously close.

§ § §

Renato ground his teeth. Goblins were noisy, wretched little beasts. He rushed along, trying to decide what to do. He could delay no longer, yet there was no doubt the sorcerer would renege on the deal once he had what he wanted. Renato knew the type well. Many years ago he'd been one of them.

They were outnumbered, and many of Belial's pets were powerful. The Asan Bosam. The Gargoyles. The disgusting ooze. Wraiths could be dealt with by fire, the ghouls by sheer force. But all at the same time? The only option was to cut off the head—Belial.

He paused, dwelling on an idea and calculating the risk. The goblins gibbered behind him, and one prodded him with a crude spear. Renato spun, fangs extended, and snarled at the little beast. It shat itself and knocked over half its allies in its retreat.

"Soon enough," he whispered.

Renato turned back to the tunnel, remembering. The right path was shorter, but after his last trip…he went left. He raced ahead, leaving the goblins to catch up. One minute without them was all he needed.

His room was as he'd left it, dusty and redolent with the chokingly pleasant scent of aged books. Setting down the lamp, he tore through his books, selecting those most precious and stashing them away in hidden recesses. His pride burned. Even now he couldn't relinquish his hard-won knowledge.

The goblins arrived, shouting, brandishing their weapons, the red of their eyes glowing with the light of the torches. Renato waved at the room. "Take them all."

It was a testament of willpower to allow the pathetic worms to pilfer his collection. Books crumbled and tore beneath their careless touch. They filtered in and left with arms burdened. He hadn't realized how many had come with him. Scores. In hardly fifteen minutes the room was bare. All that remained was air riddled with dust motes and nearly disintegrated scraps of parchment and scrolls. Renato stared at the shreds, wondering which books they belonged to and whom he had killed to get them. Throat tight, eyes watering, he knew what he had to do.

Indignation lodged like a bone in his throat, and Renato left in search of another room with a very different collection. He raced through the maze that was the second level, ignoring the screeching of the goblins as they fell behind. It didn't take long to find what he sought: a brazier an inch too low on the wall, a stone jutting from the ground, and there, the door he was looking for. Inside was a room no bigger than one of the cells above, sparsely furnished with a ratty cot and a moldering table, unremarkable in every sense of the word.

Renato dashed in, memory guiding his hands to a hidden trigger, and a grinding rumble filled the room. A portion of the floor fell, and then another, each forming a step on a winding stairwell. He'd barely made it to the bottom before the goblins burst into the room and peered down at him, both wary and riled. One threw a torch at him, and the group flooded after.

Renato strode past treasures both ancient and rare, ignoring stacks of modern currency and a hoard of gold, silver, and gems lying about in abundance enough to makes kings look like paupers. All worthless.

What Renato sought rested on a dais. Once an intriguing curiosity, now its beauty rivaled his books. Bigger than a knife, smaller than a sword, the hilt leather-wrapped and unadorned, it was a marvel. The Rose Blade, created by an alchemist that was either insane or a genius beyond his time. Renato liked to think it was both. True to its name, the metal had a faint rose hue. It shone like it had been polished just moments ago, though no hands had touched it for hundreds of years. The blade would never dull or tarnish, would never weaken or break. The metal was rare, Rhodium, altered by alchemy and perhaps by magic, though it had a different name long ago. The secret of its making was lost with the death of the alchemist. Samuel drooled whenever his eyes fell upon the weapon, lamenting letting such a prize go to waste in the treasury.

Renato tucked the sword into his belt and waited.

Goblins arrived like a burst of bile, spewing forth from the mouth of the stairs. They stopped, falling over each other, transfixed by the glittering wealth. The simple creatures were so enamored they forgot who and what they had been chasing.

They attacked the treasures, stuffing bags, filling their arms. Renato counted the seconds down. He closed his eyes, listening, waiting, and then he heard it; a faint click followed by the rasp of stone in the stairwell. He bolted, scattering the goblins from his path, and flew up the stairs. Some of the wretched beasts lurched after him, but too few and too late. The secret entrance slid shut as Renato watched in grim satisfaction. It would stay closed until he came back, long after the worms cannibalized each other and the last had starved.

§ § §

Hunger pangs knocked Kaleb to his knees. He huddled on all fours, shaking like a sick dog, waiting for them to pass. Spasms eased into tremors, tremors into shivers, and Kaleb pushed to his feet. One trudging step followed another. The absence of light hadn't eased, but the breeze was fresher, the air less fetid. Sooner or later he would find the way out.

The floor swayed beneath his feet, rolling and sinking like angry waves. The darkness shifted around him, a living creature intent on suffocating and confusing him. And mixed in the darkness was something new—a white noise, static, irritating, and distracting.

Kaleb stumbled on, hardly registering the broken bone in his shin succumbing to the constant pressure and bursting through the skin. White static roared in his ears and clouded his mind. It chased away the darkness, revealing an emptiness that went on forever. White oblivion was no better than a dark abyss.

Kaleb shook off the emptiness only to realize he'd taken a face plant in the dirt. How many times had he fallen? How many more could he get up? As if taunting him, a draft rolled over him, no longer fetid but fresh, pleasant, and carrying a slim chance of survival.

He groaned, too tired to move and trying to ignore the return of the white noise. It felt like a dream when he came back again, a sense of moving without motion, and he realized his legs were moving, shambling along with a mind of their own. He tried to stop and couldn't. And then he heard the voice. It was a whisper in the static, speaking without speaking, urging him, commanding him. *Hurry*. The static took shape, elated, ecstatic, and dominating.

"What door?" Kaleb shouted, terrified of what was happening to him. The fugue had come before, when he went too long without feeding, but nothing like this. He reached out and felt for something he could almost picture in his mind. The image became real beneath his fingers; metal, pocked with rust, and he jerked his hand back with a yelp. The damned thing had given him a shock.

The static ordered and pleaded, overwhelming his mind and forcing him to reach out again. Rusty metal tingled with an electric charge, and strange squiggles and symbols etched into the metal began to glow. A door was revealed, massive, wider than Kaleb was tall, and he fumbled with the locks. Some were so ancient they crumbled beneath his fingers. Others were newer but broke with enough force. Heavy latch bars resisted his efforts, fused to the door by time and dampness, yet even they gave in one after another.

In minutes only one lock remained. All he had to do was spin the hand wheel. A second voice shouted against the one in the static, oddly familiar, and Kaleb realized it was his own, that minuscule part of his mind that told him when to fight and when to flee. It was screaming to run.

If only he could listen to it. In a battle to control his own body, Kaleb lost. His hands reached out, touched the door, and the static faded leaving the voice perfectly clear. "*Set me free and I will reward you beyond your greatest dreams. Open this door and save us both.*"

In a way he wanted to. It was a victim just like he was. Being locked up for so long was as much a torture as being put to fire. Only this thing wasn't asking, it was telling. Worse, it was forcing him. Kaleb held onto the thought, stoking his anger and taking strength enough from it to pull away from the door.

The creature wailed, a cold and lonely sound that sent chills up his spine. He reached out, trying to feel who and what it was. His reach was limited, the images he received unclear, but he felt things nearby stir at the touch of his power—all prisoners, all hungry and weak, all scared and pitiful. On the other side of this door stirred a creature filled with malice and rage so powerful it was paralyzing. It knew no love or kindness. It knew only hatred, for humans, for monsters, for vampires, and above all it hated Emigdio.

Hunger pains came unexpectedly. Kaleb collapsed into a ball of writhing agony, muscles threatening to tear from tendons, his entire body burning as it cannibalized itself for sustenance. Rational thought fled, dulling the pain, allowing base need to take over. Kaleb clung to the vestiges of consciousness, unwilling to become a mindless beast.

After a few minutes the hunger faded, and Kaleb laid as he had fallen, recovering his strength and thinking. What did he have to lose? In hours he would be less than nothing, one of the walking dead, wandering in search of living flesh. At best he would wake over the corpse of another innocent victim. Better he should die first.

Too tired to even crawl, Kaleb dragged himself back to the door and reached for the wheel. It fought his efforts, refusing to turn, creaking and groaning and raining flakes of rust but not moving. Kaleb got to his knees and used both hands, forcing the wheel to turn. It gave with a shrieking squeal, spun until the bolts clacked, and on the other side of the door the entity roared in triumph.

§ § §

Renato, old friend, where are you? Emigdio clenched his fists to hide the tremors. Such power wasn't meant to be used in such a way, but the peace was too tenuous, held only by a show of force.

The mage flipped through a pile of stolen books, all the while crooning to his gargoyle. Beasts arrived in a constant stream, most filtering out the mansion with their arms full of plunder, a few dropping off stacks of books and oddities before dashing away to seek more.

Emigdio shifted his feet and set a stance to keep from bowing before the burden. He shot a warning glance at the others, unsure how much longer he could wait, and was surprised to see them shifting uncomfortably as well. They all felt it. Luther, Claudia, and Cora gave barely perceptible nods. Luther glanced down the back hall and Emigdio understood. Foolish. He should have known.

A horde of goblins hissed and muttered inconsolably. Wraiths circled overhead, edging closer to the light. A flicker of the eyes was all Aedan needed. The New York enforcer looked as haggard as Emigdio felt. The white flame from his hands was the only thing keeping the revolting glob at bay.

"Do you like it?"

The question caught Emigdio off guard.

"My very own creation. It took decades to perfect," Belial preened.

The arrogance, to boast of his toys at such a time. The mage was too confident. Emigdio watched, waiting for the moment when the pressure grew heavy enough. And there. Belial felt it. His gloating, smug smile fell away, and he glanced around the room realizing something was happening.

Before Belial could react, Emigdio unleashed his powers, freeing the mass of writhing tentacles to wreak havoc and sending a wave of fear cascading over the invaders. Wraith, goblin, gargoyle, or the mage himself, they all cowered.

At the same time the weight grew crushing.

Unable to withstand it, Emigdio was brought to his knees. Goblins lay gasping for air, and the wraiths descended, wailing as they entered the light and disintegrated. Of the vampyr only a few stood, and they too were being forced to the ground. Only Belial's staff kept him from being pinned to the floor. The mage overcame the fear and glared at Emigdio, astonishment becoming a childlike tantrum. The boyish face and golden hair vanished, leaving a decrepit, sickly old man in his stead. The gargoyle at his side whimpered and shrank from his touch.

And still the weight grew heavier.

Emigdio pulled back the power before he lost control of it, fighting for every inch, knowing too well the death and destruction it would cause without a master to guide it. A roiling mass of wraiths fought to escape the light, and a Bhuta cried a haunting lament as it fell to the floor in tatters, shredded by the tendrils. The goblins squealed beneath the pressure, their bones breaking and lungs bursting, and the Asan Bosam tried to crawl to the destroyed front doorway. Even vampyr were pinned to the floor one after another.

Emigdio dropped to all fours, biding his time. The mage clung to the gargoyle, muttering foul words beneath his breath, working his dark magic. The crush grew harder, pressing Emigdio onto his belly. His face and chest sank into a layer of green blood laced with red. The foul liquid wet his lips and he spat. Soon enough he could clean his palate with mage blood.

A deep guttural snarl sent shivers up Emigdio's spine, and the scream that followed drew his gaze. Maedoc. The brute shook with effort, and stood in a display of raw power. A torch in either hand, he annihilated the wraiths, grinning savagely, wallowing in their destruction.

In the back hall, blackened skin cracked and flaked with every excruciating step Vasco took. He limped along untouched by the oppressive weight.

The pressure was unbearable, constantly growing until a tsunami crashed over Emigdio. It hammered him into the floor, grinding him as a boot grinds a bug, and then receded, leaving him limp and exhausted.

But tired as he was, there was much to be done.

The black pendant burned and writhed at Emigdio's touch. Ropy black tendrils snapped out, wrapping around the last remaining Bhuta and melting through its cloudy yellow flesh. The Bhuta fell to pieces leaving only a rancid odor and patches of otherworldly skin laying in clumps. Emigdio turned to Belial. The tendrils cracked like whips, tearing strips off the gargoyle and driving it back, and then closed in on the mage, eager to flay flesh from bone.

§ § §

"Now!" Aedan shouted.

Half of the Daxes leapt to finish off wounded goblins. The other half shivered and began to split. Onwyn held his swords out, and Aedan ran his hands across them, setting them ablaze with white fire. The burning swords slashed the brown blob, splitting flesh and splattering greasy fluid, forcing the obscenity away.

Onwyn opened his mouth to make some undoubtedly smart-ass comment, and gagged instead as a spurt of slime splattered his mouth and face. Aedan grinned at Onwyn's timely bad luck, and then sent flame lash after flame lash, turning the slug's rubbery brown skin into blackened crisps oozing rancid milk.

An army of goblins flooded into the house, the pair of Asan Bosam wading through the little beasts to rejoin the fray. An enraged roar shook the very foundation of the house. Maedoc faced the incoming swarm, shifting, losing himself. He threw his arms wide. His shirt split. Leathery flesh formed webs between his arms and waist. Bones crunched and shifted beneath his skin. A monster took his place; a monster with bleeding crimson eyes and rows of teeth meant for shredding and tearing. It threw itself against the tide.

The blob heaved and groaned, trying to shy away from the fire, and Aedan plunged his hand into a gash made by Onwyn's blades. Thick, oily liquid spilled from the wounds, fat drops burning as they fell and setting the oozing monstrosity aflame. The sorcerer's wail cut through the chaos of the battle, and Aedan watched a disaster unfold before him; Emigdio's lashes whipped the enormous gargoyle without mercy, stripping flesh in a dozen places, and still the juggernaut refused to turn. Aedan rushed to intervene.

Luther swept his executioner with strong, graceful strokes, cutting heads clean off, hacking limbs, and running his enemies through. Gobbets of goblins stained the world green. Claudia fought at his side, bloodied, battered, unforgiving and unrelenting, her axe rising and falling and raining blood as they tried and failed to cut a path to Emigdio before he disappeared beneath a mountain of alabaster.

The others didn't even see it happen. Valentine, Cora, Rain, and Sarah fought beside two massive werewolves, hemmed in by the Asan Bosam. Aedan sent a flare of white fire at the gargoyle, scorching the beast's face and drawing its attention. It turned with a snarl, its cheek marred by soot.

It struck with the strength of a titan. Aedan flew halfway across the room and slammed into the wall. His ribs were broken, one jutting from his shirt. Dazed, he couldn't do anything more than watch the behemoth thunder toward him. Despite his imminent death, all he could think of was Belial standing in the midst of the slaughter, speaking in a language that made Maedoc's native tongue sound romantic.

§ § §

They would die! All of them!

They would pay for the legion of dead or wounded mire goblins and for his Bhutas, precious creatures that they were. It took a rare soul to incarnate as a Bhuta. Somehow Emigdio's power had been able to grasp them and destroy their very essence. And his Hirudinea…

Words poured from Belial, incantations seared into memory. The sight of his Hirudinea, a majestic triumph over nature, bubbling and melting before one of the vampire's powers—white flames of all things—set off an ache in his chest. It was a pain he'd never felt before, not even when he slew his family so many years ago. His vision blurred and he blinked. When tears spilled, he was almost startled into silence. His army, his pets, he'd grown fond of them.

The last words of the incantation spilled from his mouth, leaving an oily film and the taste of his own tainted blood. A powerful spell it was, and it cost him dearly, but it was a small price to pay. Pride surged as Orthrus abandoned mauling Emigdio and knocked the fire-wielder across the room. The eternal lovers with their devastating blades fell beneath a swarm of goblins. Adora, a ravishing creature, was trying to crawl up the stairs and contain her innards at the same time. His Asan Bosam had proven their worth. They were both still alive and very much capable.

A pale face caught his attention. Renato, as hungry for knowledge as himself. The vampyr gazed on the devastation in horror. Belial felt more than heard the presence behind him. He turned, slowly, the ancient vessel of his flesh weary, and stared into the eyes of a monstrous beast with bleeding red eyes and rows of needle teeth. In those eyes shone an infinite supply of savagery and the promise of an agonizing death.

Belial bared his teeth in a smile.

The vampire slashed with glinting black claws.

Dry, wheezing laughter rattled from Belial's throat. The vampire roared in pain, clumps of flesh sloughing from its hand, or rather the smoking, blackened ruin it had become. The barrier he'd summoned barely noticed the blow. Before he could take the opportunity to gloat, a high-pitched yelp sent terror into his withered heart. *Not Orthrus!* It wasn't possible.

The gargoyle whined and pawed at his face. A blade leaking white fire burned in Orthrus' eye, buried to the hilt. The almost glittering red blood that seeped around the blade and from dozens of lash marks was shocking against such alabaster skin. Orthrus thrashed his head from side to side, desperate to dislodge the blade, whining a horrible, dreadful sound that twisted Belial's stomach and drew his shriveled, long-unused testicles into his body. The pitiful sound slowed and tapered into silence and Orthrus, his faithful Orthrus, turned to a pearlescent statue.

Magic driven by emotion coalesced into blue spiders of pure energy that crawled up and down Belial's body. He screamed wordlessly. Orthrus was dead. Chimera hadn't returned. His two most loyal pets, more like children to him than his actual brood had been.

The spiders exploded into streaks of blue that left neon hazes in their wake. Bolts raked the room, striking indiscriminately. The vampyr standing over Orthrus with one short sword still blazing was hit in the chest and exploded into flames. The bolt lingered, electrocuting him, and passed through in search of a new victim. Wolves yelped. Fur smoldered. The room turned into a nightmarish landscape, snapshots of surreal carnage punctuated by flashes of darkness that hid the horror.

Foul words rolled off of Belial's tongue. Magic was his life, his very essence. White flame bounced off of the barrier. Oily black tentacles wrapped around it only to hiss and burst into smoke. The house shook. Vampyr screamed, and Belial's decimated army rallied. Walls crumbled in on themselves. The roof was torn away. Sunlight flooded in, warming, life affirming, undead destroying.

The vampyr, in all their glory and immortal grace, fled like roaches into the dark, stumbling over each other to escape the sun. The Asan Bosam shied from the light, shielding their eyes. The burnt one hissed and ran. *The burnt one.* That wouldn't do. When this was done, he would give them proper names.

Upset as he was, Belial couldn't hold back a crooked sneer. The vampire with the bloody eyes clawed and punched at the wall, tearing open a hole and cramming his considerable bulk into the drafty space behind. The replicants used their bodies as shields, leaping on the undead, creating living cloaks. And Emigdio. The master of the house was a bloody dark streak flying into the depths of the house, abandoning his *family* to seek the refuge of his catacombs. A wounded vampire shrieked piteously, unable to run, skin blackening and smoking. *The young insolent one, Valentine.* Belial spat on him and silenced him with a bolt.

They quailed, awed and terror stricken, but they had deceived him once and it had cost him dearly. There was a price to pay for such betrayal. Whispering in a language that died before men had learned to write, a faint hum filled the room, growing louder with every word spilling from Belial's lips.

§ § §

Renato had only been a few steps away. If not for being struck by a bolt this would already be over.

The sorcerer chanted, and his minions renewed the assault, trying to drag anyone they could dig their claws into out of the shadows and into the light of day. A score swarmed the guards who, despite their wounds, fought like demons. The one called Dax fought with skill, and still he was losing ground, his clones bursting with every mortal blow.

Somewhere amidst the chaos Rain shrieked unabashedly. The sound wormed its way into Renato and wriggled there. He would never say it, but she was his favorite. She had a healer's nature—kind, intelligent, soft-spoken. She was as innocent as a vampyr could be, refusing to drink human blood or do harm. And now she fought for her life. Cristo tore at her legs, trying to draw her out from beneath a table. Only it wasn't Cristo anymore. Something else animated his corpse. Black ooze dripped from his mouth, a dark stain on a discolored, slack face. Something slid beneath the skin of his bloated throat.

It had to end, now, before anyone else was hurt. He could still finish it, give penance for a few of the awful things he'd done in his many years. The faint hum turned to a buzzing. The spell was nearly complete.

Renato huddled beneath his cloak and a blanket of gore, effectively hidden amongst the corpses. It had to end. The Rose Blade hung heavy in his hands, the hilt slightly warm to the touch, and Renato readied himself for a leap that may well cost his life.

Too late. In the battle for life and death the difference is made in fractions of a second.

The air hummed with the buzz of insects. A swarm. A plague. They fell on everyone and everything, attacking indiscriminately, biting, stinging, and tearing off bits of flesh. Renato hacked at the air. Proboscises stabbed his fair skin, and stingers injected burning venom.

A deafening bang rattled the foyer and disintegrated countless insects into a wet spray of guts, wings, and limbs. And above it all, a ripple. The very sky wavered, the clouds and sun rolling like a sheet on a clothesline ruffled by the wind.

Sound returned. A ringing in Renato's ears grew lesser as the buzz grew greater. Rain still screamed. Others fought their own battles. Valentine whined, a high-pitched keening. Insects crawled over their youngest clansman, uncaring of his thrashing or the smoke roiling from his blackened flesh. Valentine, who had fallen beneath the light of day minutes ago. Valentine, inexplicably still alive when he should be no more than dust.

The way the mansion had been stripped away. Sunlight in the middle of the night. The story of the meeting in the swamp and the decrepit, leering creature seen upon leaving, the very creature that stood before them now.

Rage consumed Renato. He cast aside his cloak and dared the light, the illusion, and a bolt crackled. His muscles went numb and the floor welcomed him. A severed head with red eyes stared blankly from mere inches away.

The pain was exquisite. The bolt had left him paralyzed but still able to feel. Stingers bit into him, lighting him on fire anew. And the illusion…his skin bubbled and burned beneath the sun, and the world bled white. There was pain within this dark magic, even if it was false.

A vague shape was all Renato could see, but he imagined a leer on the sorcerer's face and a lightning bolt on his fingertips. But to actually see it…oh, that would have been glorious. For the moment he would have to be happy with a secret; something else he had seen before his vision failed. The sorcerer raised a hand covered with dancing blue sparks.

The other thing, the secret, a wavering ball of air constantly expanding and shrinking, folding in upon itself until it looked like water, exploded right behind Belial. What little remained of the room was instantly reduced to rubble. The force of the explosion slammed into Renato, tossing him like a rag doll. The sun and sky bent out, stretching and warping until it blew apart at the seams. The effects of the illusion lasted only moments longer, the searing pain, the blindness, and even the burns, fading as though they never were.

Emigdio attacked with rabid abandon, blast after concussive blast hammering the sorcerer. Then he called on his power. Darkness erupted from the skeletal vampyr, so thick he was lost within it, and with it came a creeping terror. A squirming mass of tentacles snapped out, wrapping around Belial, crushing his barrier and melting into black mist against the sparking blue shield only to have more grow in their place.

The barrier bent. The tentacles grew thicker.

Renato tried to crawl away, shaking with the effort. Flashes of electric blue raged against the darkness, lightning within a storm, and the sorcerer fell to his knees, the barrier nearly touching his skin and disbelief shining in his yellowed, bloodshot eyes. Black, ropy arms coiled tight, determined to crush him.

The others stood by impotently, unable to interfere or help. Renato struggled to sit up. What would it look like when the shield gave? Would the coils crush him? Or would they tear him to pieces? Personally, he hoped for pieces.

Emigdio revealed himself. The cloud thinned. The tentacles wavered.

Renato waited for the killing blow. He wanted to scream at Emigdio to finish it, to forget vengeance. All he could manage was a hoarse whisper. The tentacles and tendrils turned to mist and the roiling black cloud melted away. Emigdio clutched at the twisted obsidian pendant hanging around his neck, stricken helpless as it crumbled in his fingers.

Belial unleashed a scream that spoke of insanity and lost himself in a tantrum. Lightning crawled across the living and the dead, leaving sizzling meat in its wake. Bolts struck Emigdio, one after another, riding him to the floor, jolting his limp body with every strike.

The Rose Blade flipped end over end through the air. Renato watched it spinning, surprised, unable to remember throwing it.

It missed the sorcerer by a few feet.

It went right where it was supposed to.

Onwyn plucked it from the air with a practiced hand. The slashes were so quick they were barely seen. The sorcerer twitched and tried to turn, eyes wide with shock, and his body slid apart into three neatly dissected pieces.

Slightly charred and fully irritated, Onwyn kicked Belial's head, sending it flying through the broken entryway and into the night. "Prick."

Chapter 36

LISTENING TO THE voice had been a terrible mistake. The door creaked open. A blinding black light shone within, and terror radiated from the cell. Kaleb covered his eyes with his arm, but he couldn't run, couldn't even back away. He trembled on his knees, paralyzed with fear. The door swung wide. A vaguely human-shaped mass of roiling smoke wavered and spun, dancing with glee, laughing as it stepped from its jail.

Shivers wracked Kaleb, and his teeth chattered uncontrollably.

The figure noticed him and let out a throaty chuckle. A piece of smoke stretched from the mass and took shape, reaching out with a misty gray hand. "Come," the figure whispered.

Kaleb shrank away.

"Ah, I've forgotten my manners," the smoky figure rasped. "It's been so long since I've been able to use them. You may call me Kindred." It chuckled softly, maliciously, laced with contempt.

Every nerve in Kaleb's dead body quivered. His entire life he'd believed in heaven and hell, in good and evil, and for so long he had considered himself to be proof of that. Until now. This creature, this fear casting entity called Kindred, was the face of true evil.

A voice whispered not so much in Kaleb's ear as in his mind, words he'd thought long forgotten. They were words a sinner as himself should never have been allowed to read, speak, or even think. *Yea, thou I walk through the valley of the shadow of death, I will fear no evil.*

Hints of a grinning face formed in the smoke and stared down at Kaleb, seeming to judge him. Irritated but resigned, Kaleb waited, knowing there was little he could do at this point. Either the entity kept its word or it didn't. The weight of the gaze fell away, and the smoke began to fall in on itself, condensing and solidifying, growing dark gray, pale gray, and then bronze. A man emerged, nude and emaciated—someone once young and powerful who had been laid low by time and famine. Skin hung loose on Kindred's bones, and once-broad shoulders sagged. Salt and pepper hair said he was only middle-aged, but he looked decades older. The only sign of vitality was in his pale gray eyes. They laughed, but the mirth within was a lie.

He reached out, again offering a hand. Kaleb took it. As much as the touch revolted him, the feverish terror broke and the numbness eased.

197

"Shall we?" Kindred rasped. "I've been needing a night out for some time now."

Mouth dry and tongue twice the size it should be, Kaleb nodded. "Following the breeze. Too many things up top."

Kindred dismissed the idea with a shake of his head. "Bad idea. Many have tried. None have succeeded." He grinned. "I know another way. Try to keep up."

Orbs of black light appeared at the snap of Kindred's fingers. They trailed after him, glowing eerily. The nude figure stopped just a few dozen paces away, running his hands over a door. He pressed his fingers into the dense wood and ripped it from the wall.

Kaleb stared in awe. Ancient oak? Kindred had torn into it like it was butter.

Kindred turned and ran in search of the next door. Kaleb stopped short, a chill running down his spine. Insectile clicks came from the room. A trio of basket-ball-sized spiders skittered out. He'd been wrong. It was arachnid-like clicking, not insect. Bloated yellow and green bodies dragged heavily on the floor. They turned as one, peering at him with dozens of eyes, mandibles dripping with brown ichor. As one they dismissed him and scuttled after Kindred.

Even stopping to tear off doors, Kindred was hard to keep up with. Kaleb limped along, avoiding the escapees. Nightmares stalked the halls. Rare and supposedly extinct animals. Things that could only be lesser Fae from legends. Creatures that defied recognition. Some feasting on others. And rats—hundreds of them, of all sizes, long-toothed with claws. Spiders and millipedes, roaches and beetles, the floor was alive with thousands of vermin secreted by every path and crevasse, all trailing after Kindred like he was the pied piper of hell.

Something tore at Kaleb's leg and he kicked reflexively. Hundreds of legs wriggled. A shudder inducing millipede larger than his arm and venomous purple slithered away with a pound of stolen flesh. Even swaddled in his power it stung like hell.

"Come," Kindred called.

Kindred leaned against an enormous flat slab of shining metal. There were no latches or chains, only a tiny keyhole. With nothing to grip, Kindred set his feet and pushed against it. It creaked, and began to bow in. Kaleb followed his lead. They both groaned with effort, and stepped away.

Kaleb couldn't look away from the door. "If they kept you in the smaller cage, what the hell are they keeping in here?"

"I plan to find out."

They tried again and again. The door buckled. An overpowering stench wafted from the room. Blood. Meat gone bad. Animals. The lair of a predator.

Kindred backed away smiling. "Good enough. It should be able to do the rest on its own."

Part of Kaleb wanted to know what it was, but that part was too small. He limped after Kindred, his broken leg nearly useless and getting worse with every step. Still he searched from room to room for Allie, full of despair each time he didn't find her. He paused to lean on a wall, and noticed Kindred's still form in the path ahead. At the flick of a hand one of the dark lights raced ahead. A familiar voice screeched nearby. *UglyLilFucker.*

Kindred's false smile was gone. What was left chilled Kaleb to the marrow. The hate in those gray eyes, the malevolence, could only be described as demonic. Without a word Kindred dashed after the light.

Kaleb lurched after, cursing his broken leg. As hard as he tried, keeping up proved impossible. All he could do was follow the exodus and the occasional glimpse of black light. In the end he couldn't even manage that. Alone, he shuffled to where he'd seen the dark lights last and paused, waiting for a sign and trying not to think about what might be lurking nearby.

Shadows shifted within the darkness, and everything began to spin. Stopping was even more disorienting than fumbling around blind. Vertigo set the floor undulating, and Kaleb sat down hard with his head clutched between his hands. Alone with his thoughts and trying to wait out the dizziness, all he could think about was being abandoned yet again. At least it didn't sting nearly as much this time.

Caused by the wounds or fatigue, the dizziness grew worse, and the hunger made an overdue appearance. He managed to whisper a curse before the cramps set in. Muscles seized, twisting his limbs beyond their limits and snapping cartilage. A calf muscle coiled into a quivering ball, tightening until it tore loose from his heel and slithered up to his knee. It didn't hurt a fraction as much as it would if he were human. The real pain was in the acidic scald of fat and muscle dissolving as his body cannibalized itself. Emptiness clouded his mind, a frightening lack of coherence, and Kaleb tried desperately to hold on.

There was no way to tell how long the bout lasted, or if he had lapsed, but when it was over the faltering blue flame behind his eyes burned a little bit brighter, and what he hoped was drool wet his lips and chin. He reached out again with his ability, searching for Kindred or Allie, gleaning an idea of the path he needed to take. The flame faltered, his strength already waning, and touched upon the evil entity before breaking apart like mist.

The path was clear, a stairway a few dozen paces away, and above that a winding tunnel that would take him to the dungeons. If he still wanted to go…

It was impossible. There were too many vampires, not to mention the goblins, the shadows, and the giant white thing that had knocked the bejesus out of him. On the other hand, there was Kindred and all of the things they had set free—the creepies, the crawlies, the uglies, and the fuglies. All they needed now was Allie.

What choice did he have?

He made his way up the stairs, up the tunnel beyond. The chill behind his eyes became almost painful, a whiteout of unnatural beings that was too crowded and confused to pick out a lone aura.

"Do you hear it?" Kindred asked.

Kaleb startled, realizing the entity was near, and found Kindred hidden in an archway carved from the stone walls. The potential demon rested one hand against the door as though feeling what was on the other side. "The nasty little thing?" Kaleb asked.

"No. He escaped."

Fuck. Any chances they may have had were slipping away.

Kindred shoved the door from its hinges and stepped inside whispering a single word. "Cora."

Not sure if he was supposed to stay or follow, Kaleb hedged and shambled to the doorway. Inside was nothing like he would ever have imagined. Half terrarium and half lab, the room was covered with plants, tables peppered with beakers and vials, and stacks of empty cages.

"Destroy it all," Kindred said before turning and leaving without so much as waiting for a reply.

Destroy what? They were supposed to be breaking out, and now this thing was telling him to trash what was presumably Cora's garden? At best it was a petty move. Still, with a shake of his head, Kaleb grabbed a chair and hurled it. The last thing he needed was to piss off Kindred.

One good thing about trashing the room was the smell. He chopped at the plants with a piece of broken glass and smashed the pots, enjoying the scent of soil mixing with the clean, green perfume of plant blood. He hacked at a bushy, leafy plant that was bigger than he was, and barely managed to pull his swing in time to spare a terrarium that stretched along a wall until it disappeared in the leaves.

He leaned in close, meeting the gaze of a petite, opaque insect so humanesque it was unnerving. It flicked translucent wings laced with blue veins and craned its head to stare back at him. He swallowed hard. Its face was small and his eyes were starting to fail, but it seemed inquisitive. The terrarium came alive with hundreds of them pounding tiny fists against the glass. Anxious to be done and gone, Kaleb set his hands against the terrarium and pressed until it began to crack.

§ § §

The hunger returned before Kaleb even returned to the hallway. An ache settled in his belly, and his thoughts became clouded. Too soon another bout would begin, much worse than the last. Maybe he could weather another bout—he had before, but then he was only starving, not brutalized and hanging together by threads. It was a risk he didn't want to take.

He hobbled along, his limbs growing heavier, trying not to step on some of the vermin that were drawn to Kindred. A stretch of darkness turned to a puddle of light, and Kaleb looked around, not remembering getting there. One small blessing was noticing Kindred slouching against a wall not far ahead. The fearsome entity looked haggard and broken. Pitiable even. How long had they kept him? And why? What was his big sin, aside from being evil?

He looked up at Kaleb's approach. "They know."

Kaleb nodded and joined him on the ground. No big surprise there. The trio of spiders scuttled by, one parting to nestle Kindred's hand.

Kaleb shrank away. Spiders. Why did it have to be spiders? He'd hated them for as long as he could remember. Hypocrisy at its best. "What's the plan?"

Kindred looked him up and down. "You're very much useless here, aren't you?"

There was no mocking in the words, only the bitter truth. He was a shambling corpse, battered and broken with one leg sagging at every step, the bone jutting through his skin. His mental state wasn't exactly top-notch either.

"I'm going to kill them," Kindred said. "And I made a deal with you, didn't I? An interesting change of pace that was, but a deal is a deal." A grin spread, awful and nauseating. "When the time comes, run. But if you can kill a few on the way out, I would very much appreciate it." Kindred pushed to his feet and started off down the hall.

Wanting nothing more than to eat and fall asleep, Kaleb lurched after Kindred. Tremors shook his hands and his vision grew unfocused, whether from the hunger or his upcoming demise he couldn't say. Likely it was a bit of both. He slowed at every door, looking inside for Allie and cursing when she wasn't there.

He stopped at one room, the tremors spreading until his whole body shivered. It was his cell. Everything was as he'd left it—the scatter of silver tools dark and sticky with his blood, the broken manacles, the chair both Renato and Adora had sat in. Memories best forgotten came flooding back and he forced himself to turn away rather than dwell.

"Wait!" he shouted.

Kindred turned back, simmering with hostility.

"Allie," Kaleb blurted. "A friend. She's here too."

"Stay or go," Kindred growled. He pointed down the hall at a massive, wooden double door, patterned with ruins and inlaid with silver, iron, and gold. "When I open that door, our deal is complete."

Kindred stalked to the door with a plague of rodents and vermin chittering and squealing around his feet. Of those broken from their cages only a handful remained, most having slipped away to hide or perhaps seek a different route through the catacombs. More than likely a few were dead, devoured by others. Sparks flew in a sizzling spray, and Kindred pulled away from the door with a yelp, trying to shake the sting out of smoldering fingers. The rings that served as handles; cold iron by the looks of it.

Kaleb searched the tunnels for Allie, praying she was free. He felt sick. He couldn't abandon her, but he also couldn't stay. The beatings had been one thing, the silver another, but the fire…oh god, he couldn't take that kind of pain. Even worse than that, he feared the hunger, the moment when he became less than an animal and lost everything that made him who or what he was: his mind, his heart, and whatever remained of a soul.

Kindred rested a gaunt hand on the door, and a dark stain spread beneath his touch. The wood bubbled and blackened with rot, bits crawling with maggots crumbling loose. The iron rings fell with a clang, and the door collapsed in on itself.

Kindred stepped over the mess. Things crawled and skittered after him, and a few walked on two feet. A stooped and hoary old creature emerged from the darkness, gem-like blue eyes wary with distrust. Hardly a foot shorter than Kaleb, it looked to be a cousin to the little green goblins, albeit much bigger and with earthy brown skin.

Kaleb waited until it passed before closing his eyes and trying to feel for Allie. Only a few beings were near, and none of them were her. And one, something obscene, was drawing near. Nauseous with the lack of choices, and by the sight of a bloated abomination dragging itself down the hall, he stepped over the pile of rot and maggots, trying not to crush the carpet of insects swarming around his feet.

The welcome wasn't what he'd expected. The halls were empty, the rooms few. At the far end was a foyer, demolished, ripe with bodies, blood, and bowels let loose. Death was never a pretty thing.

A slaughter had happened here. Pieces of red-eyed creatures lay about the room. Scores, maybe even hundreds. And other things. A noxious, vomit-inducing blobish slug, burnt and still oozing foul fluids, quivered in the throes of death. The white beast, massive and immensely powerful, stood unmoving with a sword in one eye. Bright red blood ran like tears, dripping from its muzzle to puddle on the floor.

And no vampires.

Kindred screamed, rage bubbling over at vengeance denied. The menagerie of creatures cringed, Kaleb among them. It wasn't the scream of a man. It was inhuman voices, an overlapping chorus of them.

"They're still here," Kaleb whispered.

"Where?"

Close by. And getting closer. Kaleb backed into the hall, eyes locked on the front entrance. A horrifying, massive vampire with bleeding eyes was the first in. *Maedoc. And they call me a monster?* Maedoc eyed the army of escapees and grimaced. "This is Emigdio's great collection? Revolting."

The slender vampire followed, spinning a sword in one hand, looking equally disgusted, muttering something about spiders beneath his breath. "I've had this sword since the crusades. I'd trade it right now for a can of raid."

The other vamps filtered in, an army no matter how badly bruised. A vampire that Kaleb remembered from the invasion on his home stared daggers at him, and turned to Kindred. "Our fight is not with you. Give us the undead and we will leave."

"Cowards!" a woman cried, outraged.

"We've already been forced into one of your wars tonight."

"Claudia," Luther said, grabbing her arm. "Leave them be."

Kindred unleashed his malevolent grin. "You should have run."

A skeletal vampire who looked to be on the brink of collapse met the demon's hateful glee with a stony impassivity. One of Kindred's eyes twitched, and the battle was on. Darkness exploded from the demon, a smog too thick to see through that enveloped the room and everyone in it, and with it came fear. Terror violated Kaleb's mind to draw out every bad memory he'd ever had. Notions of fighting and saving Allie were forgotten as he bolted for the front entrance. He hadn't gotten halfway through the room before colliding with someone. They tumbled and fell, grabbing at each other. "Who are you?" a panicked voice asked. "Aedan? Maedoc?"

That voice…Kaleb dug his fingers into the man's arms. "No, Adrian, not Aedan or Maedoc." The vampire screamed and tried to pull away, and Kaleb drew him in, squeezing until bones shattered.

Kaleb blinked. He was on top of Adrian, cool, delicious blood filling his mouth. His stomach grumbled in appreciation. The vampire screeched, protesting being eaten alive, and Kaleb took another bite. A rush like nothing else raced through his dead veins, and the fog clouding his mind dissipated.

He was supposed to be running.

White light flashed in the darkness. Dim as it was, Kaleb glimpsed the madness enveloping the foyer. The seething mass of vermin flooded over the vampires— rats leaping and hissing, clawing their way up legs and gnashing away with jagged yellow teeth, and insects stinging and biting. One of the vampires glowed with an aura of white flame, holding Kindred at bay. But Kindred was no longer Kindred. He was a hovering black mass without true form, shifting endlessly, a many-armed beast lashing the vampires.

Kaleb forced himself to look away from the spectacle and found the doorway blocked by a looming shadow with arms cast wide, ready to latch onto anything that tried to get by. Kaleb slithered a wide circle around the shadowy figure, making for a window instead.

The same white light that had shown Kaleb the way flared bright enough to expose him. Maedoc's bleeding eyes found him, and somehow the vamp's night-marish maw managed to smile.

Kaleb lurched for the window, but the vampire was on him. It was the white behemoth all over again. Powerful hands dug into his flesh and lifted him off of the ground. Kaleb flailed helplessly, unable to stop himself from being slammed into a wall over and over. More than the sense knocked out of him, Kaleb twisted, clawing, searching for something to grab hold of. He grazed something rubbery and yanked with everything he could muster. Maedoc roared and loosened his grip enough for Kaleb to wriggle free. He fell to the floor and scurried away on his hands and knees, and realized he was still holding onto the bristly lump. A pointed ear, he realized, flinging it away.

Cool, sweet autumn air washed over Kaleb, and a beautiful harvest moon glowed huge and painfully bright after the dungeons. Kaleb looked over his shoulder. Maedoc was nowhere to be seen. The entire mansion heaved, inhaling and exhaling black mist. It filtered through the broken windows and shattered door and was drawn back in as if the house was alive and gasping. Light flared within, a thick bolt of pure white that left spots dancing in Kaleb's vision. The voices of a hundred men, women, children, and beasts screamed as one. Kindred. They'd hurt him bad.

Kaleb started to head for an old Chevy half ton and did a double take at the house. Something had slipped out. He spotted it slinking alongside the foundation, a tiny figure no bigger than a doll, female judging by how petite it was. The poor little thing tensed and turned to Kaleb, realizing it had been seen. It darted away before he could so much as open his mouth, so fast he could barely track it.

Unable to do anything more, he climbed into the truck, cracked open the ignition, and the old guzzler coughed to life with just a few sparks.

§ § §

He'd done it! He was free! The truck bounced and jolted, tearing through the countryside. Kaleb searched for headlights, signs, anything that would take him back to the main road. In his haste he'd cut through a field.

Fresh air whipped at his face, filling his nostrils with dust and wildflower pollen, giving him new energy borne of the night. The horizon was bright with city light. Jacksonville, if he had to guess, only ten or twelve miles away.

Kaleb patted the dashboard. "C'mon, you can make it," he crooned. The truck sputtered, and a hint of smoke tainted the country air. The truck jolted. The chassis clanged, and a rattle under the hood turned to a shrill squeal. Kaleb kept his eyes on the lights, already planning his next move. He could become lost in the alleyways until he could steal a new car.

Or...*I could go back.*

It was amazing how quickly his courage had fled. One moment he'd been ready to fight the vampires to the death. The next he was scurrying on his hands and knees, thinking only of escaping, Allie completely forgotten. He'd abandoned her.

Part of it was the hunger. It dominated his thoughts, fogged his brain. Part of it was the fear cast by Kindred, but not all of it. Kaleb was afraid even without Kindred's influence. If he'd been braver he would have at least tried. He could hurt the vamps. They all knew that. It might have made the difference... That last flare of light though, the scream. Kindred was dead. The vampires had won.

You can still try, his conscience goaded.

"Shut the fuck up!" Kaleb snarled.

Tormented by his own cowardice, he barely managed to swerve when a tree cropped up in the headlights. Branches ripped at the truck, scraping along the doors and ripping the side mirror clean free. The truck bounced uncontrollably, and Kaleb had to fight the steering wheel.

It cracked and tore off in his hands. *Karma*.

Kaleb stared at it, too tired to be shocked and unable to do anything about it. A headlight blinked out with a tinkling of glass, and an ornate fence came out of nowhere. Black wrought iron bit into the grill and clattered beneath the wheels. Metal screeched against stone, and the truck tilted and rolled.

When it was over, Kaleb was on his back staring at the floorboards. Shards of glass covered him head to toe. He soaked it all in, knowing it was less than he deserved, and listening to the night coming back to life with the chirping of crickets and the angry chatter of birds annoyed at the disturbance.

More than ever Kaleb felt broken. Irreparable. A complete and utter waste of unnatural life. He was a coward. Yellow. All meat and no potatoes. If there was any justice in the world the truck would burst into flame and put him out of his misery. He waited a minute to give it a chance and crawled from the wreckage.

The truck was totaled, the front end caved in. Oil, gas, and coolant stained the grass, pooling and spreading. Another casualty of war. And all around were bits of shattered stone. A cluster of jagged rocks. Mossy outcroppings.

Kaleb dragged himself toward a chunk of stone. Faint, fractured words had been etched onto a piece. Another had a date. It took longer than it should have to click, a sign that the hunger was back. He was in a graveyard. The country was riddled with them, from one side of America to the other. Every town past and present had one. This must have belonged to some forgotten settlement.

It was oddly appropriate.

Now that he knew, it was easy to see. Lumps on the ground, overgrown. Black and gray pillars, most fallen to ruin, decayed by time and neglect. But a few still stood. It was one of these that Kaleb crawled to and rested against. He licked his lips, savoring the taste of Adrian's blood. If only he'd taken a few more bites maybe he would have healed up a bit.

Surreal. Everything. Not just the night, but his entire life from birth to this very moment. Kaleb tilted his head to gaze up at the stars and moon, feeling as if he was back underwater and being dragged along in a languid current. A haze filled the air, streaks of moonlight falling in slow motion and putting on a show just for him. And within it a gentle murmuring—voices, he realized. Even though he couldn't make out what they were saying, he understood they only wanted to give comfort.

In the middle of nowhere, surrounded by a star-filled, beautiful night sky and no company but nature and the dead, fatigue finally caught up to him.

Chapter 37

WAKE UP, SLEEPING Beauty," a voice crooned.

Kaleb ignored it, too tired to open his eyes.

"C'mon, give him a kiss. He's just your type. Unconscious."

"One day, I'll tear that wagging tongue out of your mouth," someone else slurred. The first voice laughed.

Aches and bruises. Cuts and stab wounds. Kaleb wrapped himself in sleep, using it as a shield against the hurt, and woke with a scream.

A nightmare knelt at his side, a ragged hole bleeding where an ear should have been. Maedoc pinched the jagged piece of bone sticking out of Kaleb's leg and wiggled it back and forth. "I knew that would get you up."

Onwyn knelt beside Maedoc, looking Kaleb up and down, studying him. "Amazing. A bit of beauty sleep really goes a long way for you, doesn't it?"

Kaleb choked back the scream and resisted the chill beginning to spread through his body. He wavered on the brink of delirium, knowing he was toeing a fine line between sanity and madness, and he couldn't care less. If these moments were all that was left, he would suffer them as a human and not the monster their kind had turned him into.

Maedoc let go of the bone. Kaleb slumped against the tombstone and couldn't keep his eyes from slipping shut. He just wanted to sleep. *At home. With a cool pillow underneath my face and Jordan snuggling close. That would be a nice way to die.*

"Good nap?" Maedoc slurred.

Kaleb mustered his strength and opened one eye. "Too short," he mumbled. "How did you find me?"

"You barely made ten miles," Onwyn said. "And the truck's on fire."

It explained the orange light glowing on the vamps' pale skin. It had ignited *after* he'd crawled away. *Of course.*

The other eye snapped open. A grunt managed to get by his lips.

"Do I not have your full attention?" Maedoc asked, stepping on the bad leg.

Don't scream. Don't give in. "Just kill me!" Kaleb shouted. "Be done with it."

"That's it," Maedoc gloated. "Beg."

What more could they possibly want from him? Were they really so petty? "Wh—Why? I told you what you wanted."

The big vampire chuckled. "Why?" He pointed at the bloody hole on the side of his head. "Because you've ruined my good looks."

"Tape it back on," Kaleb snapped. "It works for me."

Onwyn shook his head. "Can't. Something ate it." He paused for a second, reconsidering. "Well, technically we probably could, but it was some really gross, slimy-ass worm thing. I chopped it into like six pieces...they just kept going... slithered right out the door. We could've gotten the ear back," he said, grimacing, "but who would want it?"

Maedoc's smile was hard to see behind his twisted mouth. "Do you have any idea how long it's going to take for my ear to grow back?" He put his weight into it and tried to grind Kaleb's leg into the ground.

The scream that erupted was enough to shock the night into stillness. Kaleb clutched his leg and never saw the fist coming; he only found himself flat on his back with blood trickling from a broken nose into his throat. It had none of the rich, vibrant goodness he was so used to.

Onwyn spoke, low but insistent. "Maedoc..."

The big vampire ignored him and kicked out.

Kaleb rolled with the force of the blow and clutched at his ribs. The chill rushed back, a pinpoint behind his eyes, flowing down his back and through his arms until his fingertips tingled. Kaleb clenched his fists and forced it back. He wouldn't die like that, numb, feeling almost nothing. He needed this. One final penance for those he'd killed. For abandoning Allie.

"Fight!" Maedoc roared.

Kaleb went limp against a flurry of kicks. Furious, Maedoc lifted him up and threw him. Kaleb soared, finally experiencing flight again after so many years. It ended too quickly, against a stone monument that had somehow survived the centuries.

"Maedoc! Enough!" Onwyn snapped.

Kaleb's breath puffed into the air, hot and steamy, alien after so many years. He reached out and touched the mist before it could dissipate. Was it life? Or only a semblance of it? He realized he didn't care. It was precious.

Maedoc loomed into view. "Pathetic. I expected more."

Kaleb wheezed laughter. Even another savage kick couldn't still it.

"Get up!" Maedoc grunted. "Die with honor!"

That set Kaleb laughing again. Honor? Did they somehow think this had been a fair fight? He tried to lift his leg. It dangled limply below the knee. "This is honor to you? I can't even stand."

Maedoc loomed over Kaleb. His voice was a whisper, out of Onwyn's hearing. "Get up and fight, or I'll take the girl back to New York and spend the better part of eternity getting to know her better."

The words sank in. Kaleb felt nauseous. Maedoc was sick enough to do it. "I broke her arm by accident a while back, you know. She didn't even notice. Whatever she used to be, she's gone now."

"I wouldn't say 'gone.' I'm sure I saw something when I tried Adora's little trick."

The ground shook beneath Kaleb. He squeezed his hands into fists to control the trembling. "No. You're lying."

Maedoc snorted laughter. "All it took was a taste of hot silver. It wasn't much; not begging or bargaining, not even words, but there was fear in her pain."

All it would take was one bite, maybe even a scratch. With luck he'd already infected the vampire when he'd torn off the ear. Either way…Kaleb lunged at the vamp, clawing for its eyes.

Maedoc danced back, out of reach. "Finally, a little spirit!"

"Fuck you!" Kaleb snarled. "We had a deal! Renato swore!"

"Ah, that. He mentioned it. Or at least he mentioned you. He said nothing of the girl."

Betrayed. He didn't know why he was surprised. They were all fiends. Kaleb glared up at Maedoc. The vampire was covered in blood and drying bits of gore. One hand was raw, the skin melted away. "Haven't you killed enough?" Kaleb shouted.

Maedoc scowled. "Goblins and beasts. Anything that counted was bled by someone else—the sorcerer and his pets. I had none of them. But you—you're why I came to this forsaken place, to face down an aberration."

So that was it? It was that simple? His life was going to amount to just another notch on this psycho's belt? Kaleb used the monument to drag himself up and leaned heavily against it. "I don't care if I die anymore. I don't want to fight anymore, but if it means you'll spare Allie then I will. But if I'm going to die tonight, I'm going to do it as a man, not a freak. You've taken *everything* from me. I won't give you that."

The big vampire leaned down. "I want to kill the aberrant, not this whimpering alter ego.

"Be done with it," Onwyn said. "I've no taste for your games."

Maedoc grunted acceptance. The big vampire's knuckles popped as they knotted into fists. Kaleb stared him down. His heart fluttered fast and shallow. The alley. His house. The dungeon. And now a graveyard. Four times was too many. The game had to end. The fear had to stop. He tried to hate Maedoc, to tap into his anger, but it wouldn't come. All he felt was tired and sad.

Maedoc slipped into a fighter's stance and Kaleb readied himself. The vamp was quick for a big guy, granite fists pummeling, sending Kaleb reeling. He swung back blindly and got knocked senseless for the effort. Without knowing when it had happened, he found himself once again on his back, looking up at twinkling stars.

"Get up."

Kaleb dragged himself up once more and squared off. What the hell made this freak tick? How could the vamp take any pleasure in this? It wasn't a fight, it was an execution, and the bastard was enjoying it.

Maedoc attacked like a boxer, refined, purposeful, and with incredible power behind every hit. Kaleb took the beating, the lacerations, crackling of bones, and the hurt that went hand in hand. He deserved it; there was no denying it. Especially after abandoning Allie. Even so that wasn't the only reason he was doing it. A haymaker came for his face. The hit he'd been waiting for. He spun. The blow glanced off his cheek, and Kaleb latched onto the arm, digging his nails deep, slicing through meat and sinew until they reached bone.

Maedoc snarled and knocked him away. What came next was no longer a fight, or even an execution, but punishment. Blow after blow. Kick after kick. Maedoc brutalized him. Through it all Kaleb was nearly senseless. All he knew was the crushing force of Maedoc's knuckles and the icy chill pressing against the back of his eyes, searching for a way out. Voices argued, the words lazily floating through the air. Onwyn didn't sound very happy. Maedoc snapped dickishly.

I hope it rots off at the shoulder, Kaleb thought. With his lifeblood leaking into the ground, he focused on the sky, entranced at a falling star. There had been a time as a boy where he'd wished on them. One night he'd seen hundreds fall, a night when he'd snuck out with Tristan and Katherine. It had been one of the best times of his life. They'd watched together, laughing, amazed by the heavenly spectacle. They all made wishes. Tristan and Katherine for wealth, adventure, love. When they asked Kaleb what he had wished for, he lied, mimicking their answers. Hundreds of stars he wished on. Always the same wish. He wanted to be healthy. To say it aloud would have ruined everyone's night, and the last thing he wanted was their pity.

Now, hundreds of years later, he looked at the same sky knowing better than to make wishes. Maybe it would be better this way. The world had no use for him nor he for it. For a few brief minutes he'd tasted freedom again, and it had left the taste of dust and ash in his mouth, flavors of cowardice and self-hatred. His freedom had cost too much. Allie. Kindred. Dozens of other creatures, good or evil.

So he didn't fight the waning. He didn't try to staunch the blood flowing out of him and into the ground. He watched the sky, waiting for more shooting stars, hoping there would be mercy in whatever came next. His heaven was a place he'd already been, in that field with his friends, his parents safe at home, all of them loving him. If he could have that, Allie, and Jordan…

Darkness came and went. A lapse. A momentary blackout. Onwyn stood over him, sword in hand. His lips moved soundlessly. It took a second to realize they were ready to kill him.

Another blackout. Maedoc was back, grinning terribly with a torch in hand. The light made the vampires look more ghoulish than normal. Maedoc kicked out, said something, but Kaleb didn't care. He listened to something else; the murmur of whispering voices. They'd been there all along, waiting for him to listen.

The pounding behind his eyes eased. The chill sought a different path to freedom, flowing through his body to mix with blood seeping from countless wounds. It stained the grass beneath him, leeching into the soil and watering the parched whispers below.

The chill touched one voice, and then another, and then another, igniting and spreading like prairie fire.

A switch flipped. A floodgate opened. The whispers grew louder, the words distinct, not only accepting him for what he was but embracing him because of it. A chorus of minds touched Kaleb's. It was no accident he'd wound up here. They'd called him. And for once in his undead life, he didn't feel alone. They were with him. They felt his pain. His fear. His remorse. And they were angry.

The dead stirred in their graves. The faint, confused remnants of who they once were coalesced into coherence. Dusty bones rattled and clawed skyward.

Maedoc lowered the torch and flames licked up. The sounds of the night seemed to magnify, the insects, leathery flapping of bat wings, the crackle of the truck still burning, and the sizzling of Kaleb's flesh.

Only the dead were silent as they rose from their graves. There were no grunts, groans, or moans, only a quiet simmering fury. Onwyn shouted. Maedoc spun away waving his torch.

Tasting fresh agony, Kaleb slapped at the flames and rolled in dirt and grass to put them out. He looked up to see Onwyn and Maedoc fighting frantically, trying to clear a path through an army of ancient corpses dressed in tattered bits of cloth and parchment-like patches of desiccated skin. The vampires were doing well against the risen dead, but they didn't see the hands erupting from the ground until it was too late.

Maedoc roared like an animal, turning bones to powder, but the dead were too many. He sank to his ankles, then to his knees, thrashing in rabid fear. They swarmed over him, peeling his flesh from his bones and eating him alive.

Onwyn swept through the dead like a force of nature, sword rising and falling in a blur as he cleared a path to Kaleb. There was no running away, not even a way to defend himself, and all Kaleb could do was raise an arm in a futile attempt to ward off the blow. Despite the mercurial shine of the blade it lacked the sting of silver, in fact it barely hurt at all. At first. A thin line of blood welled on Kaleb's wrist, and his hand fell off with a few trickling spurts of blood.

The vampire poised his sword for a clean decapitation, and Kaleb snatched up his hand and threw it. It struck Onwyn's face with a meaty slap, and the vampire's eyes widened with disbelief; a momentary hesitation that cost him his life. The dead swarmed him.

A tiny part of Kaleb felt sorry for Onwyn. He'd shown some remorse, had wanted to take pity, and he'd even argued with Maedoc over the torture. But it wasn't enough. The vampire was drawn into the ground, dirt and grass churning like turbid water as the dead fed in a frenzy. One hand thrust skyward, shaking with desperation and reaching for help that wasn't coming, until that too disappeared.

Maedoc howled. The brute fought frantically, enraged at Onwyn's demise. It did him no good. Skeletal hands held fast. He turned back to Kaleb, furious, hysterical, and terrified with bloody tears welling and spilling.

Kaleb watched it all with a cold impassivity.

The dead holding Maedoc paused as one, turning to Kaleb, waiting for him to decide. Already the others were returning to their resting spots, their voices settling into whispers. Soon they would all fade into a soft murmur.

A quick death was better than Maedoc deserved. He deserved to be chained up and taken apart one steak at a time. Maybe Kaleb could even pull a Hannibal, crack Maedoc's skull open and feed him pieces of his own brain. A gruesome if not enjoyable fantasy, but there was no time. And besides, he was very, very hungry.

Chapter 38

KALEB LINGERED ON the outskirts of Jacksonville, tempted to just leave it all behind and never look back. The cash in the safe he could do without. Maybe even the lonely few parcels of Michael in the freezer. But not Jordan. If he could make it.

Being in public in his condition? Madness. Even for a walking corpse he looked like shit. He'd had to shift again to deal with his leg, and even then it had taken fifteen minutes of trying not to retch as he slid his tibia back into place. The rest would only heal with time. Maedoc had fucked him up good. Now he was limping along, ragged, torn, covered in blood, and with a vampire's partially gnawed leg slung over one shoulder. He'd run from that if he saw it coming up the road.

Kaleb knelt in a patch of dusty scrub brush, giving his leg a break while eyeing a truck stop diner. A half-dozen semis and a handful of cars were scattered about the parking lot. He squinted, trying to take the blur out of his eyes. He scuttled out of the bushes and darted to a station wagon. It was an older model, nineties, unremarkable, a completely forgettable vehicle that no one in their right mind would steal. It was perfect.

Kaleb crept into St. Augustine like a rat. He kept to as many side streets and alleyways as he could, shunning people and light while cowering in the folds of Maedoc's shirt. It was far too large, torn in spots, and splattered with blood, but the collar folded up high enough to cover his neck and ears.

As on edge as Kaleb was, he kept drifting, letting his subconscious do the driving for him. He'd only escaped hours ago, and it already felt like a bad dream. If not for the wretched face in the rearview mirror and the gnawed leg in the passenger seat he might not believe it had really happened. Parts of it were jumbled. Insane, ghastly images flashed before his eyes. The creatures in the dungeon. Kindred. The swarm of the dead.

Movement on the street snapped Kaleb to attention, and he slammed on the breaks while a woman screeched in terror. The station wagon shuddered, tires squealing and fishtailing, leaving smoking streaks of black rubber. A small green hand stretched toward the wagon's bumper to ward it off. A goblin glared up at Kaleb. The woman screamed again, dashing into the street, straight at the little monster.

Kaleb watched, stunned. She was running right to it!

The little beast backed away a step and bolted, and Kaleb hit the gas. The wagon lurched forward, narrowly missing the goblin and smashing into a parked car.

"Run!" Kaleb shouted at the woman.

It was as if she wanted to die. She didn't even hesitate. The goblin was on her in a flash, leaping up, reaching for her neck and throttling her. What the hell were they doing in St. Augustine? There were scores of the little monsters dead at the vampire's lair. Were they swarming everything? An invasion of little green men?

Knowing he shouldn't care, that he should be running and saving his own skin, Kaleb threw open the door and dashed after the little green bastard. He hated himself enough. Sitting by and allowing it to slaughter a random woman on the street? He was cold, callous, cruel, but some things he couldn't ignore.

The woman screamed again and spun away, trying to run, but the goblin clung tight. The two were locked together, grappling as the woman stumbled away, shouting for help. Lights turned on up and down the street and people stepped from their houses.

Kaleb grabbed the goblin and tried to wrench it loose. "Let go!" he snarled. It lost its grip on the woman, and Kaleb held it at arm's length, ready to hurl it against a vehicle. The woman was on him, punching and kicking, screeching louder than ever. The goblin shrieked, a high-pitched wail, almost as loud as the woman.

This was his thanks for saving her life? He was a monster, sure, but he'd saved her…It hurt more than he liked to admit. She wrapped her arms around the goblin and desperately tried to tear it from Kaleb's grasp. "Let go!" she screeched.

Confused, Kaleb gave her what she wanted and watched her scramble away with the little green monster clutched against her chest. The beast stared at Kaleb with big eyes. Scared eyes. Pale blue eyes.

The woman's shouts seemed to multiply and Kaleb glanced around. People stood on lawns and in doorways. Groups of children huddled together while others ran away. Most were unsure of what to do, watching and waiting. Someone even held up a phone, recording everything. Kaleb turned away from everyone else, watching the little green goblin being rushed away by its mother. The mask was so realistic, so close to an actual goblin…

A few people marched toward Kaleb while others threatened and jeered, and the crowd became a mob. Baseball bats and golf clubs were brandished. Sickened by what he had almost done, Kaleb leapt back into the wagon and raced away. People scrambled out of the way, battering the old wagon with whatever they could.

"Stupid," Kaleb snarled. Hours of limping through the countryside and stealing a new set of wheels, and he blows it in the homestretch? Pathetic. Like it wasn't bad enough having to watch out for vampires and god only knows what on his ass, now he was probably the target of a state-wide manhunt. And they had pictures! Video!

A half sob, half choked burst of laughter erupted from him. Even in the few moments where he tried to do the right thing he still managed to screw it up. That kid would be traumatized. The mom too. He just wondered what they would say on the news. A one-handed zombie attempted to eat a child on All Hallows Eve? And then it made a getaway in a '91 Ford station wagon? He couldn't wait to see the police spokesman putting out that press statement.

Sirens wailed nearby. Time to ditch the wagon and hoof it. He snickered, a random thought racing through his mind. He should be able to move fast with three legs, right? He could already imagine attaching Maedoc's leg, sprinting down the street in only an oversized shirt and a pair of filthy tighty not-so-whities, three legs pumping fast and furious.

The sirens grew closer, and Kaleb pulled into an alleyway to ditch the car. He hopped out, Maedoc's leg flopping over his shoulder, the vampire kicking him even in death. He limped as fast as he could through back alleys and yards.

§ § §

Miles passed in a daze until Kaleb found himself across the street from his house, peering through the gaps in a neighbor's fence. Nothing was as it should have been, the lights off, not a single decoration put up. The one night of the year when he didn't have to hide what he was, when he used makeup to look worse so he could interact with people. Giving away treats was fun, and so was making the older kids sing or dance for their candy. He wished Halloween had been around when he was a kid.

Laughter and the standard entreaty of "Trick or Treat" rolled up and down the street. Scattered groups of children were making the rounds. Two little girls paused in front of Kaleb's house and turned away in disappointment. They called out to a larger group of older boys that Kaleb remembered from years past. The boys were all terrible singers that had played along, but always with a rebellious glint in their eyes. Every year a few houses got pranked—strewn with toilet paper, soap on the car windows, eggs, and smashed pumpkins. Typical crap. Rumor had it that one poor bastard who served up healthy snacks found a deuce in his bird bath. Kinda served him right, but still. One of the girls motioned to Kaleb's house, shaking her head. The boys just laughed and walked up the sidewalk anyways.

They rang the bell and then pounded on the door when no one answered. A few jeered, and they all turned away. They stopped halfway down the side-walk and glanced around to make sure the coast was clear before raining dozens of eggs down on the house.

Kaleb gritted his jaw and watched, unable to do anything more. Every Hal-loween for the past decade he'd given those little shits treats, and good treats, not the dinky little candies, not the healthy alternatives or tooth brushes. He misses one year and this is what happens? "Fuckers," he whispered.

He choked down his wounded pride and waited for them to move on before racing across the street. He leapt up the stairs and turned the handle. The door opened a fraction, hit something solid, and refused to go any further.

Kaleb slid around the side of the house, pausing to peer at the shattered bay window. A long time ago, when the house was built, that window overlooked the edge of the city. Now all he could see was the side of Helen's house. If only he'd had the money to buy a few more lots. At least the only person who might see it was Helen, short of the police poking around after a noise complaint or say a home invasion call.

At the back door, Kaleb dropped to his hands and knees, tossing aside a garden gnome and tearing up soil until he found what he wanted. He grabbed the fake rock, twisted it open, and drew out the spare key. Once a refuge in a never-ending stream of dark and stormy nights, now his home was the place where he'd been attacked. It was no longer his castle, a safe haven. Something else they'd taken away from him.

A stench of blood, stale musk, and shit greeted Kaleb as soon as he opened the door. Death was never a pretty thing, rather the opposite as a final indignity. He moved as softly as he could, listening, scenting the air, trying to feel if anyone else was there. The linoleum squelched under his bare feet, tacky with some unknown fluid that he had a sneaking suspicious belonged to Allie.

The hallway carpet was even worse, the fabric slick with cold congealed blood, though the living room had taken the brunt of things. From the looks of it a cow had been stuffed with grenades. The entire room was painted with blood and stippled with bits and pieces of meat. A pool covered the floor, thick and glossy and still wet. The lifeblood of a vampire, a werewolf and the clones of whatever the fuck the little man had been. The stench was unbearable, untouched by the breeze rippling the curtains.

At least they had taken the bodies.

But that wasn't quite right. A knot welled up in Kaleb's throat. A vice gripped his chest and crushed his heart. They'd left one behind. Jordan laid unmoving beside the love seat, the glow in her eyes extinguished. She'd been torn apart, eviscerated, and her tiny pink tongue lolled.

Kaleb limped toward her, numbness encroaching his mind and body and drowning out the aches. His legs gave out, and he sat hard on the love seat. He reached for Jordan, ran a finger across the side of her face, and took in what they had done to her. He tried to hold back the tears and failed miserably. A lifeless smile pulled at the corners of his mouth when he noticed bits of skin stuck to her claws. She'd gone down fighting.

Surrounded by the ruins of his home and life, time lost all meaning. Sanctuary. Work. The hope that Allie had given him. The comfort and friendship of

Jordan. They'd taken it all. All that remained was his own worthless hide. It was a poor victory.

He should be getting ready to disappear and start over somewhere else. Instead he curled up and did nothing. Every last piece of him hurt—body, mind, and shadow of a soul, enough to no longer care if the vamps came. Tears tickled as they fell over his nose, and he tried to wipe them away only to smear his face with blood from the stump of his wrist. It was bleeding again, or oozing more like. At some point he'd become human again.

He slipped through the house in a fog, not remembering getting up or taking the first step, suddenly finding himself in the garage. He fumbled with his pocket and pulled out the severed hand. What the hell was he supposed to do? He was no surgeon. His particular set of skills helped him take bodies apart, not put them back together. Threading a needle with one hand? Not likely. Staples? Wouldn't hold. Or he could go the obvious route and pull a Red Green. He reached for the duct tape, trying to figure out how to wrap his hand and wrist together, and turned to the table clamp.

The pale flesh of the severed hand looked like a Halloween prop in the metal jaws. Kaleb pressed his wrist to the stump and started winding the tape around it. It wasn't fancy, but he was whole again and wondering if it would work.

Time jumped again and he found himself back in the living room. Jordan was as he'd left her, somehow even more pitiful than earlier. He carefully picked her up and carried her to the back door.

The breeze outside was cool and soothing against the burning in his cheeks and eyes. He laid Jordan on the grass and took his frustrations out on the garden, pounding at the soil, tearing it up one handful at a time, mauling the ground until a three-foot-deep hole waited to swallow his best and only friend in this mortal and immoral world.

It took a while to work up the courage to set her inside. He sat beside her, petting her, unable to speak even a few simple words. He searched for some way to find comfort in her loss, chalk it up to a greater mercy in her long and unnatural life, but nothing made sense. She wasn't a serial killer like he was. She wasn't evil. She was just different.

As unfulfilling as it was, the only comfort he could think of was that she would have a proper burial, not be disposed of like some common roadkill. Kaleb swept the dirt back into the shallow grave, stopping to dig up a cluster of purple and blue pansies and set them in the soil above Jordan. They were her favorites, the ones she'd always stick her nose in and get a look on her face like she was about to sneeze. He patted them into place, sure they would take, and went back inside.

§ § §

Steaming hot water seared Kaleb's face, cleansing him with a punishing sting. He deserved it. He ached for it. What he didn't deserve was the gift of Maedoc's flesh. It was ambrosia. He had to stop to take a few bites every fifteen or twenty minutes, his body burning through it, healing faster than he'd thought possible. The only things that weren't healing were the gaping holes where Allie and Jordan used to live.

He attacked the wall in an abrupt burst of anger, not stopping until the shower was trashed and his fists tingled with the aftermath. Both of them. One hand was slower than the other, stiffer, but it worked. If only he could bring himself to care.

Kaleb flinched as the doorbell rang again, another group of brats demanding something for free. He was tempted to shift and open the door. Instead he turned off the water and stepped dripping from the shower. Normally he would have been embarrassed by a tantrum, even without a witness, but what was the point? It was about the least shameful thing he'd done lately. Not to mention the house was basically a write-off anyways. The bathroom didn't even have a wall anymore for Christ's sake.

He strode naked through the darkness to his bedroom and flopped into bed. He wanted to sleep. To forget.

It wasn't meant to be. Sleep wouldn't come. There were too many rampant thoughts and emotions welling up and fading only to be replaced by others. He brooded on all of them. Hating the vampires. Hating himself even more.

A shudder shook him, memories of Adora's soft hands, Maedoc's cruel sneer, and Adrian's hatred. He tried to close his eyes and forget only to have other images race through his mind: Allie being cut and burned. Jordan being ripped to shreds. The blissful embrace of nothingness remained a distant fantasy. He doubted he would ever sleep peacefully again.

Instead he dwelled on what he should have done. He should have killed them all or died trying. Kindred had fought. Some of the creeping, crawling things had fought. And he had run like a fucking coward, abandoning them all, forsaking Allie. When had he lost himself? When had he become such a cowardly shit? Or had it always been that way? It was hard to remember.

Nauseated, he sat up and swung his legs over the side of the bed. At what point was life not worth living? *Easy. Right now.* The goddamn vampires had hollowed him out. Nothing mattered anymore, not his business or his money, not even his life. He couldn't go back to being alone. It made him furious, and after all of the sorrow, the anger felt good. For the first time since the nightmare had started he was glad he'd killed some of them.

As sweet and satisfying as the anger and self-pity were, they faded before thoughts of a bleak future. Jordan was really dead. Allie was really gone.

They were lost.

But he wasn't. Not anymore.

Kaleb pushed aside everything else and stood, his mind made up. There were things to be done. Sooner or later *they* would come looking, and he didn't want to be here when they did.

Ten minutes later he looked almost presentable dressed in his finest. Still a little sickly, pale, and covered in every shade of bruise imaginable, it was still nothing short of miraculous. The clothes really did make the man. Vain or not, Armani made him look good.

An eerie silence permeated the house as he walked through it. The entire atmosphere had changed. No longer did Jordan's or Allie's presence cast a shadow. Even asleep they carried weight. At least they used to. A void had claimed the space they used to occupy.

Kaleb ignored the squishing beneath his shoes and made his way to the kitchen, wondering just what, if anything, he should say to Helen. She was a good neighbor, and she would come looking eventually. A note on the fridge? *Hi, Helen. Got attacked by vampires and had to move.* Maybe not. But what excuse could he come up with that sounded even remotely feasible? What could possibly explain the carnage scattered throughout the house or the chains in the basement?

Nothing. Mere words couldn't explain. And while it would have been nice to say goodbye, he didn't really owe anyone anything. The best option was probably to burn it all down. If there wasn't a decent chance of taking out the entire neighborhood he probably would have.

The Mercedes was where he had left it, a slumbering lion ready to awaken and roar at a moment's notice. It was surprising that one of them hadn't stolen it. Kaleb backed onto the driveway and then the street. His gaze was drawn back to his house, dark and empty, once a cabinet of curiosities hidden from the world. He doubted if he would ever see it again. He watched the flap on the front door, almost waiting for Jordan to come prancing out and dash across the lawn, and stomped the gas pedal knowing she never would.

St. Augustine was silent in the late hours. A few homes were still bright inside, but the parties were few. Only a handful of people still strode the streets, the hardcore crowd of partiers and misfits.

That was when he saw *them.*

§ § §

Kaleb ditched the car and bolted for a cluster of bushes like his life depended on it. *They* were close. Their voices grew louder as they drew near, cursing and whispering. How could they wander so brazenly, unworried about whom or what might see them?

Kaleb stopped breathing and willed the change. It came easily and eagerly, flowing over and through him. When it was done, he was as he had imagined, bloated and wet, truly rancid and revolting.

They paused.

"What the hell is that?" one of them said.

"Alex, you dirty bastard!"

"Not me!"

Kaleb lurched out of the bushes, arms outstretched, groaning. They screamed, scrambling backwards, bags of loot dropped in shock. Kaleb staggered toward them. The little shits fled, knocking each other out the way in their haste.

Grinning, Kaleb ran after them. He swiped at the kid at the back of the pack dragging soft, swollen knuckles over the kid's coat. The brat screeched like Satan himself had scratched his ass and the kids scattered, every man for himself style. They disappeared around corners and over fences, and Kaleb watched them flee, taking a bit too much pleasure in it, glad to be on the giving side for once. It was mean, probably scarring, but it sure felt good. The little vandals probably wouldn't go out after dark again until they were in their thirties.

Kaleb shifted back and jogged to his Mercedes with his spirit fractionally buoyed. He hadn't given any treats, but that had been one hell of a trick.

One more quick stop and he'd be on his way.

Chapter 39

KALEB HELD A hand through the open window, feeling the press of the wind through his fingers, and took a deep breath. Why hadn't he spent more time enjoying the little things? Florida was a beautiful place, full of parks and wildlife, and outside of St. Augustine the air was sweet and pure.

It was a scent he might never enjoy again.

He pulled his hand back inside, trying to stay focused. Already the calm was wavering and the fear was coming back. He called on the experience of spending years hiding in plain sight, of being sure everyone knew who and what he was, and turned the inner turmoil into a façade of placidity. It was the cowardly piece of his soul that had dictated so much of his life, and it wouldn't control him any longer.

For all of the devastation Renato and his clan had caused, they had also shown him some important truths. So many years lost, pretending, feeding an insatiable hunger yet starving of basic human necessities. The friendships he'd had as a child had been brief and ended badly, and still they had been crucial in making him the man he was. He missed the companionship, shared secrets, and contact with another person, if only a clap on the shoulder or a hug. And while a true, deep friendship was its own kind of intimacy, he craved the sense of touch, the physical desire for romantic closeness, and as an extension, he needed love.

Jordan had given him part of that. She was family, a little sister, a child.

And Allie, she wasn't much yet, but she'd given Kaleb hope. He liked her, had from the start. The dimple in her chin. Her heart-shaped face. The fire in her eyes. And when she died…she'd smiled at him. She hadn't been afraid. Ever since then he'd been able to sense something inside of her, some piece of her unconscious mind that didn't hate him. And now she was just like him. Maybe it was fate. Maybe they were meant to be together.

Kaleb couldn't live without knowing.

He pulled off the highway and eased down a dusty gravel road. They were down there. He could feel them. It was strange. It should have been a courageous moment, maybe even noble, but he still felt cowardly. His legs were rubbery and he couldn't stop his hands from trembling.

He got out the car and looked at the lights in the distance. The mansion glowed in the night, an eerie flickering orange that came with the stench of diseased flesh roasting. A funeral pyre blazed, piled high with tangled corpses.

Gravel crunching beneath his shoes, and he strode at a steady but quiet pace, waiting for the moment when shouts rang out to announce his arrival. They never came. There was no one to greet him outside, nor at the gaping hole where a door used to be. He crept up the front steps, listening to men grumble inside. Two by the sounds of it, both setting off a tingling behind his eyes.

Kaleb stepped inside the mansion he'd escaped only hours earlier. Two wolves scraped at layers of flesh, blood, and a carpet of crushed insects and rats, bitching about the job. It was the behemoth that drew his attention. That it could turn at any moment, maul him, tear him to shreds with its incredible strength stole his courage. He backed up a step, two, and realized it wasn't moving, not even to take a breath. A hilt protruded from one eye, and both scars and scorch marks laced its thick hide. In a way it was tragic, such an amazing animal dead. Would it have a place in Emigdio's dungeon? He shook his head. Of course it would.

His attention was drawn again, not by something he saw or heard but by the silence. The wolves were fixated on him, no doubt stunned by his sudden reappearance. A whirlwind of emotions enveloped Kaleb—grief, hatred, self-doubt, and a hundred more. One of the wolves was covered in festering red scratches and bloody furrows. Kaleb had seen marks like those before, not nearly as bad, but similar to ones he'd suffered over the years.

Why? What reason could he possibly have had? Not that it mattered. There was nothing the wolf could say that would save him. The tempest within possessed Kaleb and he charged, a spectator in his own body.

He felt like he was watching himself attack more than actually doing it as he smacked aside the wolf's hand, gripped him by the jaw, and lifted him off of the ground. The wolf kicked and shouted, reaching for Kaleb's arms and trying to pry them free. A fist rocked the back of Kaleb's head, and the other wolf shouted for help. He ignored it all, trying to enjoy his revenge but feeling an empty satisfaction.

In one harsh movement he threw the wolf to the floor. The jaw, though, stayed in his hand. Unintelligible shouts turned to unintelligible screams. Blood gushed out. Kaleb spun on the other wolf, using his nails like a blade to slash from crotch to throat, and turned away, barely paying attention to the waterfall of innards spilling behind him. His only concern was the jawless wolf with the face full of festering scratches. With one hand he grabbed its hair, with the other he went for the spine. Fingers sunk into flesh, and with a wrench they were sliding up, severing meat and ribs. Without those bonds to connect them, the spine snapped with a wet pop and the body peeled away. Kaleb held on to the severed head, accepting that one small measure of closure as a victory.

He didn't have to turn to know the vamps were flooding into the room, coming from the floor above and a room near the stairs to the basement. He threw the head at Emigdio's feet, his uncertainty gone. This was the right thing to do no matter the consequence. There was still fear, but it wasn't his anymore. It was theirs.

The vamps were haggard, covered with fresh cuts and bruises, tokens of Kindred's gratitude for their hospitality. None were unscathed.

Adrian pushed through the group, only staying on his feet by holding onto the arms of the others. Dark bags had formed beneath his hateful eyes, and blood soaked his clothing, not all of it his own. It smelled of older and stronger vampires. Flashes of biting and scratching came to Kaleb, of veritably ravaging the vamp. Everywhere he'd broken the skin was burned to a char. They had tried to heal the wounds through blood and then by fire, and judging by the dark, swollen streaks, they had failed.

It begged a question: what did it mean? Was his bite fatal to vampires? Or…

"Not my fucking problem," Kaleb muttered. Either Adrian died or he was theirs to execute.

Adora grimaced and held a hand over her nose. "Gods, the smell," she complained. The small, robed man threw back his cowl. Seams split his cheeks and blood dribbled.

Aedan rested a bloodied hand on the ashen man's shoulder. "Wait." He met Kaleb's eyes. "Maedoc and Onwyn?"

"Gone," Kaleb said, taking no pleasure in it. The bloodsucker sagged at the words like he'd been punched in the gut.

"You should not have come back," Renato said, weary.

"You took everything I care about. Allie, Jordan, my home. I have nothing to live for."

"You are strong," Emigdio said, "but not strong enough. You cannot win."

Kaleb appraised the vampire. He looked different. Granted their introduction had been brief, but something had changed. "Kindred really took a bite out of you, didn't he?" Kaleb shook his head. "I should have stayed with him and fought. What happened to him anyways?"

"Gone," Adora snarled from behind the others.

Damn. Odd, feeling sorry for Kindred. Even if he was pure evil, he'd also been an ally. "That's too bad. I bet he had a lot of reasons to hate you all. He said he was down there for a long time." Kaleb focused on Adora and gave her a lopsided grin. "But I'm glad you're still around, Adora. I've been thinking about you."

Renato slid in front of his hell spawn. "What do you want?"

Emigdio spun back with a snarl, "Mind your place, Renato!"

The old poet was unfazed. "How many must die tonight? How many of us will you sacrifice?"

"Renato!" Claudia snapped. "You know what he is! He cannot be allowed to live. We only do as we must."

"Please," Renato pleaded. "No more blood. Settle this another way."

Emigdio closed his eyes, struggling with indecision, and struck Renato with the back of his hand. The only vampire in the bunch that Kaleb didn't want to murder spilled to the floor and lay still.

Their bickering was as annoying as it was irrelevant. "What do I want?" Kaleb mused aloud. What did he really want? He'd come in expecting to die. He really hadn't expected a conversation. He allowed them a glimpse of the hatred burning inside of him. "I came here for two things." He glanced at the severed head covered with scratch marks. "He was one. The other is the girl."

A vampire pushed to Emigdio's side, a hideous mass of raw flesh and melted skin. "So, this is the aberrant," the burned man rasped, "the pestilence that plagues our house." The tension in the room amped up. The vampires began to spread out, preparing, steeling themselves for yet another battle.

"You're right," Kaleb admitted with a smile. "I'm not strong enough to take you all, not at once anyways. Hell, I doubt I can get more than one or two of you like this. But what makes you think I came alone?"

He set his power free. It moved with a mind of its own, calling out, connecting. *They* felt his need, his hurt and hate, and *They* answered. The dead flooded into the mansion, through the doorway, spilling from the windows, settling their hollow, sunken gazes on the vampires.

Finding them had been easy once he'd let loose. This country was a burial ground. There were bones deep down, ancient, so far removed from who they used to be that only the barest trace of energy remained. And there were bones not so deep, not so old, and most of those were at least a shadow of their former selves while some were more coherent, purposeful, and even malevolent. All were connected by a similar need; a palpable ache for life. Kaleb realized with a start that their numbers had grown along the way. Fleshy. Skeletal. Hanging together by scraps of skin and clothing. There was even one without a body, ghostly and intangible, less substantial than mist, a malevolent entity.

The vampires attacked.

Kaleb charged the crispy bloodsucker. He was old and powerful. The others had stepped out of his path. As wounded as he was, no one had tried to hold him back or protect him. He was dangerous.

Crushing weight collapsed onto Kaleb just as he reached the vampire. He managed to grab the vamp's clothing and drag him down. They tumbled to the floor, grappling, either unable to overpower the other. Aedan charged in, hands glowing with white flame, and Claudia readied a gore-soaked axe for a decapitating blow.

Kaleb twisted and heaved the vampire to arm's length, right into Aedan's outstretched hands. The white flames leapt, setting the burned vampire and Kaleb afire in a burst of heat and light. The vampire screamed and chomped at Kaleb's face, driven mad with fear. Only an elbow jammed below its chin kept the fangs away.

The dead swarmed around them. The house rattled and shook, jarred by piercing explosions. Bones and rancid flesh fell in a constant rain, joined here and there by puddles of cold crimson. An axe skimmed Kaleb's head close enough and sharp enough to take a swatch of hair, and a woman warrior angled herself to swing a second axe. She swore, unable to get a clean shot, and shouted in frustration as the dead forced her back, the same dead who dug their bony fingers into the burning vampire. The vicious bastard let go of Kaleb to attack the swarm, killing with every wild blow only to find more fighting to take their place.

The weight returned with pulverizing force, shoving Kaleb back down just as he was getting up. Ribs cracked beneath the pressure, as did the floor beneath him. The entire house groaned while plaster and dust sprinkled down. Certain a killing blow was imminent, he twisted and turned, straining just to turn on his side.

There was no fatal blow on its way. There was no one even capable of delivering one. All but the burning vampire had been struck down, and he had turned into a pillar of flame. A few of the dead clinging to him were old and dry, so desiccated they were essentially kindling.

The vampire staggered and fell to his knees screaming in a horribly high pitch. The weight eased, just for a second, and hammered down, an impossible weight that knocked the air from Kaleb's lungs and some of the fluids from his body. Torrents of ichor shot from his mouth, nose, and other places. A pyre of white flame streaked with red and yellow, the vampire toppled, the terrible whine tapered to nothing, and the oppressive weight broke.

For a long moment the only sound was the sizzle of meat cooking.

There was no time to recover. Kaleb fought to get up, to defy his battered body, fearing the moment when the vampires would come at him again. His army was in ruins. Literally. But more were coming. A dozen. A score. And more behind. Already the vampires were settling murderous glares on him, and he scuttled back to hide behind his ranks and wait for their numbers to swell.

This was what he'd come for. He drew upon the faltering energy Maedoc's flesh had given him and threw out his power. He felt everything around him: the vampires, faltering despite their unnatural powers, and his dead, scores destroyed but hundreds clustered and pressing to get in. Beneath them all, creatures stirred and waited, listening to the turmoil above and feeling Kaleb's power tracing over them. So many creatures, great and small, many set free and roaming for a safe way out and even more still caged up. One of them was Allie. His mind touched hers, saw as she did, and he crawled on all fours around the fighting. He slipped down the hall he had escaped through earlier, past closed doors and the vampires' den, through the door Kindred had disintegrated, and down into the dungeon.

She was close, on this very floor, and she knew he was coming. She struggled against her chains, metal that burned and clanked but would not break. Monsters scurried away at his approach. He let them. His task was elsewhere.

Alien creatures ran deeper into the dungeons. A white behemoth had found its way down several levels, where there were no rooms or hallways, and pushed through caverns, pools, and tunnels, trying to get away from the nightmare stalking it. Hidden horrors barely sensed watched in the darkness, waiting for a battle and the inevitable carcass that would be left behind.

He slowed to glance up at the revolting little beast that had tormented him. It whimpered and one eye rolled to peer at Kaleb through a veil of sticky webs.

A burst of fear from above distracted Kaleb. The vampires were worried, hemmed in on all sides, but a particular source had his attention. In his mind's eye he saw the spectral entity, so angry, so full of hate, and it had Adora cornered alone in the upper level of the mansion. Already others were headed that way, drawn by the promise of blood. She was already wounded, scraped and gouged, bleeding where yellowed teeth had cut into her pale skin. Even so, it wasn't the dead she was seeing. Nor the entity. She was lost, fighting another losing battle within her own mind. Tears ran down her cheeks. It was almost enough to feel pity for her.

Almost.

The specter seemed to be looking back at Kaleb, waiting, even though Kaleb knew this one did not need his permission for anything.

He gave it anyways.

Kaleb felt it all happen as though he was there. He felt his fingers sinking into Adora's silky flesh, and the moment when the skin broke and his teeth cut into meat. He tasted her blood on his tongue, setting it tingling. Her energy filtered into him, swelling his veins, nipping at the heels of the fatigue. Taken so unaware, he fell to his knees.

It was over too soon. He almost licked the blood off of his fingers and stopped, knowing that it wasn't really there. But he felt it, on his skin, under his nails, and in his belly. To his eyes he was clean, relatively for a corpse, but he had no illusions about his responsibility for her death.

She was weak, nothing compared to Maedoc, but she was more than human and that was enough. He pushed back to his feet having gained another wind.

Twisting turns took Kaleb down hallways he hadn't seen the last time. He strained his power and his ears, listening for the clatter of chains, trying to match what Allie saw to what was before him. Her door was already broken down when he arrived. She stopped thrashing when he stepped inside and waited calmly, for once not trying to kill him.

It was the other thing in the room that wanted to destroy him. Barely recognizable, it lunged, clawing at the space between them. The Rose Knight, no longer so noble or rosy. He was taken by infection and somehow still alive. The question loomed again whether a vampire could come back as he had. They were kin in a dysfunctional way. But none of this had precedent. At least not that he knew of.

He felt the presence coming, old, vampiric, and had just enough time to think of sighing. Renato grabbed him by the hair and wrenched his head back. The sting of silver punctured the side of Kaleb's neck, just below the jaw. It wouldn't take the vamp much effort to bury the blade in his brain. A fatal wound? Or would it just hurt like a motherfucker? "Call them off," Renato hissed in his ear.

Kaleb looked into Allie's cloudy blue eyes, almost regretting what he'd done. He hadn't thought of it in the moment, but Adora held a bit of Renato's scent, as had Michael. Now he had murdered both of Renato's children. The pain he'd inflicted on the vampire was the very same he knew he couldn't bear himself.

"That won't stop me," he bluffed. "Now put it away. You're the only one here I don't want to hurt. Don't change that."

"Please!" Renato implored, choked with misery.

Bullshit. He had no right to ask any such thing. They'd brought it on themselves. "Why should I?" Kaleb shouted. "You said it yourself. They'll do anything they can to kill me. It's us or them."

The tip of the blade pulled away, and the knife clattered to the floor. Renato sagged to his knees, weeping red tears. "I'm sorry," the vampire said, "so sorry for what we've done to you. But I can't lose anyone else. I cannot bear it."

Kaleb glowered at Renato, despising the pain he was causing the vampire, and even more, the misery that would come when he discovered Adora. What would the vampire do then? Seek revenge? It was foolish to take the chance, but after everything, could he really kill him?

Disgusted once again by himself, Kaleb kicked at the blade and sent it spinning across the floor. He spun on Renato. "I'll give them one chance," he snapped. "If they lie, I swear I'll kill every last fucking thing in this house!"

"You will call them off then?"

Kaleb nodded, and reached out. The dead balked at his wants, confused by the change and wallowing in the blood and death, but they listened, and they waited.

Renato got up slowly and wiped at his face, ashamed at the display. With their combined strength the chains broke on the first try. The second she was free Allie threw herself at Renato, reverting to her usual snapping, clawing self. Kaleb threw his arms around her and held tight. "Go," he said. "Warn them."

§ § §

All eyes fell on Kaleb as he and Allie emerged into the first-floor hallway—vampire, dead, and whatever the hell the ashen man was. The army of walking dead were so silent and still it was unearthly, and yet their collective gaze spoke volumes. So many had fallen, destroyed in battle. So many more were wounded. Their patience was wearing thin with the need to know if they could feast.

If the vampires looked battered earlier, now they looked brutalized. Renato was emotionless, gazing at something very far from the nightmare they were all in. *He knew.* Emigdio swayed on his feet, barely able to stand, one bloodied hand pressed against the side of his neck. The burned vampire was huddled into a charred ball on the floor, miraculously still alive, though how Kaleb would never know. An elderly vampiress tended them all, refusing to look up. The others were no better, fatigued, bled, on the verge of collapse, and both wolves were gone, reduced to bloody bones scattered amongst those of the less recently dead. It had been a bad night all around. They were hurt, badly, but most still had a spark of defiance in their eyes.

Kaleb walked through them as if they weren't even there. He paused at the doorway and turned back. "What will it be?"

Emigdio tried to speak and wound up coughing instead. Blood foamed on his lips. "What do you want?" he croaked.

That was the question they came up with? Like he was the one who wanted something? Kaleb let his contempt show. "I don't want anything from you," he said. "I never did. I would have been happy never having seen any of you. All I want is to be left alone."

"No!" someone snarled.

Kaleb searched for the voice and grimaced when he found it. Adrian.

"He killed my brother! Maedoc and Onwyn! And we've been commanded by Lord Harlow to destroy him!" Adrian had about an inch of life left in him, and he was all too willing to waste his last minutes doing everything he could to settle up. More lingered on the tip of his tongue, but the words wouldn't come. They never would again. Shocked and dismayed, he tried to look over his shoulder. Tics and twitches took over his body, worsening into a seizure, and a hand covered in white flame burst from his chest.

Aedan pulled his hand back and the flames snuffed out. Earlier he had fared better than the others. That time was past. "We've heard your terms. Now hear ours."

Kaleb nodded, more curious than anything.

"Do you even understand what you are? The risk you pose?"

Kaleb glanced at Allie. "Yeah, I do."

The vampire sighed, grateful for that little concession. "Then you understand that you cannot breed. You cannot make any more like you, either of you."

An eternity of solitude. It was unfair to ask of anyone. What if Allie didn't want to stick around? Now that he knew what would happen, he wasn't allowed to make some companions? But he knew better than most that life wasn't fair. It did as it pleased, good or bad, giving or taking. He didn't want to accept what the vampire was saying, but he understood it. Everything had spiraled out of control, and it had started with a mere scratch. If Allie had gotten loose…or if he had the will to spread the disease…the potential for disaster was limitless.

"Fine," Kaleb said. "I get it. But where does that leave us?"

The vampire looked surprised. "Nowhere. You were destroyed tonight after a long and costly battle. Your body was burned." He nodded at Allie. "As was hers. The threat has been eliminated." He turned, looking to the others for agreement. One by one they nodded, some grudgingly, some in relief.

Kaleb held tight to Allie's hand, sensing her desire to eat them alive, and walked from the mansion. He resisted the urge to make threats, to swear vengeance should they break their truce. It was implied.

§ § §

Five minutes later they were on the road. Kaleb willed the life to come back to his body and gasped for breath. His heart pounded and his entire body shook. If he wasn't already sitting, he was sure his legs would have given out beneath him. He clutched the steering wheel, trying to control tremors so bad he could barely drive. Allie moved beside him, a sudden lunge, and Kaleb flinched, waiting for teeth to sink into his flesh.

Three times. Shame on him.

The attack never came. She squirmed and twisted her way into the back seat. She landed with a flop and came up a moment later slurping happily on the gnawed remains of Maedoc's leg.

The clock flashed four. It hardly seemed possible for so much to have happened in one insane night. He yawned suddenly, feeling the drag of the sun even though it was hours away. It wasn't only his tiredness he was feeling. Some of it was theirs, the dead trudging behind him, splintering off as they returned to their graves. Their hunger wasn't sated. He wasn't sure it ever could be, but they were ready to slumber again.

Mile by mile his nerves began to settle. The knots in his stomach began to untwist. And for once the ride home wasn't quite so empty.

Epilogue

THE SCENT OF drywall and fresh paint still lingered in the air, but it was fading a little more every day. Tomorrow would mark a full month since Halloween, and aside from flashes of certainty that someone was coming—justifiable paranoia in his opinion—Kaleb hadn't seen or heard anything out of the ordinary. The mosquitoes were keeping their word. So far.

"You're gonna love this," Kaleb said. "I can't believe you've never seen it."

"*Planet of the Apes*? That crappy Wahlberg movie?"

"Ew, no. This is the original. It's way better."

"Why don't I believe you?"

Exasperated, Kaleb threw up his hands and found a spot on the couch. "Just give it a fair chance, alright?"

Allie rolled her eyes. "Whatever. I'm going to grab a snack. Want some?"

He wasn't particularly hungry, but what's a movie without a snack? "Yeah. Can you grab me a drink too?"

Allie took off without answering. Her manners were a little rough yet, unrefined, no doubt the after effects of growing up as a commoner. Still, considering where she'd been a month ago, it was nothing short of miraculous. She'd gone to town on Maedoc's leg, refused to give it up once they got home, and within a day not a scrap was left. It had worked wonders. He'd been tempted to pass the information on to the vamps, see if they could save the Rose Knight, but eventually he'd decided against it. The Knight had tried to kill him, had damn near eviscerated him, and if he'd gone for the neck—well—that would have been that. In time he might change his mind, give them a heads up; something told him the Knight wasn't going anywhere. Hypocrites.

Kaleb fiddled with the remote while he waited for Allie to come back, and absentmindedly set a hand on the cushion at his side. It wasn't the first time he'd reached out without thinking, still expecting Jordan to be curled up there. He'd even had moments when he'd done double takes, sure he had seen her. Wishful thinking.

Allie came back and divvied up the snacks. "What's with you?" she asked.

With his excitement for the movie suddenly subdued, Kaleb shrugged. "Nothing. Just thinking."

"Are you still worried about them coming back?"

It was a distinct possibility, but he didn't want to worry her too much. Besides, he'd been taking some precautions in case they broke their word. "Nah. They'll be nursing their bruises for a few years yet."

Allie eyed him until he shifted uncomfortably. She knew he was holding back, she just didn't know what. It was unnerving how she could see through him sometimes. Before she could press the issue, he hit play. The cheese started to roll.

Not for the first time in the past month, Kaleb's heart began to race. Allie nestled in close, slipping her hand within his. They were both still a bit confused by what had happened, and by where it left them, but they were trying to figure it out. The biggest step had happened only days after the showdown. She'd spoken, not perfectly, a bit choppy and disconnected, but the gist had been about forgiveness. They'd talked a lot since then. She seemed to know more than she should have, like she'd been able to peek inside his memories. He could see into her as well, not her memories per say, rather he could read her moods and pick up on how she felt.

Allie groaned at the special effects and the moments of overacting, but as the movie rolled on, she lost herself in the story. Kaleb spent half the time watching her, reliving the first experience of the movie through her reactions.

He nearly leapt off of the couch when a chill ran up his spine. A weight hung over his head, bearing down on him. Eyes were on him, he was sure of it.

Allie squeezed his hands, startled. "What is it?" she whispered.

The vice squeezing Kaleb's throat eased. The gaze he felt crawling over his skin turned away. But the chill behind his eyes was still screaming at him, warning him that something was coming. He let go of Allie's hand and stood, searching and listening. A creak. In the kitchen. The faintest squeal of a hinge swinging.

His fears were realized when a shadow flickered in the hallway. It slipped along, barely seen, moving fast. Kaleb called on his power. It surged through him, and just as quickly it went away.

How?

The last time he'd seen her she'd been little more than scraps of fur and bone. Jordan leapt into his arms purring madly, rubbing her face against his chin and hugging him for all she was worth.

"Jordan, right?" Allie said, clearly unimpressed.

It was more than he could process at the moment. He glanced at Allie, not exactly sure what she had just said.

"She scared the living hell out of me," Allie went on. "You ever step on a cat before? Try doing it when you're escaping a psycho cannibal's dungeon. My heart almost popped." Confusion crossed her face for a moment. "Didn't you say she died? The vampires?"

Kaleb nodded, overwhelmed, a missing piece of his life slipping back into place.

Also by Divertir Publishing

The Entropy of Knowledge
Mark Dellandre and Britton Learnard

We've all had moments when we felt like we were surrounded by idiots...Babylon Briggs feels that pain every day because his town, his planet, even his galaxy, is jam-packed with the most thick-headed simpletons imaginable. So when his home world is invaded by a group of equally clueless conquerors, it's up to Babylon to save the day. The only question is:

Is he smart enough?

Bonebelly
Christine Lajewski

A sinner transformed into a hideous creature, with an unfortunate craving for human flesh, condemned to a private hell in a wooded corner of Rhode Island; An outdoor haunted attraction—the creature's only respite from his suffering; Two young aspiring graphic novelists trying to record it all. Will the sinner find redemption by stopping the evil he chose to ignore so long ago...